NEVER
BE ALONE

PAIGE DEARTH

ISBN 10: 1983422843

ISBN 13: 9781983422843

SOME DIRT ON THE AUTHOR:

Born and raised in Plymouth Meeting, a small town west of Philadelphia, Paige Dearth was a victim of child abuse and spent her early years yearning desperately for a better life. Living through the fear and isolation that marked her youth, she found a way of coping with the trauma: she developed the ability to dream up stories grounded in reality that would provide her with a creative outlet when she finally embarked on a series of novels. Paige's debut novel, *Believe Like A Child*, is the darkest version of the life she imagines she would have been doomed to lead had fate not intervened just in the nick of time. Paige writes real-life horror and refers to her work as: Fiction with Mean-ing. She hopes that awareness through fiction creates prevention.

CONNECT WITH PAIGE:

Visit her website at www.paigedearth.com and sign up for updates

Friend Paige on Facebook at www.facebook.com/paigedearth

Follow Paige on Twitter @paigedearth

Find all of Paige's books here: Books by Paige Dearth

Dedications

For my child…You will always come first. You are the love of my life.
~Mom

For my husband and best friend.
What did you wish for when you threw that rock?
I love you.

Acknowledgments

To all those who have been homeless or even close to it: may you find the peace you so deserve. We can make a home anywhere as long as it's filled with love and laughter.

Many thanks to all the people who continue to read my work—without all of you, my dream would be nothing more than a bunch of lonely words.

For all of the book bloggers and reviewers, I would still be hidden in the darkness if you hadn't shined your light on me—thank you all so much!

Big E, thanks for standing by me! Love you, brother!

Just A Child

She's a girl, just a child, no older than fifteen.

She's dirty. Her clothes are frayed. She wears her hair long. It's knotted and greasy. You don't want to get too close—you may catch what she has. Can you catch homelessness? You tell yourself it's a ridiculous thought, but you still don't dare approach her. Although she is weak and fragile, the girl scares you.

One day, the girl catches you watching her. Your eyes meet for a split second, and blood rushes to your face, guilt filling every crevice of your body. She's a girl, just a child, no older than fifteen.

As summer fades and the first autumn frost chills you to the bone, you wonder where she will go, how she'll stay warm.

By early November, it's been weeks since you've seen her in the alley-way begging for money, the same spot she sits in every morning. You wonder what happened to her. Two weeks go by, and still there's no sight of her.

At the end of the third week, you panic. You should have helped her. She's just a child. You find the courage to venture closer to her edgy friends, the others that know her, the ones that are like her. You ask, "Where is she?" But they do not answer. One of them holds your gaze steadily until you look away. You can't stand the pain in those eyes, such weathered skin on a teenager, the bony face and neck— because food is a luxury for them and they don't have enough of it.

Now, every day, you stop on your way to work and stare at the spot where you last saw the beautiful girl who looked so lonely. You wish you would have asked if she was okay. Maybe you would have helped her find a shelter, said a kind word…made her feel like she was human.

Months later, buried deep inside the newspaper, you see a picture of the homeless girl. Her body was thrown away on the side of the railroad tracks, like garbage. In the picture, she is homeless—you recognize the alleyway where she sat. She is smiling, but her smile reveals her pain.

The news story says the girl's death was no accident. She'd been beaten, tortured, and sexually assaulted—reduced to nothing. She was left naked in the mud next to the train tracks.

Later that night, you awake from a nightmare, sweating...but you're safe in your home. You pull the covers up to your chin and settle back to sleep. But sleep rejects you, and all you can think about is the girl and the other children living on the streets.

She was a girl, just a child, no older than fifteen when her life ended. If only you had helped.

~Paige Dearth

The New Family

Jamie pulled up in front of a dilapidated house and parked. Eight-year-old Joon held her breath and looked around at her surroundings. Her insides felt weightless. The little girl hunkered down in her seat, determined to stay inside the confines of the metal-and-glass box that stood between her and this other, unknown life.

Joon peeked out the car window with unblinking, wide eyes. So much had changed since her parents had died. She had been ripped away from her friends and teachers, her sense of security torn away. She was reeling from the rapid changes in her life. She fought the urge to scream. Her anguish and loss overwhelmed her as her eyes roved over her new home.

The house was weathered. The small yard was neglected, with patches of overgrown weeds poking out of the dirt where grass refused to grow. Joon's gaze followed the broken walkway to the porch and the screen door hanging from a single hinge. She looked over at Jamie with apprehension, wishing she were back in the modest but well-maintained home where she'd lived with her parents, where she felt safest.

Hot tears stung her eyes. "Is this it?" Joon squeaked out.

"Yes." Jamie rested her hand on Joon's shoulder. "Now don't worry. It's going to be fine. Your foster mother, Aron Remmi, is excited for you to live with her. You have two foster brothers too. I think you'll love it here."

"But the house looks scary," Joon said, her bottom lip quivering.

"Well, I'll admit, it's a bit run-down on the outside, but Aron keeps her home very clean inside, I made sure of that," Jamie said proudly. "When I place a child in a clean home, that's when I know I'm doing my job right. Every child deserves a good family and a clean home. You'll have both of those things here, so don't worry."

Joon's eyes dropped to her lap, and she rubbed her sweaty palms on her thighs.

Jamie leaned toward the child. "I know this a big change for you, Joon. I'm sure it feels very scary, but I need you to trust me on this. Being in a single-family foster home is better than all the other places you could have been placed. You're one of the lucky kids. There are a lot of kids just like you that end up in group homes. Here, with Aron and her two sons, you get to have a real family." Jamie patted Joon's shoulder. "Now put on your best smile and let's go meet them."

As Jamie and Joon walked up the porch steps, Aron pulled the front door open. The woman wore a warm smile, and Joon noticed she had large teeth. They weren't unattractive, but they stood out against her blotchy, white skin, wide nose, and big ears. Her long, wiry, brown hair hung below her shoulders. She wore a beautiful yellow-and-white sundress and smelled of honeydew and cucumber lotion. The smell reminded Joon of her mother, Gwen, and sadness pressed in on her until she felt weighed down with it. She fought the urge to drop to the ground and cry.

Aron stooped and rested her fingers on Joon's shoulders. "You must be Joon. Welcome home, sweetheart."

The tears building in Joon's eyes spilled over. It didn't matter how nice Aron was—Joon feared her new home. Until now, she hadn't known where she would live, but she'd been comfortable at the temporary shelter. The people who worked at the shelter had told her it was temporary housing, but now that she was at her new "home," the reality, the permanence, of her situation was all too real. In the first days following her parents' deaths, she'd hoped they were still alive, that it was all a big mistake. As the shelter workers had waited for a foster home to become available for her, Joon had waited for her parents to come and rescue her.

Now, Joon looked at Aron, and her guts knotted. She wanted her mother and father. She didn't want to live with strangers.

Aron narrowed her eyes. "Are you gonna say hello, honey?"

Although Aron was smiling, Joon noticed the tightness in the woman's jaw, and her senses went berserk. The woman gave her the willies, and she instinctively stepped toward Jamie for protection.

"Come on, Joon. Say hello to Aron," Jamie urged. The social worker gently pushed her toward Aron again.

Joon looked up at Jamie, her eyes pleading for her to stop. The case-worker, feeling sorry for the girl, tried to comfort her, forcing a smile on her face again, and nodded in Aron's direction.

Joon turned to Aron. "Hi," she said in a small voice.

"Well, I see that you sent me a shy one," Aron said, her lips in a tight line.

Jamie stepped closer to Aron. "Joon has been through a traumatic experience, losing both parents suddenly. I think she needs some love and care. She's going to adjust just fine in your capable hands."

Aron bent, took Joon's hand, and moved toward the front door. Joon tried to dig her heels into the aged wood of the porch, but Aron steadily pulled her along.

"Let's go now," Aron said. "I want you to meet your new brothers."

For Joon, going inside the house meant closing the door on her old life—the life she'd loved. She had cherished being an only child, as her mother and father had given all of their attention to her. But her life was different now, and knowing she had foster brothers made her more nervous. Joon clenched her teeth, worrying that the boys would be mean to her or even hate her. She wasn't used to living with other children and all the changes about to happen overwhelmed her.

Aron tugged on Joon's hand, and her muscles tensed as she guardedly followed her new foster mom into the house. Just inside the door, Aron turned back to Jamie and stared into the other woman's eyes. "I can take it from here. I think it'll be easier for my new foster daughter," she said kindly.

Jamie nodded. "You're right. Bye, Joon. I'll be back to check on you in a month or so."

Joon's eyes grew double in size, and she clutched at her own neck to contain the bile burning the back of her throat. "Do you promise to come back and see me?"

Jamie nodded. "I'll see you real soon," she said, before turning and leaving the house.

Aron shut the door and pulled Joon into the living room. "Boys, this is your new foster sister. Her name is *Joon*," she said and cackled. "Such a stupid name. I don't really like it. In fact, I hate it. I'll have to think of another name for her. Anyway, this is Deen and that's Dobi," Aron said, pointing to one boy, then the other.

Deen, the older of the two, eyed Joon. "Yeah, Joon is a dumb name," he stated.

"I love my name," Joon mumbled, wrapping her arms over her chest and pressing her lips together. Her new foster family glared at her, and she felt the world around her darken—she could feel their coldness through their dead stares. She felt trapped, and fear rose from her stomach, pushing harder at the bile in her throat. Her body trembled.

Aron raised an eyebrow at the child. "Looks like we have a girl with no manners. I'll need to tame that if you're going fit in here. You need to tell Deen you're sorry."

Joon shook her head. She wasn't sorry. She didn't want to lie. Besides, he was the one who'd been mean. *Shouldn't he apologize?*

"Okay. I'll show you to your room, and you can sit in there until you're ready to tell Deen you're sorry for being rude to him."

Minutes later, Joon was sitting alone in her dingy bedroom. Aron had instructed her to sit on the edge of her mattress, feet flat on the floor and hands in her lap. So Joon sat still, her heart hammering away in her small chest, fear creeping up her spine and clenching tightly around her heart. Aron scared her. She was nothing like her own mother had been.

As she waited, Joon thought about her name. She had always loved it. She replayed a story her mother had told her often over the years: "Before you were born, your dad and I only had each other. Both of our parents were gone, and being only children, we had no one else…well, we had each other but we wanted a family. The doctor that delivered you laid you on my chest, and my heart filled with a love I had never known before, and I started to cry. Your father and I looked at each other, and he said, 'We finally have a family.' We were so excited to have you in our lives. The nurse gently touched the top of your head and asked what your name was. Your father and I felt silly because we hadn't decided on your name yet; we wanted to wait until we saw you. The nurse smiled at us and said, 'What about Joon? Joon means 'life.'' That was it for us. The name settled into our hearts, and we knew we'd love you forever—our Joon, our life."

Joon's parents, Gwen and Rich, had met at a bowling alley when they were in their early twenties. They moved in together the following year and married six months later. They had a solid marriage and great love for each other. And they were good to Joon. Rich was a third-grade teacher and Gwen had quit her job as a secretary for an insurance company to stay home and raise Joon. Even though they had little money, they had an endless amount of love for their daughter. They always made certain she had decent clothes and plenty of food.

Joon's favorite memory was of Christmas morning when she was six-years-old, when her parents had given her a new bicycle. It was pink and purple, with a white basket on the front. For Joon, the bicycle represented fun and freedom. Over the summer, she had seen the other girls riding their bikes up and down the street. They had all looked so happy, riding along with their hair blowing in the wind as they raced to an invisible finish line. Now, Joon could zip through the streets too. Rich had taught Joon how to ride it as Gwen stood on the sidewalk and cheered her on. When she'd fallen off, her mother had taken her inside, made her a cup of hot cocoa, and told her to try again. After, Joon had rushed outside and climbed back on her bike. That night at dinner, Rich and Gwen told Joon how proud they were of her.

"Remember," Gwen had said, taking the child's hand, "you can do anything you want in life as long as you don't give up."

Chapter One

Joon's teeth were clenched and her lower lip trembled as she sat on the floor waiting for the pain to follow. She would have welcomed death, but instead, all she could do was cram herself farther into the corner of the kitchen, between the cold plaster wall and the wooden door that led to the dreaded basement. She wanted the hurt to stop. It had been three months since she'd been placed with her new foster family—three long months of terror and torture for anyone, let alone an eight-year-old.

"You rotten, ungrateful, little bitch. What did I tell you about stealing food?" Aron yelled. The woman pulled back her leg and kicked. The pointy toe of her shoe landed on Joon's thigh.

Joon let out a muffled yelp and scurried from the corner like a spider being chased by a broom. She scuttled under the kitchen table, hoping to find shelter beneath the pressed wood.

"I'm sorry. I'm hungry, Aron," Joon cried weakly.

"You don't know what hungry is, girl." Aron crouched, clamped her hand around Joon's ankle, and pulled the child out from under the table with one forceful yank.

Exposed in the middle of the kitchen floor, Joon curled up, knees and elbows pressed together, hands clasped behind her head, trying to protect herself from the fury brewing in Aron.

Aron opened the door to the dark, dank basement. "Get. Down. There."

Joon, willing to accept isolation in the darkness over another beating, quickly rose to her feet and stepped through the opened door. As she moved toward the first step, reaching for the railing, Aron elbowed her in the back. Joon tumbled down the wooden stairs and hit the bottom with a thud.

1

"You can stay down there and think about what you did. Ain't nobody gonna steal from me. I told you before—you get to eat when I say you can eat."

As the basement door banged closed, the cold blackness rushed in on Joon. She had sharp pain in her back. On her hands and knees, she dragged her aching body to the closest wall. She closed her eyes against the pain and the fear of being alone in the basement. Things moved around in the dark down there. There were rats and bugs. After moving in, she'd learned swiftly that Aron enjoyed punishing her. It made her foster mother feel important, powerful. Joon had also learned there would always be another punishment, no matter how much she tried to please Aron.

During the long hours of the night, Joon focused on her breathing to calm her frazzled nerves.

She must have eventually drifted off, because the sound of a toilet flushing above her brought Joon back into the moment. Tears dribbled from her chin at the fading memory of her parents. She sat in silence, hoping that someone would come and take her away from the hell she called home.

Chapter Two - Three Years Later

In the early hours of the morning, the pain of Joon's cracked rib and sprained ankle gave way to a numbing disillusionment. Aron had pushed her down the basement steps again the night before. Joon was injured, but she no longer feared the dark space, the wet dirt floor of the basement, where the bugs and rodents crawled around her. In fact, the creepy-crawlies reminded her she was still alive. They made her feel like she wasn't alone.

Joon had slipped in and out of sleep all night. When the basement door was flung open later that morning, the light from the kitchen startled her. She squinted up at the shadow at the top of the steps until her eyes adjusted. Her thirteen-year-old foster brother Deen was staring down at her with a sickening smile. Deen was almost as mean as Aron—the boy thrived on the power his mother gave him over Joon.

"Mom said you gotta get up here now, maggot," Deen said, taunting her.

Joon got to her hands and knees, and used the old, wooden railing to hoist herself up. She limped up the stairs slowly.

Deen sneered as he watched her painful climb to the top. As Joon walked past, he whacked her on the side of the head with his open hand. "Mom said to get this kitchen cleaned up. She said it better be spotless."

Joon remained silent. She only spoke when given permission, a rule Aron established in the first few days after her arrival. The only time Joon broke this rule was when her hunger overpowered her fear.

With her body aching, Joon hurried to clear the dirty breakfast dishes from the kitchen table and put them on the counter next to the sink, then filled the sink with water and soap.

"The water needs to be hotter, scumbag," Deen growled. "Are you trying to get us sick?"

Joon turned the hot water higher and Deen shut off the cold water. The kitchen faucet spewed steamy water into the basin. When it was half-filled, Deen turned the water off.

"Get washin'," he demanded.

Joon studied the steam coming from the sink. She knew there was only one thing to do. The girl shoved her hands into the scalding water and washed the dishes. Her feet danced in place; her hands felt like they were on fire. Satisfied that Joon was being tortured properly, Deen spit on her and left the kitchen.

As soon as he was gone, Joon turned on the cold water and let it run over her hands, instantly relieving the throbbing burn. She hurried to finish cleaning the kitchen before Aron came in to inspect her work. Joon had just put the last dish away when Aron waltzed into the room followed by Deen and her twelve-year-old son, Dobi.

"Well, lookie here, boys. Pathetic, scruffy Joon looks a little hungry this morning," Aron said. "Should we give this animal something to eat?"

Joon's eyes grew bigger. The very thought of food, any food, made her hopes soar.

"Nah," Deen said. "I think she needs at least another day before she can eat."

Aron turned to her younger son. "How about you, Dobi? What do you think?"

Dobi squirmed. He pushed his hands into the front pockets of his jeans. "I think she looks real hungry, Ma. We should give her something now."

"Okay, Dobi, we'll do that then," Aron said, opening the cabinet under the sink.

She pulled out a bag of dry dog food and poured it into a bowl. Then she opened another cabinet and grabbed a bottle of Tabasco sauce. She drizzled it over the food before pulling the refrigerator open and grabbing a bottle of fish sauce she used to make seafood soup. The amber contents splashed onto the dog food. The smell made Deen and Dobi take a few steps back from the concoction. Aron mixed the three ingredients together and placed it on the kitchen table.

"You're hungry?" Aron sang, leaning into Joon. "Now you got food. I'm giving you two minutes to eat, starting now."

Joon stood over the bowl and looked at Aron.

Aron gave her a grave look, and Joon stared back, her eyes pleading for mercy. "Stop eyeballing me. You're hungry, and you wanted to eat, so eat. Who knows the next time you'll get food. Sooo, you better get to eating."

Joon looked down at the bowl, pinched her nose closed with her left hand, and grabbed a glob of the food with her fingers. She shoved it into her mouth and chewed. The Tabasco pierced her tongue and gums with fiery heat. She flung her mouth open and fanned at the garbage splayed over her tongue and lodged between her teeth.

"You got another minute left. You better hurry and eat up," Aron said, laughing.

Joon's eyes were watering. The heat was unbearable. The smell and taste of the fish sauce was strumming her gag reflex. Joon stepped away from the bowl and fell to the floor.

"Please," Joon pleaded, "I need water."

Aron put her hands on her hips and stared right through the child. She took a few steps and, with her foot, pushed the dog's water bowl over to the girl.

Joon cupped her hands and slurped the water. She was in too much pain to care about the food particles and thick, stringy saliva left by the dog that were floating in the bowl.

Aron stooped, so she could put her face close to Joon's. "You're a disgusting pig. Those mother fucking people that sent you here to live with me should be paying me way more money to keep you." She straightened up and turned to her two sons. "This here is what you call white trash. You remember what it looks like because you better never bring a little slut like this home as your girlfriend."

Deen snickered, grabbed a scoop of the rotten mixture from the bowl, and threw it onto the side of Joon's face. Most of it was in her hair, but a bit landed on her eyelid, and when Joon pushed it off her face, a small piece lodged in her eye. The Tabasco sauce scorched her eye, and as she rubbed it, the heat spread. Joon rolled around on the floor crying from the blazing agony.

Aron turned and left the kitchen. "Let's go, boys. Leave this piece of shit here for now. I'll deal with her later."

Joon flailed around, rubbing her face, but when Deen and Dobi obediently followed their mother, Joon got to her feet, grabbed a dish towel, soaked it with cold water, and pressed it against her eye. She dropped to her knees and trembled on the floor. Her heart felt like a lump of useless clay inside her chest, like it would continue to get heavier and heavier and, eventually, just stop beating.

Chapter Three

Joon rarely found relief from Aron's daily humiliations. It was almost the end of summer though, and she hoped that middle school would be better than her years in elementary school had been. Aron had stopped hitting Joon in the face weeks before school started, to avoid the bruises that had become as normal to Joon as her nose.

After the incident with the Tabasco sauce, Joon never felt hope again when being offered food by Aron. When Aron did feed her, it was only discarded scraps from the family's plates, and while it wasn't ever enough to satisfy her hunger, Joon at least knew the food was safe to eat.

Joon's bedroom was on the main floor of the house, the room that Aron had showed to Jamie before they placed Joon with her and when the social worker returned for visits, which was rare. But the small girl rarely slept in the bed. Most nights, she was sent into the basement and, on rare occasions, the family dog, Kensey, went into the darkness with her. When this happened, Joon and Kensey slept together, the dog providing her warmth through the night.

On the first day of middle school, Aron opened the basement door before the sun was up. "Get your ass up here," she demanded.

Joon ran up the steps and stood before Aron. Her head hung and her long, blond hair was matted and covered her face.

"Look at you. You're a disgrace. Today is your first day at a new school. There's a couple things you better not forget. Keep your fucking mouth shut. I don't want nobody knowing my business. The other thing is if anyone asks you how you like living here, the answer is that you love it. Understand?"

Joon raised her head to look at Aron and nodded.

"Then say it!" Aron yelled.

"I love living here," Joon repeated in a small voice.

Aron shook her head. "Let's go. You need to take a bath so you look human. It ain't gonna be easy for you in school given that you're so ugly."

Joon was so exhausted from the beating she'd taken from Aron the night prior, without thinking, she said, "My mom and dad thought I was pretty."

Aron spun on her. "Your mother was either a lying bitch, or as stupid as you. Besides, where's your precious mother now? I'll tell you where she is—she's dead, lying in the ground, rotting next to your loser father. Look around you. Do you see your wonderful parents here? Taking care of you? Making sure you're raised right?"

For a split second, Joon thought of protesting but knew it would only ignite Aron's fury further.

"No," Joon mumbled.

"That's right. Besides, they were too dumb to teach you how to act like a nice girl instead of a dirty pig. But I know how to raise you right. You ain't an easy one to help because you're the most stupid child I've ever known." Aron shook her head. "Get moving. I want you cleaned up before the bus comes."

Joon followed Aron into the bathroom and watched as her foster mom ran water into the tub. Her body tingled as she thought about cleaning off the grime caked on her skin. The buildup made her flesh feel too tight for her body.

Aron turned from the tub. She put her hands on her hips and scowled at Joon. "What are you waiting for? Get those filthy clothes off."

Joon undressed, and Aron's judging eyes bore through her, making the child feel self-conscious.

"Hurry up!" Aron screamed.

Joon removed the remainder of her dirty, worn clothing quickly and climbed into the tub. She hadn't taken a real bath in close to seven weeks. The warm water felt heavenly against her crusted flesh. Aron handed her a small bar of soap and placed shampoo next to the tub. Then she reached into the bathroom closet and tossed a washcloth into the water. "Make sure you wash up real good. Get that stink off of you." Aron put down the toilet lid and placed a thin bath towel on top. "That's for you to dry off with. Now get a move on. You ain't got a lot of time."

As soon as Aron left and closed the door behind her, Joon put her whole head under the water. She used the soap and washcloth to scrub her skin. Then she picked up the shampoo and washed her long, blond hair quickly and dunked her head under the water again. Joon felt released from the filth that had held her skin hostage. Being clean was a luxury that she yearned for in the long time between each bath. She leaned her head back against the tub and smiled, as she often did when she was allowed to bathe, and let herself get lost in the glorious moment. Then she heard footsteps coming toward the bathroom.

"Let's go," Aron yelled through the door. "Your time is up."

Joon hurried out of the tub and grabbed the thin towel, her sense of peace snuffed out by the crude sound of Aron's shrill voice. She dried herself and opened the bathroom door. Aron was waiting, staring down at her. Joon followed her foster mother into the bedroom. On the bed were a pair of secondhand jeans and a purple T-shirt.

"Get dressed, then get your ass into the kitchen. Breakfast needs to be cleaned up before you go to school," Aron barked. She glared at the child as Joon combed her tangled hair with her fingers. The older woman opened the top drawer and took out the brush that Joon's mother had gently ran through her hair. Aron stomped over to Joon and grabbed the top of her head. She raked through Joon's hair in long, hard strokes. Joon could feel the hair being pulled from her scalp. She squeezed her eyes closed, enduring the sting as her head jerked back and forth until Aron finished.

"There," Aron said, looking satisfied. "Now, hurry the hell up."

Joon finished dressing and paused in front of the mirror hanging on the back of the bedroom door. Her reflection was jarring. She had grown taller over the past seven weeks. Her jeans were two inches too short and her T-shirt was baggy. She was much thinner with dark circles under her eyes. Her once vibrant blue eyes were now faded to a dull gray. She no longer recognized the girl in the mirror—the person looking back was stripped of all humanity, a shell of the girl she once was. She only had access to a full-length mirror when she was in her supposed bedroom, and she was always curious to see what she looked like and hated to find the monster looking back at her. She pushed the wet strands of hair behind her ears, just like her mother had done for her when she was alive.

When Joon walked into the kitchen, Deen and Dobi were almost finished eating. Aron took a bite of her toast and motioned for Joon to sit in the empty chair at the table.

"You're ugly even when you're clean," Deen remarked.

Aron smirked and nodded.

Egged on by his mother's reaction, Deen continued. "All the kids are gonna pick on you. I already told my friends that you're a mutant, that there's something wrong with you. Everybody already hates you. Welcome to middle school."

Aron shoved the last of the toast into her mouth. "Okay. Finish your breakfast, boys."

Deen and Dobi finished eating while Joon was made to sit and watch. The smell of toast was glorious, and her mouth watered and her stomach gurgled thinking about taking a buttery bite or just one spoonful of the colorful, sugary cereal Deen and Dobi were eating. When the three were finished, Aron told the boys to get ready for school.

"You get this kitchen cleaned up. I want to see this place sparkle before you leave."

Alone in the kitchen, Joon cleared the dishes from the table. She thought for sure that Aron would have let her eat breakfast before going to school, as she had in the few years prior, even if it was just a banana or half a slice of dry toast. Joon considered drinking the milk left in the cereal bowls but knew if she was caught, the consequences would be severe.

A little later, at the bus stop, Joon stood far away from the other kids. The boys threw pebbles at her that stung, and the girls giggled and pointed at her clothes. Joon crossed her arms over her chest as the bus pulled up. Until now, school had been a short escape from her foster home, but nothing more. As the bus doors opened, she tried to be optimistic about her new school, hopeful that something would change for the better.

Chapter Four

———————■———————

Joon's classmates rejected her from the start. She wasn't outgoing like many of the other girls in her class. But the real problem was that Joon's appearance made her a target of ridicule. Her unstylish, shabby clothes and unkempt, mangled hair gave the other girls all the ammunition they needed to be mean. While it hurt Joon's feelings, compared to the three months of isolation without her basic needs being met, just being around people was a step in the right direction. She remained quiet though, trying her best not to be noticed.

At lunchtime, Joon stood outside the cafeteria as the kid's voices melted into a buzz of noise. She waited off to the side of the doors, not wanting to enter. One of the volunteer moms bent down in front of Joon and looked into her face.

"You're new here, huh?"

Joon gave her a small smile. "Yeah, today's my first day."

The lunch mom studied her. "You have beautiful eyes," she commented.

Joon blushed; her parents had always told her that looking into her eyes was like staring into the soul of an angel.

"Thank you," Joon whispered.

"Well, are you going to eat lunch?" the mom asked.

Joon shrugged. "I didn't bring my lunch. I…I forgot it."

The lunch mom gave her a warm smile. "Well, that's not a problem. I'm pretty sure you have a lunch ticket, just like your foster brothers."

Joon looked down at the brown floor. "How do you know I have foster brothers?"

"Oh, hon, news travels fast in this school. Besides, we always keep an eye out for the kids starting here. Let's get your lunch ticket so you can eat."

"Really?" Joon said sharply, delighted to have a lunch ticket.

"Yep. Come on. Just over there," she said, pointing to an older lady sitting in a chair behind a small table. "Every day, you go right there, and Mrs. Evans will give you the ticket."

Aron had applied for free lunches, and because of her financial situation and the fact that she was a foster parent, the children were accommodated.

"Hello, Mrs. Evans," the woman said. "This is Joon Taylor. Today is her first day of middle school."

"Oh, yes," Mrs. Evans said. "Deen and Dobi are your foster brothers, right?"

Joon nodded.

"Well now, Dobi seems like a nice young man, but Deen—that boy is just trouble waiting to happen. You steer clear of him," Mrs. Evans advised.

Joon smiled politely at Mrs. Evans, avoiding any conversation about her foster family. She was afraid that one of the adults would find out about her living situation and Aron would kill her, as she had threatened.

"Here's your ticket," Mrs. Evans said, handing the small blue card to Joon. "Go on and get your lunch. Have a nice day."

Joon extended her hand and took the card. "Thank you," she said and took a few steps before she stopped. She turned back to Mrs. Evans and the lunch mom. "Have a nice day," Joon said.

"I like that kid," Mrs. Evans whispered to the lunch mom as Joon disappeared into the cafeteria.

Joon took a plastic tray from the holder and walked toward the food line. She looked through the glass at the food on the other side.

A lady with netted hair leaned toward her. "Hot dog or grilled cheese?"

Joon eyed them both. Her stomach felt like it was coming up through her throat.

"Honey? What's it gonna be?"

Joon pointed. "Grilled cheese."

"Fries or mashed potatoes?"

"Can I have some of both?"

The woman cocked her head and looked closely at Joon's thin frame. "Sure. Why not?" she said, putting a mound of mashed potatoes next to a pile of french fries. "Looks like you could use some fattening up."

Farther down the line, Joon grabbed a vanilla pudding and carton of chocolate milk. She proceeded to the register, where another woman punched a hole in her lunch ticket.

As Joon held her tray of food, the wonderful smells made her belly dance with delight. She felt giddy. She looked into the vast room filled with rowdy kids. Her anticipation around eating a real meal grew with rapid intensity as she searched for a place to sit. She found four open seats midway through the cafeteria. She sat in the seat on the end, farthest from the kids at the other side of the table.

After she placed her tray down, she shoveled food into her mouth as if she were possessed, barely taking the time to chew it before swallowing. For Joon, it was as if the whole world went pitch-black and the only things in existence were her and the tray of food. She grabbed, snorted, and shoveled the meal into her mouth. When she drank the last drop of chocolate milk, it was as if a light had been switched on, and she looked around her. The kids closest to Joon were staring at her with their mouths hanging open.

A girl Joon's age broke the silence. "Ew. You're disgusting. What's wrong with you?"

All the kids around her laughed. Though hidden under the canopy of her long, blond hair, Joon's cheeks were bright red. She thought about how she must have appeared to the other kids, eating her food like an animal, but it didn't matter to her—she'd gotten to eat real food and enough to fill her belly. She stood silently and took her tray to the front of the cafeteria, where other kids were dropping them off.

Joon followed the flow of kids down the hallway and back to her class. She sat at her desk, her belly bulging from its unaccustomed fullness, and she put a hand over it. She hadn't felt so good in a long, long time. School was exactly what Joon needed. It was an escape from Aron's and Deen's cruelty and a place where she'd finally be able to eat. Joon looked around her sixth grade class. Everyone had their pencils out, ready for their first math lesson. Joon was eager to learn everything the teacher taught.

She looked down at the open book on her desk. Her parents had taught her that the best thing she could do for herself was get a good education. They'd instilled in her a belief that the one thing no one could take from her is knowledge. From them, she had learned that no matter how little control over her life she thought she had, if she did well in school, she'd always have power. Joon's parents had taught her that, with a good education, came freedom. Her parents' beliefs ran through Joon's mind as she turned her full attention to the teacher. She was determined to learn and take a small bit of control over her own life.

Chapter Five

---■---

When Joon returned home with Deen and Dobi from the first day of school, Aron was standing at the front door waiting for them. Deen shot through the door first.

"The whole school was talking about Joon today. They were sayin' she ate everything in the cafeteria. I heard she was really disgusting and people had to go to the nurse because it was so gross they threw up all over the place," Deen said, exaggerating.

"Is that so?" Aron said, giving Joon a scathing look.

Joon's heart sank, and the sudden wispy feeling in the pit of her stomach overwhelmed her.

"So you think that you have a right to eat anything you want 'cause I'm not there to watch over you? Well, I won't have no fatty as a foster kid. There's no way that's going to happen," Aron said. She grabbed Joon's arm and dragged her into the bathroom, opening the medicine cabinet and pulling out a small bottle. "Put your head back and open your mouth."

Joon stared at Aron in disbelief, afraid of what would happen next.

Aron pinched the back of Joon's upper arm. The child reeled from the intense pain. "Head back and open your fuckin' mouth!"

This time, Joon did as she was instructed. Aron lifted the bottle and poured in a hefty shot of ipecac. Joon choked down the foul liquid and rushed to the toilet, where she began to violently vomit. Any food left in her stomach spewed out of her in putrid, smelly chunks. The child kneeled before the toilet until there was nothing left in her. With tears streaming down her face and snot stringing from her nose, she looked at Aron with a bewildered gaze.

"You didn't like that much, did you?" Aron spat.

"No. I'm sorry," Joon cried.

Aron looked down on the child, pitiless. "Damn straight you're sorry. Here's how it's gonna work from now on. When you go to that fancy cafeteria in school, you can get one thing from the line. What I mean by one thing is a sandwich or a piece of meatloaf or some other shit they're serving. You can take three small bites of whatever you get. No milk either. You can get a drink from the water fountain. Now, if I find out you eat more than three bites, we'll do this routine again when you get home. I'm giving you three bites 'cause if I don't, those nosy bitches that run the place might get suspicious and start trouble." Aron pointed her finger in Joon's face. "And if you do eat more than three bites, I'll find out. You can bet your blubbery, nasty-looking ass that I'll find out about it. Now, get up off the floor and clean this house up. It's a mess."

Joon followed Aron out of the bathroom. Her stomach was aching and her mouth was filled with the vile taste of puke. Pushing past her discomfort, Joon set about her chores, starting with making Deen's and Dobi's beds. By dinnertime, Joon was just finishing the housework. She walked into the kitchen slowly and stood in the doorway. Aron, Deen, and Dobi looked over at her.

"Are you hungry?" Aron asked in a sweet voice.

Joon looked at her with wide eyes, unsure how to answer. Her foster mother could easily be playing her usual trick, so she carefully managed her expectations. "Yes, I'm very hungry."

Aron threw her head back and laughed. "Well, that's a shame because you ain't getting nothing to eat tonight."

Deen grinned from ear to ear while Dobi looked down at his plate of half-eaten food.

Joon's chin dropped to her chest and her shoulders slumped forward.

"Get downstairs, you little bitch. You're ruining our family dinner," Aron snapped.

Joon opened the basement door and descended the stairs. In the pitch-black basement, she sat on the dirt floor and leaned against the cinderblock wall. Her hope that school would be an escape was gone. Aron was the cruelest person she'd ever known, and Joon fed the hate she felt for the woman who was supposed to be her caretaker, sating herself on her emotion in lieu of food.

She sat in the basement until the door opened, only to be summoned up to clean the dinner dishes. Joon cleaned up from dinner with a renewed sense of energy fueled by her anger. She had a burning, gnawing feeling in her gut as she made Aron's kitchen spotless. When she was finished, she went back into the basement without being told. She was still scared to death of Aron, but she had taken a tiny piece of control back.

Joon heard Aron walking into the kitchen overhead. "Joon?" she bellowed, her voice echoing through the house.

"I'm down here," Joon yelled toward the door.

Aron opened the door and looked down at Joon. She rushed down the steps and grabbed the child by the back of her shirt. "Did I tell you to come down here?"

"No, but I finished the dishes," Joon mumbled, her bravery slipping away.

"What are you supposed do when you're finished cleaning the kitchen?" Aron said through clenched teeth.

"Squat against the kitchen wall until you come and inspect my work," Joon said, her voice cracking from the anxiety consuming her.

"That's right. You squat until I tell you that it's time to stop. I told you, it'll help those flabby thighs of yours," Aron said, slapping the top of Joon's leg.

Tears rushed over Joon's cheeks, and Aron's twisted face softened as she experienced a hateful release at hearing Joon's anguish.

Aron put her hand on Joon's shoulder and dug her fingers into the muscles there. "I want you to get upstairs and get into your squat position. When I'm ready for you to stop, I'll let you know."

Aron followed Joon up to the kitchen and waited until the girl leaned against the wall and into a squat. Her bone-thin legs felt fatigued almost immediately. But Joon did as she was told, because if she didn't, a worse punishment awaited her.

Aron looked Joon over. In the short moments that had passed, the child's legs were already trembling. At the sight of Joon's agony, Aron felt a surge of power. She loved the way her control over the child made her feel. *And the government pays me to do this shit,* Aron thought with a sinister smile.

Chapter Six

Over the next six months, Joon's body changed. Her twelfth birthday had come and gone with no acknowledgment, but despite the dark circles under her eyes from lack of sleep and stress, Joon was turning into a stunning preteen. The more the girl developed, the greater Aron resented her. The woman's punishments focused on dehumanizing Joon. She was often made to wear clothes too small for her or forced to go to school after Aron teased out her hair into a matted and tangled nest. Several nights a week, the girl was forced to stand in the doorway of the living room, her arms held out horizontally while her foster family watched their television shows.

Shortly after the new school year had started, Deen rushed through the front door screaming for his mother.

"Calm down, Deen. What the hell's going on?"

"Today, a boy in my class told me my foster sister was hot. She's a little slut, Mom. I won't deal with this shit. Do you know how embarrassing it is that she acts like a whore?"

"Is that so? Well, I'll put an end to this right away. This is the problem when you take in stray kids. You never know where they came from. Besides," Aron said, cracking her knuckles, "I think Joon is one of the ugliest girls I've ever laid eyes on. But I guess if you're willing to give it up to anyone who pays attention to you, then it doesn't matter what you look like." Aron put her arms around Deen's shoulders. "Don't worry, baby. I'll take care of this as soon as she gets home. I made her stop at the corner store on her way home to pick up bread."

Deen smiled affectionately at his mother. Secretly, he wanted to be the first boy to have Joon and had been waiting for the right moment, when his mother was out grocery shopping or visiting with one of her, what he considered annoying, girlfriends.

Deen and Aron sat on the sofa waiting for Joon. The woman was livid that the boys at school were noticing Joon. Her jealousy simmered in the pit of her belly, and when the young girl got home, the woman attacked her.

"You think you're hot shit, huh?" Aron screamed at her.

"I don't know what you're talking about. I didn't do anything," Joon said. She looked across the room. An icy chill ran through her at the smile on Deen's lips. Joon shuffled her feet, slowly backing away. The hateful look on Aron's face made her palms sweat and her legs tingle.

Aron moved closer and pointed her finger in the girls face, seething. "Well, you little whore, Deen told me that the boys in his class were talking about you. They're fourteen, and you're twelve. Do you know why boys that age talk dirty about girls your age?"

"But I swear, I didn't do anything. I don't even know any of the boys in Deen's class."

Aron slapped her across the face. "Liar! I'll tell you why they're talking about you. Those boys like you because they know you're easy. I bet you'll suck a dick quicker than eat all the food in my kitchen. Yeah, I bet you're a real dick tease. Aren't ya?"

Joon had never seen Aron so mad. Her heart was thumping thunderously inside her chest. Her palms were slick with sweat, and she felt as though her airway had closed. Pressure built in her head as a high-pitched ringing drowned out her thoughts.

Aron pushed her against the hallway wall. "So ya think you're so goddamn hot? Well, you're gonna show us how hot you are then. We'll see if you know what the hell you're inviting when you shake that fat ass of yours all over school. Come in here."

Joon crept in slowly. Her mind raced. She couldn't remember talking to a boy, not even in her own grade.

"Boys, take a seat on the couch," Aron ordered. Deen quickly took his seat, but Dobi hesitated. At thirteen, the boy was just showing an interest in girls, but over the years, his empathy for Joon had grown. He wanted to help her but felt powerless against his mother and wasn't willing to put himself in harm's way.

"What are ya waiting for, Dobi? I said sit down," Aron growled.

Dobi sat on the opposite end of the couch from Deen.

Aron sat on the edge of her reclining chair. "See, Sons, what we have here is what's called a loose girl. That means she'll have sex with anyone who tells her she's pretty. I personally think she has some kind of sex disorder. And as her foster mother, it's my responsibility to stop her from being a tramp." Aron turned to look at Joon. "I want you to take all of your clothes off."

Joon shook her head with conviction. The thought of getting naked in front of Deen and Dobi was more than she could handle. "No, I won't do it."

"You'll do what I tell you to do. I want you to remember that, as long as you're in my custody, you're my property. I own you. Now, take your fuckin' clothes off before I rip them off your body."

Joon crossed her arms over her stomach. She couldn't make eye contact with Aron. She squeezed her eyes shut as if she could transport herself to another place if she concentrated hard enough. But that wasn't what she was doing. Joon was repeating, *Let me die. Let me die. Let me die,* in her head.

She was so lost in wishing death upon herself that she wasn't prepared when Aron punched her in the shoulder. The twelve-year-old flew backward into the wall and crumpled to the floor. Stunned, her eyes sprung open and landed on Aron standing over her.

"Stand up," the woman commanded.

Joon put her hands against the wall to steady herself as she lifted her body from the floor. The girl had gotten much taller since she'd arrived at Aron's house, and she stood looking down at her foster mother.

Aron fell a few inches shy of five feet tall, but she reached out with her stubby fingers and pulled at Joon's shirt. The cheap, thin fabric ripped effortlessly, and as the front fell away, exposing her undershirt, Joon cried. Joon needed a bra, but Aron had refused to acknowledge any of the girl's needs. Through her hostile treatment of the child, Aron made herself feel whole.

"It's up to you, Looney Jooney, you can undress yourself, or I can do it. But you can bet if I have to do it for you, I'll beat you with a belt once you're naked." Aron narrowed her eyes at Joon. "A whipping you won't soon forget."

Joon's hands were shaking. The threat of the belt against her bare skin brought back the memory of a few years ago when Aron had pulled Joon's pants down, made her lay facedown on the dirt floor in the basement, and whipped her raw.

The young girl unbuttoned her jeans and slid them off as best she could—she was shaking so hard from fear that it was difficult to do. Her face was bright red as she stood before Deen and Dobi in her underwear, sobbing.

"Everything," Aron said. "Take everything off."

Joon removed her undershirt and underwear and then put one arm over her chest, using the other hand to cover her crotch.

Aron walked back to her chair and sat down. Joon stood awkwardly, trying to steady herself as her head spun. She had a stabbing pain in the pit of her stomach when she glanced at Deen. He licked his lips, and the way he looked at her made her sick. She didn't know exactly what the look in his eyes was telling her, but her instincts sent panic coursing through her veins.

"Hands to your sides," Aron said as she sat back and relaxed in her chair.

Joon shook her head. Before Aron could say anything, Deen snorted. "Did you hear what my mom told ya to do? Put your hands to your sides. Do I need to come over there and punch ya in the gut?"

Joon reluctantly dropped her hands, exposing her naked body to the three of them. Dobi quickly averted his eyes, but after a few seconds, his curiosity won out, and he took a long look at Joon. It made him feel like a rotten person, and he peeled his eyes away from her body.

"Look at those tits, guys. I bet that Joon is the president of the Itty Bitty Titty Committee at school," Aron said, taunting her and cackling a high-pitched laugh like Joon imagined a witch taking flight on her broom would.

Deen sat on the edge of the sofa. "So, is what my mom said true? Are you sucking guys off? Do you use the boy's locker room to do it? Is that where you take them?"

Unable to control her embarrassment, Joon let a sob escape. "I don't know what you're talking about. Please stop doing this to me. I didn't do anything wrong, I swear. I would never do anything with the boys in school. I don't even like them."

Aron watched intently—her hateful soul was being replenished with the anguish of a twelve-year-old soul. The woman smiled and stood. "Come on, you two. I want you to help me make dinner."

Joon bent down and reached for her jeans, but Aron stopped her by banging her foot on the floor.

"What do you think you're doing, Looney Jooney?" Aron hissed.

"Putting my clothes on so I can start my chores," the girl mumbled, still blubbering openly.

"No, no, no. You'll stand there naked until I say you can cover up. That way, every time one of us walks by you, we can gawk at that disgusting body of yours." Aron leaned in so close to Joon's face that she feared the rotten smell of Aron's breath would make her faint. "See, you ruined yourself when you acted like a slut at school. Ain't no decent boy ever going to want you now."

Aron left the living room, and Dobi practically ran to keep up with her. He felt uncomfortable for Joon and wanted the torment to end. Deen, however, took his time walking across the living room. When he was only a few feet away from her, Joon covered her breasts and crotch with her hands.

Deen grabbed her wrists. "What were you told about keeping your hands at your sides? Don't you know how to listen?"

Joon could barely breathe, she was bawling so hard. She felt subhuman.

Deen pulled on the arm over her breasts and pushed it to her side. Then he did the same with the hand covering her crotch. He started to walk away but stopped and turned back to her. "Since you're already ruined, I figure a little taste won't hurt anything," he said. The boy shoved his fingers inside of her. Joon reared back against the wall behind her. Deen pulled his fingers out and stuck them in his mouth. "Yummy. I guess little whores taste good too. Don't worry. I'll be back to taste more."

That night, alone and naked on the dirt floor of the basement, Joon couldn't sleep. It wasn't the rodents and bugs keeping her awake—Deen's threat had scared the hell out of her. She lay awake all night, morbid thoughts of Deen consuming her now that Aron had opened a new door for her twisted son. Joon knew enough about sex to be very afraid of what he might do to her.

Over the years, Aron had severely abused and neglected her. But now Deen was about to bring her torture to a whole new level—one that made her need for safety as important as the air she breathed.

Chapter Seven

———————————————————■———————————————————

The following morning when the basement door opened, Joon looked up at that shadow standing at the top of the stairs. She blinked against the light from the kitchen and held her breath as she waited for what came next.

"Get up here, Looney Jooney," Aron screeched.

Joon ascended the stairs with trepidation. She was cold and self-conscious. When she reached the top, she looked at her foster mother. There was a frosty deadness to Aron's eyes as she stared back through narrowed slits, her lips tightly pressed together. Aron grabbed a handful of Joon's hair and pulled her into the center of the kitchen.

"Put your fuckin' clothes on, you animal," Aron said, pointing to the T-shirt and jeans on the kitchen table.

Joon quickly dressed and turned back to Aron.

"What are you looking at? Move it. Go wash your ugly face and get ready for school."

Joon moved quickly through the house and into the bathroom. She shut the door behind her and leaned over the sink as she splashed water on her face. She ran her fingers through her hair and tucked the long strands behind her ears. When she opened the bathroom door to leave, Deen was standing just outside.

"Did you hear?" Deen said. He snarled at her, his facing turning into a twisted mass of pimply flesh.

"Hear…hear what?" Joon stuttered.

"Mom is going out tonight with her friends. So we're on our own after dinner and I'm in charge. I'm gonna make sure that Dobi goes over to that little asshole's house down the street to play, so that you and I can be alone," Deen whispered.

Joon's legs felt weak and she steadied herself against the doorjamb. Her voice was trapped deep within her belly, but she willed herself to speak, finally forcing out: "I don't want to be alone with you." She took a deep breath. "If you touch me, I'll tell your mom," she said, her voice cracking.

Deen smiled at her. "My mom doesn't care what I do to you. She's let me do whatever I want to you for years. And here's the deal." Deen leaned into Joon with his mouth next to her ear. "If you say a fuckin' word, I'll kill you. Who cares if you're dead or alive? Nobody, that's who. From now on, you're gonna be my little bitch. You're already a slut, screwing around with every guy you meet. So instead of you slutting around with the boys at school, you can slut around for me. Ya know, like my private sex slave."

Her blood felt boiling hot as it flooded her face. Her hands shook and her mouth drew downward. She shook her head, as if refusing to let his words sink into her brain. "No," she managed. "No. I won't let you."

Deen put his arm around her waist, pulled her close to him, put his mouth over hers, and grabbed her ass. Then he grabbed one of her breasts through her shirt. "You ain't got no say. You'll do what you're told. Period."

He gave her a hard shove, and she flew backward into the bathroom and fell to the floor. After Deen stomped off, she sat on the bathroom floor and cried. *What am I going to do? I would rather die than let Deen touch me again.*

On the walk to the bus stop, Joon was sick with worry. She stood in her usual spot, off to the side, away from the other kids. She took in the neighborhood she had lived in for the past four years. The street was narrow. There was an endless line of battered row homes. They all blended together, with their dark-red brick and stained, beige stucco. The small lawns in front were uneven, with overgrown grass in some yards and barely any in others. Litter from overflowing trash cans clung to the edges of the uneven sidewalks. Joon followed a woman's voice and watched as a bone-thin lady in an oversized housecoat screamed at her grown son for not coming home the night before.

She was surrounded by chaos, a tornado of unstable and erratic activity. Joon had been so caught up in her own hopeless situation she hadn't noticed anything outside of the house where her life was pure hell. Now, she saw things clearly, and while the neighborhood was in shambles and nothing seemed cared for, neither people nor structures, Joon felt less alone. The buildings and broken-down cars, the trash on the streets, and even the emptiness and hopelessness gave her a sense of peace, for she was the same as her neighborhood: broken, neglected, and longing for repair.

Joon got onto the bus and took a seat near the front. She leaned her head against the window and watched without really seeing as the scenery buzzed by. She took in a sharp breath and held it as a thought hit her: *The worst poverty isn't about not having enough money to survive. Real poverty is when there is no one in the world who loves you. When there is no other human to make you feel like you matter. As if you aren't worth the air you breathe. Poverty of love is the worst thing you can be deprived of.*

As the hours passed in school that day, Joon's dread of going home heightened. When the bell rang for the end of school, Joon walked outside into the sun. The school buses were lined up and down the city block, Joon's bus sixth in the line, as always. As she walked toward it, she suddenly stopped short and turned around, heading in the opposite direction.

Just like that, she walked off of the school grounds and kept on walking. Joon didn't know where she was going nor did she care.

Chapter Eight

Joon walked for an hour and a half before she stopped to sit on a bench at Carpenter Hall on Chestnut Street in Center City, Philadelphia. She looked around at the old but well-maintained buildings and the skyscrapers beyond. The air was filled with the sounds of people talking and laughing. In the distance, there was music playing. The aroma of hot dogs and popcorn floated through the air, pulling people toward the smells and making Joon's belly rumble. She felt as though she were in another world. It wasn't the dreary streets of the neighborhood where she had lived with Aron. It was filled with life, and there was an exciting energy all around her. She took comfort in all the strangers nearby, feeling camouflaged inside the sea of people.

As dusk covered the city and the tall shadows of the buildings thrust night upon Joon, her serene afternoon faded. The crowds of people milling about had thinned. She looked around her, wondering where to go. The shade chilled her, and she rubbed at her bare arms to generate heat. She looked around again and began panicking, taking in gulps of air through her mouth. She pulled her knees up to her chest and wrapped her arms around her legs. The thought of having nowhere to go now scared her.

Joon sat and sobbed. She cried for all that she had lost in her real mother and father and all that she had endured at the hands of her foster mother. Then, she laid on the bench until she cried herself to sleep.

"Hey, girl, what are ya doin' here?"

Joon opened her eyes. It was so dark, at first, she thought she was in Aron's basement. But then the cool, gentle breeze of the night air brushed across her face. She sat up quickly and looked at the black lady who stood over her.

"What?" Joon said.

"I asked what you're doin' here."

Joon put her hands over her face. "I came here to...I had to come here."

"You a runaway?"

Joon nodded. "I guess so." She started fidgeting and looking around, a bit worried that the woman would drag her back to Aron's house.

"You okay, kid?"

Joon nodded. Her body was tensed so hard that her muscles ached. "What are you gonna do to me?"

"I ain't gonna do nothing to ya, kid." The woman cocked her head to the side and placed her hand on Joon's shoulder.

Joon flinched and put more distance between them.

The woman gave her a tender smile. "You ain't gotta be afraid of me. Now, let me ask you: Are you runnin' from your daddy? Did your daddy touch ya in your private place?"

"No. My daddy was great. He died a long time ago," Joon said.

"Your momma givin' ya a hard time?"

"No. My mom died too."

The woman sat on the bench next to Joon. "Then who ya runnin' from, girl?"

She stared at the woman for a few seconds and finally admitted, "My foster mom and brother."

The woman scooted closer and put her arm around Joon's shoulders. "What they do to ya?"

Joon leaned away and looked closely at the woman. Her clothes were weathered and her long dreadlocks went to the middle of her back. But her honey-colored eyes were warm and made Joon feel safe.

"My foster mom has been mean to me since I moved in."

"And your foster brother? He mean to ya too?"

Joon nodded. "Yeah, but he did something to me and I can't stay there anymore."

"How they mean to ya?"

"Aron, my foster mom, she beats me and doesn't let me eat. I sleep on the basement floor. When I'm really lucky, the dog sleeps down there with me. Dobi's nice to me, but he's too scared of Aron to help me."

"Wait! Hold on now. You tellin' me this woman—bitch I mean—beats ya, starves ya, and makes ya sleep with the dog? What kinda no-good, rotten whore is she?"

Joon stared into the woman's eyes. She liked how outraged the stranger was by a few simple facts about her living situation. "Aron isn't normal. I mean, she looks normal, but when no one is watching, she's a monster. Nobody can see how she really is. She's tricky and people believe her lies. She's selfish. I think she's ugly. I hate her. And she does and says things to me and never feels bad about it. It makes her happy to see me in pain."

The woman's mouth pinched tight. "What about your foster brother? What he do?"

Joon's face turned red. "He touched me in my private place. Then he said he was gonna do more to me later, when Aron went out tonight. So after school today, I left and came here."

"When did he touch you?"

"Last night. Deen and Aron said I'm a slut."

"Do ya even know what a slut is?"

Joon shrugged and nodded. "Someone who does dirty things with boys."

"Lord have mercy. People are so fucking fucked up," the woman said.

Joon thought about how violated she'd felt when Deen touched her. She lowered her chin to her chest and cried.

"Come on, now. Ya don't need to cry. Look here, my name is Ragtop." The woman ran her long, slim fingers over the bandana covering her head, holding her dreadlocks.

The girl wiped the tears from her eyes and gave her a small smile. "Nice to meet you."

"Well? What's your name?" the woman asked.

"Joon."

"Joon...that's a great name. Is it your real name?"

Joon nodded. "My mom and dad named me Joon, J-O-O-N. Aron hates my name. She says it's stupid."

Ragtop pulled Joon closer to her. "Aron is a piece of donkey shit."

Joon giggled. "Yeah, she smells like donkey shit too."

"See that, baby girl, now you're catching on." Ragtop leaned forward and rested her elbows on her knees. "So, here's the thing—if you wanna come stay with me tonight, you can. I got a couple blankets I can share with ya. I ain't got much to offer, but I'm willing to share what I got."

Joon considered her options—she was cold and hungry, and she could stay on the bench or go with Ragtop. The thought of staying on the bench alone all night scared her. However, she didn't know Ragtop. What if the woman was out to hurt her and she fell for it and walked right into her trap?

"I don't know you," Joon said.

"So what? There's lots of people on the street that don't know each other. Ain't mean we don't try to help people out. Listen, girl, out here"— Ragtop waved her hand to the vast city around them—"you gotta find your people and stick together. There's all kinds of crazy on the streets, but it ain't usually the people who live on 'em that's crazy. It's the assholes that got themselves a home to live in and just like messing with us. You can stay here if ya want, that's fine with me, but don't say I didn't warn ya."

Ragtop stood and looked down at Joon, but the girl didn't move from the bench. "Okay, have it your way. Maybe I'll see you around." She turned and walked away.

"Wait!"

Ragtop turned back. "Well, are ya coming or not?"

Joon got to her feet and joined the woman. She was relieved that Ragtop was so nice to her but also scared to be walking off with a stranger. Her senses were on high alert, but with nowhere else to go, she had to follow the woman.

They walked silently through the streets of the city and eventually turned down a dark alley. Even in the dark of night, Joon could see sloppy graffiti on the walls. There was a man lying on his side, his back to the brick wall, and she stopped short, staring at him.

"Where are we going?" she asked as she watched him.

Ragtop looked over at the homeless man. "You ain't gotta be afraid of him. His name is Thatch. He sleeps there almost every night. He wouldn't hurt a fly. In fact, he'll be the first person to help someone out when they need it."

"But where are we going?"

"See that underpass?" Ragtop pointed down the alley, and in the distance, Joon saw where the highway rose above the street. "That's where we sleep. I got my stuff tucked up in there so nobody steals it. Besides, most of the people around here know it's my spot, so they don't fuck with it."

As they approached the underpass, Joon looked at the steep ledge, where black plastic was hung. She followed Ragtop up the incline, and at the top, the woman pulled the plastic to the side.

"Go on in," Ragtop said. She lit a candle and let the plastic swing shut. The small space was dimly lit by the solitary flame.

Inside the confines of the concrete-and-plastic home, Joon looked around. To the left, two blankets were folded neatly on the ledge. To the right, across the remainder of the ledge, she noticed two water bottles, a bar of soap, an old cooler, and a small cardboard box.

Ragtop shifted to the cooler. "You hungry?"

"Kinda," Joon said.

"What do you mean 'kinda'? Did ya eat today?"

"Yeah, I had lunch at school. I only took three bites though, in case I chickened out and went back to Aron's house."

Ragtop tilted her head and scrunched her nose. "What?"

"Aron only lets me take three bites of my lunch at school. She said if I eat more, she'll know. Then I have to go through a washout when I get home."

"A washout?"

Joon fidgeted, scared to tell anyone what Aron put her through. "She makes me drink this yucky stuff so I throw up until there isn't any food in me."

Ragtop's mouth dropped open as she stared at the frail child. The shocked look on the woman's face somehow encouraged Joon, who continued with her story. "Anyway, Aron says I'm fat. She calls me thunder thighs, fatty, Joon the balloon. She told me I can't eat too much or I'll be uglier than I already am." She lowered her head. "It's okay. I can go for a lot of days without eating…I've been doing it since I moved in with Aron. She would only let me eat when she felt like it."

"Sweet Jesus. What has that woman done to you, child?"

Joon shrugged her shoulders. "A lot of stuff. So that I'm raised right."

Ragtop sat on the ledge and pulled Joon down next to her. The woman opened the cooler and pulled out a few broken chocolate chip cookies. She pushed them toward the young girl. "Here ya go. Eat these. I got it from one of the trash cans in front of a fancy sandwich shop that gives out a cookie with every meal."

Joon wanted to rip the pieces of cookie from Ragtop's hand, but was embarrassed and slightly nervous to take the offering. Slowly, she started to reach out but suddenly snapped her hand back.

"What's wrong? I said you can have it," Ragtop said.

"You're not just teasing me?" Joon said, tears burning her eyes.

"Why would I tease 'bout a damn cookie?"

Joon's eyes were focused on the cookie. "Aron used to hold out food for me, and then when I would reach for it, she would hit my knuckles with a belt or a metal spoon. Sometimes she would shove the food into her mouth and just laugh at me. She would do it when I was really hungry, when she knew I'd fall for it."

"Well, this ain't no trick. I don't do that kinda sick shit to kids or to anybody. Now go on and take the cookie." Ragtop placed the cookie on Joon's thigh and turned back to the cooler to get two stale crackers for herself.

Joon's small fingers wrapped around the sugary substance and pulled it back quickly, holding the cookie against her chest.

Ragtop chuckled. "Ain't nobody gonna steal it from you. Go on and eat it. You ain't gotta worry about me. I ain't gonna play no tricks on ya. I promise."

Joon shoved the cookie into her mouth. As she chewed, she closed her eyes and savored the sugar, butter, and chocolate that made her taste buds dance. After she swallowed, she opened her eyes to find Ragtop watching her.

"Are you sure ya took those three bites of food at school today?" Ragtop said, half joking.

"Yeah, I swear I did," Joon said with fire in her tone. Her shoulders slumping, she let her hair hang in front of her face.

The woman patted Joon's leg. "Okay, I believe ya," she said quietly.

"You do?" Joon said, raising her head.

"Course I do. Why wouldn't I? Oh wait, let me guess—Aron never believes anything you tell her," Ragtop said.

"How do you know that? Do you know her?"

Ragtop grinned. "No, sweetie, I don't know that evil bitch. It was just a good guess. Why don't you settle down on the ledge right here and get yourself some sleep?" She laid a blanket over the concrete and had

Joon lay on top of it. Then she covered her with another blanket. "You sleep tight. Everything is gonna be just fine."

Joon pulled the scratchy, wool blanket up under her chin. She looked at Ragtop, who smiled down at her and started humming the Beatles song "Hey Jude." Joon was lulled by the soft murmur. She wanted to listen to Ragtop hum—she could've listened to her forever—but within a few short minutes, she was sound asleep.

Chapter Nine

———◼———

The next morning, Joon woke with a start. She sat up quickly and looked around, forgetting where she was briefly. Ragtop was lying next to her, on her back, snoring softly. Joon lay back down and snuggled up closer to the woman, cold from the chilly morning air.

Ragtop stirred and opened her eyes. "Good morning, Joon."

Joon smiled. "Good morning."

"How are you feeling today?" Ragtop asked, readjusting herself on the hard concrete and closing her eyes again.

"Fine, I guess." Joon was up on her elbow, looking into the woman's face.

After a few seconds passed, Ragtop opened her eyes. "What are you starin' at, darlin'?"

Joon giggled. "I was just looking at you and wondering something."

Ragtop closed her eyes again. "Oh yeah? What's that?"

"How old are you?"

Joon was so serious Ragtop tried to conceal her smile. "How old do you think I am?"

Joon shrugged. "I don't know. Twenty?"

Ragtop gave her a toothy smile. "I knew I liked ya, kid. Yeah, let's just say you're close enough." She was twenty-five, but age had never meant much to her.

"How long have you lived here?" Joon asked.

"You mean right here or out on the streets?"

Joon gave her a shy grin. "On the streets, I guess."

"Oh, I've been houseless since I was sixteen-years-old," Ragtop said.

"How come? Did you run away from home like I did?"

As Ragtop sat up and hung her feet over the ledge, Joon moved in beside her and looked up at the woman. Ragtop looked over at Joon, whose lips were turned downward and whose eyes held a deep sadness. Ragtop understood Joon more than the child could know. She knew Joon couldn't go back to her foster mother. She felt a bond with the girl she hadn't felt with anyone in a long time. She took in a deep breath before answering. "Yeah, I ran away from home too." Her shoulders slumped and she started rubbing the back of her own neck as she recalled the past.

"Were your mom and dad mean to you?"

"Yeah, kind of. When I was sixteen, I had a baby. A little boy. My mom and dad didn't have no money, so when I got pregnant, they were really mad. They let me live with them until he was born. Then, they made me leave the house, called me all kinds of names, said that God couldn't stand the sight of me and neither could they. I had broken the rules and had sex. Even though they let me live in the house until I had the baby, neither of them talked to me for the whole nine months. My brother and two sisters weren't allowed to talk to me either. I didn't get to leave the house from the time I found out I was pregnant until they took me to the hospital to have the baby. After the baby was born, a nurse brought a plastic bag into my room with some of my clothes and a letter. Want me to read it to you?"

Joon nodded.

Ragtop reached inside her bra and took out a piece of paper and unfolded it. Years of folding and unfolding the paper had made it wear thin along the creases, so she opened it gently, careful not to rip it, then cleared her throat.

"'Dear Brenda'—that's my real name—'you are no longer our daughter. You gave that up when you spread your legs like a piece of trash before you were married. You have been our greatest pain and biggest embarrassment to God and all others who know us. Your brother and sisters shouldn't have to bear the burden of your sexual misconduct. Our family will be forever damaged by what you have done. We have prayed to God to help us understand why you were ever born, and he has answered our prayers by letting us know that you were a mistake. You should have never been born and we must shun you. We are certain that you will go on to ruin your life and the lives of others. God has granted us the freedom from watching you walk the earth and destroying everything in your path. You no longer have a family. You are no longer welcome in our home. Sincerely, Sherri and Pete.'"

Joon had watched Ragtop intently as she read the letter. Tears had slipped from the woman's eyes and down her cheeks as she recited the words she had read so many times. The child put her hand over Ragtop's.

"I'm sorry," she said.

Ragtop looked at her through bloodshot eyes. "I ain't never read that letter to nobody. You're the only one."

Joon inched closer to the woman. "Can I ask you another question?"

"Sure."

"Where's your baby?"

Ragtop rubbed the back of her neck and rocked back and forth. "He died not long after he was born."

Joon drew in a sharp breath and covered her mouth with her hand.

"My baby boy—I named him Chase—he died a couple hours after he was born. His heart was on the outside of his chest. Grew that way for some reason. My mother, when she came to see me right after he died, told me that Chase was a child of Satan, not God, and that's why he died. She said my baby didn't have no heart, just like his mother. Then my mama turned and left me in the hospital room. Never saw her again after that. It's been nine years now. "

"Who's Satan?" Joon asked, wide-eyed.

"The devil. I ain't never believed her though. My boy was an angel. He was gonna be adopted by a real nice couple. They were really sad that he died." Ragtop paused to reflect, then shook her head slowly. "The couple told me my mother tried to convince them it was my fault, that I had brought death to my baby because I was such a horrible person. They thought my mother was a crazy fool. I was broken up about Chase dying and losing my family. It was a really bad time for me. That couple was right—they said my whole damn family was nuts. Took me a while after I left the hospital to get my shit together. I got hooked on heavy drugs. It almost killed me. Thatch, the guy in the alley last night, is the one who helped me stop getting high. I haven't done nothin' for three years now."

Hearing the sadness in Ragtop's voice as she told her story, Joon clutched her stomach. She wished there were something she could do to make the woman feel better. "I'm sorry, Ragtop. I think you're a really nice person. I'm real sad that your baby died." The girl paused for a long moment. "Your mom and dad don't know you at all. I think you're great.

I wouldn't have known where to go yesterday if you didn't invite me here."

The woman raised her eyebrows and gazed at Joon. "Thanks, kid. Enough of this sad shit. How about we go find some breakfast? That sound good?"

Joon pushed herself to her feet. She was unsure what would happen after they found breakfast or where she would go when she had to leave Ragtop's home under the bridge, but she was happy she had met Ragtop, so she didn't have to be alone on the streets—it scared her to think about being on her own.

Chapter Ten

As Joon and Ragtop walked back down the alley, they saw Thatch sitting up against the wall, nibbling on a piece of bread.

"Hi, Thatch. I want you to meet Joon," Ragtop said.

Thatch looked the child up and down, saying nothing. He turned his attention back to Ragtop. "Where'd ya find her? You better be careful. We don't need no cops comin' and givin' us any trouble 'cause they're looking for this kid."

Ragtop put her hands on her hips and her eyes bulged. "You know, Thatch, this little girl needs some help. I told her that you watch out for us and now you're making me look like a liar. I don't know if anybody will be lookin' for her, but I can tell ya, from what she told me, we'd be real assholes to let anybody take her back to where she came from."

Thatch flushed with embarrassment. Ragtop had a way of making him feel like he was a protector of the streets, and he strived to live up to her vision of him. He leaned forward and extended his hand to Joon. The child put her hand in his. "Nice to meet ya, Joon. I like your name."

"Nice to meet you too, Thatch. Just so you know, Aron doesn't ever come into the city. Well, only to fill out paperwork so she can get money for keeping me. But even when she has to do that, she complains about it for a long time before she comes here. She says Center City is for rich people who think they're better than everyone else. She likes to stay home, where she's the boss."

"I don't know who Aron is, but it sounds like she's got her head up her ass," Thatch remarked. Then a huge grin spread across his face, revealing his missing front teeth.

Joon's eyes got big as she stared at the space where his teeth belonged.

He laughed. "Yeah, I'm missing a couple of teeth, but I don't need them 'cause I got swag," he said, rocking his shoulders back and forth.

Ragtop laughed and reached for Joon's hand. "Come on, little girl. Let's get moving before this fool starts telling more jokes. Besides, we gotta get some breakfast before there ain't none to be found."

As the two walked down the alley, Thatch yelled, "If ya find anything good, bring some back for me."

When Ragtop and Joon stepped onto the sidewalk, the sun hit them with a burst of warmth.

"What happened to Thatch's teeth?" Joon asked as they walked.

"Sometimes it ain't easy to take care of yourself when ya ain't got the right stuff to do it with. You just learned your first lesson in street living: always take care of your teeth. That means whatever little bit of money you got, make sure ya have toothpaste and a toothbrush and use 'em every day. Thatch, well, he likes his booze, so he prefers to drink liquor over having all his teeth."

"Do you drink liquor?" Joon asked.

Ragtop pursed her lips and looked up into the blue sky, relishing the heat from the sun on her face. "Sometimes I like to indulge. What do you know about liquor anyway?"

"I know that Aron liked to drink it when she had a date over to the house. I got to take a bath and sleep up in the bedroom when she had a man friend over. She mixed her liquor with soda. When she drank enough of it, she would be kinda nice and really goofy. She would say stupid stuff to her man friend's like: 'If you wanna see skin, then pour me more gin.' When she told her man friends that, they would rush to get her more to drink. Sometimes, she wouldn't be able to walk, and the guy would carry her to the bedroom and they didn't come out until the morning. The day after she had liquor, she was the meanest. One time, after one of her man friends left after sleeping at the house for two nights, she was really bad."

Joon's voice trailed off, and Ragtop stopped walking and knelt on the sidewalk in front of the child. "What did she do that was so bad?"

Joon turned her head, attempting to avoid the woman's gaze. She took several seconds to find the courage to speak, wringing her hands together and squeezing her eyes shut tightly as images of the past ran like a movie in her head.

Ragtop gently pulled Joon into her arms. "I think it might make you feel better if you told someone. Do ya think that's true?"

Joon nodded slightly as the tears streamed down her cheeks.

"Tell me what she did when her man friend left after two days. It's okay. You can trust me."

Joon wiped her nose on her arm. "She dragged me into the bathroom by my hair. Then she filled the bathtub with really hot water, and while it was filling, she tied my hands behind my back and tied my ankles together." She gazed at the sidewalk and took in a long breath as she recalled the memory.

"After the tub was full, she threw me into the hot water. It burned so bad, and I was underwater, so I couldn't breathe. She'd pull me up, so I could catch my breath, then shove me back under again. She did it a bunch of times, until I couldn't breathe anymore and I thought I was gonna die. Then all of a sudden, she pulled me out of the tub and I landed on the floor. My body was burned from the hot water. I had blisters all over the place, even my face." Joon paused and touched her cheeks where the blisters had been. Then she shook her head, as if she could knock loose the pictures in her mind.

"It took a while for them to all go away. Aron gave me some medicine to put on them, but it was awful. The only good thing was she didn't hit me until all the blisters were gone 'cause she said she didn't want to get any of my 'gooey cooties' on her hands."

Ragtop shuddered, despite her will not to react. She had seen and heard a lot of stories over the years, but Joon's stories were by far some of the worst. The older woman pulled Joon into her and softly rubbed her back. "Why would she do that to you?" Ragtop asked mindlessly.

Joon shrugged. "When she was filling the tub, she kept screaming that she saw me looking at her man friend like I wanted him, and it took away from the attention he was supposed to give to her. She wanted to kill me that day."

"How old were ya?"

Joon thought for a moment. "I was nine. I really hated living with Aron. I felt sick all the time there. You know, not sick like I have a cold, but sick in my head. I never know when I'm gonna get in trouble and I'm afraid all the time that Aron is gonna do something really bad to me."

"Nasty bitch!" Ragtop said, devastated that an innocent child could be treated so horribly. "All right, enough about that woman. Let's go find us some food."

43

Joon was sniffling and wiping at her nose. She looked up at her new friend with a forced smile.

Ragtop ran her hand down her dreadlocks and gave Joon a heartfelt smile. "Look, Joon, I want ya to know you can talk to me anytime you want to. Maybe talkin' about this stuff will help ya feel better. Ya know? I mean, the things that woman did to you, it just ain't right."

Joon nodded half-heartedly. There were so many stories about the things that Aron had done to her over the years. She was worried that Ragtop would be scared off if she shared too much. Aron had drilled into Joon's head that no one wanted to hear her whiny, little stories about how bad things were and if she ever told anyone, Aron would kill her. "What goes on in my house is my business. I'll kill your fat ass if you ever tell people things about me," she'd say while pinching the back of Joon's arm.

"Hey. Joon. Let's get moving," Ragtop said, interrupting the child's gruesome memories.

Joon smiled. "Yeah, I'd like that." She took a deep breath. "Thanks for being nice to me. Other than my teachers at school once in a while, nobody's been nice to me since my mom and dad died."

Ragtop knew what it was like to be unwanted, unloved, and left on her own. "Well, Joon, you ain't never gotta thank people for loving ya. In this life, there are all kinds of people, and you'll learn that the ones worth keeping around don't ever need nothin' from ya but being nice in return."

Joon nodded. She felt comforted with her hand firmly grasped in Ragtop's.

Ragtop stopped on the sidewalk and crouched to Joon's level. "See that Dumpster over there?" she said, pointing to the alley opening. "That's where we're gonna find us some good breakfast. Go on and climb on the side. Get us something good."

Joon didn't hesitate; she walked over to the Dumpster with Ragtop looking on. The child climbed up the side and hung over the top, pushing boxes and paper around, searching for food.

Ragtop stared at her. "Now all of a sudden you know how to find food in the trash."

Joon nodded. "Most times, it's the only way I get to eat anything at Aron's. I dig through the trash when no one is looking."

"You're gonna be just fine, kid. Now, tell me what's on the breakfast menu this morning."

Joon grabbed a half-eaten bagel close to the top of the trash. She handed it to Ragtop.

"What else ya see?" the woman said.

Joon reached farther across and plucked an apple that was missing one bite and handed it over. Then she saw half a donut on the other side of the Dumpster. Getting down, Joon walked to the other side and grabbed the donut, smiling as she handed it to Ragtop, then dug deeper through the trash layers, in search for more.

"No, Joon. You can't do that," Ragtop said.

Joon froze, concerned that she was in trouble. "Do what?"

"You always gotta take food from the top. Once ya start digging lower, that's when you get yourself food that's too old and contaminated."

Joon gave her a perplexed look.

"What I mean is that the food below could be bad, ya know, nibbled on by rats and such. That could make you real sick," Ragtop explained.

Joon was still confused. "But I always dug through the trash at Aron's and never got sick."

"Yeah, well, that's 'cause it was a trash can in the house. Out here, we gotta share with animals and bugs. You see what I'm sayin'?"

Joon jumped down from the Dumpster. "I guess so. Is it because they got cooties? Aron says I have cooties."

"Yeah." Ragtop scratched at the bandana on her head. "Except these are real cooties. The cooties that bring disease from rats and bugs in real dirty places, like the sewer. The cooties that crazy woman talked about you havin'…they're not real."

The girl smiled. "Okay, so where to next?" She was determined to do whatever Ragtop said. She wanted to stay with the woman.

"Let's take a walk down to the park, see what's goin' on today."

As the two walked toward their destination, they ate the food that Joon had pulled from the garbage, and Joon took in her surroundings. There were all kinds of people. At a corner, waiting to cross the street, Joon watched as a mother in a red dress held her daughter's hand and spoke to her child. Joon edged closer so she could hear them.

"So, after school, daddy is going to take you to your ballet class. Then, I'll come and meet the two of you, and we're going out to dinner," the mother said.

45

"Yay!" the little girl, who was much younger than Joon, replied. "I love when Daddy picks me up from school."

The mom leaned down and kissed her daughter on the forehead, and as the light turned green, they walked to the other side, hand in hand, seemingly worriless.

"I hope someday I can be happy like that little girl," Joon said.

Ragtop looked over at the mother and daughter. "Happiness is about bein' grateful for all you got…even if it ain't much. The thing you gotta remember is most of the people who ain't got nothin' act the way human beings are supposed to act. We learn to be grateful for things that don't really matter to folks with jobs and money. For instance, take this food ya got us. You're grateful we ate this morning, right?"

"Yeah, that donut was really good," Joon said.

"That's what I'm sayin'. People who are grateful for what they got and not lookin' at what they ain't got are the happiest people on earth. Remember that," Ragtop said.

It had been many years since a mother figure had talked to Joon about anything with meaning. The child felt as though her life were just beginning.

Chapter Eleven

On Joon's first day living on the streets, she learned how to scavenge food from Dumpsters and made two new friends. Ragtop begged for money, and with it, they each had a hot dog from a street vendor for dinner. When they finished eating, Ragtop stood from the bench they had been sitting on.

"Well, it was a good day."

Joon looked up at her. This was the moment she had dreaded. She nodded and tried to give Ragtop a genuine smile. "Thanks for letting me stay with you." She took a deep breath and asked, "Where do you think I should go to sleep tonight?"

Ragtop cocked her hip to the side and studied the child. "Baby, do you think I'm gonna throw you away or something?"

Joon met Ragtop's gaze. Her shoulders lifted to her ears. She turned her eyes away from the woman and felt heat spread over her neck and face. "I...I don't know."

"Let me tell you somethin'. You're just a little girl. Ain't no grown woman with an ounce of brains in her head gonna throw you to the wolves. I guess you ain't learned nothing from that selfish bitch ya lived with, and that's okay. But you need to understand that I don't do that. Now listen, I ain't got no idea if I can help ya, but I'm sure as hell gonna try. You'll stay with me until we can figure out what to do."

"Really?" Joon said, jumping to her feet and wrapping her arms around the woman's waist.

Ragtop hadn't felt genuine gratitude from another human in a long time, and she slowly wrapped her arms around the girl, and the two stood joined as a mother and daughter would.

"We best get going," Ragtop finally said. "I wanna get back to our cement palace early to make sure you know how to get there. We can't be together every minute of every day, so I'm gonna teach ya how to find your way back."

On the way to the underpass, Ragtop pointed out the landmarks so Joon could remember the route.

"You any good in school?" Ragtop asked, as they walked.

"Yeah. I always get A's and B's. Mostly A's though. Aron says I'm stupid, so I work really hard to do well in school. I thought if I got good grades, she would think I'm smart. But whenever I brought home good report cards, she said that I got good grades 'cause I cheated." Joon looked up at Ragtop and put her hand over heart. "I swear I don't cheat. I told Aron, but she never believed me. She got real mad and slapped me in the face 'cause I talked back to her."

"Well, I believe you." Ragtop tapped her chin with her index finger. "Ya know, I got a friend, lives over on the other side of Broad Street. Her name is Ginger. She used to be a school teacher, but she got laid off 'bout three years ago. She ain't got no family and didn't have nothin' to fall back on. Anyway, all she does is read. She's always at the library getting books. Maybe I can see if she'll teach ya for a while. You're just a baby, and someday I expect ya to get off the streets, and you ain't gonna do that if ya stop learning."

"Wow. I would love that," Joon said. "Do you think she would teach me?"

"Don't know. Can't hurt to ask though. I'll take a walk over there tomorrow and see if she'd be willing."

"What am I gonna do tomorrow?" Joon said, wringing her hands together.

"You're gonna go out and get yourself acquainted with your surroundings. Like I said, kid, we can't be together all the time. It just ain't possible. I'm an adult, and sometimes I gotta go out and do grown-up things," Ragtop explained.

"Like what?" Joon asked.

"Like things you don't know about yet. Let's just leave it at that," Ragtop stated firmly.

Joon didn't want to press the issue, afraid Ragtop would make her leave their place under the bridge.

When they arrived at the underpass, Joon set herself up on the concrete and pulled the wool blanket over her. With fall upon them, the days were getting shorter, and the cooler evenings too. Joon shivered under the blanket as Ragtop took inventory of their food. The woman looked over at the girl and saw her small body shaking.

"You cold, baby?"

"Yeah. It's okay though. I was always cold in the basement, so I'm used to it."

Ragtop's stomach flopped at the visual she got of Joon sleeping on a dirt floor. She knew homeless people slept in undesirable places, but sleeping on benches or a slab of concrete was a choice that didn't take away their freedom. The thought of the child being kept in darkness like a dog chained to a tree made her insides crawl. The older woman pulled a sweatshirt out of a bag on the ledge. "Here, let's put this on ya. That T-shirt ain't enough."

Joon sat up and slid the large sweatshirt over her head. It went down to Joon's knees, warming most of her body.

"Thanks. This feels really nice," Joon said, sliding back under the wool blanket.

Ragtop waited for more than an hour after Joon fell asleep to sneak away. When she did, she walked down the alley and stooped in front of Thatch.

"What's goin' on?" Thatch asked.

"I need to go out and make some money. This child, she needs more than I got. I need you to keep an eye out that nobody bothers her. Ya understand?" she said, pointing to the half-full bottle of cheap whiskey he was holding.

"Aw, come on now. Why do I gotta be the babysitter?"

"Because the child ain't got nobody. That's why. Ain't gonna kill you not to drink for a couple of hours," Ragtop scolded.

Thatch shoved the bottle into the canvas bag that held his belongings. "Okay, fine. But hurry the fuck up."

Ragtop shook her head at the man.

He sat up straighter against the wall. "I don't know who you're shaking your head at. I know what you're gonna go do now, and I don't like it. Remember how I found ya. I want ya to be real careful. Ya ain't done that in a long time."

"I know. But this time I ain't all fucked up on drugs. I'm gonna go out, take care of business, make some money to buy that child some warmer clothes, and that's it."

"Uh-huh. Ya remember what I just said. Once ya got real money in your hands, ya might be tempted to go buy some dope. I want ya to be aware 'cause bad habits come back on ya real fast," Thatch warned.

"I got this, old man," Ragtop said. She continued down the alley and onto the main street. *I'll sell my services to some dudes and I'll head right back,* she told herself.

Chapter Twelve

When Joon woke on the second morning, Ragtop was sipping on a cup of hot coffee. Joon stretched and shook her arms to bring them back to life. She wrapped herself in the wool blanket and sat down beside Ragtop, their feet dangling over the ledge.

"Good morning, Joon," Ragtop said. Her eyelids were heavy as she fought off sleep after being up all night.

"Good morning." Joon eyed the cup of steaming liquid and her stomach growled.

Ragtop produced a cup for Joon. "Mine's coffee, but I got you hot chocolate," she said, handing the Styrofoam cup to her.

Joon took the cup and pulled the lid off gently. The chocolatey smell filled her nose and awakened her senses. She breathed the scent in harder and then took a sip. The liquid slid down her throat and warmed her empty belly. She glanced at Ragtop. "Thank you. This is the best drink I ever had in my whole life."

The woman nodded. "I bought ya a couple of things this morning. By the way, you're kinda a late sleeper. You're gonna need to get moving earlier than eleven if ya wanna get yourself breakfast."

"I never slept much at Aron's house. I feel safe sleeping now 'cause I know you're here."

Ragtop considered her answer for a moment, not wanting to frighten the child by letting her know she had been away all night. "That's good. But here's the thing, Joon—we need to work on you being okay when you're by yourself. I ain't going nowhere soon, but we never know what life will hand us. Look at you, for instance. I bet you never thought you'd be livin' out on the streets with some black woman ya don't even know, and I never thought I'd be trying to help some little white kid neither, but that's the way things go sometimes. You understand?"

"Yeah, just like you never thought I knew how to get food out of the Dumpster. Like that, right?"

"Yep, that's what I'm saying. My point is that you're a strong, little force and you got through some really fucked-up shit on your own. I mean, you were just a damn baby when that witch got her hands on you. Hell, you're still a baby." Ragtop pushed her fingers through the dreadlocks and scratched her scalp. "I figure we was meant to meet for a reason. I ain't got no idea what the reason is yet, but I guess we'll find out in time. So for the time being, until we figure out something better for you, we'll take care of each other."

Ragtop grabbed a small shopping bag from the Salvation Army and handed it to Joon. She pulled out two pairs of jeans, one sweater, three pairs of socks, and a very used winter jacket. Joon looked at all the goodies, and her heart almost burst in her chest. She threw her arms around Ragtop's neck. "Thank you," she cried.

The woman returned the hug. "No problem, kid." As her eyes welled up, she turned her head so Joon wouldn't notice. She wanted to set an example for the child of a strong female figure. Since quitting drugs, she'd tried to be known on the streets as a woman of strength and compassion. Now, with Joon in her care, she could prove to herself that her parents were wrong about her. Ragtop wanted to make people's lives better, not destroy them, as her mother had said.

"Wait. I got one more thing for you, Joon."

Joon watched as Ragtop reached into the front pocket of her jeans.

She pulled her hand out and put her fist in front of Joon. "Close your eyes and hold out your hand," Ragtop said.

Joon complied. She felt the woman lay something soft in her palm.

"Go ahead. Open your eyes," Ragtop said.

Joon looked down at the bandana in her hand and smiled. "Wow. Will you put it on for me?"

"You like it?"

"I love it. Now I can look just like you."

Ragtop laughed. "It's gonna take a little more than a bandana for you to look like me. I'd say it would take a damn miracle."

Joon didn't get the joke but smiled anyway. Ragtop tied the bandana around Joon's head the same way her own was tied. "There," she said. "Now if anyone asks, you just say you're with Ragtop."

Joon jumped from the ledge and ran down toward the alley, where Thatch was usually slumped. She looked at her reflection in a window that was boarded up from the inside. Joon smiled at her own image and ran back to the underpass.

"This is so cool. I look like you. Maybe people will think you're my mom. Wouldn't that be great?" Joon gushed, excited.

Ragtop beamed with happiness. "Not likely, but that's okay, honey. If you're gonna dream, then you may as well dream big."

Joon leaned into the woman. "You're the best person I've met since my mom and dad died," the child said.

"Yeah, yeah. After a week with me, ya might change your mind," Ragtop said.

"No. I'll never change my mind." It had been a long time since Joon wasn't afraid and worried about her well-being, and now, she had such a strong sense of safety with Ragtop. She looked up at the woman who appeared so strong and sure of everything. Joon couldn't see beyond the present—living with Aron had taught her how to survive day to day. She hadn't been taught to think about the future, and in this case, she didn't want to either. She liked her new friend and wasn't about to give her up so easily.

"Honey, you don't even know me that well. Listen, ya can't trust too easy out here on the streets. You'll get eaten alive. Do ya understand?"

Joon shrugged and shook her head.

Ragtop drew in a deep breath and released it. "When you're living on the streets and you ain't got no doors or windows to keep the bad people out, you gotta be on your toes." The woman put her hand on Joon's stomach. "When you meet people or somebody talks to ya and you get a bad feeling here in the pit of your belly, ya get away from those people as quick as you can. You understand now?"

Joon was thoughtful. "Yeah, when the lady brought me to Aron's house, my belly felt like it had bugs in it. I was little, but I remember that I didn't want to live with Aron. I wanted to leave with the lady who brought me there, but she made me stay. Do you mean that feeling?"

Ragtop, still deeply disturbed by Joon's situation, lost her cool. "Yes, that's exactly what I mean. Too bad that no-good whore-bag left ya to stay with that punk-ass bitch. I'm tellin' you, if I ever met that woman, Aron, I'll be forced to kick the shit outta her. I'd fuck her up real good!"

"You curse a lot," Joon pointed out.

"Yeah, I know. I can't help it. Makes me feel better," Ragtop admitted. "You know what else makes me feel better?"

Joon shook her head.

"Food! Child, don't ya ever get so hungry that you wanna chew your arm off?"

Joon shrugged. "Yeah, I guess. I learned how to be hungry. That's how Aron raised me. I can go for a long time without food…not that I want to," Joon added quickly.

"All right, well, let's get us something to eat. Then, I'm gonna teach you how to beg, so you can earn some money," Ragtop said.

"Can I get in trouble begging?"

"No, but if anybody asks you how old you are, just run as fast as ya can. Otherwise, they might call the cops, and they'll take you back to that asshole—or it could be a pimp, trying to turn ya out on the streets."

"What's a pimp?" Joon asked, suddenly feeling surrounded by danger.

"People that get you to have sex with men and take all of the money. You know what sex is?"

"Yeah. I learned about sex in school. When Deen put his fingers inside me, I knew he wanted to have sex with me," Joon said.

Ragtop rocked back and forth for a moment. Her repulsion made her nauseous, and she took a moment to collect herself, then pulled Joon into her. "I'm sorry that happened to you. You did the right thing by running away, 'cause Deen would've done exactly that to ya. Anyway, the pimp will tell you that they'll give you a nice place to live and buy your food and make sure that the men you have sex with don't hurt you. But it's all bullshit. You'll end up in a place worse than being on the streets and the pimps will beat you and use you and make you feel like you're nothing. Having sex with someone should be special—you know, when you love somebody. You're too young for sex now, but when you're older, you'll want to experience it with someone great."

"I don't know about that," Joon said, her eyes on the ground. Ragtop's lesson was scaring her…and making her feel a little embarrassed. "I miss my mommy and daddy."

"I know you do, baby. What happened to them? How did they die?"

Joon tilted her head to meet Ragtop's eyes. "Aron told me my mom and dad died because they were poor white trash who did stupid stuff.

She said my mom probably caught a disease from being a slut and gave it to my dad. And she told me that I would end up just like my mom 'cause I'm a slut too."

"Oh for fuck's sake! That woman is unbelievable. I hope someday I meet her, just so I can teach her a lesson. Didn't anyone from the state ever check on you after they left you there?"

"Yeah, they did," Joon said sadly. "Before the lady would come, Aron would let me get cleaned up and she even let me eat a little. When the lady came to talk, Aron made me tell her I loved living there and that I never wanted to leave."

"Did you ever think about ratting the bitch out?"

Joon scrunched her eyebrows and tilted her head.

"Tattling. You know, telling the state woman what was happening to you in that house."

"No way. Aron said they would never believe me, and if I ever told, she would find out and boil my hands in hot oil on the stove." Joon spread her hands open and looked down at them then she turned back to the older woman. "She would have too."

Ragtop shook the images from her mind. "Back to your parents, Joon. You know that Aron was lying to you about how they died. Maybe one day you'll figure out what really happened."

Joon leaned her head on Ragtop's chest—the child was starved for love and human contact. "All I know is I remember my mom took me to school one day and she never came back. I remember my third grade teacher crying when she told me that my mom and dad weren't coming home that night and that someone was coming to pick me up. I was so scared that I didn't talk to anybody. All I did was cry because I wanted my parents. Next thing I knew, I was living with Aron."

"I'm sorry, Joon. It sounds awful. At least I know my mother was crazy and threw my ass out for no good reason. I was old enough to understand some of it. But you were so young…makes my heart feel heavy to think about you being out there without your mama to love ya."

"Yeah, but maybe you'll love me," Joon said, desperately wanting to be loved by the woman.

"What? I love ya already, sugar."

Joon beamed.

"Come on, now. Let's go teach you how to beg."

Chapter Thirteen

—————————◼—————————

If there were such a thing as the perfect beggar, it would have been Joon. She was a likeable child, shy and distant, with a sadness that tore at the hearts of men and women. Joon held a small sign that read: *I'm Hungry*. Ragtop had insisted that Joon write it herself, so people would know it was done by a child's hand.

Joon would sit on the sidewalk on South Broad Street with her cardboard sign, with its large, black wording, and a rusty coffee can. She had been begging for a few weeks in the same spot when a woman approached her.

"How are you today, honey?"

Joon looked up at the stout, cheerful woman with long, brown hair staring down on her. "I'm fine," she mumbled.

"Would you like me to buy you a sandwich from the deli across the street?"

"That would really nice." Joon smiled.

"Good. You wait right here and I'll bring it back for you."

Several minutes had passed when Joon noticed the woman coming out of the deli holding a bag. When she approached and handed Joon the bag, she said, "I got you a turkey and cheese hoagie. There are chips, a soda, and a pack of cookies for dessert."

"Thank you," Joon said, opening the bag and looking inside.

"So, honey, where's your mom and dad?"

Joon got that sensation in the pit of her stomach, the one that Ragtop had warned her to recognize, and she rolled up the bag and focused on the woman out of the corner of her eye. "They're coming to meet me here soon."

"I don't see them anywhere. Are you lying to me?"

There was an edge to the question Joon didn't like. "No, my mom and dad are meeting me here." She rose to her feet slowly, but the lady stepped closer, and Joon backed up against the wall.

"I think you should come with me. I'm sure I can help you find a place to sleep. I hate seeing children like you out here on the streets." The woman was still smiling, but there was something off about it, like when she'd first met Aron.

"No thank you," she said, trying to squeeze between the wall and the woman.

The woman's hand clasped down on Joon's wrist, and she put her mouth next to Joon's ear. "Listen, you little shit. I just paid eight bucks for that food you're holding. You need to relax and walk with me. My car is parked at the end of the block. Now, get moving."

Joon yanked hard on her arm, trying to pull her wrist away, but the woman held tight as she moved down the block. "If you make a scene, this will be much harder for you," she whispered.

"Hey!" a voice boomed from behind them.

Joon turned and saw Ragtop rushing up to them.

Ragtop stood in front of the lady, her feet set apart and hands clenched into fists. "Well, if it isn't Bailey. Always looking for new blood to satisfy that lousy prick pimp of yours." Ragtop's teeth were bared and she was swaying from side to side, like a boxer waiting for the fight to start. She kept her eyes locked on Bailey as she spoke. "Joon, baby, I want you to go over and stand with that big black man. See that real tall one standing over near the bench?"

Joon looked behind her, and sure enough, there he was. "Yes."

"Good. His name is TeTe. He's a good friend of mine. Now you go on like I said, go over to him."

TeTe waved Joon toward him, and Bailey reluctantly let go.

Joon ran to TeTe, and he took her small hand in his own. They both stood watching the two women a short distance away.

Ragtop leaned in close to Bailey. "Let me be real fuckin' clear with you. That is a child. She ain't old enough to know her ass from a hole in the ground. I don't wanna see you around her again. That girl is with me, so you can take your fat ass back to Richy Love and tell him that she's off-limits. You tell him if I see ya bothering that girl again, I'm gonna go to the cops and tell them where to find him. Richy Love will know that I mean it too. Now, get yourself off this block before I whoop your ass."

"Fuck you, Ragtop. Who do you think you're talking to? You can't get over that Richy Love left you for me. Besides, you ain't the boss. You don't own this block, bitch," Bailey said.

"Oh, I own this motherfuckin' block every time that child over there is on it." For good measure, Ragtop pulled back her arm and punched the other woman in the face.

Bailey cupped her nose with both hands as blood gushed through her fingers.

Ragtop stepped back and lifted her fists in front of her. "You want more?"

Bailey, with her hands still over her nose, rushed away. Before she was too far, she turned back and screamed, "Richy Love isn't gonna let you get away with this, you whore!"

"Yeah, I'm a whore. You a whore. We all whores except for that child standing over there. Go home. Be grateful that I smashed that pig nose of yours. Consider it a free nose job," Ragtop yelled back before joining TeTe and Joon. She looked at the girl with a serious expression. "Joon, you remember what that woman looks like. If you see her on the streets, you leave in a hurry and go back to the underpass. If you can't get to the underpass, ya look for TeTe here or Thatch. You got me?"

Joon nodded. "Yeah. She bought me lunch, but then she grabbed my wrist and I couldn't fight her."

"I know, kid. That's how fast it happens on the streets. Remember when I told you about pimps that turn young girls out?"

"Yeah, but I thought pimps were boys."

"Yeah, well, sometimes pimps put girls out on the streets to find girls like you. It's easy for kids to trust women. But once they get ya in their car, they take you to their pimp. He beats you and does awful things to you, then he turns ya out. So stay the hell away from her."

Joon trembled, imagining what would have happened to her if Ragtop hadn't been there. She crossed her arms over her chest and held tight to keep herself from shaking.

Ragtop stooped and embraced the girl. "It's okay," she said, soothing her. "You're safe, but I gotta explain these things to you; otherwise, I ain't doing you no good."

Joon held on to the woman tight. Once she calmed down, she adjusted the bandana on her head and looked at Ragtop with a forced smile. "I saw you punch that lady."

Ragtop let go of the embrace to crack her knuckles and smile. "I wanted to knock her lights out."

"Yeah, Ragtop can beat a man's ass. I'm even scared of her," TeTe said.

Ragtop and Joon looked at him. Joon was mesmerized by his size. TeTe stood over six feet tall. He wore his curly hair cropped tight to his head. His facial expression was serious and Joon thought that maybe he was angry with her.

"Don't worry, baby. TeTe ain't mad at you," Ragtop said, reading the girl's expression. "Stop looking at her like that, TeTe. Can't you see you're making the kid nervous?"

Joon continued to watch the man, taking in his dark-brown skin and high cheekbones. Then TeTe gave the girl a smile to die for, and Joon relaxed and smiled back.

Ragtop shook her hips back and forth. "You two ain't been properly introduced. TeTe, this is Joon. Joon, meet TeTe."

"Is TeTe your real name?" Joon asked.

"It sure is." TeTe bowed, took Joon's hand in his own, and kissed the top.

"You are a damn fool," Ragtop said, laughing. "Thanks for hanging around to help me out."

"It was my pleasure. Miss Joon, I have to be leaving now. It was nice to meet you and I'm sure we will be seeing each other real soon. If you ever need me, I'm at Rittenhouse Square at some point every single day, even holidays," he said and gave her bandana a gentle tug.

"Nice to meet you too," Joon said, then turned to Ragtop. "Will you show me how to get to the square where TeTe goes?"

"Yeah, course I will."

A short time later, Ragtop and Joon were walking back to the under-pass. Joon had had enough of a scare for one day, and she clung to Ragtop's hand as they made their way through the city streets in silence.

A few blocks away, after careful consideration, Ragtop spoke. "What happened today ain't good. Living on the streets, you're gonna come across some really mean people. There are gonna be people who wanna hurt you so they can get something. Do you know how to fight?"

"No. I've never hit anybody, but I've been hit. I know that if you really want to hurt somebody to punch them in the ear or mouth. It always hurt really bad when Aron punched me in one of those places. But you can teach me to fight. I learn real fast."

"Oh Jesus," Ragtop said, looking up into the sky, then back at Joon. "You sure had to learn things the hard way. Don't you worry none. Your time has come."

"So you'll teach me how to fight?"

"Yeah, Joon. I'll teach ya how to fight. Knowing how to protect yourself comes in handy out here," Ragtop said.

That night, as Joon lay on the cool concrete, she thought about how much better her life was away from Aron. The way Joon viewed it, she'd never had a home at Aron's house, and here, in the streets of Philadelphia, at least she felt like she was a part of a small family.

Chapter Fourteen

A s the weeks wore on and Thanksgiving approached, even Joon knew they couldn't sleep at the underpass anymore.

"Can we go somewhere else, Ragtop? I'm freezing here. It makes my bones hurt, and I can hardly sleep during the night because it's too cold." Joon pressed her hands between her thighs to keep them warm. "Do you remember a couple of weeks ago when I told you that I met a girl named Avery?"

Ragtop rubbed her eyes. "The girl who's going blind. It's a damn shame about that, kid. What about her?"

"I saw her this morning, and she said that a bunch of them are going to start riding the trains at night for as long as they can to keep warm. Maybe we should do that too."

While Joon was jabbering, Ragtop's mind was somewhere else. The woman was thinking how much easier it had been when she had only herself to take care of. She'd go to a shelter or even camp out at an abandoned house with some other homeless people. But now that she felt responsible for Joon's well-being, it was more difficult and risky to take Joon, because the places she normally went were filled with adults.

"Ragtop? Are you listening to me? Did you hear what I said about the trains?"

"Yes, child, I heard you. I got other things on my mind. You're too young to be riding around on a train all night. Besides, that could be dangerous. Gangs take trains. I have something else in mind."

Joon smiled and clapped her hands together. "Really? What?"

"Nothin' I can tell ya about right now. You'll just have to trust me. I promise, tonight will be our last night at the underpass. After tonight, I'll get us somewhere we can stay warm and take baths. How's that sound?"

Joon had been with Ragtop for almost two months, and having gotten to know her well, she sensed Ragtop was hiding something from her. "It sounds great, but how are we gonna pay for it?"

"You know what your problem is? You worry too much for a kid. Where I get the money isn't your concern. I said I'll take care of it," Ragtop said with a tone of finality.

"Okay," she said, but there was a touch of doubt to it. "I have to get going. I'm gonna be late for my lessons with Ginger, and she gets really pissed if I'm late. We're working on math this week."

"Oh yeah? That makes me real happy to hear. I saw Ginger last week. She said you're a real smart girl. I told her, 'You ain't gotta tell me that Joon is smart. I know she's smart. That's why you gotta keep teaching her. Because someday, she's gonna make a difference in this world.'"

Joon put her arms around Ragtop and squeezed her tight. "Thanks. You're the best friend I've ever had. Gotta go. Love you," Joon sang as she started to walk in the cold November morning.

She alternated between running and walking fast to the other side of Broad Street to meet Ginger. Ginger had a job at a local donut shop. She didn't make enough money to get off the streets, but it helped her take care of herself, and it was convenient for the two to meet there. Ginger's friends behind the counter always gave Joon a donut and glass of milk when they met, which was four times each week. Ginger had to work a day shift on Fridays, so that was Joon's day to study and get all the homework done that Ginger had assigned to her.

Joon didn't have a strong connection with Ginger—she was a good teacher, but most times, she was rather brash with the young girl. Ginger always wanted to know what the girl was thinking, but Joon was very guarded about what she shared. After Aron, she needed to completely trust an adult before she'd open up to them, and Ginger hadn't gained her trust. Joon was quiet—Aron had raised her to be silent unless told to speak—but she missed nothing.

That night, after her lesson and after she and Ragtop shared a can of tuna and the last of their bread, the older woman got Joon settled and left her alone. By morning, Ragtop was lying next to Joon on the concrete, and together, they were generating just enough heat under their blankets to keep them from freezing to death. When they woke, they gathered their things together and headed across town.

The unlikely duo walked into the lobby of an old, unkempt motel. The man behind the counter looked over his reading glasses and eyed them up and down. "How can I help you?"

Ragtop pushed her long dreads behind her shoulders and stepped closer to the counter. "I need a room."

The man cleared phlegm from his throat. "Oh yeah? For how long?"

Ragtop fidgeted with the waistband of her jeans. "I'm not sure yet. At least a couple of months."

"Well, you don't get a deal for staying longer. It's thirty-seven dollars a night, whether you're here one night or a hundred. The price goes up twenty bucks in the summer, when all the tourists visit the city."

"Fine. What do you need?"

The man pulled out a clipboard. "Fill that out and I'll need thirty-seven dollars for tonight. If you don't pay by eleven a.m. tomorrow, you'll be thrown out. That's how it works. Every day, you make sure I have that night's money." The man turned and stared at Joon. "This your kid?"

Joon shrank back and pushed her body against Ragtop. The older woman put her arm around Joon's shoulders. "Something like that. What's it to you?" she snapped.

"Listen, lady, I don't give a good goddamn if that's your kid or not. But don't let me find out you're doing anything to hurt her."

Joon was annoyed at the accusation. "Ragtop would never hurt me."

"Whatever you say, kid. I heard that song before."

Ragtop had filled out the few lines of information, writing her parent's home address on the form.

The man looked at it. "You live kinda close to be renting a room here."

"Are you renting rooms or writing a book? Here," Ragtop said, pushing two twenty-dollar bills across the counter. "Can I have the key?"

The man opened a drawer, pulled out a single key, and counted her change. "Take that hallway down to the end and make a left. Your room is on the right. Don't forget I need your money by eleven a.m. every day or you're outta here."

Their room had dark-brown paneling, and the floor was covered in light-blue carpet with dark-brown stains in various places. A queen-size bed sat in the middle of the room with a thin, red-and-yellow-plaid bedspread. A small television sat on top of a battered dresser. They both looked around, and Joon placed the shopping bags that held all of her belongings on the bed.

"This is nice," she said.

Ragtop raised her eyebrows. "Yep, it's a lot better than the underpass. I'm gonna put our stuff in the drawers while you go and check out the bathroom."

Joon rushed to the only door inside the room. "It's got a tub and a toilet and a sink, but they're dirty. I can clean really good, so I'll fix it all up."

"You gotta have stuff to clean with, and we need to use our money to keep sleeping here...get us through the winter. We'll see how it goes."

Joon turned back to Ragtop. "Okay. What do you wanna do now?"

"I wanna sleep. I'm tired as hell. How about if you watch TV and I'll take a nap?"

Joon pulled semi-clean clothes from her shopping bag. "First, I'm gonna take a bath, and then, I'll watch TV."

"You do that," Ragtop said as she fell asleep.

Joon went into the bathroom and undressed. She hadn't taken a real bath in months. The air on her skin raised goose bumps. When she stepped into the tub of warm water, she savored it. She used the products that they'd bought, and it wasn't long before the water became murky. She opened the drain, then turned on the shower and basked in the feeling of being clean.

Chapter Fifteen

Their first night in the motel, at eleven in the evening, Ragtop left Joon sleeping peacefully. She didn't return until five o'clock the next morning. Ragtop opened the motel room door slowly, and when she did, she found Joon lying on the bed awake, staring up at the ceiling.

"Where were you?" Joon asked, propping herself up on her elbows.

"I had to run out," Ragtop said.

"Why are you dressed like that?"

Ragtop looked down at her miniskirt and low-cut top and tried not to get irritated. "Why are you asking so many questions?"

"Because…I woke up and you weren't here. I was scared. I thought something bad had happened to you."

Ragtop sat on the edge of the bed next to the girl. "Nothing happened to me. I'm fine. See?"

"Are you dressed like that because a pimp turned you out?" Joon asked. "That's the way the girls you showed me dressed, and you said they were turned out."

Ragtop let out a heavy sigh. "No. I do not have a pimp that turned me out."

"Do you promise?"

Ragtop rubbed her temples and considered what to tell the child and went with the truth—or at least, part of it. "Look, Joon, the only way we can stay inside, in this motel, during the winter is if we can pay for it. I'm doing adult things so we can afford it."

"You mean you're selling sex." Joon sat up in the bed. "You told me never to do that."

"That's absolutely right. You are never to do it."

Joon scooted closer to her. "Then why are you doing it?"

"Joon...baby, I was almost grown when my momma and daddy threw me out of the house. The only way I thought I could survive was to have sex for money. I did pretty good for a long time. Then, Richy Love came along and turned me into one of his girls. That's when things went bad for me."

Joon laid her head on Ragtop's shoulder. "Why did things go bad?"

Ragtop grabbed one of her dreadlocks and rubbed it between her fingers. "Because Richy Love started giving me drugs. Holy shit, they made me feel real good too. Before I knew it, I couldn't go a day without getting high. That's when Richy took over my customers and all the money I made."

"How did you make it stop?"

The woman took in a long breath, held it for a few seconds, and let it out slowly. Reliving the experience gave her anxiety, but she thought it may help Joon stay out of trouble. "I met Thatch. I tried to get him to pay me for sex, but instead, he took me to a restaurant and bought me a hot meal. He took me to TeTe's house—he rented a house back then, before he got laid off from his job. TeTe let us crash there for a couple of weeks. TeTe helped Thatch get me off drugs. TeTe lived in another part of the city and kept me away from Richy Love for a couple weeks," Ragtop explained.

"Were you and TeTe in love?"

Ragtop grunted and chuckled. "Nah, it wasn't nothing like that. We were just really good friends—still are. TeTe has been with the same girl for as long as I've known him. Once they lost their house, they moved around the city, sleeping in different places, but they stayed together. TeTe helped me because, when he was hooked on drugs, somebody helped him. When Thatch brought me to his house that day, high and trying to sell my ass, he felt he needed to help me. I was young. I was so scared..."

Joon put her arm around Ragtop's waist. "TeTe and Thatch were really nice to you just like you're nice to me."

"Yeah, well, when I first saw ya, I thought you were lost. Then when I found out what your story was, I wanted to help you."

Joon's street smarts over the past months had progressed. She was tempted to let the subject drop but couldn't—she had to know for sure. "You're selling sex. That's why you're dressed like that, right?"

Ragtop nodded and lowered her chin to her chest. "Yeah, baby, that's what I'm doing." She looked Joon in the eyes. "But it's only for the winter, so we can keep warm. That's it. Once spring comes, I'm gonna stop."

"I think you should stop now. We can go live somewhere else. Maybe we can live at the train station or maybe we can both get jobs," Joon said, her voice weighted with desperation.

"I wish things were that easy, but they ain't. For now, this is what I'm gonna have to do. You don't need to worry. I know how to take care of myself," Ragtop said, assuring the girl.

"But what if something happens to me when you're not here?"

"Ain't nothing gonna happen to you. Keep the door locked. I have the key and I won't knock. That's the deal."

Joon's belly swirled thinking about Ragtop out on the streets, alone in the night. "I'm scared, Ragtop. I'm afraid something is gonna happen to you," she said and collapsed into the woman's lap.

Ragtop rubbed the girl's back. "Fear is just our imagination playing tricks on us. There ain't no such thing as fear. As you get older, I want you to remember that facing fears, running them out of your mind, is the only way you can really enjoy the life that you have. Now go on and get yourself cleaned up. When you're finished, I'll walk you over to Ginger for your schooling."

Joon obeyed, and as she showered and dressed, she fought back her fears, trying to convince herself they were useless. She vowed to herself that she would battle her fears. No matter how scared she was, she'd remember that Ragtop said it was just her imagination playing tricks on her. More than anything, Joon wanted Ragtop to be proud of her.

Chapter Sixteen

By Thanksgiving, Joon was alone every night in the motel room while Ragtop worked the streets. The girl tried to sleep, but always found it difficult when Ragtop wasn't with her. She didn't understand how Ragtop could get naked with so many men. She had done research at the library about prostitution, which helped her discuss it more openly with Ragtop. Joon couldn't understand how her friend could have sex with strangers, especially because Ragtop had told her that it wasn't enjoyable, but it paid the rent and kept them fed.

It was Thanksgiving Eve and Ragtop was getting dressed to work the streets, looking in the mirror, applying her makeup.

"Thanksgiving is tomorrow, you know," Joon said. "Maybe we can have a turkey dinner."

"That's the plan, sugar. I'm gonna work my ass off so we can go have us a real good dinner at one of those nice restaurants."

"This will be the first Thanksgiving I've ever celebrated," Joon stated.

Ragtop stopped brushing the mascara along her eyelashes and turned to face Joon. "I'm sure you had Thanksgiving when you lived with your mama and daddy."

"Probably, but it's hard to remember now. After I moved in with Aron, I wasn't allowed to eat with them, and definitely not on the holidays. Anyway, I'm excited we're going to have our own Thanksgiving."

"You can bet on it. You know, I've been saving money from all this work I've been getting. I thought maybe I could save enough to rent us a real apartment."

"Wow!" Joon breathed. "That would be great. Then we'd never have to live outside again. How much money do we need?"

"Well, let's see. We need first and last month's rent and maybe a security deposit. I don't know. About three thousand dollars?"

"Three thousand dollars? That's a lot. How are you going to get all that money?" Joon's shoulders slumped and she looked at the floor. She felt bad questioning Ragtop, but then, she had another thought. "I know! I can beg more and help us save money," she said excitedly.

"Nope," Ragtop said definitively. "I don't need ya begging any more than you do right now. You need to stay focused on learning. I already saved eight hundred dollars. I wish I could charge more, but these clients are just downright cheap. Anyway, I figure by the spring, we can leave this motel and find us something better."

Joon looked around the room. "I don't think it's so bad here. We got lights and heat and a toilet and a shower..."

Ragtop kissed Joon on the forehead. "That's what I love about you. I've never met anybody so grateful for the small things."

Joon shrugged. "I never had any of these things living with Aron, so I think having them now is great."

"You hang on to that feeling. If you can, your life will be much happier. Simpler too."

After Ragtop left that evening, Joon lay in bed watching the distorted images through the haze of poor TV reception, but her thoughts drifted to how lucky she was that Ragtop had found her.

When Joon awoke on Thanksgiving morning, Ragtop was lying next to her in the bed, snoring lightly. The child snuggled closer to the woman, who opened her heavy eyelids for a moment.

"Happy Thanksgiving," Joon said in a soft voice.

"Same to you, baby. It was a long night and I need a little more sleep."

"Okay. I'm gonna take a walk."

"Yeah, yeah. Be careful. Don't be too long," Ragtop said, easily falling back to sleep.

Joon dressed in the bathroom and slipped quietly out of the motel room. Once outside, she walked toward Center City. She only planned to be gone for an hour at most and didn't want to wander too far from the motel. It was early, but there were already homeless people lined up outside shelters and soup kitchens to enjoy Thanksgiving dinner. Joon said hello to a few homeless people she knew through Ragtop. As she approached the subway, she could hear angry voices coming from below. She hesitated for a moment, then went down to find out what was going on. At the bottom of the steps, a girl was pressed up against the wall, a teenage boy holding her there as he slapped her hard in the face. When Joon gasped, the boy quickly turned and glared at her.

"What the hell are you looking at?" he growled.

Joon backed up a step, but then remembered what Ragtop had said about not being afraid. Using it to bolster her confidence, she took a step forward.

"You better leave her alone," Joon said, pointing at the girl against the wall.

The boy let go of the girl's shoulders and turned toward Joon. "Oh yeah? Who the hell do you think you are, kid? I suggest you take your gangly ass back up those steps before you're sorry."

When Joon didn't move, he took two steps toward her, and as he did, the girl who he'd been hitting raised her backpack and brought it down on his head. The boy was knocked to the ground, and in a flash, the girl grabbed Joon's hand and raced up the subway steps with her.

When they got to street level, the two kept running hand in hand. When they made it to Rittenhouse Square, they flung themselves onto a bench, both girls panting. The teenager pulled her backpack into her lap and turned to face the younger girl.

"My name is Gia. You got balls the size of this city, kid."

Joon smiled. "I'm Joon." She waited a few more seconds to catch her breath before asking, "Why was he hurting you?"

"Because he's an asshole. Sometimes you run into people like that. I met him at a party last night. We hooked up and the jerkoff thought that because we spent a night together, he owned me. When I tried to leave him in the subway, that's when he started hitting me. Good thing you came along. I was sure as shit that he was gonna beat the hell outta me. Thanks."

"You're welcome," Joon said, looking up into the blue sky. "Do you live around here?"

"Sure, I live anywhere around here that I can lay my head at night."

Joon nodded. "I thought you were homeless. So am I. Well, not right now 'cause I'm living at a motel with my friend for the winter."

A trickle of dread crept up Gia's spine. She'd heard about the sickos that took children and made child porn. She told herself that Joon wouldn't be free to roam the streets if that were the case, but just in case, she was compelled to ask, "Oh yeah? That friend of yours. Does he have a name?"

"It's not a he; it's a she. Her name is Ragtop. She found me after I ran away from home and she lets me stay with her. When it got too cold to sleep outside, we moved to a motel."

"Oh yeah? So how does your friend pay for this motel?"

Joon lowered her chin, her hair swinging down to cover her face. She was ashamed to tell Gia the truth, scared that the girl wouldn't like her. "Ragtop sells sex," she said quietly.

"Huh. Yeah, I know a lot of girls my age who do that too. Most of them are on drugs and their pimps treat them like they ain't even human. A couple of them tried to get me to do it too, but if I'm gonna do that, then I'm keeping all the money. So I just stay away from hooking. Ya know?"

"Do you have people you stay with?" Joon asked.

"Sorta. I mostly stay with the kids under the bridge near Thirtieth Street Station during nice weather. Then when it gets too cold, we kinda go our separate ways 'cause there ain't nowhere that we can all stay together. I go to the same abandoned house every winter. There's a neighborhood not far from here where a lot of the houses are empty. I'm living with two girls from my group."

"What's it like to live there?" Joon was curious how others lived and was always looking for ideas to bring back to Ragtop. In particular, she wanted to find a way for Ragtop to stop selling sex but for them to still be warm enough through the winter.

"Ha. It's almost the same as living outside. There ain't no electricity or water, but at least it saves us from the wind and snow. There are lots of other kids who live there too. The three of us keep to ourselves. Living in those abandoned places ain't too great. There are lots of drugs and shit. Do you wanna see it?"

"How far away is it?"

Gia pointed to the west. "About a mile or two that way. Come on. It won't take long."

Joon considered what she should do. "Okay, but I have to be quick, or Ragtop will get pissed at me."

Chapter Seventeen

Joon and Gia walked for almost thirty minutes before they reached the building where Gia was squatting. They carefully wound their way around to the back of the house and entered through an opening covered by thick, blue plastic. As they stepped into what was once the kitchen, dirt and debris covered the floor. There were no longer cabinets or countertops—they had been stolen long ago—and the only item in the room that let Joon know it had been a kitchen was an old refrigerator with the doors missing, the inside caked in rust and dirt.

There were homeless people throughout the downstairs, mostly teens who sat in small groups on the floor. They huddled tightly together to keep warm and seemed not to even notice Joon and Gia as they made their way to the wooden staircase. When the girls reached the third floor, Gia led the way to a room that, like the others in the house, was occupied by clusters of teens.

A grumpy girl named Fipple glared at them. "What's up, Gia? Why are ya bringing that kid here?"

Gia grinned, exposing her stained, crooked teeth. "Shut up, Fipple. The kid just saved my ass and she ain't staying. I just wanted to show her where we live."

Fipple got up and walked over to Joon. "Okay, now you saw it. Go home."

Joon flinched and took a step back in the direction of the door. "I better go now," she said.

Gia put her arm around Joon's shoulders and looked at Fipple. "Stop being a dick."

Fipple put her hands on her chunky hips. "What the hell's the point of you bringing her here? She sure ain't homeless. You can smell that she's clean. You can still smell, can't ya, Gia?"

Joon felt bad that Gia was getting in trouble for bringing her, so she piped up. "I lived on the streets before Ragtop rented us a room at the motel. And I did take a bath this morning, but that doesn't mean I ain't homeless. If we can't save enough money to get outta the motel by the spring, we'll be living on the streets again."

Fipple's top lip curled. "Oh, boo-hoo-hoo. Cry me a fuckin' river. Poor little brat might be homeless after the cold winter is gone. How old are you?"

Joon straightened and pushed her chest out. "Twelve. I'll be thirteen soon."

"Well, me and Gia are fifteen. When you get to be our age and are still living on the streets, then you'll know what being homeless is all about. Until then, just keep your trap shut."

Joon shoved her hands into her pockets and looked away, so the older girls didn't see the tears welling in her eyes. She turned to Gia. "I have to go. Maybe I'll see ya around."

"Sure thing, Joon. I'll walk ya downstairs."

Once the two girls were outside, Gia looked at the girl seriously. "Hey, thanks again, Joon. Ya know Fipple doesn't mean anything. She's just bitter she ain't got a house and parents like other kids our age. Sorry if she took it out on you."

Joon shrugged. "It's fine. I know someone a lot meaner than Fipple."

"All right, cool," Gia said, nodding. "I, ya know, owe you one."

As Joon traced her route back into Center City, she thought about Fipple and Gia. It was too bad they didn't have someone like Ragtop to take care of them, but at least they had each other. When she got back to the motel room and opened the door, Ragtop was sitting on the bed, leaning up against the wall.

"Where did you go?" she asked. "You've been gone awhile."

"I met a girl named Gia. Some boy was beating her up in the subway and I helped stop him," Joon said proudly.

"What?" Ragtop looked jarred. "Wait. Back up. You went down into the subway?"

Joon heard the edge in Ragtop's voice and nodded apprehensively.

"I told you flat-out that you're never to go into the subway without me," she said.

"I know. But I heard the girl crying and the boy yelling at her. You also told me never to be afraid, so I went down to help her."

"For the love of God, girl. I didn't mean that you should walk straight into danger. I meant that fear doesn't do jack shit for ya. It's okay to be scared of real things, like someone being violent in front of you."

Joon's forehead wrinkled and she tilted her head to the side, tears welling in her eyes.

Ragtop softened. "I just don't want you to get hurt," she said. "Who was this girl?"

"Her name is Gia and she lives a mile or two from the square," she said. "I walked to a boarded-up house where she lives. There's a bunch of other people living there too. Gia's friend Fipple wasn't very nice to me, but I didn't let her see that she hurt my feelings."

Ragtop flew off the bed and stood next Joon, resting her hands gently on the child's shoulders. "Now wait. You went off with a girl that ya just met to a house that you never been to before. Do you have any idea how dangerous that was?"

Joon's eyes grew wide. "Gia is really nice. She was excited that I helped her with that boy."

Ragtop led Joon over to the bed, and they sat together. "Sugar, it don't matter how nice somebody is to you. Don't ever go off with people ya don't know. What if Gia were working for one of the pimps?"

Joon thought about it a moment and her eyes clouded with fear. "I didn't think about that. I'm sorry."

"I don't need you to be sorry. I need you to think about what you're doing when you're alone. It's okay this time, 'cause it worked out, but next time, you might not be so lucky. You pay close attention to me: don't you ever go off with people you don't know."

Ragtop stood in the bathroom doorway. "I'm gonna take a bath, and then we're gonna watch the parade on TV together. After that, we'll go out and get us a big turkey dinner."

Joon sat on the bed. "Okay," she mumbled, and the woman walked to the bathroom. "Ragtop?"

"Yeah, Joon?"

"That girl, Fipple—she said that if I'm still on the streets when I'm fifteen, then I'll know what being homeless is all about. Do you think I'll still be homeless when I'm fifteen?"

"I don't know, Joon. Getting off the streets ain't easy," she said, shaking her head. "Don't matter how old you are. People see ya different than them."

"Like how?"

"People who don't live on the streets think that you wanna be homeless or that you made yourself homeless somehow. They don't understand that, for a lot of us, we don't have nowhere else to turn. Just like you. You didn't have a soul in this world who could help you. After you're homeless for a while, it gets hard to pick up your life again. You're just a kid. You gotta have a future planned; otherwise, you'll be on the streets for a long time. But I ain't got the perfect answer—all I know is that you gotta keep learning and moving forward."

Joon knew what it was like to be thought of as different. She'd never fit in at school and certainly not with Aron and her sons. "How do we make people stop looking at us like we're different?"

Ragtop rubbed her temples. "Well, I don't know exactly, but what I'd say is, if you wanna change the way people think, you need to make a difference somehow. Ya know, do something that's so special they can't help but see you as a real person."

Joon thought about that for a few seconds. "Do you think someday I can do that? Something that's real special?"

Ragtop smiled at the girl. "I sure do, Joon. I think you can do whatever you set your mind to, and someday, somebody is gonna see how great you really are. Just don't forget me when you're all rich and famous," she teased.

"I'll never forget you. That would be like forgetting my real mom. You're my other mom."

Touched by Joon's words, Ragtop teared up and turned away quickly. "I'm gonna get cleaned up."

Joon scooted onto the bed and leaned up against the wall. *Someday, I'm gonna do something special and show all the people that just because you don't have a home, it doesn't mean you're not the same as them.*

Chapter Eighteen

B y mid-December, Joon had noticed a change in Ragtop. The woman had been distant since Thanksgiving, and she slept whenever she wasn't working, to the point where Joon felt as though she lived on her own. It was nine o'clock on a Wednesday morning when Ragtop entered the motel.

"Where have you been?" Joon asked cautiously.

"Working," Ragtop snapped, throwing her purse on the floor.

Joon recoiled and watched the woman to gauge how angry she was, but Ragtop wouldn't make eye contact. "You used to come home when it was still dark outside. How come you don't anymore?"

Ragtop undressed quickly, refusing to look at Joon. "I got more clients, that's how come. I don't wanna talk. I need to sleep."

"You always sleep when you're here. Then you wake up and go out again. It's not like it used to be," Joon complained.

"Yeah, well, things change sometimes. When you get older, you'll understand that."

Joon was quiet. Her angst at being alone again stifled her voice. She wondered if she would be less afraid when she got older. Joon's years with Aron had instilled in her a sense of paranoia about trusting people, but she also had a fear of being alone, terrified she'd continue to be abandoned by those who loved her. While Joon acted pleasant outwardly, on the inside, she grappled with her insecurities—she had a hard time feeling like she deserved it when good things happened. Her past experience had taught her that good things eventually left and bad things hung around.

Ragtop glanced over and saw the vacant look in Joon's eyes. "Come on, now. Everything is gonna be fine," she said before turning her back to Joon to finish undressing.

Joon watched Ragtop and noted that there was a lack of emotion in her words. *Maybe Ragtop is just tired from working every night,* she thought, trying to convince herself. But then her paranoia took over and she asked, "Did I make you mad?"

Ragtop threw her shirt on the end of the bed and shrugged. "Nah. You didn't do nothing wrong. Look, I'm going through some shit. Ain't everything about you all the time, okay?"

"But it feels like you don't ever wanna be around me anymore. We never have any fun together and we never—"

"Stop it!" The woman pushed her dreadlocks over her shoulder, turned with her hand on her hip, and stared at Joon. "I'm sick of you asking a million questions and actin' like I don't take care of you. You have a place to live and food to eat. Ain't that enough? What more do you want from me?"

Hurt to the core and feeling like her fears were coming true, Joon left the bedroom and went into the bathroom. When she was alone, she thought about how much Ragtop had helped her and she felt bad for how she'd spoken to the woman. After she collected herself, she sat on the floor next to the bed, where the woman was already sound asleep, and took comfort in the steady sound of Ragtop's breathing.

Over the next week, Ragtop made more of an effort to acknowledge Joon. She didn't want the kid to feel bad, but she had needs too. Her own needs had become her priority after she'd taken that first hit of crack a few days after Thanksgiving. She had blown through the money she'd saved—nothing, not even Joon, was more important than getting high now. She'd been clean for a long, long time. Once Ragtop was making money to stay in the motel, all the cash in hand drew her to the dope pushers on the streets. At first, she thought she could handle it. Just one hit was all she was looking for to get relief from the pressure she'd placed on herself. She hated prostituting, and being high made it a lot easier. A week before Christmas, she pledged to stop getting high.

I quit this shit before and I can do it again, Ragtop told herself.

Chapter Nineteen

On the morning of Christmas Eve, Joon woke early and turned on the television. She watched all the happy holiday commercials with a heavy heart. People getting ready for Christmas were depressing. Toys, food, Santa, clothes—the ads were nonstop. Everyone looked so content, and it put her at odds with her ability to be grateful for what she had and made her want more of what the people on TV had. Joon couldn't help but think about how nice it would be to have just a few of the things she saw on TV. The young girl walked over to the dresser and grabbed the last breakfast bar. She settled back down and flipped through the channels until she came to a movie: *A Christmas Story*. She was captivated by Ralphie and his parents. Joon imagined herself in Ralphie's life, with a mother and father and brother. What seemed so burdensome to Ralphie would have made all the difference for Joon. Ralphie made her angry, and she wondered why he couldn't see how good his life was with his family.

When the movie ended, it was close to ten thirty in the morning. Ragtop still hadn't come back from the previous night, so Joon took a bath and dressed, expecting to see the older woman asleep in the bed when she emerged from the bathroom. But when she was ready, Ragtop still hadn't returned. Just before noon, there was a knock at the motel door.

"Who is it?" Joon asked.

"Motel manager," a gruff voice responded.

Joon eased the door open and looked into the man's face.

"I need to talk to that woman who stays here."

"She's not here right now, but she'll be back soon."

"Well, I don't give a damn when she's coming back. She didn't pay for the room today, so you gotta leave."

"I…I can't leave. I have to wait for her," Joon stammered.

"You can leave and you will leave. I'll stand here and you can get your things together," he said as he pushed the door wide open.

"Go on. Get your stuff or you're leaving with nothing." He glared at Joon. "Your choice."

Joon hurried around the room, placing their few belongings into a large bag and filling a smaller bag with the little food that was left. When she was finished, she looked at the man, her eyes wide and her bottom lip trembling.

"How will Ragtop find me if I leave? Please let me wait for her."

"Listen, kid, I ain't in the charity business. What goes on between you and that lady is your business. I have people who are willing to pay for this room, given that it's Christmas Eve."

The motel manager gave her a forced smile that made Joon want to spit on him. She grabbed her bags and walked to the front of the motel. She prayed that Ragtop would walk in and clear everything up, but her prayers went unanswered. When she stepped outside, the icy wind cut through her thin clothing, and she dropped her bags and hugged her body. After waiting several minutes to see if Ragtop would appear, Joon walked away from the motel to look for shelter.

After about five blocks, she stopped and looked down an alley, her eyes finding a Dumpster. Her winter coat wasn't enough for the below-freezing temperature. She looked around her on the streets, to make sure that no one was watching, darted into the alley, and squatted next to the large container of trash. She could smell the waste inside the steel box, but instead of being repulsed by the smell of rot, she focused on the small relief she got from the cold wind biting at her flesh. She stayed beside the Dumpster for over an hour, until she ventured back to the motel to look for Ragtop. Not finding her, Joon went into the motel.

The motel manager threw his magazine aside and propped himself up on his elbows as she walked in. "What's your problem, kid? Didn't you hear me? You're not welcome here."

Joon pushed her windblown hair away from her eyes. "I just wanted to know if she came back looking for me."

"Ha!" the man grunted. "Get lost, kid. That woman ain't coming back for you. The party's over."

The man's words felt like a punch to the gut. Joon turned slowly and walked out onto the streets again. She quickly made her way into the heart of the city, hoping that she'd find one of Ragtop's friends. The only people out were the last-minute shoppers. Joon sat outside a designer clothing store, and as women entered and exited, she looked up at them, her blue eyes revealing the pain buried deep within her soul. Some women gave her money, but others just shook their heads in disgust.

Joon had hoped to make enough money to have a meal and get out of the cold, but she hadn't realized that everything, even most fast-food restaurants, were closed early on Christmas Eve. So she wandered the streets, ducking into doorways to catch her breath when the cold was too much for her to take. Her mind whirled like a tornado, thoughts of how to survive coming and leaving in flashes. She kept walking until she was standing in front of a major department store. People were flowing in and out of the doors, and she fixed her hair neatly under the bandana and entered the store behind a family, pretending to be part of the group.

The heat inside rushed at her and her skin prickled. Although grateful to be out of the cold, the sensation was unpleasant, almost painful. She kept close to groups of people as she roamed around the three-story building. It was three thirty in the afternoon when an announcement came over the speakers telling shoppers the store would close in thirty minutes. Joon had been inside just under an hour. She slumped as she realized she would have to go back out into the cold. As she sat on the floor off in a corner, camouflaged by racks of clothing, she pulled out a bag of half-eaten pretzels and dipped them in the last of the peanut butter.

Just before the store closed, Joon made her way out onto the street. She looked left, then right. There were very few people out. Two young women passed Joon, and she heard one say to the other that they were only a ten-minute walk from their destination. Not knowing what to do, she followed the two older women, and ten minutes later, they turned down a residential street. Christmas lights canopied the street for the entire block, creating a warm glow and giving her a kind of joy that Joon hadn't experienced before.

Joon kept her distance as she watched the women disappear into one of the row homes. She stood on the sidewalk for a moment before she noticed a narrow alley between the houses. She snuck around the side and, as she did, a window covered with sheer fabric gave her a view inside.

She listened to the laughter and the steady hum of the voices in the house. She closed her eyes and imagined herself inside with the party-goers, enjoying the food and warmth on this cold Christmas Eve. She slumped against the brick wall just under the window. Then she pulled the clothes from the bag she was carrying and laid them on top of her.

She was lonely, and as her unknown, new reality began to take root in the pit of her stomach, she worried about what she'd do next. She was scared that something bad had happened to Ragtop. Joon envisioned Ragtop lying dead somewhere in the city—she was sure that death was the only thing that would have prevented Ragtop from coming back for her. Joon let out a heavy sigh, fearful of the uncertainty she faced, and cried. As her chest heaved with uncontrollable sobs, she remembered what Ragtop had told her: *Fear is just our imagination playing tricks on us.*

She gave all of her attention to the statement and slowly regained control over her emotions. When she did, she was again aware of how cold it was outside.

Joon sat for a while longer listening to the murmur of people inside, and she didn't feel so alone anymore. Her fear of where to go next slinked away as she focused on the frozen breath coming from her mouth and escaping into the darkness of night until she lulled herself into a frigid sleep.

When she awoke, her body was stiff. There were still people inside the row home, and as she stood and peered in the window, she saw the crowd had thinned. After shoving her clothes back into the bag, she walked—Ragtop had taught her that in the bitter cold, you can rest, but moving is the only way to avoid death.

Joon had been walking for fifteen minutes when she saw a group of people walking together. She paused for a moment and then followed the crowd.

Chapter Twenty

It was almost eleven thirty that night when Joon entered Saint Monica Roman Catholic Church. The pews were already filling with parishioners for midnight mass. She slid into a pew midway down the side aisle, shoved her bags under the pew in front of her, and sat quietly, hands folded in her lap.

Joon had never been to a mass before and she felt peaceful as people kneeled, hands together and eyes closed as they prayed. She wanted to pray too but didn't know how. She watched everyone around her. Praying seemed so simple to other people. *Maybe God only teaches good people to pray and doesn't let the rest of us know how to do it,* she thought.

She looked to the front of the church and watched the priest talking about the relevance of Christmas Eve. "On this night, so long ago, God and man were united. It gave us hope. God fills us with wonder and promise. He has shown us that love will win over hatred and life over death."

The words penetrated Joon's thoughts, and she contemplated the meaning: *Hope. Wonder and promise. Love over hatred, life over death. Maybe if I believe, God will let me be happy too.*

Joon bowed her head like she'd seen the others do and prayed. *God, you don't know me. But can you please help me find Ragtop? I don't know what I'll do if I can't find her. I don't have anybody. She's the only mom I've had since my real mom died. She's all I have in this world.*

The people in the pews in front of her were nodding as the priest spoke. She wondered why she hadn't learned about God in school. Then the priest talked more about the birth of Jesus and Joon felt a connection. *That lady Mary and her kid had to sleep outside just like me. They slept with the animals to keep them warm, just like I slept with the dog in Aron's basement. Maybe I already am normal. If the church guy up there says it's okay and everyone is agreeing with him, maybe people won't think that I don't matter because I'm homeless.*

When the mass was over, Joon sat in the pew as the families filtered out of the church. Waiting until the last moment, she finally stood and walked out with the remaining people. Outside on the steps, there were kids about her age wishing people a Merry Christmas. Some of the older kids stood on the sidewalk and smoked cigarettes while others leaned against the stone railing, joking with one another. Joon forgot about the cold as she stood off to the side and observed them.

A voice came from behind her. "Hi."

Joon looked over her shoulder at a teen girl. "Hi."

"Merry Christmas. I'm Giselle."

"I'm Joon," she responded nervously.

"You homeless?"

Joon would have been surprised, but she supposed, showered or not, she probably looked homeless at this point. She nodded. "I have to go."

"Why? You can stay here tonight. Father John let's all of us sleep inside on Christmas Eve. He lets us stay here when it snows too," Giselle explained.

Joon looked at the girl in the dim light spilling from inside the church. "Are you homeless too?"

"Yep. We all are," she said, pointing to the kids Joon had just been observing on the other side of the elaborate cement staircase.

Joon backed away with hands raised and looked around to locate the quickest way to get away from the church. "Why do you care what I do?"

Giselle tilted her head and looked at her intently. "Look, I was just offering you a way out of the cold tonight. If you don't wanna stay, then leave."

Joon tapped her fingers on her thighs, weighing her options. "What do I have to do to stay here? I don't have any money."

"You don't need money. It ain't like that here. This is a church."

Joon's brows drew closer together and her face tightened. She thought about her options. She didn't know Giselle or anyone else at the church, but staying on the street in the cold seemed like a dumb choice too. "Okay. As long as I don't have to pay."

"Well, come on. I'll introduce you to Father John." Giselle started walking toward the entrance and, turning back, saw that Joon wasn't following. "Are you coming or not? The other option is to walk around all night and from the looks of your chapped cheeks, you wouldn't make it until morning."

What if someone hurts me here? But what if I die in the bitter cold on the streets? She looked at Giselle through squinted eyes. "I don't know you."

"Well, you can get to know me. I ain't an ax murderer if that's what you're thinking."

Joon crossed and uncrossed her arms, fighting her desire to flee. Finally, she decided the better of the two potentially bad situations was to stay at the church. "Okay, but I can leave if I want to, right? I don't have to wait until morning?"

"Sure. You can leave anytime you want. It's a church not a prison."

Joon followed Giselle back inside and down the center aisle, where the group she'd seen outside was laying out blankets and sleeping bags. Giselle spotted Father John at the closet, handing out blankets, and called out to him. "Father John, this is Joon," she said as they approached.

Father John looked into Joon's eyes. "How are you, Joon?"

Joon shrugged.

"It's okay. You're safe here with the other kids. No one will bother you. Here, take a blanket," he said, handing the item to Joon.

He hesitated before he asked, "When is the last time you ate something?"

"I had pretzels with some peanut butter earlier. I don't really have any food left...I mean, I have some licorice, but only a couple of pieces."

"Well, how about if Giselle takes you into the kitchen?" He turned to Giselle. "I think there are some sandwiches left that the Women's Auxiliary made for all of you."

Giselle smiled. "Thanks, Father John. Come on, Joon."

When the girls got back into the kitchen, Giselle led Joon over to the refrigerator and pulled out a tray. "There's tuna salad, turkey, or roast beef. Personally, I love the tuna."

"Doesn't matter," Joon said, gleefully anticipating how good it would be to have her belly full.

Giselle placed a whole sandwich on a paper plate and laid it on the table. Joon stood near the counter, watching.

"Can I use the bathroom first?" Joon asked.

"Sure, down the hall on the left."

Inside the bathroom, Joon turned on the hot water and washed her hands. She looked in the mirror at her red cheeks—they were peeling. Her hair was tangled from the wind. "You have to find Ragtop," she said to herself.

When she got back to the kitchen, Giselle and Father John were sitting at the table talking.

Father John stood. "Joon, sit and eat, please."

Joon slid onto the chair next to Giselle.

"How old are you?" Father John asked.

Joon tensed and looked at Giselle. "How old are you?"

Giselle smiled. "Fourteen."

Joon looked back at Father John. "I'm fourteen too," she lied.

"I see," he said, relaxing his posture a bit. "I must say you're a very youthful-looking fourteen-year-old."

Joon took a bite of the sandwich, barely chewed, and swallowed. "I was a preemie. I'm small for my age."

"Oh?" Father John said, nodding. "You see, Joon, it doesn't matter how old or even how young you are. There aren't enough shelters in the city to accommodate all of our homeless youth, but you won't find any trouble here. You're always welcome to come here during the day if you find yourself in need of God's love."

Joon took another bite of her sandwich. "I don't know God and he doesn't know me either. Even if we did know each other, I doubt that he'd love me."

Father John's green eyes shifted, sadness shadowing his face. "God knows all of us, Joon. We're all his children. God takes care of us and helps guide us so we can achieve all that He's planned for us."

Shocked, Joon placed her half-eaten sandwich on the plate. "God doesn't know me. Maybe no one told him I was born. I don't know. But he took my mom and dad away from me, made me live with Aron, and then took Ragtop from me, so if that was His plan, then I don't want to know Him."

Father John reached out to touch Joon's hand, but she instinctively pulled away. He pulled his hand back and sat up straight. "I hope someday to convince you that God does know you. He loves you and has a plan for each of us."

Joon went back to eating her sandwich, and Father John stood to leave the kitchen. At the door, he turned back to the girls. "When you girls are done, make sure you clean up and turn off the lights. It's time for everyone to sleep."

When he was gone, Joon looked at Giselle. "I hope I didn't piss off Father John. But I don't wanna hear about God who takes care of lots of rotten people and lets good people be hungry and cold and have no one."

Craving sleep, Giselle shifted in her seat and tried to keep her heavy eyes open. "The only thing that upsets Father John is when us kids who live on the streets are suffering. You ain't gotta worry about him. He's a good guy. Maybe if you stick around long enough, you'll get to know him."

That night, as Joon lay on the church floor, she couldn't sleep. Not knowing where she would go in the morning burned at her insides. She cried silently, missing Ragtop and knowing that, once again, there was no one in the world who cared about her.

Chapter Twenty-One

On Christmas morning, Joon sat up slowly and looked around. The other kids were already folding their blankets and carrying them over to the closet. Joon followed the others into the kitchen, where muffins and pastries were set out on large trays, and got in line for her breakfast. After eating, she grabbed her bags and headed toward the door.

"Hey, Joon. Where are you going?" Giselle yelled from behind her.

Joon turned around and walked toward her, closing the gap between them. "I'm going to find Ragtop."

"Oh. What's a ragtop?"

Joon looked down at her feet. "She's a person; she's like my mom. You know, she takes care of me."

The girl nodded and looked at her seriously. "What if you can't find her? Where will you go?"

Joon shrugged. "Don't know yet."

"It can get real scary on the streets by yourself," Giselle warned.

"Scary how?"

Giselle stepped closer to Joon. "Just watch your back. Be careful and stay away from the older kids. They can be trouble. And stay clear of the rowdy packs. They'll get you in deep shit." Giselle turned to walk back into the church. "Maybe I'll see you around sometime."

"Sure, I guess," Joon said, noncommittal.

As Joon left the shelter of the church and walked out under the overcast sky of the cold Christmas morning, she felt an uneasiness she hadn't felt since she ran away from Aron's house—the anxiety that comes with loneliness.

She walked until she was back at the motel, where she took a deep breath before entering the lobby again.

The motel manager looked up from the television show he was watching. "What the hell's your problem, kid? I told ya yesterday to get outta here!"

Joon stopped right inside the entrance, slid down onto the floor, and wept. "She didn't come back for me?"

The manager came around from behind the counter, bent down, lifted Joon by her arm, opened the door, and pushed her back onto the sidewalk, where she collapsed in a heap. As she sat on the cold pavement, a light freezing rain began to fall.

Not knowing what to do next, she stumbled to her feet and walked the city streets, searching the back alleys for cover. Ice clung to her everywhere. Finally, she spotted a cardboard box that had held a refrigerator— *probably just this morning,* she thought.

Joon lugged the large box into the narrow alley behind a row of houses, climbed inside it, and curled into the corner farthest from the opening. She lay shivering as she listened to the freezing rain tap on the outside of box. Inside, the cardboard kept her safe from the wind, but the frosty temperatures provided no relief from the freezing rain that had frozen her hair and clothing. She looked in her bags and, pulling out one of Ragtop's T-shirts, noticed her bright-red hands. They were blotchy, and Joon quickly wrapped the T-shirt around them. After a couple of hours, the temperature rose just enough so rain splashed against the cardboard instead of ice. A cold dampness now took up residence in her bones. It was already dusk when Joon crawled to the opening of the box and peeked outside. The streets were dark and wet as she wandered around looking for something to eat. Houses were lit inside with holiday celebrations, and she paused to stare into windows from the street, wishing she could be part of a real family and feeling sorry for herself.

Close to seven o'clock that evening, Joon got onto a bus with the money she'd gotten from the women in the high-end store the day prior. As she boarded, the bus driver watched her closely.

"Kind of young to be out on your own this time of night on Christmas," he remarked.

Joon gave him a lame smile. "Um, I have to get to my aunt's house."

"Oh yeah?" the driver said. "Well, why don't you have a seat behind me?" He bent over and lifted a lid from a plastic box next to his bucket seat and pulled out a blanket. "Here. You look like you can use a little warming up."

She took the blanket. "Thanks." She wrapped herself in the blanket and settled into the seat behind him.

"You eat today?" the driver said, looking in his rearview mirror at her.

"Early this morning," she said.

"My cooler is behind me. Go on and open it. I have a couple of sandwiches in there. You can take one."

Joon rushed to the cooler and pulled a sandwich out. She ripped the waxed paper open, her mouth was watering.

"You eat and rest. My shift isn't over until two in the morning. It'll give you some time to sleep."

"Thanks, mister." When she finished the sandwich, Joon settled on the seat with the blanket up to her chin. She suddenly sat up and stood beside the driver. "How do you know that I don't really have anywhere to go?"

The driver cleared his throat. "I see kids like you all the time. You're younger than most." He sighed. "I know the look on your face when you got nowhere to go. When I was a teenager, I lived on the streets for a couple of months until I decided I'd rather go home and put up with my parents' rules. Your eyes are tired and glazed over. That's a sure sign that you have the weight of the world on your shoulders. Maybe you can go home too. Like I did. All I had to do was put up with a couple of stupid rules."

"I don't have a home," Joon said. She slumped in the seat and tears streamed down her raw cheeks. "My mom and dad died. I've been on my own since I was little."

"Oh, I see." He sounded genuinely sorry for her as he said, "I'm sorry to hear that, kid. Like I said, you're welcome to ride until my shift is up."

Joon hunkered back down in the seat. Her clothes and hair were wet from the melted ice. It was an uncomfortable feeling, and it made her skin itchy. Blocking it out, she wrapped herself tighter in the blanket and fell into a deep sleep.

Chapter Twenty-Two

Hours later, Joon was awakened by the bus driver.

"Hey, kid," the driver said in a soft voice. "Kid, you gotta wake up."

Joon opened her eyes and sat up quickly. She looked around her. She was still on the bus. "What's wrong?"

The bus driver shoved his hands into his pockets. "My shift is over. You have to get off the bus."

Joon looked out the bus window trying to orient herself. "Where are we?"

"We're in Old City. This is a pretty safe area."

"Okay. Thanks."

Joon gathered her things and walked toward the door. She unwrapped herself from the blanket and handed it back to the driver. "Here, mister. Thanks for letting me use it."

"You keep it, kid. It's really cold out tonight. I hope you find some shelter," he said. The driver looked away, his guilt over leaving a child in the middle of a cold, dark night churning his stomach. "I wish I could help you out. I really do. I got a wife and kids at home, and they'd never understand. I'm sorry."

"You did help me. You let me ride the bus for a long time. Thanks." Joon walked off of the bus and into the night.

She had walked a short distance when she came upon a brick wall with a locked gated entrance. She looked around for any sign of other people, threw her bags over the wall, and quickly shimmied up the brick surface by grabbing the ledge. She jumped down on the other side and looked around her at the tombstones inside of Christ Church Burial Ground.

She scanned the cemetery, which was dimly lit by the old-fashioned-looking lanterns mounted to the top of the wall.

She walked over to the gravesite she'd visited many times prior and sat down next to the grave, covering herself with her new blanket. She'd had plenty of sleep on the bus; it was now a matter of not freezing to death by morning.

She ran her fingers over Benjamin Franklin's name engraved in the stone. A few months prior, when Joon read that Ben Franklin had run away from his home in Boston in 1723 to come to Philadelphia, she had felt inspired.

Joon had told Ragtop, "Just think! Ben Franklin ran away from home and became a successful newspaper editor and printer right here in Philadelphia. He got rich after he published *Poor Richard's Almanack*. I read some of them in the library. They had really good puzzles too. And did you know that he stopped going to school when he was ten and educated himself by reading? I'm almost thirteen. That means I went to school two more years than him. Can you believe it? This means I can do anything too. Right, Ragtop?"

"Sure, baby," Ragtop had said. The woman pulled Joon onto her lap. "You're the smartest kid I know. There ain't nothing you can't do if you set your mind to it. You just keep learning everything you can, so that someday, you'll get to make choices about the life you wanna live."

Because of Joon's interest in and connection to the late Ben Franklin, Ginger, her homeless teacher, had taken her to visit Franklin's grave. She thought about all that Ben had accomplished and was certain if she stayed focused, she too, could turn her life around. Slowly, Joon's self-pity, fear and loneliness faded and was replaced with hope. She imagined herself lighting a candle and thought of all the good things that had happened to her. She had found a refrigerator box to get shelter from the freezing rain, got a new blanket, spent hours sleeping on a warm bus, and ate a muffin and a sandwich that day.

"Thanks, Ben. When I left the church this morning, I didn't expect that anything good would happen if I didn't find Ragtop. But so many good things happened today that made my Christmas special," Joon said.

She snuggled up against the long tombstone in the ground. She clung to the hope that her life would get better. Even alone, without Ragtop, it was better than being in her foster home with Aron. *I'd rather die on the streets than ever go back there again.*

Chapter Twenty-Three

As the sun rose the day after Christmas, Joon gathered her things from the cemetery and went back out onto the street. Her small, thin body was stiff and aching from the cold. She walked around the block and entered a hotel lobby on Arch Street.

Joon quickly moved through the hotel and found a bathroom. She darted into a stall, locked it, and sat on the toilet, waiting for her body to thaw. She had been taught by Ragtop how to use bathrooms in public places. She stayed in the stall for an hour before emerging. At the sink, she washed her hands and face. While brushing her teeth, she looked at herself in the mirror and wondered who the broken child was that gazed back. Her eyes were ringed by dark circles, her cheeks and lips cracked and peeling. Her long hair looked like a cheap wig. She tried her best to clean herself up and look presentable, but it was no use. There was little she could do without a hot shower, soap, and shampoo.

After leaving the hotel, she made her way to Rittenhouse Square, remembering that TeTe said he hung out there. As she walked through the square, she spotted him on the other side and ran to him.

"Joon? Are you okay?" TeTe asked.

"No. Ragtop never came back on Christmas Eve. I don't have anywhere to go. I've been walking around for a couple of days."

"Oh, I'm so sorry, baby."

"Have you seen Ragtop?" she asked, holding her breath as she waited for an answer.

TeTe rubbed at his chest. "No, I haven't. It's so damn cold that I've been staying at the men's shelter. Me and my girl had to split up until this weather breaks. It's gonna be bitter cold straight through New Year's. We have to find you a place to stay."

Joon nodded. "I didn't know where to go."

"Well, why don't we take a walk down to a youth shelter? I know where one is. Maybe we can get you a bed there for the time being."

"Okay, but…" Joon looked away from TeTe.

"But what, Joon?"

"I'm really hungry."

"Well, we'll grab donuts on our way there. How's that sound?"

"That sounds good. I got some money."

"Nah. This one is on me. You keep your money. You'll need it later," TeTe said.

When Joon and TeTe arrived at the youth shelter, a line of kids ran two full city blocks. He walked her to the back of the line.

She looked up at him. "What time will they let us in?"

A girl in front of them turned and looked at Joon. "Not until two o'clock. So they won't be giving us any lunch. They usually have snacks though." She looked up at TeTe. "You know this is a youth shelter. They ain't gonna let you in."

TeTe smiled. "Yeah, I know. This is my friend Joon. She doesn't know her way around too well, so I walked her down. She's new at this."

Joon gave the girl a shy smile.

"Oh. My name is Pringle. I have a lot of experience. I've been home-less for almost two years." She didn't say it with much emotion, just matter-of-factly. "How long have you been out here?"

Joon got great vibes from the girl, something she didn't normally feel about someone she'd just met. "About four months. Where do you live when you aren't at the shelter?"

Pringle glanced at TeTe. "I can't say. It's a secret."

"Oh," Joon said, suddenly embarrassed. "Sorry."

The other girl pushed her hair out of her eyes. "It's cool. Anyway, I'm thirteen. How old are you?"

"I'm almost thirteen. My birthday is in February."

As the hours passed and the sun shifted in the sky, the shadows from the large buildings made the waiting teens much colder. Joon and Pringle talked most of the time, getting to know each other while TeTe watched and engaged occasionally. He knew that Joon needed to find people her own age if she was going to survive on the streets. Just like the part of society that lives in houses, homeless people had to have a support net-work too.

At one thirty in the afternoon, TeTe put his hand on Joon's shoulder. "I have to get over to the men's shelter or I'll be screwed for the night. Will you be okay here by yourself?"

"Yeah, I'll be fine," Joon said in a weak voice, mentally exhausted after all that had happened since Ragtop disappeared.

Pringle smiled at TeTe. "Don't worry. I'll look after her. Joon can hang with me. The doors are gonna open soon anyway."

TeTe gave Pringle a nod. "I appreciate that."

Joon grabbed TeTe's arm. "What about Ragtop? Will you look for her…tell her where I am?"

TeTe knelt beside Joon. "Sure I will. I'll ask around to find out where she might be. But listen, Joon, sometimes things happen with people. Ragtop taught you how to manage on the streets as best she could, and you need to take all those things you learned and use them now."

Joon's eyes welled and she lowered her head to not let Pringle and TeTe see she was upset.

"Don't worry about it. You'll be fine," Pringle said as they watched TeTe leave. "I know lots of people, and sometimes they disappear and you never see them again. That can't stop you from living. Shit happens, ya know?"

"I don't know what I'll do if I never see Ragtop again," Joon confessed.

Pringle put her hands on her hips. "You ain't got a choice but to keep on living. You'll see… Being homeless sucks sometimes, but there are times when it's really good."

Joon shoved her hands into her jean pockets. "I hope you're right."

Chapter Twenty-Four

Joon and Pringle were a short distance from entering the shelter when a man in jeans and a flannel shirt stepped out onto the pavement in front of the door.

"Sorry, everyone. We're filled up. There's a soup kitchen down on Porter Street if you want to try and grab a hot meal. We heard there are a few churches that have some room in West Philly. It's cold, and the shelters are filling to capacity. I'm sorry. We open again tomorrow at two o'clock."

Joon was shivering, not only from the cold, but also from the sudden realization that she would have to spend another night wandering the city in search of shelter. From her bag, she pulled out her blanket and wrapped it around her shoulders.

"Are you gonna share that or what?" Pringle said.

Joon extended her arm and the two girls huddled together in the blanket on the sidewalk. "Where will you go?" she asked her new friend.

"I have some options. I mean, they aren't great, but there are a couple of places. You can come with me."

Joon, flooded with relief, nodded. "Thank you. I feel like my bones are frozen."

"All right, come on. Let's get moving. We're gonna make a stop and try to warm up a little before we make the walk. You got any money?"

"Yeah," Joon said through chattering teeth. "I've got about twelve dollars."

"Good, let's go. We can stop at Wendy's, grab something to eat, and sit in there for a while."

Inside the restaurant, the girls went up to the counter and ordered. They took their food and sat in a corner away from everyone.

Joon took a bite of her burger. Her eyes closed as she chewed the warm meat. "Where are we going?"

Pringle shoved fries into her mouth and took a few chomps. "Over near Thirtieth Street, next to the train tracks. There's a group of kids that live there, but mostly when it ain't cold. Lots of people move outta there in the winter, if they can find shelter, but there's always someone there, and they got a couple of barrels that we light fires in to keep warm. It ain't the greatest, and you're still outside, but at least you can warm up by the fire and get some sleep. It's mostly boys."

A while later, when the two girls arrived at the site, there were barrels with blazing fires just like Pringle had said. Joon followed her new friend and stood in front of one of them.

"Welcome to the Tracks," Pringle said, stepping closer to the fire.

"Who's the new girl, Pringle?" Booz, the perpetually drunk boy, asked.

"Everybody, this is Joon. Met her waiting to get into a shelter. Fuckers closed the door when we were almost there. Anyway, she ain't got nobody," Pringle explained.

"Nice to meet ya, Joon. You're cute," Booz said, breathing the smell of whiskey into her face. "Do you need me to keep ya warm?"

"Knock it off, Booz. You're scaring her," another boy said as he moved next to Joon.

"I'm Quinn," the boy said, giving Joon a warm smile. "Booz is harmless. He's drunk, like always. Anyway, it's good to have you here. Better than freezing to death."

Quinn was just under six feet tall. His long, brown hair partially covered his brown eyes, and Joon couldn't help but notice how cute he was—and she liked that he stood up for her.

There was trash scattered all over the ground, and tires and logs were sporadically lying about.

Pringle grabbed her arm. "Come on. We gotta help get shit set up for the night."

Joon and the others pulled the tires and logs closer to the fires. Pringle dragged a large piece of cardboard in front of one of the logs to use as a mattress and looked at Joon. "We can share your blanket. I got an extra pair of gloves you can use. With the fire and our body heat, we'll be fine.

It's nice having another girl to share with. Sometimes the boys can get grabby, not that boys being grabby is totally a bad thing."

"I'm definitely not interested in boys."

Pringle giggled. "Sometimes it's good to kiss and stuff. It makes me feel closer to someone and I like that. Besides, it's no big deal. Anyways, let's settle in. The others who don't get into a shelter will be coming here, and we wanna spot close to the fire."

Joon followed Pringle, and the two girls covered themselves with the blanket. The frozen earth felt like concrete beneath them. As the minutes passed, Joon became uncomfortably numb. "The ground is so hard and cold," Joon said.

"You'll get used to it. Besides, after we lay here a while, the ground will soften up some."

Joon thought for a moment. "Let's spread my clothes out under us. That'll make it warmer."

Pringle smiled. "You're smart as hell."

Once the girls settled down again, Pringle fell asleep quickly. Joon watched the boys as they sat and talked. Knowing she needed to sleep, she concentrated on the puffs of vapor as her breath was released into the night air. She was comfortable with Pringle, but she missed Ragtop terribly. Her eyes welled, and as she sucked in a sharp breath, Pringle's eyes sprang open and she looked over at her.

"What's wrong?" she asked.

"You wouldn't understand."

"Try me. All of us here have been through crazy things," Pringle assured her.

"When I ran away from home, I met Ragtop. She's like a mom to me, ya know? I've been living with her since late September. Then, on Christmas Eve, she never came back for me. I don't know what happened to her and I'm worried she's been hurt."

"Look, Joon, all kinds of things happen to people living on the streets. Where did Ragtop go when she left?"

"She was out...making money for us," Joon said.

"Making money how?"

"Selling stuff."

Pringle pressed herself up on her elbow. "Is Ragtop a hooker?"

Joon nodded. "Yeah, but she wasn't working for a pimp," she added quickly.

"That doesn't mean anything. She's probably into drugs," Pringle said.

"Why would you say that?"

"'Cause I know lots of hookers. Most of them take drugs so they can sell their bodies. I mean not all of them. I know a couple of hookers that don't take drugs, but *they* mainly stick to hand jobs and blow jobs."

Joon's eyes bugged out and her mouth was gaping open. "What do you mean?"

Pringle scratched at the dry, cracking skin on her hand. "A hand job is where you, ya know, pull a guy's thing and a blow job is where ya suck on it." She lowered her voice into the slightest whisper. "Sometimes, I'll do things for guys to make a little money, but only when I really have to, like when I'm so hungry that my stomach feels like it's eating itself."

Joon's own stomach fluttered with nerves. This was more than she wanted to know, yet she wanted to know more at the same time. "How is that different from selling your body?"

"Those are the girls who will do whatever the buyer wants. You know, they have sex with guys, real sex. Those are the ones that get into drugs. How else could they get through that kinda stuff?" Pringle pulled in a long breath. "Those girls, some boys too, will let the buyers put their things anywhere they want."

Joon pulled her head back and pushed her shoulders forward. "Boys do that too?"

"Yeah. I know hookers that are boys and girls. I mean, I think they're all called hookers." She tilted her head to the side. "I guess I'm a hooker too. I don't do it all the time, but I still do it. Anyway, that's just life. It's part of being on the streets. We all do shit we don't wanna do. You will too."

Joon shook her head slowly. "I'm never doing that. Not ever." The thought of anyone touching her in that way made her queasy. She'd never understood how Ragtop went through with it. Now, hearing Pringle did it too, her stomach churned. It wasn't that Joon thought she was better than either of them, but it seemed like the worst violation that anyone could endure—all she could compare it to was when Deen had assaulted her.

Pringle gave Joon a sad smile. "You'll do all kinds of crazy shit when you're hungry enough…or cold enough. It's not something I like doing, but man, when you feel like you can't live another day without something decent to eat, that's when doing nasty things doesn't seem so bad."

Joon thought back to the time that Aron fried up worms from the yard. "If you want to eat, this is your only option. Otherwise, you can just starve," she'd said.

Joon hadn't eaten in four days at that point, and she'd eaten every last worm that Aron put on the plate. *Pringle is right*, she thought. *We are all capable of doing awful things when we're hungry.*

She propped herself up on her elbow and looked into Pringle's face. "Do you think that Ragtop sells whatever people want? Do you think she's that kinda hooker?"

Pringle shrugged. "I don't know. I ain't never met her before. I think since she never came back for ya she probably is."

Joon lay back and pulled the blanket up under her chin. The moon was covered by thick clouds, and she gazed up into the starless sky. "Ragtop told me she used to take drugs but that she stopped doing that a long time ago."

Pringle lay flat on her back next to Joon. "Maybe she started again. You never know. But look, you're here now. If you stay cool, this group will take you in. We watch out for each other. And I'll tell ya right now, it's better than being alone."

Joon curled into a fetal position and closed her eyes. She tried to clear her mind the way she'd done when she lived with Aron. She needed sleep. *Tomorrow is another day. Besides, Pringle is right—I have new friends,* she reminded herself.

As she lay there trying to sleep, it snowed. The flakes came down hard and quickly covered the surfaces. Joon and Pringle got up and scurried around, picking up cardboard. They crawled back under the blankets, laid all the cardboard they'd collected on top of them, laid back, and watched the snow fall.

"I remember when I lived with my foster family," Joon began, "when I was in school and it snowed, my teachers would let us look out the windows. They said that the snow made everything look new, it covered up the bad things, and that should make us happy. The snow never made me happy though. I always knew that under the pretty, white covering, there was ugly stuff waiting to come out again."

Pringle snuggled closer to Joon. "Yeah, I know how you feel. But for me, the darkness ain't so scary because that's where I always lived. At least in the darkness I know what to expect. I get to know the bad guys and stay away from them. Out there in the light, there's no telling what can happen."

Chapter Twenty-Five

Joon woke early the next morning. Her body felt as though it had frozen into the fetal position, which she had slept in. Her bones felt brittle. The raw skin on her face burned and her chapped, split lips bled when she opened her mouth. Pringle stirred next to her, her eyes slowly fluttering open.

"Hey," Joon said, her jaw was tight from the cold. "Let's get outta here. It's freezing."

Pringle stretched her hardened limbs. "Yeah, it's fuckin' cold."

The two girls had to work to get the cardboard that lay on top of their blankets off them. Two inches of new snow had fallen and was frozen solid. It took them a few tries to break free. As they stood at the Tracks, the girls each put an arm around the other's waist and, with their other arm, held the blanket tightly around their shoulders.

"Now what?" Joon asked.

"Now we walk until we find somewhere we can hang out for a while."

"Let's go to the library. I always used to go there. You can get washed up in the bathroom. Maybe sit down and read," Joon said.

"Yeah, okay. But I ain't reading. I don't like to read."

Joon jerked her head sideways, her mouth hanging open. "You don't like to read? It's great. You find a book and you get lost in it. You know, like you're living someone else's life. Makes you forget about your own shitty life for a while."

Pringle looked away.

"What?" Joon asked. "Do you think that's lame?"

"No." Pringle shook her head. "I just never learned how to read that good. I mean, I can read a little, but I never read a book or nothing."

Joon smiled, and in doing so, her chapped lips cracked further. She ignored the metallic taste of her own blood as it touched her tongue. "I can teach you how. It'll be fun."

As the girls made their way to the library, there were people walking the city in their warm down coats, hats, scarves, and mittens, and Joon tightened her grip around Pringle's waist. "I wish I were like all these people out here, wearing warm clothes. They look happy, ya know? I wonder what it would be like to have a normal life—not the kind in a motel, but live in a real house where people care about you. All I want is a decent place to live, food, and people to love. What about you?"

Pringle gave her a sideways glance. "I had all of that. I mean, it wasn't anything great, but I lived with my dad in public housing. Most of the time we had heat and hot water."

Joon gasped. "Wait! What happened? Why aren't you living with your dad?"

"It's a long story, but my evil stepmother moved in with us. She hated my guts. Used to hurt me and yell at me whenever my father wasn't around. She said that I was ruining their life. Anyway, she tried to turn my dad against me, and for a long time, he didn't give in. But then she got pregnant and my dad was so excited and I was forgotten. Before I knew it, my dad was sticking up for the bitch and my life sucked. I was constantly being attacked by her and my father would back her. The more pregnant she got, the meaner she was, and so I packed some shit and left."

Joon's heart felt heavy. "Did your dad look for you?"

Pringle shrugged. "I doubt it. I don't really know and I don't care either. I'm happier being away from them. It was just gonna get worse, so I figure I'm lucky I got outta there before things got really bad."

"What about your mom? Why didn't you go live with her?"

Pringle took a deep breath. "My mom died in a car accident when I was six. I had the greatest family when she was alive. I don't remember that much, but I do remember being happy, and we didn't have to live in public housing. After she died, my dad couldn't work anymore and we lost everything. When my stepmom came along, he was happy again and that made me happy. Then everything turned to shit. I know my mom's in Heaven, and I bet she's pissed as hell at my dad for turning his back on me. I think my stepmom hated me because my dad loved me. Anyway, enough of that crap. We're here," she said, pointing up at the library.

The girls were walking up the steps of the library when Joon stopped. Pringle was on the step above her and turned around. "Why are you stopping?"

"I was just wondering why we're being punished."

"I don't know, girl. We just got a bad deal. Maybe someday we'll grow up to be something great, and it'll be because we had to put up with so much shit."

Joon nodded. "I hope you're right. I wanna do something really special. You know, something to help people. Lots of bad things happened to me after my parents died. I just want to be happy."

Pringle took Joon's hand and pulled her along. "You can help me right now by walking, so we can get inside where there's heat."

The library hadn't been open long, and only a few other people were inside. The woman at the desk looked up from her paperwork, eyed the two girls, and looked back down at her desk as the girls rushed into the ladies' room.

They washed themselves at the sink while studying their reflections. Pringle, a redhead with green eyes, watched her friend. Joon was pushing misplaced hair back in her bandana. Finally, Joon smiled at herself. Then she caught Pringle staring at her in the mirror. "What?"

"Nothing." Pringle rubbed the ghostly white skin under her eyes and looked back up at Joon again.

"Come on. What?" Joon said.

"It's just that you're really pretty."

Joon blushed. "I think there's something wrong with your eyes."

"Nope. I see just fine. You're really pretty. I wish I was pretty like you. I hate my red hair and super-white skin."

Joon studied Pringle for a moment. "I think you're nuts. Your eyes are beautiful, and your hair is like a burning flame around your face."

The two girls stood a moment longer, watching each other in the mirror. Then they smiled at each other. They were lighthearted and feeling pretty.

Chapter Twenty-Six

———————◼———————

As winter passed, Joon became integrated into the group of homeless teens. She and Pringle made it into youth shelters one night each week, and there were always different teens that stayed at the Tracks alongside the regulars. Joon felt at home when Pringle was with her. One night, a boy they hadn't seen before came with a radio blaring. He approached the group with an air of confidence, bobbing his head to the music.

Pringle grabbed Joon's hand. "Let's dance."

But Joon pulled her hand away, feeling suddenly shy. "I don't know how to dance."

"Sure you do. Everyone knows how to dance. Just listen to the music and move your body. Come on, Joon. Don't be such a downer."

Joon smiled, unsure of how to respond. Then she took a deep breath, grabbed Pringle's hand, and got to her feet. When Joon danced, she felt awkward and silly, but as she watched Pringle flailing and shaking her body, she giggled and started to lighten up.

She leaned into Pringle. "Everyone is watching us."

"So what? Let them watch. Come on, girl. Ignore all of them and let yourself go."

Joon tried to mimic Pringle's dance moves, but she imagined she looked like she was getting an electric shock. She closed her eyes and focused on the music. Quickly, she found her muscles relaxing and her body flowing to the music. The girls danced for the next thirty minutes.

When they finally sat against a log to catch their breath, Joon said, "That was so much fun."

"Yeah, I love to dance. It helps me release all of that crazy shit that gets caught up in my head."

Quinn had been mesmerized watching Joon dance. He made his way over to the girls, sat down next to her, slung his arm around her shoulders, and moved his lips close to her ear.

"You're a great dancer," he whispered softly, his wispy breath tickling her ear.

Joon smiled at him. "Thanks. I never danced before. It was a lot of fun."

He cocked his head. "It didn't look like you've never danced before. I bet you could be a real dancer at a strip club. You have the body for it."

Joon flushed a deep red. She glanced down at her rail-thin body and small chest. "I don't think so."

Quinn watched her intently. "They'll grow more," he confirmed, nodding toward her breasts.

"Shut up, Quinn," Pringle snapped, partly to protect her friend and partly because she was jealous of the attention he was giving Joon.

He smiled at Pringle. "I'm just being honest."

She snarled at him. "That might be true, but you're embarrassing her. You can't look at a girl's boobs and tell her they'll grow. You're an idiot."

"Come on, Pringle. Your boobs are gonna grow too," he said with a smirk.

"Fuck you, Quinn," Pringle shot back.

Joon's happy feeling quickly faded. "Stop it, you guys. We were just having fun." She turned to Quinn, her eyes sparkling with adoration for the older boy. "You better be nice to Pringle if you want to be around me. Pringle is my best friend."

Pringle sat up straight. "I am?" She smiled. "I've never had a best friend."

Joon gave her a warm smile. "Me neither. Well, I mean Ragtop was my best friend, but she was a lot older than me. More like my best mom-like friend."

Pringle jumped on top of Joon and gave her a bear hug. "You and me are unstoppable. Ain't nobody ever coming between us."

Joon giggled and returned the hug.

Quinn gave an exaggerated pout. "What about me?"

The two girls looked at him and laughed. "What about you?" Joon asked.

Quinn pushed his long hair behind his ears. "Can't I be part of the circle too?"

Joon locked eyes with Pringle. Mischievous grins grew on both of their faces. Joon exhaled loudly. "I guess so, but only if you treat us nice."

Quinn put his arms around the two girls. "I promise. I'll always be nice."

Later that night, nestled inside a cardboard box, the girls lay side by side, snuggling together not only for warmth, but also to feel the love of another human. Joon rolled over to face Pringle.

"Tomorrow is my birthday," she said.

Pringle sat up. "Really? Wait! What's the date?"

"February third. When I turned five, my mom told me that the night I was born, there was a big snowstorm. She knew that I was ready to be born and rushed to the hospital. She was with a nurse in the elevator on her way to the room where moms have babies. She told me that I didn't want to wait and started pushing my way out when they were in the elevator. By the time they got to the room, I was already born." She smiled sadly, thinking of her mother. "I can't remember what my mom looked like. I try really hard to remember her face and her hair, but I can't see her anymore."

Pringle threw her arm over Joon. "Maybe there's a picture of her somewhere."

Joon shook her head. "I don't know what they did with all the stuff from our house when my mom and dad died. I bet someone threw it all away."

"I'm sorry," she said gently. "But hey, tomorrow's your birthday. What do you wanna do to celebrate?"

"Have a home," Joon joked, but Pringle saw the sadness in her eyes.

"Hey, listen, we're houseless not homeless. The streets are our mom and dad. This cardboard box is our heavenly comfort at night, and we have a home because we have people here that care if we live or die. We may not live in a 'real home'"—Pringle air quoted—"but this home gives us the things that a building can't. We have each other."

Joon welled up. "You're right. When I lived with Aron, there wasn't anyone there who loved me. I was living in a house—well, if you consider living in the basement part of living in a house. Anyway, I was really lonely and scared."

"Was Aron ever nice to you?" Pringle asked.

"Only when someone from social services was coming to check on me, which was hardly ever. And she wasn't really nice to me then, but she'd let me take a bath and eat a little bit, so I didn't look so ugly."

"'Look ugly'—what does that mean?"

Joon shrugged. "I don't know. She said I looked ugly all the time. But when the people were coming to check on me, she said a little bit of food would put color back in my pasty face."

Pringle was quiet for a moment as she crossed her arms over her chest. "Aron's a piece of dog shit and a big, fat liar. She just said that to you 'cause she was jealous that you're pretty. We hate her."

Joon barked out a laugh. "Yeah, we hate her."

Pringle intertwined her fingers with Joon's. "Back to your birthday. We gotta do something real special. How much money you got?"

"I think I have eight dollars."

"Okay, I have six. I say we have a hot breakfast and then get a bakery cupcake to eat tomorrow night."

In the darkness of the cardboard box, Pringle couldn't see the smile on Joon's face. "That sounds perfect."

Pringle rolled over on her side. "Tomorrow is gonna be our best day ever. I promise. Night, birthday girl."

"Night, Pringle." Joon put her hands over her heart and smiled. A sense of happiness fell over her as she closed her eyes.

Chapter Twenty-Seven

———————————————————————

"Happy birthday, Joon!" Pringle sang as she came back into the cardboard box. "It's about time you woke up. Man, you were sleeping for a long time."

"I guess all that dancing made me tired." She stretched her arms and yawned.

"Come on. Let's get moving. It's your birthday…we got lots to do."

Joon crawled out of the box and looked up. Even though the temperature was below thirty degrees, the sky was clear and the sun shining brightly. Joon wrapped her arms around herself. She lifted her face to the sun and let its warmth penetrate her skin. She walked over to a barrel with a fresh fire roaring inside and soaked up the heat.

Pringle, who had been talking to Quinn and some of the other boys, moseyed over next to Joon. "First stop, Little Pete's Restaurant for breakfast."

"Then where are we going?" Joon asked, her joy evident in her tone.

Pringle nudged Joon's ribs with her elbow and winked at her. "None of your business. But now that you're thirteen, you're officially a teenager, and that's pretty special."

When the girls walked into Little Pete's, the aroma of bacon and toast drifted into their noses and took hold of their stomachs. Holding hands, they made their way to the booth farthest from the door. A waitress approached and quickly assessed the two disheveled girls.

"Hi, girls. You eating breakfast?"

"Yes," Pringle said with a victorious smile.

"Okay then. What can I bring ya?"

Several minutes later, when the waitress laid the plate in front of Joon, Joon's eyes grew large and her mouth watered. There were pancakes with butter melting on top, bacon, and scrambled eggs. She picked up her fork, and, without a word, both girls dug into their breakfasts.

Coming up for a breath, Joon looked over at Pringle. "I think this is the best food I've ever had in my whole life. I can eat this until I throw up."

Pringle crinkled her nose, then let out a loud burp. Her hand quickly flew up to her mouth, and she looked around. "Oops. Sorry," she said with hearty laughter.

When they finished eating, the waitress came back, took their plates, and gave them the check. The girls counted out their money, then stood and headed back toward the bathroom.

"Um, girls," the waitress yelled after them.

Joon and Pringle turned around.

"Where are you two going?"

Joon pointed. "To the bathroom."

The waitress sighed heavily. "Okay, now I know that ya ain't just going in there to take a piss. I can see you two need a good cleaning," she said as she waved her hand at their clothing. She paused, and, sensing trouble, Joon's heart pounded hard. But then the woman's gaze softened. "You go on and get cleaned up," she said, handing each of them a dish towel. "But you leave that bathroom clean when you're finished. My fat ass doesn't want to clean it again."

"Thank you," Joon said politely.

"Yeah, thanks," Pringle said. "Today's her birthday."

"Oh yeah, well, happy birthday, kid."

Joon smiled and the girls rushed into the bathroom to wash up. It was rare that someone inside a business accepted the homeless teens, and Joon felt grateful. "This is already a great day," she said. "Can you believe she's actually letting us get clean?"

Pringle pushed the hair back from her own face. "Yeah, I wish it was this easy all the time. Even when you buy shit, these people don't let you clean up in their bathroom. I think you're my good-luck charm."

Joon glared at her friend in the mirror. "Ha! Now you've lost your mind. The last thing I am is lucky. If you knew everything I've been through, you'd know that I'm the most unlucky person alive."

Pringle ignored the comment, and the girls left the restaurant to continue the birthday celebration. They walked to Edgar Allan Poe's house and toured the building, Joon imagining what it would've been like to live in his house in 1843.

"I bet there weren't many other buildings here then," Joon said, "and he could see the river from his front yard. Could you imagine how great it would've been to live here?"

Pringle, less enthused by history, shrugged. "I don't know, I guess. This place is pretty cool though. It'd be perfect if all the kids at the Tracks could live here."

When they left Poe's house, they visited the Liberty Bell. Joon had walked by these places before, but now, she actually focused on these landmarks and was interested in their significance.

"Okay, last stop before we go back to the Tracks," Pringle said, running ahead.

Several minutes later, Joon and Pringle stood gazing into Elfreth's Alley. As they took in the old-fashioned flower boxes, shutters, and Flemish bond brickwork, it was as if time had stood still.

"Wow," Joon breathed. "I never knew this street was here."

"Yeah, I saved it for last. I knew you'd like it given how *obsessed* you are with houses. Anyway, people have lived in these houses longer than any other street in America, and they still do. How cool is that?"

Joon's mouth hung open as she scanned the scenery. "I thought you didn't like history."

Pringle bumped her shoulder lightly into Joon's. "I don't, but this place is awesome."

"Let's look," Joon said, grabbing Pringle's hand. They walked slowly by each row home, taking in the architectural details of the buildings. "This is the most beautiful place I've ever seen in my life. The people who live here are so lucky." She smiled wistfully. "Maybe someday I'll live on this street."

"Whoa! Dream big, why don't you!" Pringle said.

"Hey, why not? I'm still here and going strong."

The day was special, and Pringle told anyone who would listen that it was Joon's birthday. So many strangers said happy birthday to Joon that she was overflowing with joy.

They got back to the Tracks just before dark. There were three barrels with roaring fires inside. As they walked closer, Joon watched a dozen of the regulars stand in two lines facing each other. They raised their arms above their heads and joined hands with the person on the opposite side.

"What are they doing?" Joon whispered.

"It's your birthday canopy. When you walk underneath their hands, you need to make a wish."

Joon stopped short. "I don't know how to make a single wish. I mean, there are about a million things that I wish for every day. How am I supposed to pick one?"

Pringle put her arm around Joon's shoulders and led her to the birthday canopy. "Close your eyes." When Joon's eyes were closed, Pringle asked, "What is the one thing you want most in the world? Don't tell me. Just think about it. You got it?"

Joon smiled and nodded.

"Okay, now when you walk underneath your birthday canopy, that's what you wish for."

Joon giggled. "I swear, Pringle. I would be lost without you." She looked at the human canopy. The teens were smiling and cheering for her, and as she walked underneath, she made her birthday wish.

Later that night, after sharing her birthday cupcake with Pringle, Joon walked over to a barrel where Quinn was standing alone.

"Did you have a good birthday?" he asked.

Joon rubbed her hands together near the fire. "Yeah, best one ever. It was really nice that all of you helped me celebrate."

Quinn moved closer to her. "I got you a present."

Her eyes widened. "You did? Why?"

He pulled something from his pocket. "Because I really like you, and I wanted to give you something." He let a bracelet made of multicolored thread dangle from his fingers. "It's a bracelet. I thought you'd like it."

Joon reached out gently and took the present, rubbing it between her fingers and feeling the thick threads before sliding it onto her wrist. "This is really nice. Thank you."

Quinn gave her a nod. "You're welcome. I have something else for you too."

She gave him a quizzical look. "You do?"

"Yep." Then, he leaned in, closed his eyes, and gave Joon a kiss on the lips. When he pulled away, he studied her reaction. "Was that okay?"

Joon let out a nervous giggle. "Yeah, I guess. I mean it was nice." She was flustered by it, even though she was happy he'd done it, and she looked around awkwardly for a moment before turning around. "Hey, I have to get back to Pringle. I'll see you later."

She felt warm all over her body. It was a simple kiss, but it had made her feel special. She licked her lips and could taste the beer that Quinn had been drinking. It made her feel connected to him.

She'd had a crush on Quinn since they'd met, and the fact that he was three years older than her made her feel even more special. She always felt safer when he was around, and that night, as she tried to sleep, all Joon could do was think about the kiss. She was content as she drifted to sleep in her house made of cardboard.

Chapter Twenty-Eight

———————◼———————

The next morning, Joon woke up with butterflies in her belly thinking about Quinn, and it didn't go unnoticed by her friend.

"You got a secret you wanna share?" Pringle asked.

"No," Joon said with a sly smile.

"Oh. My. God. You do have a secret. Tell me."

Actually dying to share, she easily conceded. "So, last night, before we went to sleep...Quinn gave me this bracelet." Joon pulled her jacket sleeve up so Pringle could see her present. "Then he kissed me."

Pringle grabbed Joon's shoulders. "What? Did he tongue you?"

"No, ew, don't be gross." Joon lowered her voice so she wouldn't be overheard. "He kissed me on the lips...mouth closed. It was really nice. Can you believe it?"

Her friend shook her head ruefully. "Yeah, I believe it," she said. "But you know, he's sixteen. He's had girlfriends before. I've met a couple of them. They never last. You better be careful," Pringle warned.

Joon felt deflated. "You don't want me to like Quinn?"

"It's not that. I just think that maybe he's taking advantage of you."

"How?"

"'Cause you're thirteen and not very street smart," Pringle said with an edge to her voice.

Joon was starting to get irritated and wondered if her friend was jealous. "Are you mad 'cause Quinn likes me?"

"No. I'm mad because, just when I get a best friend, that asshole tries to come in and steal you from me."

Joon put her arms around Pringle and pulled her close. "No one will ever come between us, remember?"

Pringle pouted and fluttered her eyelashes, her green eyes exuding innocence. "Do you promise?"

"Yes, I promise," she said, laughing. "I love you, Pring. Now, what should I say to Quinn when I see him?"

"You're such a rookie," Pringle said, pulling the collar of her jacket up around her neck. "I mean, really, you just say hi. Just act the way you always do. You seriously have no social skills at all."

Joon looked away. "I can't help it. The only person that's ever even talked to me before you was Ragtop and some of her friends, but they're all old. I'm still getting used to it."

"Hey, I didn't mean to hurt your feelings. I was just messing with you."

Pringle stood and put her hands out to Joon, pulling her to her feet.

"Let's get our day started. We need to earn some money to make up for what we spent on your birthday yesterday."

Joon groaned and her shoulders slumped forward. "I don't feel like begging."

Pringle put her hands on her hips and glared at her friend. "You feel like eating?"

"Yeah."

"Then you better start feeling like begging. It's not so bad. People like to give *you* money. Think about some of the other kids having to sell their asses to eat. That should make you feel better."

Joon couldn't handle the thought of letting someone touch her private places. The memory of Deen touching her made her skin crawl and scared her. It made her stomach fill with acid.

"I feel like I would die if I had to do anything like that to eat," Joon said.

"Exactly!"

When the girls joined the other teens, Quinn approached them and gave Joon a hug.

"Morning, you beautiful creature," he whispered. "Are you gonna hug me back? Everyone is watching. You're making me look like a fool."

Joon glanced at Pringle, who was staring at them. Then she put her arms around Quinn and gave him a quick squeeze.

Quinn looked down at Joon. He placed his index finger gently under her chin and tilted her head up to meet his eyes. "Where are you off to today?"

"Market Street to beg."

Quinn smiled. "I like a woman who knows how to make money. That makes you independent. It turns me on."

Not able to take it anymore, Pringle stepped closer to the couple. "Quinn, you're like liquid sugar. I mean, really. You're so weird. Yuck!"

Quinn laughed at Pringle's remarks. "Okay, you two go on and earn some money. I'm doing some work for Pug today."

"Oh, that's just great," Pringle fired back at him. "You better watch your ass with that snake. I don't know why you don't stay away from him."

Quinn ran his hand through his long hair. "Because I can make more money quicker without having to beg or take a chance getting caught stealing. That's why. Maybe you should try it sometime."

Pringle put her hands on her hips and shook her head. "I'd rather die. I don't want nothing to do with him. Pug is a mean bastard, and he'll do anything to make money. He doesn't care about nobody but himself." With that, she grabbed Joon's hands and turned her back to Quinn. "We're out of here."

"What's wrong with you? You're being kinda rude to Quinn," Joon said when they were far enough away that nobody else would hear.

"Quinn is acting like he owns you, and I don't like it."

"How's he doing that?"

"Being grabby with you like you're his girlfriend. Plus, all that shit he said about you being independent and earning your own money. One kiss doesn't mean you're getting married," she fumed.

Joon was quiet. She had liked that Quinn greeted her with a hug even though she'd been embarrassed that he did it in front of everyone. He made her feel special. After all, Quinn was one of the oldest boys in the group. He was charming and good-looking, and several girls had a crush on him—she had watched them flirt with him while she'd been living at the Tracks.

"It didn't bother me, Pringle. I kind of liked it. Everyone looks up to Quinn, and he likes me of all people. That makes me feel...I don't know...special, I guess."

"Special how?"

"Special like I matter. I've never had anyone my age that wanted to be around me. Now, I have you and Quinn. I feel...really lucky. Ya know? Like my life might be changing. That's all."

The girls spent the remainder of the day moving around the city and panhandling. Before going back to the Tracks, they stopped at a dollar store and bought a loaf of bread and a jar of generic peanut butter. It was expected that each person bring something to the Tracks and was a long-standing way the children of the streets survived.

Chapter Twenty-Nine

That night at the Tracks, Quinn sat next to Joon and took her hand in his. He threaded their fingers together and took advantage of his popularity to impress her. The other boys would listen to everything he said, and when Quinn asked the others to do things, they did them. He was better off, so to speak, because of the money he made working for Pug.

He opened two beers and handed one to Joon, but she shook her head. "Come on, Joon. It ain't gonna kill you. It's a fucking beer."

Hesitantly, she took the can from Quinn and lifted it to her mouth. She took a small sip and scrunched up her face. "Ew. That's gross."

"It grows on you. Give it a chance. Finish that one and I bet you'll change your tune," Quinn said.

Joon took small sips of the bitter liquid until she was halfway done, but by that time, she was feeling the effects of the alcohol, finished the beer quickly, and asked Quinn for another. She'd drank three beers in under an hour. She stood to go pee and swayed on her feet. Quinn got up quickly and grabbed her arm.

"Whoa! Easy does it. Let me walk with you."

Joon looked over at Pringle, who was making out with Booz. Not wanting to interrupt her friend, she took Quinn up on his offer. Off to the side, but still where they could see the crowd, Joon stopped and turned to Quinn.

"Ya gotta turn around," she slurred.

Quinn gave a forced laugh. "You don't have anything I haven't seen before."

Feeling dizzy, Joon shrugged and lowered her pants and underwear. She squatted low and emptied her bladder. When she finished, she looked up to find Quinn handing her a napkin he'd dug out of his coat pocket.

Joon took it from him, did a quick wipe, and attempted to stand. As she did, the blood rushed from her head and she fell back into her puddle of urine. Quinn quickly helped her up. As she leaned on his shoulders, he pulled up her underwear and worn jeans. Before he zipped them though, he reached inside and touched her softly, between her legs.

"What are ya doin'?" she asked.

"Nothing…just wanted you to know that I'm really into you," he purred.

Too drunk to process much, she leaned her body against his. "I wanna lie down. I'm so tired."

He walked her back toward the group, and when Pringle glanced up and saw Joon hanging from Quinn's arm like a rag doll, she got to her feet and rushed over.

"What the hell happened, Quinn?" Pringle seethed.

"I didn't do shit to her. She had a little too much to drink. Don't get your panties in a bunch."

Pringle put Joon's arm over her own shoulder and half dragged, half carried her friend over to their cardboard box. After Pringle got Joon settled, she went to find Quinn.

"What the fuck is your problem, Quinn? You know she never drinks. How many beers did you let her have?"

"Shut up, Pringle! Joon is old enough to make her own decisions. So she had a little too much. Ain't like you haven't been seen staggering around here before."

The green of Pringle's eyes was blazing. "We're not talking about me. Joon ain't never had nobody. Do you get that? She trusts us and you know better. Why did you take her over to pee?"

"So she could take a fuckin' piss. Why the hell else would I go over there?"

Pringle pointed her index finger in Quinn's face. "You better not have done anything to her. You get me?"

Quinn let out a sinister laugh. "Why? What are you gonna do? Kick my ass? Cut me a break, Pringle. You're just a jealous girl who can't stand to see me with somebody else."

"Fuck you, Quinn. Breaking up with you is the best thing that I ever did. You're a player and you're never happy with who you have. I'm happy I followed my instincts. You always gave me the willies and you still do. I ain't jealous—I'm looking out for my friend," Pringle yelled, spittle flying from her mouth.

Quinn grabbed a beer from his bag and opened it. The crackle and fizzle cut into the silence as he looked Pringle in the eyes. "You want one?" He held out an open beer.

Pringle looked at the beer, then at Quinn, then back down at the beer. Finally, she put her hand around the can and tried to take it, but he wouldn't let it go.

"Friends?"

Pringle took a swig of the beer. "*Friend* is a strong word. I'm telling you Quinn, don't fuck with her."

Quinn cocked his head to the side. "You don't own Joon. She has a mind of her own. Besides, in case you haven't noticed, Joon's into me."

"Joon's into you because she doesn't know any better. You can be a real asshole. I've seen enough girls come here for a while and then never come back just a couple months later. You use people to get what you want."

"You're being a bitch just because you and I didn't work out. It's not like I treated you bad."

"Yeah, you did treat me bad. Every time I turned around, I either saw you with another girl or heard you were with another girl. You're a prick," Pringle spat.

"Whatever. You didn't want to commit when I asked you to leave with me. You wanted to stay at the Tracks for the rest of your fucking life. You're just bitter."

Pringle turned to walk away but stopped short. "She's not some piece of trash for you to use up. Joon is different, and she doesn't know enough about boys to get caught up with a jerk like you. Just remember, I'm watching you."

Chapter Thirty

A month later, as the late-March air warmed, Joon was happy to have survived the harsh winter. The girls were panhandling outside the train station on Market Street, and the morning had been good. They'd earned four dollars between them. Pringle always pushed Joon to be front and center. She'd lived on the streets long enough to know that people will give more money to girls and even more to pretty girls. Joon was pretty, and her eyes revealed her hard life—she wore a mask of sadness that a veteran actress couldn't mimic.

After several hours, they called it a day. As they walked toward Thirtieth Street, Joon shoved her hands into her jean pockets. "Pringle, I'm dying for a shower. There is dirt imbedded in my pores. It makes everything feel tight." She leaned close to her friend's ear. "And my ass is so itchy I can't stand it anymore."

Pringle nodded. "Yep, gets like that after the cold weather breaks and you can actually feel again. There's something we can do. It's cheap, it ain't a shower, but it's close enough."

The girls stopped at a drugstore on their way back to the Tracks. Pringle placed a long piece of cardboard against a tree to shield them from the main area where the teens hung. The girls stepped behind the cardboard.

"You first," Pringle said.

Joon quickly stripped off her clothing.

"Ready?" Pringle asked.

Joon nodded and Pringle poured some of the water from the gallon jug they'd purchased over her head.

"Now you have to soap up quick," Pringle instructed. "Don't use too much soap in your hair. It'll be too hard to rinse out."

Joon used the bar of generic soap they had bought to wash her body and hair. When she was finished, Pringle poured more of the water over her, and Joon rubbed her hair and skin. "How much water is left?"

"A little more than half."

"Okay, pour some on my back and keep half to take your shower. Let's keep the other gallon for next week."

When Joon turned, Pringle gasped. Both girls stopped and looked at each other.

"What's wrong?" Joon said, crossing her arms over her chest.

"Those marks on your back. It looks like...like you were whipped. Where did you get those?"

Pringle moved closer and touched the raised lines of skin on her friend's back. They looked like the roots of a large tree. They were four shades darker than her uninjured flesh.

Joon flushed as embarrassment coursed through her. She lowered her head. "Aron did it."

"How? Why?" Pringle shrieked.

"Lots of reasons."

"Like what? You have to tell me," Pringle pushed.

"When I pissed off Aron, sometimes my punishment was a whipping." A tingling swept up the back of Joon's neck and across her face. "She'd make me strip and lay facedown on the bed. Then she'd tie my legs and arms to the bedposts, so I couldn't move. She whipped me with different things...whatever was in reach. Sometimes it was a hairbrush or a long metal spoon, but mostly it was a thick belt with a big buckle. Joon absently rubbed her arms as the painful memory played through her mind. "The worst was when she'd whip me before my cuts healed from the last whipping. That made me wanna die."

"Yeah, but like, what did you actually do to piss her off?"

Joon let out a big sigh. "Different things. I got caught eating from the dog's bowl. Didn't clean a counter good enough. One of her son's left a glass on the kitchen table after I was already put in the basement. I don't know, Pringle. She beat me for anything. She beat me because I was me."

Joon broke down and wept for the piece of her that Aron had stolen— her innocence. It was hard to relive the things her foster mother had done to her. But most times when she talked about what happened, she felt better afterward.

"I'm sorry," Pringle announced. "Let's get you done so I can clean up."

When Joon was finished, she shook off the excess water and wrung out her hair. Then she pulled her dirty clothes on over her wet skin. Joon helped Pringle take a shower, and when they were both finished, they sat on a log in the sun, hoping their clothes would dry before day turned to night and the air turned chilly.

"Do you feel better?" Pringle asked.

Joon was raking her fingers through her wet hair. She held her hands up for both of them to see. Joon stared at the dirt embedded under her fingernails. "Well, my skin feels a little better, but I wouldn't say I'm clean. It'll take a lot more than a bottle shower to get rid of that dirt."

"Anything's gotta be better than what that lady did to you," Pringle said, still reeling from Joon's story.

Joon nodded. "Her name is Aron. I always use her name to remind myself of the person I will never become, and every time I say Aron's name, I become less and less afraid of her."

Quinn watched the girls from a distance, wondering how long it would be before Joon fell head over heels for him.

Chapter Thirty-One

A few days later, Joon woke up alone. She rubbed her eyes, stretched, and crawled out of their box. Several teens were sitting on the logs and tires. Joon approached the group Quinn was sitting with.

"Where's Pringle?"

Quinn looked up at her and shrugged. "Haven't seen her this morning. Last time I saw her was last night after you went to sleep. She was hanging with some guy that stumbled in here. Looked like she was really into him. Maybe she slept somewhere else last night."

Joon shook her head. "Pringle wouldn't do that, not if she didn't know the guy."

"Well, then it beats me where she's at."

"Anybody else see her?" Joon asked the rest of the group sitting there.

They all shook their heads.

"I'm gonna take a piss, then look for her. You wanna help me?" Joon asked Quinn.

"Sure. I'll help. I ain't got nothing else to do today. We can check the train station. Maybe she headed out early this morning to beg."

Joon nodded and walked off to pee. As she squatted, she thought about the places they could look, and when she finished, as she pulled her jeans up, she noticed something in the distance. As she stared, she realized it was Pringle's sneakered feet.

"Girl," Joon yelled. "You better get decent. You and that boy you're with better be ready 'cause I'm coming over there."

As Joon got closer, her heart raced. No one was lying next to Pringle. She ran toward her friend.

"Pringle!" Joon stood over her friend, who was lying facedown. She dropped to her knees and shook the girl, and when Pringle didn't wake up, Joon flipped her over—Pringle's face was purple and black. A guttural scream escaped from Joon.

Seconds later, Quinn and the others ran to her.

"What the hell happened?" Quinn asked.

Joon looked up at him in shock. "I think she's...she's dead."

"No. She can't be," Quinn replied. He dropped to his knees and pushed Joon out of the way. He looked into Pringle's face and was visibly horrorstruck as he felt for a pulse.

"Is she alive? Does she have a pulse?"

"Wait. Give me a minute." Quinn continued to move his hand to different places on Pringle's neck, checking for a pulse while Joon and the others looked on waiting for him to deliver good news. Finally, he turned to Joon and shook his head.

"Noooooo!" she cried. "No, no, no, she can't be dead." Joon sat on Pringle's hips and tried to pull the dead girl into a sitting position.

Quinn looked at the others who had gathered. They were all deeply saddened that Pringle had died, and Joon's reaction tore at their hearts. Quinn stood and put his hands under Joon's armpits. "Come on, Joon. She's gone."

Joon snapped her head to the side and glared at him. "No. You don't understand. Pringle can't be dead. I won't let her be dead. You have to do something to help her."

"There's nothing I can do." He looked around the group and Joon followed his gaze. "There's nothing any of us can do. It's too late. Now, I'm gonna take you back over there," he said, pointing to the main area. "I'll take care of you. I'm gonna help you. I won't leave you, and we'll figure everything out together, okay?" he said in a soothing voice. Quinn led Joon back to the main area and sat next to her. His arm wrapped protectively around her shoulders, he looked up at Booz and the other boys. "Joon, I need to talk to Booz for a minute," he said gently. "I'll be right back."

Joon stared off into nothingness, her tears a relentless stream. She barely heard what Quinn said to her.

"Joon? Did you hear me?"

Joon nodded but was clearly still in a state of shock.

Quinn pulled Booz off to the side. "We're gonna need to take care of her body. We can't just let her lay there, and Joon will need closure.

Take some of the other guys about two hundred feet down the tracks to that small patch of trees. Tell them to bring whatever they have to dig a grave. We'll bury her tomorrow. We gotta give Joon a little time to let this all sink in."

"What the fuck happened to her?" the other boy asked.

Quinn lowered his head and shook it gently. "Not sure. There wasn't any blood that I could see. She has a mark around her neck. Maybe a rope or something like that. I can't really tell. Looks like she was choked or suffocated. I don't know. That dude she was with last night—where'd he go?"

Booz shrugged. "Not sure. I got drunk and fell asleep."

Quinn nodded. "Get the guys together and take care of the grave. Okay?"

"Sure, man," Booz said, placing his palm on Quinn's chest. "This is some real fucked-up shit."

"Yeah, it really is. We all loved Pringle, and now, we're gonna need to help Joon get through this."

Booz called some of the other boys and explained what they needed to do. As they walked toward the patch of trees where Pringle would be buried, Quinn settled in next to Joon and took her in his arms.

Chapter Thirty-Two

The next morning, Joon stirred in the cardboard box. She'd had a restless sleep and kept waiting for Pringle to come back and join her. When she opened her eyes, Quinn was lying next to her. He hadn't left her side since she'd discovered Pringle's body. He rolled onto his side and found Joon was staring at him with a blank expression.

She felt dread as she thought about facing another day without Pringle.

"You okay?" he asked.

Joon pulled the wool blanket tighter around her. *Please just leave me alone with my misery*, she thought, but finally answered. "No. I'm not okay. I keep waiting for her to come back. I feel...broken. I don't know what I'm going to do now."

"You're going to stay with me. I'm gonna take care of you. I don't want you to worry," he said, moving closer and putting his arm over her. "I made arrangements for Pringle."

Joon's eyes widened. "What do you mean?"

"She deserves a decent funeral, and I had some of the guys dig a place for us to lay her to rest. Everyone is gonna gather at noon today."

Joon startled a bit at the news. She couldn't really remember her parents' funeral and hadn't even thought of one for Pringle yet. "What? We're burying her today? I'm not ready, Quinn," she cried.

"Joon, listen to me. We can't just let her lay out there in the grass. We have to show her respect. I know this is sudden and that you need time to accept that she's gone. But leaving her body there to rot or be eaten by animals just isn't right."

The thought of either thing happening to Pringle's body made Joon grimace. "You're right," she said sadly. "I just miss her so much already."

"I know you do. We all miss her. Let's get outta here and go grab something to eat at the train station before the funeral."

Joon shook her head. "I'm not hungry. Just go without me."

"No. I won't eat either. I'm staying right here so I can take care of you."

At noon, the group gathered at what would be Pringle's grave. Quinn was holding Joon's arm as he brought her to stand beside the open grave. Joon looked into the hole. Pringle's body was wrapped in a thick, black tarp that the boys had found near the train station.

Booz looked around the circle of teens. "Somebody's gotta say something."

They all looked at Joon, but her grief was too heavy.

Quinn cleared his throat, and the others bowed their heads.

"Pringle, we will all miss you. Everyone here loved you. If there is a God, we hope you're with Him right now." He pulled Joon into him. "I don't want you to worry about Joon. I'll take good care of her. Amen."

"Amen," the group murmured together.

Joon pulled away from Quinn and climbed into the grave. She laid on top of Pringle's body. Her sadness was overwhelming, not only for herself, but also for those who watched her grieve.

Quinn hurriedly climbed in and scooped Joon up into his arms. She leaned into him, her arms locked around his neck in a death grip.

"Everything will be okay," he murmured, stroking her hair. Then with the help of Booz, they lifted Joon out of the grave and Quinn walked her back to the cardboard box she no longer shared with Pringle.

Chapter Thirty-Three

That night, the teens sat around a barrel fire. Joon just stared. She hadn't talked much since she'd found Pringle the morning prior. Quinn approached her, and she looked up at him.

Her bottom lip quivered. "I feel so alone. Pringle was the only best friend I ever had in my whole life."

Quinn made an exaggerated pouty face. "I can be your new best friend."

Joon, still crying, looked away. There was a deep ache in her chest, and the sobs ripped through her, as if the sorrow were trying to escape.

"Come on," Quinn said. "Let's take a walk. We won't be gone long. You need to eat something."

After much encouragement, Joon finally agreed to go with Quinn. The two walked to a fast-food restaurant, and while Joon sat with her head in her hands, Quinn ordered two burgers and fries. When he returned, he sat across from her.

"You should eat," he said, pushing the plastic tray toward her.

Joon unwrapped her burger and took a bite. "Where did you get the money to pay for all of this?"

"I work for Pug, remember?"

"Whatever that means," she spat, remembering the negative reaction Pringle always had to Pug.

"It means that I always have money in my pocket."

"Pringle didn't like that Pug guy."

Quinn set his burger down. "Pringle didn't even know Pug. I know him. He's a good guy. You know I loved Pringle, but there weren't many people she trusted. You're different in that way, I think. You trust people more than she did."

Joon shrugged. "I don't know. I guess it depends on who it is."

"Do you trust me?" Quinn asked, his tone gentle as he placed his hand over hers.

Joon eyes softened as she looked at him. "I guess. I mean I've known you for a little while. But I don't really know that much about you."

"I don't know that much about you either…doesn't mean I don't trust you."

The two finished their meal and headed back to the Tracks. That night, when it was time to sleep, Joon went off to her box, climbed in, and pulled the blanket over her. Joon had the chills even though the air hung heavy with the heat from the day.

Quinn ducked his head inside the box. "Hey…you want some company?"

Joon was feeling a little uneasy being in the box by herself, but she also remembered Pringle's warning about getting too close to Quinn too soon. Pringle had never trusted him, but Quinn was the only person who Joon could depend on at that moment. She scooted to the side and waved him in.

"Joon, its ninety degrees outside," he said, exaggerating. "Why are you covered with a blanket?"

"I don't know," she mumbled. "I'm freaked out. I'm cold. I can't help it." She started crying again.

"Come here." Quinn lay next to her and wrapped her in his arms. "I'm here now. You're not alone, and I'm not going anywhere."

"It's not the same," she said heavyhearted. "I mean, I'm happy you're helping me, but I miss Pringle. I just want her to come back."

"I understand. Girls are different than guys. You and Pringle were really close. No one can ever replace her," Quinn soothed. "Hey, look on the bright side—I make enough money working for Pug to buy food and keep my belly full. I can take care of you too."

"What do you do for Pug?" she asked.

"I sell stuff for him."

"What kind of stuff?"

"Just stuff."

Joon wanted to know exactly what Quinn was selling. She had her suspicions but decided not to press the issue. Right now, she needed a friend and didn't want to chance chasing him away.

She dug her fingers deep into her thick hair and scratched her scalp. "I think I have lice," she moaned.

"That sucks. Tomorrow we'll go down to the youth center on Broad Street and get you one of those kits. If Albany is there, she'll let you use the sink in the bathroom to wash your hair with that shit they give you to kill those little fuckers."

Joon scratched at her scalp harder. "I hope Albany is there tomorrow. I've had them for a couple of weeks and my head is sore from scratching."

Quinn pulled Joon closer to him. "We'll head down there first thing when we wake up. I told you I would take care of you, and I mean it. I really like you." He lifted her chin and pressed his lips to hers, licking at her lips.

Joon turned her head away. "Knock it off."

"I'm sorry. I was just trying to get closer to you. I want to be able to comfort you."

In the darkness, she flushed. Secretly, she enjoyed the feeling of Quinn's tongue softly passing over her lips, but she was still grieving and couldn't concentrate on Quinn and how she should react to his kiss. The deep emptiness caused by Pringle being so suddenly gone overpowered all other feelings.

Chapter Thirty-Four

The next morning at the youth shelter, Joon felt hopeful when Quinn walked her over to a lady and greeted her with a bear hug.

"Hi, Albany," Quinn sang.

"Oh, hey, baby. How you holding up?"

Quinn smiled at the older woman. "Well, you know, it's always easier in the warmer weather."

"Yeah, I remember those cold winters on the streets. You need something?"

"Yeah," he replied, grabbing Joon's hand. "This is my girl, Joon. She's got lice. We need a kit and I hope a sink to shampoo that crap in."

Albany looked Joon over. "How old are you, child?"

Joon scratched her head. "Thirteen."

Albany looked back at Quinn. "A little young for you, Quinn. Don't you think?"

Quinn stood firm and shook his head. "Nope. Not at all. You know that the streets age you quickly. Joon might be thirteen, but she acts more like sixteen."

Albany put her hands on her wide hips. "I don't know about all that. Listen, child, this boy here, well, he's a real charmer. You gotta watch out for him. Don't let his good looks make you do anything you don't wanna do. He's a hustler."

Before Joon could respond, Quinn kissed Albany on the cheek, pecking at her until she giggled. "You know you're my best girl," he teased the older woman.

"Quinn, don't give me none of that shit. You've been a ladies' man since you were Joon's age. Now, I want you to be sweet to this girl. Looks like she has seen some dark days in her young life."

Joon shoved her hands into the pockets of her jeans. "How would you know if I had dark days?"

Albany put her arm around Joon's shoulders. "It's all in the eyes, baby. The harder the life, the more it shows in your eyes." The woman pushed Joon back to arm's length and kept her hands gently on her shoulders. She stared at the child. "See now, the blue in your eyes is bold and real vibrant—you're a true survivor. But the small flecks of white and gray inside that blue is where you find the pain."

"My best friend just died," Joon said so quietly it was almost a whisper, her lower lip quivering.

"Come here, child," Albany said and gave her a lingering hug. "It's gonna be okay. Your friend will live on in your heart." The woman turned to Quinn. "Anybody I know?"

"Pringle."

Albany clasped her hands together and pulled them to her chest. "Dear Lord, Pringle was a good kid. What happened to her?"

"A guy came to the Tracks. Pringle hooked up with him, and she was with him when we all crashed. Joon found her the next morning. All the guys are looking for the dude, but we haven't had any luck."

Albany turned her attention to Joon. "You're gonna be okay. This is an awful thing that happened to Pringle. There ain't nothing worse than losing someone we love, but the thing is, child, you still gotta live."

Joon gave the woman a watery smile and felt her tense muscles let go a little. Albany's words gave her comfort—she wanted to believe what the woman was telling her.

Albany took Joon's hand as she spoke. "Come on, baby. Let's go get those little critters out of your hair. You'll feel much better."

In the bathroom, Joon bent over the sink while Albany washed her hair with the lice killing shampoo. After she finished, Albany sat the young girl in a chair as she combed the unhatched eggs from her scalp. It took a long time, and Joon's head was soon throbbing.

"Okay. We only got to do the base of your neck. Lean forward and lower your head."

Albany pushed Joon's hair over, starting on the right side of her head. She paused, gently running her fingers along a thick, ugly scar in the child's hairline that ran from behind her ear to the nape of her neck.

"Girl, where did you get this nasty scar?"

Joon just closed her eyes. "My foster mom."

"How?" Albany asked, trying to remain calm.

Joon let out a loud breath. "One time, I didn't vacuum the carpet right. The lines from the sweeper had to be perfect, but one of the lines crossed into another line, and Aron grabbed an old curtain rod she kept in the closet to whip me with. When I saw her coming, I curled into a ball, and she laid into me. She hit me until she almost collapsed on the floor next to me. I had lumps and bruises all over the place. Then I noticed that I was bleeding from my head. When Aron saw the blood, she dragged me by my feet into the kitchen, so I didn't bleed on her carpet. When it wouldn't stop, she was really mad, so she got her sewing kit and pulled the skin together real tight and sewed it back together."

"Dear Lord," Albany gasped, forgetting herself for a moment and letting her emotions get the better of her.

Joon continued. "I got punished again for screaming when she was sewing my skin back together. It hurt so bad, but every time I yelled, she punched me and told me to shut up. I started begging her to take me to the hospital to get it fixed. That got her really pissed off. She said she wasn't going to pay a dime for anyone to fix my cracked skull because I wasn't worth it. And, that I was already stupid and it wouldn't matter."

Albany was incensed and disgusted by the story. All the kids living on the streets had a story, but she wasn't immune to cruelty. Albany lifted Joon's shoulders and sat her upright in the chair. "You've been through a lot for a kid. I want you to know that you can come and see me anytime. You hear?"

"Thank you," Joon muttered.

"All right, now let's finish up."

Joon bent over again, and Albany, mesmerized by the scar that was an inch thick and rose up like a bulging vein below the skin's surface, imagined the pain and suffering the girl withstood to have the wound sewn back together.

When she was finished, Joon stood and faced the woman. "You're a good kid. You remember that not all people are bad. Your foster mom, she's a real monster, but there are good people in the world. You use this," Albany said, putting her hand on Joon's stomach. "This will always tell you if you're facing good or evil. Sometimes, we get fooled for a while and think we're with good people, but then if your belly feels different, then you know you're dealing with trouble and you get away as quick as you can."

Joon smiled, thinking of Ragtop. "My sort of mom told me that once. She was homeless too. She took care of me when I first got to the city." Joon wrapped her arms around Albany's waist. "I'll come back and see you again."

"Good," Albany said, then turned to Quinn. "This is a special girl here. You best take good care of her and don't let me hear nothing different. I'm as badass as you are. I don't care that you're younger. I spent fifteen years on the streets."

"Don't worry so much, Albany. I got this." Quinn kissed the older woman's cheek. "Thanks for your help."

As Joon and Quinn left the shelter, she turned to the older boy. "Where are we going now?"

"I have some work to do for Pug. You can come along."

Quinn grabbed Joon's hand as they headed down Market Street to sneak onto the train that would take them into North Philadelphia.

Chapter Thirty-Five

Joon followed Quinn off of the train when they arrived in North Philadelphia, and they walked awhile until they reached North Water Street. Quinn grabbed Joon's hand as they stood facing a brick row home that had been painted dark brown. The paint was chipped away, exposing the brick in random places. Next to the house was a lot filled with rejected household items, trash, wood, and broken tables and chairs. The house was two stories high. The black-shingled awning across the front of the home was detaching from the brick. Joon looked up. Some windows were boarded up with plywood, and others were gone, leaving large, gaping holes in the building. A porch ran the length of the house. Joon followed Quinn as he stepped over the missing floorboards of the porch.

Joon's skin prickled—she knew she was in dangerous territory.

Quinn looked in through the ripped screen door. One of the older guys inside noticed him and yelled, "What's up, Quinn?"

"Hey, Blast. I'm here for Pug. Is he home?"

Blast took a sip of beer and gestured for Quinn to come inside.

Quinn hesitated. "I got my girl with me. Is it okay to bring her in?"

Before Blast could answer, Goldie, the main girl blurted, "Sure, bring your bitch in so we can see her."

Quinn turned to Joon. "Just be cool. Everything's fine."

Joon's heart strummed rapidly, but she nodded as she took in the neighborhood; she didn't want to stay out on the porch by herself.

Inside, teenage boys and girls were sitting around a darkened living room. The once-white walls were streaked with water stains, and the long wall to the right was covered in graffiti. In the middle was the word SLAYERS, and the artwork around it included blood, knives, guns, and faces with mouths that had pointy teeth. The room fell silent as they all stared at Joon.

"Pug!" Blast yelled.

Quinn looked around the room. All eyes were on the couple as they waited for Pug, who finally appeared and stopped halfway down the steps. He looked at Quinn, then at Joon, and grinned. "Why don't you two come upstairs?"

Quinn took Joon's hand and pulled her toward the steps. Right behind them, a couple of the other boys followed. When they got inside Pug's bedroom, he nodded to Joon to sit down on a ripped beanbag chair in the corner.

"So you have a new girl," Pug said to Quinn.

Quinn nodded proudly as some of the other guys collected at the doorway. "Yeah, we...you know...met on the streets. This is Joon."

Joon glanced up at them but didn't smile. The group was standing around her. One boy squatted in front of her.

"You're pretty," he said in a slimy tone as he brushed the hair away from her face.

Joon shrank back, but the boy got closer.

"Come on, man. Leave her alone," Quinn said, glancing at Pug.

Pug snickered. "You thought you'd bring this sweet thing to our house and we would all ignore her?"

"Well, you all got a good look at her. Here's the money from the last run. Just give me some more shit and we'll get out of here."

"Not so fast," a boy named Snake Eyes said. He got on the beanbag next to Joon and put his arm around her. Joon pushed him away as he kissed her neck. "You know who we are?"

Joon shook her head.

"We're a gang. The Slayers. We run these streets. Maybe you want to come and stay with us for a while."

Joon's blood went cold and she shivered. Her eyes darted around the room, as if looking for an escape. Regret for following Quinn to the house raged through her, and she took several deep breaths to try to calm herself.

"I just want to leave. We have to go."

"Aw, come on, Joooooon. We just want to get to know you better. Ain't no harm in that, now is there?"

Joon made eye contact with Quinn. "I want to go," she said in a weak voice.

Quinn moved toward Joon, but one of the other boys blocked his way and Quinn stopped. Three of the other guys moved onto the floor and touched Joon's arms and torso. The girl's breathing became labored. She took long, uncontrollable breaths. Then Snake Eyes put his mouth over hers. When she tried to move away, the other boys held her down while Snake Eyes lifted her shirt and unbuttoned her jeans. Joon arched her back and jerked from side to side to break free. Snake Eyes slapped her across the face, dazing her briefly, but she shook it off and screamed for help.

Chapter Thirty-Six

———————————————— ▬ ————————————————

Just as Joon felt her chance of escape slipping away, a handsome boy with thick, brown hair and green eyes charged through the bedroom door. He was taller than the others and his chest and arm muscles bulged under his shirt. "What the fuck is going on?"

"Get the fuck outta here, Bruno!" Pug yelled.

"I don't think so. Leave her the hell alone," Tony Bruno yelled back.

That's when Blast stepped into the room. "Come on. Get the fuck off of her." He was an older and respected member of the Slayers, and he spoke with authority. The boys backed away one by one.

Tony stepped forward and extended his hand to Joon. "Come on. Let's get you out of here."

Outside on the porch, he turned to her. "I'm Tony. This ain't a good place for you to be. As soon as your stupid ass boyfriend gets done, he needs to get you outta here."

Joon nodded, trying to slow her pulse and stabilize her weak legs. "I'm sorry. I didn't know. I just came here with Quinn."

Tony's warm green eyes met Joon's. "How old are you?"

"Thirteen."

"I'm fourteen. You live on the streets?"

"Yeah. Ran away a while ago. I don't have anywhere to go," Joon admitted.

"Yeah, I get that. I was homeless for a while. Then"—he lowered his voice to barely a whisper—"I met these assholes and came to live here."

"Why do you stay here if you think they're assholes?"

Tony shrugged his shoulders. "I guess it's better than livin' on the streets. I was scared, and once I got into the Slayers, it was too late for me to go back out on my own. A couple of the guys that live here are decent. Like Blast, the one that came into the room after me—he's a good guy. So it ain't all that bad."

"Those guys would've really hurt me if you didn't come in there, huh?"

Tony pushed his brown hair from his eyes. "Yeah, they would've hurt ya real bad. You're a pretty girl, and I suggest you don't come anywhere near here again. And another thing: your boyfriend ain't too smart for bringing ya here. He should've known better."

"I won't come back again. I promise." It wasn't a hard promise to make—she wanted to get out of there as fast as possible. Her hands probably weren't going to stop shaking anytime soon.

"Good. Hey, listen. Do you ever go into South Philly?"

Joon looked at Tony more closely, afraid to tell him too much. "I guess sometimes I do," she said cautiously. "Why?"

Tony rubbed his chin. "I work at a bakery there. It's called Donata's. If you ever get out that way, come on in and see me. I'll give ya a deal on some bread and shit."

"Thank you," she said, meaning it but not sure she'd do it. "Where is Donata's?"

"In the Italian Market. You know where that's at?"

"Yeah, that's some of the best Dumpster diving in town. Problem is every other person living on the streets knows it, and it's just luck if you get good food or not."

"Yep, that's the place. Anyway, stop by and see me sometime."

The screen door opened, and Quinn stepped out onto the porch. He extended his hand to Tony, who returned the gesture. "Thanks, man. I appreciate your help."

Tony's eyes turned dark and he leaned into Quinn. "Don't you ever bring this girl here again. She could've been raped seven times over."

Quinn jerked his hand from his grip. "Yeah. I won't."

Tony knew Quinn wasn't sincere and that pissed him off. To make his point, he grabbed Quinn's arm and pulled him closer. "After they were done with her," he whispered, "they would've done the same to you." Tony released his grip. "See ya later, Joon."

"Bye, Tony. Thanks again."

Blast came onto the porch and stood with Tony as they watched Quinn and Joon head back to the train station that would take them into the heart of the city.

"That boy's a real fucking loser. I don't like him," Tony said.

Blast lit a cigarette and blew out the smoke. "Yeah, I don't like him either."

Chapter Thirty-Seven

When they were far enough from the Slayers' house for her to feel safe, Joon stopped and turned to him. Her eyes were red from crying and her teeth were clenched together.

"Why did you take me there, Quinn? I couldn't protect myself and you couldn't either. Why would you do that to me?"

Quinn reached for her hand. "I knew they wouldn't really do anything. They were just messing with you. Besides, I wouldn't have let them hurt you. I'm sorry."

She jerked away from him. "You're not sorry. You knew a gang lived there. We all talk about gangs at the Tracks. I could've been raped and killed."

Quinn placed his hands gently on Joon's shoulders. He looked into her eyes for several seconds. "I know. It was really dumb. I thought we would be in and out. I wanted to show you off to Pug. It's just that you're so pretty, and I wanted him to be jealous of me for having you as my girl."

Joon was still shook up, but the compliment was doing a good job of distracting her. It was rare that anyone was complimentary of her looks. She folded her arms over her chest and tried not to smile. "I'm not pretty."

"You're more than pretty. I think you're, like, the prettiest girl I've ever seen," Quinn said, flashing her a charming smile.

Joon watched him, a small smile playing on her lips. "Do you really think I'm pretty?"

"The prettiest," he said, sliding his arm behind her back and pulling her into him. When they were so close that their breath became one, Quinn kissed her. The scare Joon had just gone through made her want to be close to him, to feel as though he could protect her. Joon kissed him back, and this time, when he opened his mouth, she followed his movements, and their tongues danced with each other. When they parted, Joon was breathless.

"I really am sorry," Quinn said, kissing her forehead. "Let's get outta this shit hole."

He paid the train fare on the way back into the city because Joon was still shaken and he didn't want to put more stress on her by having to sneak onto the train.

Back at the Tracks, tucked inside the cardboard box, Quinn pulled his jeans off and threw them to the side, and a bag fell out of his pocket, revealing small, white packets.

Joon's eyes hardened with judgment as she stared at the bag. "I knew it! You're selling drugs. I figured that's what you're doing. That's not good, Quinn. Do you know what can happen to you if you're caught? And what about all of the kids' lives you're ruining?"

Quinn scooped the bag up and shoved it back into the pocket of his jeans. "It's not a big deal. So what if I'm selling dope for Pug? You'll be happy when you aren't hungry all the time. Besides, I'm building a pretty big customer base. If I keep going, I'll be able to buy my own house and get us off the streets."

"Us?"

Quinn nodded.

Joon was torn—she strongly felt how wrong it was that Quinn was selling drugs, but she suddenly had hope—real hope—that he could buy a house and she could move in with him. She was searching for something to make her feel better, and the hope of a real home for the first time since her parents had died was seductive. Just as she was about to give in to it, a thought crept into her mind and a cold slice of fear edged up her spine.

"Do you take drugs too?" Joon asked.

"I have a little taste every now and then, but I ain't hooked on them if that's what you're asking."

"Ragtop took drugs and it really screwed her up. I don't want you to ruin your life. Why do you take them at all?"

Quinn sat beside her. "Because sometimes, when I get sick of living like this, it's a nice little escape. I've been homeless since I was twelve. It gets to you after a while and I need something to pick me up."

"What happened to your family?"

Quinn lay on his back and let out a loud breath. "My dad was a businessman. I was never close to him. He traveled a lot, and my mom got lonely. While he was in other cities on business, she would, you know, have guys over. Anyway, when I was eleven, my dad was on a business trip, but he came home a few days early and caught my mom in bed with this dude she picked up at a bar. They got into a big fight that night. My dad said she was a whore and told her that I probably wasn't his real son. After he left, we didn't have money, and my mom brought guys home every night. Sometimes they'd pay her with money, and other times they'd pay her with drugs."

He shrugged. It didn't seem to bother him. "In less than a year, she was hooked on cocaine and couldn't get enough of the dope in her. She would leave me in the house for weeks at a time and not come home. I was still young enough that my friend's parents would let me eat at their house and stuff. Anyway, while my mom was on one of her binges, the landlord evicted us. I couldn't find her, so I took whatever shit I could carry and moved to the streets."

"Have you seen your mom since then?"

Quinn's face pinched tight—the first emotion she'd seen since he started telling her about it. "Nope. I haven't seen the whore since I left. But, you know, I didn't have it half as bad as some of the kids around here. Look at you. I mean, I know your foster mom hurt you... I don't know everything that happened, but it had to be worse than just being left alone and thrown out."

Joon put her face closer to his. "I think they're both bad. We're a lot alike, all of us kids—we all left something bad to find something better. Somedays, when I have enough to eat and I can wash up, I think it actually is better. I get to eat more now than when I lived with Aron. She starved me most of the time. It's amazing what you'll do when you're hungry enough."

Quinn kissed her on the cheek. "I hear you. People who've never lived without food have no idea how much pain there is when you haven't eaten in a couple of days." He was quiet for a moment and looked down, as if shy as he said the next part. "Joon, you're the only girl I ever met that's made me feel like a real person."

Joon melted into Quinn's body. "I don't know what I'd do without you. You've been so good to me and I love being with you."

That night, the two of them lay quietly, each thinking of the demons from their past until they fell asleep hoping that the next day would bring something better.

Chapter Thirty-Eight

All through summer and well into the fall, Joon and Quinn were together most of the time. Their lives became intertwined, and while Joon wouldn't have sex with him, they had experimented plenty.

As fall neared, one night, Joon and Quinn sat by a fire at the Tracks, talking. "Winter's coming again. I hate this time of year. It's starting to get cold already. Maybe we can find a shelter this year," Joon said.

Quinn shook his head. "No shelters for us. Those places are more dangerous than living on the street. You know what happens there. Remember last year when Pringle had her shoes stolen? Beats the hell outta me how she let that happen. She knew better than to take her shoes off."

"Her shoes were too small and her feet hurt. She was just trying to get some relief," Joon said, defending her deceased friend.

"Yeah, you're right." Quinn kissed her gently on the lips. "Have I told you today how much I love you?"

Joon smiled and shook her head. "Nope. Not today."

Quinn pulled her onto his lap. "Well, then, I love you, Joon. You make me whole. These past months have been the best of my life."

"I love you too, and we'll always be together. We'll have little Joons and Quinns running around someday."

Quinn kissed her deeply. "I'm counting on it. I know you'll make the most beautiful babies."

Joon rested her head on Quinn's chest. "So, if we aren't going to spend time in shelters, then what are we gonna do for the whole winter?"

"We're gonna stay right here. When the temperature gets really bad, we'll figure something out. I have some things in the works."

"Like what?"

Quinn gently ran his hand over her breasts, and the sensation made Joon's body tingle. He whispered, "You don't need to worry all the time. Just let me take care of you. It makes me feel good to provide for you."

Joon held Quinn tighter. She knew they belonged together. A smile she couldn't contain spread over her face. "You're amazing," she said.

They stared at the flames poking out from the top of the barrel, and Joon couldn't help but wonder what was in store for the two of them as winter approached. But she felt whole with the thought that her boyfriend would take care of her.

The next morning, as Quinn made his way into North Philadelphia, Joon set out to see Tony Bruno in the Italian Market. After meeting him at the Slayers' house, Joon had made it a point to visit once every two weeks, while Quinn went to see Pug. Joon liked Tony and enjoyed being around him. Not in the same way as she liked Quinn, but as a friend who she could share easy conversation with.

"Morning, Tony," Joon crooned as she walked through the door.

"Hey, Joon! How are you?"

Joon stood for a moment, taking in the smells of the bakery. "It's starting to get cold again. I hate the winter."

Tony placed a large tray of cinnamon buns on the counter and walked over to her. He gave her a quick embrace as Donata stepped into the store from the kitchen.

"Oh, hello, Joon," the older woman greeted. "How are you doing? The weather will be changing soon. Where will you stay when it snows?"

Joon laughed. "I don't know yet. Donata. My boyfriend is trying to figure that out."

"*Boyfriend.* Every time you tell me that, I don't like it. You're too young to be with boys," Donata remarked.

"I'll be fourteen in February."

"Fourteen? You're a baby. How come I never see this boy?"

Joon looked at the floor and let her hair hang over her face. "He works. That's how I have money to buy goodies from you."

"I see. If he works, then why are you livin' on the streets?" Donata asked with an edge to her voice.

Joon gave a helpless glance in Tony's direction, who jumped in. "Whoa. Now come on, Donata. Leave her alone. You sound like a mom."

"I was a mom, and now I'm a grandmother." Donata was raising her granddaughter, Ruth, after the girl's parents were killed in a car accident that had left the child a severely injured orphan.

"Yeah, I know you are," Tony said, sliding his arm over Donata's shoulder. "I only wish I had a grandma like you."

"Oh, knock it off with that sweet talk," Donata said, shooing Tony's arm off of her. Then she turned back to Joon. "I mean it. I think you're too young. But it's none of my business, so I won't bring it up again if I can help it." She made her way behind the counter and pulled a bag from the shelf behind her. "What's it gonna be today, Joon?"

Joon picked her goods carefully. Quinn made money for them to eat, but not enough for her to be frivolous.

That night, back at the Tracks, Donata's worry played over in Joon's head. "Quinn, I'm nervous about the winter. At least with Pringle I stayed at a shelter one night a week. I know you said you're working on something, but can you please tell me what it is?"

Quinn took her in his arms. "I hate to see you worry. I have some connections in Kensington. I've been working there a lot lately and I met some people. I'm not saying it's a done deal, but I think it might work out to keep us both inside this winter."

Joon smiled, trying not to let her hopes get too high. "When will we know for sure?"

"Hopefully by Halloween."

Quinn handed Joon a beer while he lit a joint. "You want some?"

She shook her head.

"Oh come on," Quinn coaxed. "Take a hit. It's not gonna kill you."

Joon took the joint and sucked on the end. As the harsh smoke hit the back of her throat, she coughed uncontrollably. Joon took another drag and held it in her lungs. She felt herself relax and a haze gently settled over her mind and thoughts. The world looked different through high eyes; it wasn't as scary, and life seemed filled with possibility.

"That's it," Quinn said. "Take another hit. Before you know it, you won't be worried about a thing."

Chapter Thirty-Nine

———————————————

Joon took several more hits of the joint before she looked at Quinn, her eyes drooping and her mouth hanging open.

He chuckled. "How're you feeling, babe?"

She tried to form words, but nothing came out right. Her tongue was dry and stuck to the roof of her mouth.

"All right, come on. I think we need to call it a night," Quinn said, chuckling. He helped Joon up from the ground and got her snuggled into her cardboard home. She couldn't command her body, and she drifted into a state of limbo, allowing herself to relax in Quinn's arms. As she did, Quinn started to gently undress her.

"Stop it," she said, her voice garbled.

He kissed her on the lips. "Now is the perfect time. There's nothing more phenomenal than having sex when you're on the kind of high you're on right now."

She tried to shake her head but couldn't be sure she actually did. "No sex. I'm not ready."

"That's the A-bomb talking."

Joon lifted her head from the floor of the box. "What?"

He gave her a sexy smile. "I took a little heroin off the top of my bags and sprinkled it on the joint we smoked. Great shit, isn't it?"

Joon shook her head, which set off a wave of queasiness. "I don't feel so good."

Quinn grabbed a warm soda from his backpack. "Here, drink this."

She sipped the lemon-lime drink and her stomach settled. When she finished it, she handed the empty can to Quinn and lay back.

He set the can aside and ran his hand down her chest. "So, I want you to relax. I'm gonna make you feel better than you ever felt in your life."

Joon opened her eyes a crack and shut them again as Quinn kissed her neck. Before she knew what was happening, he had undressed her and himself. He stroked her body softly, and as Joon moaned from the glorious feeling, he put his mouth between her legs. His tongue glided over her crotch like a satin ribbon. Joon arched her back and put her hand on the back of his head, pulling his mouth to her.

With Joon on the verge of orgasm, Quinn entered her. Her insides clenched down on him, and Joon let out a small gasp. She knew what they were doing, and something in her told her to make him stop. But she couldn't find the strength to fight her way through the drug-induced fog that made her body and mind go limp. Besides, what he was doing made her feel so good.

Joon woke late the next morning. Her head was throbbing and she was disoriented. Feeling sick, she crawled out of the cardboard box to find Quinn.

"What happened last night?" she asked.

"You know what happened. You participated, remember?"

Joon glared at him. Her legs were planted wide, her hands balled into fists. She felt like a bull ready to charge a matador. "Yeah, I remember. You wouldn't take no for an answer." She got on her tiptoes and put her mouth close to his ear. "What if I get pregnant?"

Quinn chuckled. "You haven't even gotten your period yet, so I don't think that'll be a problem. In fact, we should be doing it all the time before you start to get your period."

"Okay, so I can't get pregnant, but I wasn't ready to do it yet."

He ran his hand over her hair. "It's not a big deal, Joon. Don't make it more than it is. You liked it. And when you came, I couldn't help but explode."

Joon was embarrassed. "Having sex is a big deal to me. I just thought it would be special."

Quinn was losing his patience. He'd done everything for Joon—he paid for them to eat and made sure she was safe. He stepped away from her. "It was special, Joon. Man, girls get so twisted about sex. It's just sex.

Look, if you don't want to be with me anymore, that's fine. You can go find someone else to take care of you."

Annoyed that he had violated her and was showing no remorse, Joon put her hands on her hips. "Fine," she yelled. "I guess we're breaking up then." She turned on her heel and walked off.

When she got to Rittenhouse Square, she flopped down on a grassy area, curled into a fetal position, and fell asleep under the warmth of the fall sun.

"Hey, Joon!"

She bolted upright out of her sleep and looked around.

"TeTe!" she said when her eyes landed on him. "Where have you been?"

TeTe sat on the grass next to her. "I've been all over the damn place. After I left you at the shelter last year, I heard about a shelter in Camden that allows couples. I got my girl, and we made our way over there. We stayed there all summer too. I'm back in Philly for a couple of days. I need to get my birth certificate, so me and my girl can get one of those public housing apartments in Camden. I worked for a company over the summer that paints houses, and they're keeping me on for the winter. If I'm lucky, this could really turn into something for us." He smiled as he updated her. "My girl got a job too. She's waitressing at a local joint." He looked carefully at Joon. "How've you been? You don't look so great."

Joon tried to sit up straighter and smooth her hair down. "I'm doing good, TeTe. Have you seen Ragtop?"

He shook his head. "No. Nobody's seen her. Hey, how about that girl I left you with…Pringle, right? She still around?"

Joon cringed at someone else mentioning her friend's name. "No, she died."

TeTe looked around the park. "Wow. I'm sorry to hear that. She seemed like a real nice girl. You got people you're hanging with?"

Joon's eyes welled with tears. "I did. But I blew it. I had a boyfriend. We broke up this morning."

"How come you broke up?" TeTe asked gently.

Talking to TeTe was as close as she could come to talking to Ragtop again, so details started pouring out. "We had sex last night," she confided.

"You're kinda young for that." He rubbed the back of his neck. "But when you're living on the streets, things tend to happen sooner. Did you break up because the sex was bad?" he said, trying to lighten her mood.

"No." Joon blushed and her shoulders slumped forward. "I never said I wanted to have sex. I smoked weed last night. I got real messed up… and we did it. I wasn't ready." She sighed. "I wanted to wait." She hugged her knees and rocked back and forth.

As they sat in silence, Joon remembered bits and pieces of what had happened the night prior. She had wanted Quinn to stop, but her body wouldn't listen to her brain, and all too quickly he had been inside of her. She tried to put together everything that had happened, but she had been too high to remember all the details. She felt broken and used—and dirty.

TeTe interrupted her morbid thoughts. "Do you love him?"

"Yeah. I know it sounds stupid after what happened, but we love each other a lot. After Pringle died, he watched over me, made sure I ate, and stayed with me every night so I wouldn't have to sleep alone. He's a really good guy." Her situation was starting to sink in more, and she was trapped between loving him and not wanting to be on her own again. "Maybe I'm overreacting."

"Sounds like he isn't a total dick. Look, we all mess up. So you had sex before you wanted to. I know it sucks, but if he is good to you, maybe it's not the worst thing in the world."

Joon leaned into the man. "Thank you, TeTe. Other than Quinn, I don't have anyone else to share secrets with."

"Sure thing. I'm happy to help." He paused briefly. "But one thing is bothering me."

"What?"

"What are you doing smoking dope, huh? Don't you know that shit will fuck up your life?"

"I didn't mean to. I just got carried away. I didn't like it much; it made me feel sick. I didn't have control over my body. I was stupid."

TeTe bit his bottom lip. "Yeah, you were real stupid. Look, it's okay to have a beer once in a while, but once you start doing drugs, it's all over. Your life on the street becomes hell 'cause you need a way to get more dope, and if you don't have any money, you'll do real crazy shit to get high. Things you'll regret…like the stuff Ragtop did before I met her."

Suddenly overwhelmed, Joon threw her arms around TeTe's neck and let herself cry. She cried for all she'd lost and all she never had, and the large, gentle man let her take as long as she needed.

Before the two parted, TeTe treated Joon to a slice of pizza and handed her a five-dollar bill.

"I'm not sure when I'll see you again, given that I'll be living in Jersey," TeTe said. "You take care of yourself, little Joon."

They were the last words she heard before TeTe stepped onto a bus and left her standing alone in the streets of Philadelphia.

Chapter Forty

When Joon got back to the Tracks, Quinn was sitting on a log with a girl she hadn't seen before. They were laughing, and the girl was hanging all over him. Joon glared at the two-some as she made her way over to another barrel fire and stood over it, rubbing her hands together. Every now and again, she glanced at the two of them—he seemed not to notice, and that left Joon with overwhelming sadness. Unable to take it anymore, she walked over and looked down on the two of them. The girl looked at Joon and then back at Quinn.

"Can I help you?" Quinn insisted.

"We need to talk," Joon said meekly.

He guzzled from his beer and scooted closer to the girl. "About what?"

"About us."

"What about us, Joon? We broke up this morning, remember?"

Joon looked at the rest of the group sitting around the fire. "I...I need to talk to you for a few minutes."

Quinn glared at her with a stone-faced expression.

"Please," she said quietly.

Quinn pushed himself up from the ground. "Fine, but only a couple of minutes." He turned to the girl he had been partying with. "Keep my seat warm. I'll be right back."

Joon's heart sank into her stomach, the full impact of losing Quinn hitting her hard. They walked out of earshot from the group, and Joon turned to face him, but she stared down at her ratty sneakers.

"So what do you want?" Quinn asked.

"I was upset this morning. I mean, I always imagined that when we finally made love, we would be somewhere special and it would be the most fantastic moment of our lives."

"Really, Joon? Are we talking about that again? I get it's different for girls, but we both enjoyed it last night. When you moaned in my ear, I could hardly contain myself. Then when I felt you clamp down on me as you came, it was the greatest feeling I'd ever had with a girl. That's how I know that you're the one for me."

Joon eyes welled. *Have I blown everything out of proportion? I feel like a fool for getting so upset with him.*

Quinn softly rubbed his thumb over her cheek. "You're still the prettiest girl I've ever seen."

Joon blushed and relief coursed through her. "Really?"

"Yeah, really, and making love to you last night was very special to me."

Joon pushed her long, blond hair away from her face. "So what are we gonna do now?"

He rested his hand on her shoulder. "We're gonna tell that bimbo over there waiting for me to piss off. Then, we're gonna go into our box and make love, just like we did last night. How's that sound?"

"Scary, if I'm being honest. But I want to be close to you." She reached up and held on to his arm, keeping it in place on her shoulder. "Just one thing. I didn't like that you put heroin in the joint and didn't let me know. I would've never smoked it."

"You're right. I'm sorry. I thought it would be fun. I won't do that again."

The two stood in silence for a few moments, and Joon finally made a decision. "I love you, Quinn."

He wrapped both his arms around her. "Yeah, I love you more than you'll ever know," he replied into her hair as they hugged.

Joon smiled. "I like that...you loving me."

"Good. Let's call it a night. I wanna make love to you," Quinn stated.

Joon's belly swirled with anxiety.

Quinn watched her. "What's wrong? I thought we just talked everything through."

"Yeah, we did. It's just that...I'm nervous I won't be good at it."

He kissed the tip of her nose. "That's impossible. It's like you were born knowing how to be the best lovemaker on the planet."

Joon giggled and touched his chest gently. He led her into their box and undressed them both, and before she knew it, she was lying on her back and he was taking both of her hands. "Just kneel, okay?"

As Joon rose to her knees, she glided her hands up his thighs and over his ass.

Quinn rubbed his hand over her hair. "Just take it into your mouth."

She hesitated for a moment, then sucked on the tip.

Quinn let out a loud groan. "More, Joon. Please. The whole thing. Please."

Joon looked up. His eyes were pleading for her to do what he wanted, so she took him into her mouth again. This time she took all of him, and he moved her head back and forth until she understood and did the motion on her own. Suddenly, he pulled her head away and laid her back. Quinn got on top of her and put his tongue between her legs while she took all of him into her mouth again. They found a steady rhythm, and several minutes later, Quinn came into her mouth and Joon came into his.

They both collapsed. "That was great, wasn't it?" Quinn asked.

"Better than I ever could've imagined." She took a moment to regain her breath. "Oh my God, Quinn. I love you so much."

"I love you too, babe."

The two lay naked in each other arms, and Joon stayed awake most of the night. She had given herself to Quinn and, because of this, she felt much closer to him. By morning, she was more relaxed.

Quinn's eyes slowly opened.

"Morning," Joon said.

"Morning, gorgeous. How long have you been up?"

"Most of the night."

"Doing what?" he asked, surprised.

"Thinking about us."

"All good thoughts, I hope," he muttered.

Joon rested her hand on his shoulder and giggled. "Of course. I was thinking about how much we love each other. You know what I mean?"

Quinn leaned into Joon, and they shared a deep kiss. He pulled his head back slightly to look into her eyes, then softly ran his hand down her chest, over her abdomen, and across her pelvis and slid his fingers into her. Joon closed her eyes, welcoming the love she was about to receive.

Chapter Forty-One

———————————————■———————————————

B y Thanksgiving, the cold temperatures had returned and the kids on the street were getting ready for another hard winter. Some migrated south, and others found different forms of shelter. This would be Joon's second winter at the Tracks, and she and Quinn were still talking about where else they could stay. Being outside was hard on the body. The frigid temperatures also played with Joon's mind—when all she could focus on was being cold, she literally couldn't think about anything else.

"Hey," Quinn grunted as he woke. "Happy Thanksgiving."

Joon snuggled into him. "Happy Thanksgiving. I'm freezing."

"Yeah, it's pretty cold. I'll go out and light a barrel."

"What are we going to do all winter? You don't want to go to a shelter, and we don't have enough money to stay anywhere. You said that you were working on something. Did you figure it out?"

Quinn looked deep into her eyes. "I did. I got us a small place in Kensington. It ain't much, but it'll be ours.

"Oh," Joon moaned, leaning into him. "I don't care where we go as long as we're together."

"Have you ever been there?"

Joon shook her head. "Is it nice?"

Quinn laughed. "We're homeless teenagers that haven't had a real bath in months and have no money. How nice do you think it's gonna be?"

"Oh, man. Is it at least as nice as the worst shelter?" she teased.

He laughed. "Not sure I'd say that either. These places aren't run by people like Albany. They're run by people who wanna make money."

"How will we pay them?"

"I'll make money from Pug, and the rest we can pay in trade," Quinn explained easily. "You worry too much. You need to learn how to go with the flow."

"Well, when are we leaving?"

"We're all set for tomorrow morning, so let's enjoy our Thanksgiving. I'm taking you to a diner for a turkey dinner."

That night, Joon sat in a booth at a diner looking at a plate of round turkey slices, yellow gravy, lumpy mashed potatoes, and limp vegetables. She leaned forward and took a whiff of the food. "This smells so good," she said, digging her fork into the mashed potatoes.

Quinn didn't comment. He kept his head down and shoveled the dinner into his mouth, barely swallowing before taking in the next mouthful.

Later, back at the Tracks, they packed their meager belongings and settled in for sleep.

"I'm so excited to go somewhere new," she said, content from the food and the prospect of sleeping inside soon.

"Yeah? Good. I like making you happy."

Joon took off her clothes as Quinn removed his own. She laid on top of his body, and with deep, unrelenting passion, they made love.

Chapter Forty-Two

———————◼———————

Joon stepped onto the street in Kensington.

"Welcome to life under the El," Quinn announced. He was swaying to the loud music coming from a parked car.

Joon looked around, then stared above them. A massive steel structure ran the length of the street as far as she could see. "What is that?" she asked.

Quinn looked up at the seemingly endless, prehistoric-looking steel centipede above them.

"That's the Market–Frankford Line."

Joon gave him a blank stare.

"It's the subway, stupid. This is where it rises aboveground."

Joon gazed at the people on the sidewalk. There were prostitutes and drug addicts everywhere. It wasn't like Center City, where the prostitutes were more discreet. In Kensington, no one seemed worried about hiding in the shadows. The people and the seedy part of town were jarring to Joon, and she reached for Quinn's hand.

But as he pulled his hand away, his demeanor changed and his voice was low and deep. "Don't be so needy. People will notice it. You gotta learn how to stand your ground. We ain't at the Tracks. You see the people around here? They'll destroy you if you don't keep it together."

Fear surged through Joon. She didn't like being in such a dangerous area. She and Quinn walked for several blocks before they turned onto Diamond Street and stopped in front of a dilapidated home. There were teenage girls on the porch and men who undressed Joon with their eyes.

"We're here," Quinn said, looking up at the house with a smirk. "This is where you're staying."

"What do you mean it's where *I'm* staying?"

"I don't think I spoke Spanish? It's where you're staying," he growled.

Joon spun to walk away, but Quinn grabbed her arm. "Where are you going?"

"Back to the Tracks," Joon said, her voice becoming shrill. "I'd rather freeze to death than live here."

"That's not possible. I made a deal with Pug."

Joon tried to pull her arm away, but he clung tightly. "I don't care, Quinn. I don't know what deal you're talking about, but tell Pug that I'm not staying here. Why the hell would he care if I stay here or not? I'm leaving."

Quinn backhanded Joon across the face, and she landed on the concrete. Stunned, she sat on the broken sidewalk and cried.

A few seconds later, a girl's voice above her said, "Look, bitch, I ain't your babysitter. Get the fuck up. Time to go."

Joon struggled to her feet and used the sleeve of her coat to wipe the blood from her mouth.

"You got this?" Quinn asked the girl, who grabbed Joon's arm.

"Yeah, I got it. Just head out."

Quinn clasped Joon's shoulder and squeezed hard. "Don't be a fool. Well, I mean, you've been a fool since Pringle died, but try not to keep it up."

"W-what?" Joon said, her eyes bulging. "We love each other."

"Love each other? Please." He laughed. "You made it so easy, like stealing candy from a baby."

It took a few seconds for Joon to process what was happening, but her first reaction was hatred—pure and simple. "I hate you," she screamed. "If Pringle were alive, this never would have happened to me."

"That's why I killed her, *Joon*." Quinn sneered.

Joon pulled her arm free from the girl and lunged at Quinn, but he took a quick side step and she landed on the pavement. "You motherfucker! How could you kill Pringle? You fucking prick," Joon screamed as she watched him walk down the block. She wanted to run after him and choke him to death.

"Listen, bitch. If I gotta stand out on this sidewalk for another minute waiting for you to get your shit together, I'm gonna fuck you up."

Joon looked at the girl incredulously. "Didn't you hear what he just said?" she demanded. "He killed my best friend. Leave me alone. I'm leaving. You can forget you ever saw me. He killed her. He killed Pringle!"

The older girl laughed. "Girl, I don't care who the fuck that piece of shit killed. You're here now, and you ain't goin' nowhere. Now get the fuck up," she said and kicked Joon in the thigh.

Joon glowered at the girl. "I didn't agree to come here."

She barked out a laugh. "I've had enough. Let's go." She bent down, grabbed a handful of Joon's hair, and yanked until she was on her feet. Then she gripped her arm tightly and pulled her toward the house. "I'm Angie. What the fuck's your name? Not that I really care, but I gotta know what to call ya."

Joon didn't answer, and the attractive black girl with a large gap between her front teeth dug her fingers into her arm harder. "What's your fucking name?"

"I'm Joon. Stop squeezing my arm so tight. You're hurting me."

Angie smacked Joon in the back of the head. "How 'bout that? Does that hurt too? I'll hit ya more if ya don't shut up."

Joon felt dazed as Angie dragged her up the porch steps and into the house. The other girls inside gave Joon dirty looks. Some held their nose as she passed. "You smell like you just crawled out of a sewer, girl," one girl said. "You a ratty mess."

Joon realized that, compared to the others, she was in an awful state. She hadn't had a real shower in a long time. Now, self-conscious, she followed Angie into the house. Just inside the door was a room with large cloth sofas and a small television. There were blankets and discarded fast-food wrappers scattered over the floor.

Angie put her hand on Joon's elbow. "That girl ain't joking. You stank, girl. You're so filthy I can't even tell what ya look like. Let's go upstairs. You need to take a shower."

Chapter Forty-Three

Joon wrapped her arms tightly over her chest. As she followed Angie to the second floor, she held in a scream churning in her throat. Things had moved too quickly since she'd arrived in Kensington.

Angie led her into the bathroom, and Joon looked around. There was tub with a mildew-stained shower curtain, a sink crusted with rust, and a toilet that hadn't been cleaned in a long time.

"Put your shit in the corner and get undressed," Angie instructed.

Joon turned to the girl. She closed her eyes tight, and a shallow whimper escaped from deep within her belly.

Angie raised her eyebrows and stepped forward. "Are you fuckin' deaf? I said take your goddamn clothes off."

"I don't want to," Joon said quietly.

Angie slapped her across the face. "I don't give a shit what you want. Did I ask you what you wanted, princess? No! I gave you an order. Now do it!"

Joon quickly shed her clothing and stood naked in the middle of the bathroom, shivering even though her nerves were making her sweat. Angie turned on the shower and looked back at Joon. "Get in. We don't waste water here. Everything costs money."

Joon stepped into the tub, and the cold water drenched her hair. She stood clutching her body. "The water is freezing."

Angie grunted. "Girl, you don't get a hot shower until you earn it." She handed Joon a bar of cheap soap. "Wash your hair and your nasty body. When you earn money, you'll buy yourself some shit to shower with, but until then, you can deal with that bar of soap."

Joon followed her instructions like a robot, showering quickly and drying off fast when Angie handed her a damp bath towel.

"Come to the room across the hall. Pug bought some clothes for you. As for that shit you came in, it all goes in the trash."

"Why would Pug buy me clothes?"

Angie snickered and shook her head. "I ain't your mommy and I ain't here to answer all your stupid questions. Just hurry the fuck up."

Joon stared at her reflection in the small mirror above the sink. She looked like someone she'd never met—her eyes were crazed, to match the feeling in her belly. She quickly went over to her bag, took out a large comb, and pulled it through her hair, then brushed her teeth until her gums bled.

Joon found Angie sitting with four other girls in the bedroom across the hall. She walked in and closed the door behind her, clinging to the wet towel wrapped around her shivering body. The other girls watched her closely.

Angie broke the silence. "This bitch's name is Joon. She's gonna be staying with us."

A light-skinned black girl named Cinnamon stood and put her hands on her hips. "Um, not so fast. She ain't no better than the rest of us just 'cause she's young and white. She ain't gettin' no special privileges. When she earns her way in here, that's when she can stay."

The other three girls nodded in agreement.

"Cinnamon, I know what the fuck I'm doin'," Angie spat. "Just 'cause Pug didn't pick you to bring her into the house doesn't mean ya gotta act like a nasty bitch. I know how it works here. She's gonna be in holding like any other new girl."

Cinnamon walked toward the bedroom door but stopped right in front of Joon and put her nose a few inches away. "Good. You ain't getting no special treatment here. I don't like you. I want ya to remember that."

Cinnamon left the room and the other three girls followed.

Joon covered her face with her hands, letting go of the towel and dropping to her knees. Her body heaved with sobs.

Angie sat back and watched her. After a few minutes, she spoke angrily. "Let me be clear. Ain't nobody here, especially me, care about your tears. You don't get no respect from the girls that live here until you earn respect. In fact, you're pretty annoying. Stop all that crying and whimpering shit. Ain't nobody wanna be around that all day."

Joon was still on her hands and knees, but she slowly stood and bent over to grab the towel to cover her body.

"What's on your leg?" Angie asked.

Joon looked down at her right thigh and instinctively put her hand over the scar. "I got burned."

"Oh yeah? How'd that happen?"

Joon glared at the girl. "What do you care?"

Angie shrugged. "I don't really, just curious," she said, turning away.

"My foster mother threw hot oil from a frying pan on my leg…said she was trying to melt away my fat thighs," Joon spat.

"Oh, I see. You get your crazy from your foster mom?" Angie laughed.

"I'm not crazy. I'm nothing like her."

"Uh-huh. Whatever. You're a damn fool."

Joon stood awkwardly, still trying to hide her scar. "Do you have some clothes?"

Angie threw a pair of jeans and a crop top at her.

Joon looked the garments over. They were clean. The shirt was skimpy for cold weather, but she didn't want Angie to hit her again, so she put the clothes on. The jeans were skin tight, the waistband sat low on her hips, and the shirt hit her two inches below her breasts.

Joon rubbed her arms, as if to warm herself. "Now what?" She looked around the room, eyeing the four single mattresses on the floor. "Am I sleeping in here?"

Angie laughed. "No, girl. You don't sleep in the house. You heard Cinnamon. You're new. You sleep out back in the shed with the other new girls."

"Shed?"

The girl pointed out the window. "You sleep outside."

Joon's mouth dropped open. "Why do I have to stay outside? I came here to live inside for the winter."

"We covered this already. You stay out there 'cause you're new. There's two other girls out there to keep ya company," Angie said with a chuckle.

Joon's insides trembled, her belly twisting and a large lump forming in her throat. Then she pushed her mind to the safe place she had discovered when she lived with Aron. Quickly, her thoughts shut down, and she focused on the task in front of her, removing all emotion and presence.

Angie watched Joon and threw a skimpy coat at her. "Time to go, bitch."

Joon pulled the coat on, grabbed her wet hair, and twisted the long strands, placing a knot on top of her head with the one hair tie she always kept on her wrist.

"Ready to meet your roommates?" Angie said sarcastically.

Joon didn't reply. She mechanically followed Angie out to the shed in silence and watched as Angie undid the lock on the outside of the shed door.

"It's locked from the outside?" Joon asked, startled.

Angie laughed. "God, you're pathetic. The door stays locked to keep the new girls from running."

"But what if something bad happens, like a fire or someone has a heart attack or something?"

Angie shrugged. "Shit happens, and there ain't nothing you can do about it. People are here one minute and gone the next. Welcome to Kensington."

Chapter Forty-Four

Angie pulled the shed door open and pushed Joon inside. Joon just barely managed to stay upright and quickly sized up the other two girls. One girl immediately jumped to her feet and faced Joon. Then she turned to Angie.

"Ya ain't sticking her in here too. This fucking shit hole ain't big enough for three people," the girl growled.

"Shut up, Tori. It ain't like you have a say in this. This here is Joon. That's Tori, and that," she said, pointing to the girl squatting in the corner like a scared cat, "is Elf. She's scared of everything and everybody. Ain't ya, Elf?"

Elf averted her eyes and buried her face in the nook of her arm.

"Well, I'll leave you to get to know each other." Angie laughed, closed the door behind her, and snapped the lock closed.

Joon looked around. There was a large bucket in the corner she assumed was a toilet—and the source of the foul odor. There was a light bulb overhead and a small space heater near the door. Against the back wall was a milk crate that held a double-burner hot plate. Next to the crate were canned goods, a can opener, and a few gallons of water. Extension cords stretched across the dirt floor.

Tori glared at her. She was a beautiful mixed-race girl. She had long, wavy, black hair, a round face, and plump lips. Her green eyes made her look exotic. Joon turned away from Tori and took another look around the shed.

Elf shyly met Joon's eyes. "Your sleeping bag and pillow are over there." She pointed.

"Who said she can have those?" Tori thundered.

"We...we...we...all get them," Elf murmured.

"She can get one if I say she can," Tori yelled.

Joon had spent enough time on the streets to know this was a test. Her next action would determine her existence with Tori.

"No. Elf is right. They're mine."

When Joon walked over and grabbed the sleeping bag and pillow, Tori grabbed a fistful of Joon's hair. "What did I just tell ya, bitch?"

Joon acted swiftly. She pulled her hand back and punched Tori in the gut. Instinctively, the girl let go of her hair and bent over, holding her stomach.

"I don't want to fight with you," Joon stated, teeth bared. "But I will if I have to." She was pretending to be much tougher than she felt—it was a technique Ragtop had taught her early on. "I'd like us to be friends."

"Fuck you! I ain't never gonna be your friend," Tori hollered.

Joon took her belongings and moved to the other side of the shed, where Elf was sitting. She settled in next to the other girl.

"How did you two end up here?" Joon asked.

In a voice just above a whisper, Elf responded. "I ran away from home. I was only on the street for two nights when I met Pug. He gave me food and brought me here."

Joon turned and looked at Tori.

"What are you looking at?"

Joon let out a heavy sigh. "Well, it looks like we're gonna be living together for a while. Maybe if we got to know each other, things would be easier."

Tori snarled as she stared at Joon.

"Look, none of us asked to be here. I thought I was coming here to live in a house for the winter." She lowered her voice. "I trusted my boyfriend, and now I don't know what he's gotten me into. All I know is he fooled me, he never loved me, and I fell right into his trap."

Tori still stared at her with hatred.

"How long have you been here?" Joon asked Tori.

Tori snorted a sarcastic laugh. "I told ya already, we ain't friends. You and that dumb bitch there," she said, gesturing toward Elf, "can build your little girlfriend bullshit thing. Leave me the fuck out of it."

Joon shimmied into the dirty sleeping bag. It smelled like dried-up saliva and piss. Then she tucked the thin pillow under her head and faced Tori.

"Sure. We'll leave you alone, then. We don't want to bother you." Joon looked at Elf. "How long have you been here?"

Elf was Asian, and as Joon took in her details, she could see the pain of the past in the girl's dull brown eyes. Elf pushed her black hair behind her ears. "Since right before Halloween."

"You've been living in here for *a month?*"

Elf nodded. "Tori came here the day after Halloween."

Tori was on her feet, standing over Elf, who put her arms over her head to protect herself. "Bitch! Did I ask you to tell that girl anything about me?"

"No. I'm *sorry.*"

Joon jumped to her feet. "Whoa! Come on. She's just trying to be nice. Leave her alone."

Tori took a few steps toward Joon and, with both hands, pushed Joon backward into the wall of the shed. Joon smacked into it with a thud that sounded much worse than it felt.

This is my second test, Joon thought. She composed herself and stepped closer to the girl. "Tori, there isn't anything you can do to me that will ever hurt as much as I've already been hurt. I think you're an asshole who is mean for no good reason. I've met a lot of people like you, so if you're gonna be a jerk-off, then I won't bother with you. I just thought that if we stick together, it would be easier for all of us. Maybe we could even figure a way outta here."

Tori grunted and retreated to her side of the shed.

Joon settled down and looked at Elf. "Why are we here? And when do we get out?"

Elf placed her hand over her own chest. "You don't know. Do you?"

Chapter Forty-Five

Elf clutched at her own neck. "You really don't know why you're here?"

Joon shook her head.

Elf looked at her fingers and nibbled on a nail. "We all..." She paused and looked at Tori, who was glaring at her. "We, you know...we...have sex for money."

Joon was stunned. "Who is 'we'?"

"All of us. The girls in the house and...us," Elf explained.

"I don't understand. I didn't agree to come here for that. Quinn never told me anything about this place. That asshole brought me here and left."

"Who did you say?" Tori barked.

"What?" Joon asked, confused. All she could concentrate on was what Elf had just told her. She couldn't even remember what she'd just said.

"Did you say Quinn?"

"Yeah, why?"

Tori's nostrils flared and her hands balled into fists. "Does Quinn have long, brown hair and brown eyes?"

Joon nodded cautiously.

"He works for Pug, right? Sells dope for the fucker."

"Yeah. How do you know him?"

"Ha! That asshole pretended to be my boyfriend. He would come to my cousin's apartment where I lived. We'd go out on dates and shit."

"Dates?" Joon asked, staring in disbelief.

"Yeah. What are you, dense? Dates. You know, where you go out and eat, party and have sex?" Tori snapped.

Joon flinched. She instinctively leaned away from Tori and looked over at Elf, who was watching intently. "That's impossible. Quinn is my boyfriend. He was with me all the time." It was too much for her to process all at once.

"Yeah, except when the bastard wasn't with you, that's when he was here, in my fucking city, selling his drugs and pretending he loved me."

Joon rubbed her jaw and flopped back against the wall. "Oh. My. God. He's lied about everything. He killed my best friend too." Then, she lay down in the sleeping bag and curled onto her side, turning her back to the other girls. But Tori and Elf knew by the way Joon's shoulders shook that she was crying.

Joon suffocated in the darkness that suddenly clung to her, working its way inside her soul. *Why did I trust Quinn? Pringle knew he wasn't a good person.*

Her regret over falling for him was all consuming. After two hours, she sat up and looked at Tori. Joon's eyes were red and swollen, but Tori returned the gaze, her eyes narrowed and her eyebrows pinched together as she concentrated on Joon.

Tori leaned forward. "You ain't the only one here that's been played, so don't go thinking you're all special and shit. We've all been made a fool, or we wouldn't be sitting here on this dirt floor in this cold-ass wooden box."

"But I loved him," Joon moaned.

"Love. What the hell do you know about love? Quinn is a selfish prick. He does whatever it takes to get what he wants. He told me he loved me too, but I wasn't dumb enough to believe it. I was just dumb for thinking I found me a dude that was willing to take me out and treat me good for some damn sex. There are others who thought Quinn was their boyfriend...others who live in the house."

Joon sucked in a quick breath. "Others? How many?"

Tori shrugged. "I don't know. Four or five."

Joon turned away and covered her mouth with her hand. "He brings girls to Pug, and he's a killer."

Tori was seething. "It doesn't surprise me a bit that he's a killer too. Anyone who works for Pug is a piece of shit."

Joon glanced over at Elf, who shook her head slightly. Left to face her own regret, Joon's hands trembled, and she rocked back and forth. To stop her hands from shaking, she crossed her arms, hugging herself and tucking them under the opposite elbow. She was taking fast, shallow breaths.

"It's not that bad," Elf said, trying to comfort her.

Joon turned to her. "What?"

"I said it's not that bad. All you have to do is lie there."

"You're kidding me, right?"

Tori could practically smell Joon's fear. "What? Are you a virgin or something?"

Joon paused. "No. But I don't wanna have sex with people I don't know."

"Yeah, well, join the club," Tori snapped.

"What's gonna happen? I mean, when? Please tell me," Joon begged the other girls.

Elf sat up straight. "They take us inside almost every night. You get to shower and put on clean clothes. Then they bring in all kinds of men."

Joon's guts twisted, and she wretched.

"Ew, girl. Clean that shit up. I better not step in your puke," Tori growled.

Elf got to her feet and went to help Joon. "You'll be okay," she whispered.

"I want to believe you, but I can't do this. Do you understand me?" she demanded, her voice rising. She felt the hysteria taking hold, and she was sure she was close to passing out or somehow physically flying apart.

Elf nodded and rubbed her back. "It'll be easier if you don't fight them."

Tori smirked. "That's the only smart thing I've ever heard come outta your mouth."

Elf grabbed her sleeping bag and placed it next to Joon, snuggling up close, trying to give the new girl comfort.

Chapter Forty-Six

Joon lay on the dirt floor next to Elf. She didn't know if hours or days had passed. No one came to check on them. The shed had been rigged so no light could get in under the door, and there were no windows. The only sounds were wind and an occasional car honking or police siren screaming in the distance. Joon's stomach felt like a black hole as she anticipated the degradation to come. When the shed door opened, the girls looked up to see Angie standing in the doorway.

Immediately, Joon looked beyond the girl. Outside, it was partially dark, but she could still see blue sky in the fading light.

"How long have I been here?" Joon asked.

Angie shrugged. "What difference does it make?"

Joon scooted out of the sleeping bag. "This is all a big mistake. I want to leave."

Angie grabbed Joon's face. "Quinn brings lots of girls here. It's not a mistake. It's called business, and Quinn does it better than anyone else. You was just stupid enough to listen to him. Your fault."

Joon stared at Angie with watery eyes filled with desperation.

Angie glared at her. "Girl, those tears don't mean nothin' to me. Right now, you just do what you're told. Period. Now, you and Tori gotta come with me. Time to get showered and dressed."

Tori stood, and with her head held high, she followed Angie.

"Move it!" Angie screamed at Joon.

Joon's feet stayed planted. Elf stood beside her. "Please, Joon, go with her. Please. You don't have any idea how bad they'll make it for you... for all of us. We all get punished when someone doesn't go along with it. Most of the girls hate me because I refused in the beginning, and no one got to eat for two days and practically everyone got a beating. Some of the girls beat me when no one was looking. Please. For all of us."

Joon couldn't bear the burden of others suffering for her actions, so she slowly followed Angie back into the house. After she took her cold shower and dressed, she sat on the toilet while Angie roughly applied her makeup and fixed her hair. When she was finished, Joon looked in the mirror. Her eyelids were covered in pink eye shadow and accentuated by thick, black eyeliner. Her cheeks were covered in a pink-orange blush, her lips slathered in bright-red lipstick.

"I look ridiculous. Why do I have to wear makeup?"

Angie pushed Joon's face against the mirror. "Because that's what Pug expects. I ain't your personal fucking stylist. Next time, you'll do it yourself."

Back in the bedroom, Angie gave Joon a pair of six-inch heels. Joon turned one shoe over in her hand, then looked across the bedroom at Tori. "I can't wear these," she stated.

Tori looked at her. "Girl, you just ain't getting it. There is no *can't* or *won't* in our world. Put the fucking shoes on and shut the hell up."

Joon sat on a small wooden chair in the corner of the room and strapped herself into the shoes. Slowly, she tried to stand, but the heels were so high she wobbled, her ankles shaking until she lost her balance and landed on the bedroom floor. As she fell, Angie walked back into the room and scowled at her.

The older girl walked over to Joon and slapped her on the back of the head. "What the hell is wrong with you? You better practice walking until it's time to go downstairs."

Joon clomped unsteadily around the room for a bit. Then carefully descended the steps to the first floor, clinging to the railing every step of the way. She sat next to Tori on the battered sofa. She could feel her heart throbbing inside her chest. Two men entered the gloomy living room from the kitchen, each holding a can of beer.

Pug lagged behind them. When Joon saw him, her whole body tensed.

"Look here, boys. We got a new one tonight," he said, pointing to Joon.

Joon unstably stood in her too-high heels. "I want to go back to the city."

Pug waltzed up to Joon and backhanded her. She landed on the floor and curled up into a ball. He loomed over her, pressing his shoe down hard on her ankle. "Get up, whore."

Joon wiped at her mouth, and the back of her hand came away blood-ied. Tears streaked through the blood dripping from her lip and down her chin.

Angie stood nervously off to the side. She glanced at Pug and gave him a small, fearful smile. His eyes met hers as he scowled at the older girl. "What the fuck are you hanging around for? Go get your fat ass ready."

Angie nodded and scurried off to change her clothes.

"Now, let's get to business," Pug announced. He grabbed Joon's chin and pulled her head up, roughly pushing her hair back from her face with his other hand. "Pretty. Ain't she?"

Both men nodded and grunted.

"How much, man?" the heavier man, Warren, asked.

"Two hundred."

"What's she got, gold between her legs?" Warren said.

"Why don't you give me two hundred bucks and find out? You won't be disappointed."

Warren wavered.

Pug spun Joon around and slapped her ass hard. "This is her first night here. You gotta pay for that, you know what I'm saying?"

Warren beamed. "Yeah, all right. She know what she's doing?"

Pug gave Warren an evil grin. "I just said it's her first night here, motherfucker, so no, she don't know what she's doing. You get to teach her, big fella."

Warren slinked up to Joon. His eyes roved up and down her body. Joon's head spun and sweat was dripping from her armpits down her sides. She looked at Tori with pure terror, but the other girl turned away quickly. Joon whimpered and Warren smiled.

"Yeah, that's good. I like that innocent thing you got going on. How old are you, girl?" When Joon didn't respond, Warren grabbed a handful of her hair and pulled her face close to his. "I asked how old you are."

"Four...Fourteen," Joon stuttered.

Warren let go of her hair and ran his hand down her back and over her ass. "You are a fine piece of ass." He looked over at Pug. "I'm ready to get this party started."

Pug nodded. "You yell if you have any problems with her."

Warren grabbed Joon's arm and headed toward the stairs. "Don't worry. We ain't gonna have no problems, and if she decides to give me any, I'll take care of her myself."

Joon threw one last desperate glance at Tori, but there was nothing any of them could do. The girls were at the mercy of a group of unpredictable men. Knowing she had no choice, Joon walked up the stairs with trepidation.

When they reached the second floor, Joon focused her thoughts on the darkness, going to her safe place where pain didn't exist and her mind slipped into nothingness.

Chapter Forty-Seven

Inside the bedroom Warren glowered at Joon, like a hungry lion in dense cover waiting to attack his prey. She backed away from him slowly, feeling his hunger for her. Anxiety rushed through her body and her insides quivered. Feeling dizzy, she tried to control her short, rapid breaths as Warren thumped across the bedroom and put his arms around her waist. He pulled her into him, and when she resisted, his jaw stiffened and his eyes grew hard. "Don't make me hurt you."

Warren's long, fleshy fingers roughly undressed her, and then she lay on the bed as she was told. His desire for the young teen took over. He quickly undressed and covered her thin body with pounds of hairy fat. He grabbed a handful of her hair at the top of her skull and pulled back hard. Joon thought her head would snap off as she sank deeper into the mattress.

"Yeah, you're a dirty, little thing, aren't ya?"

Joon looked at Warren with bulging eyes and her chin quivered.

"You gonna cry? I make all the girls cry," he taunted.

Joon held back her tears. She had spent years hiding her emotions from Aron, and tonight, that ability was going to come in handy. Joon's lips went taut and her eyes narrowed.

Warren clamped down on her breast, trying to break her. But she wouldn't give him the satisfaction. One thing Joon knew was physical pain, and this was nothing compared to the pain Aron had inflicted on her. Frustrated that he couldn't make her cry, Warren slammed himself inside of her. Joon held her breath. It was nothing like when she'd had sex with Quinn, who had pretended to be caring and loving. She ignored the pain. She focused on how repulsive it was having Warren inside her. She felt dirty and cheap. When Warren came, he collapsed on top of the fourteen-year-old like a hippo napping in mud. Eventually, he let her out from under him, and she scurried into the bathroom. She grabbed a dirty washcloth, soaped it as best she could with cold water, and rubbed between her legs to remove any remnants of Warren.

In the weeks that followed, some of the other girls told Joon that giving herself over to the men willingly would make it easier. But, after Warren, she refused to give in, and no matter how long she was forced to have sex with strange men, it never got better. It felt as disgusting as the first night.

Within a couple months, Joon was being forced to sell her body up to six times a night. She still lived in the shed with Tori, but Elf had moved into the house with the last rotation of girls. Joon learned there were several houses throughout North Philadelphia. Pug would rotate the girls to keep the johns from getting bored.

She had stopped dreaming about going back to live on the streets of Center City and no longer beat herself up about being fooled by Quinn. It had been almost two months since she'd walked the streets freely or saw any of her old homeless friends, and Joon missed her freedom.

Joon had just been returned to the shed after a long night. Her body was used up. She got into her sleeping bag and lay quietly, trying not to disturb Tori. The girls hadn't become friends, but they had learned to live together, although Tori's moods were delicate, and Joon tried her best to keep things neutral between them.

Tori rolled over onto her side. "I gotta get outta this shit hole."

Joon looked over at her. "That's never gonna happen." She pulled the sleeping bag up to her chin.

"That's why I don't like you," Tori snapped. "You say stupid stuff."

"What do you want me to say, Tori? Pug keeps us under lock and key. He has taken our bodies and freedom away from us. We never get to go anywhere other than to the house and back into this shitty shed. How do you think we're ever gonna get out of here?"

Tori's hateful glare burned into Joon. "First, I'm gonna get into the house on the next rotation. Once I'm in there, they'll let me work the streets. Then, when the time is right, I'm gonna get the fuck outta here."

Joon leaned up on her elbow. "Do you know what Pug would do if he caught you?"

"Nope. And I don't care. Anything is better than this."

Joon considered that. "Where would we go?"

"We? Have you lost your damn mind? I ain't going anywhere with you. We're all in this alone. You understand? Nobody here cares about you or me or that little shit stain Elf. Do you see Elf trying to help us out?"

Joon scrunched her brow. "What do you expect her to do?"

"I expect her to help."

"How, Tori? How is Elf supposed to help us?"

Tori was on her feet. "I don't know how. All I know is that she should."

Joon sat up. "Because you would help the girls out here if you were inside? You just said you're not going anywhere with me and that we're all in it alone. Is that what you mean by 'help'? You can be a real asshole."

Tori lunged at Joon, and the girls wrestled on the dirt floor. Tori sat on Joon's stomach, pulled her hand back, and clocked Joon in the face. Blood splattered from her nose.

Brought to the edge of rage, Joon heaved her hips up and bucked Tori off of her, and the girl landed against the shed wall. Joon jumped to her feet and rushed the other girl before she could get up. She slapped Tori, then pushed her head against the shed. The thud of Tori's skull coming in contact with the wall made Joon stop abruptly. She sat back on her heels and watched as Tori held the back of her own head.

She took a moment to catch her breath before she spoke. "I'm sorry, Tori. I don't want to fight with you." Tears clung to Joon's cheeks. "I don't know what happened. I didn't mean to hurt you. But you hit me first." She reached for an old T-shirt to wipe her own bloodied nose.

Tori rubbed her head and looked at her hand, checking for blood, but there wasn't any. She shook uncontrollably and wrapped her arms tightly around herself.

Joon leaned forward and placed her hand on the girls shoulder. "What's wrong? Are you okay? I said I'm sorry," Joon said with sincerity.

Tori shook her head. "It ain't you." Suddenly, it was like all the energy was drained out of the girl. "I can't be here no more. This shit that we're doing—I can't live with it. I ain't no whore. That guy, the last guy I was with tonight, he…he stuck things in me."

"What?"

"You heard me. He stuck things in me—a huge dildo. He was all into it and then he fucked me with a soda bottle before he actually fucked me with his dick. He pulled my nipples so hard I thought he was gonna rip them off."

Joon sat next to Tori and put her arm around her shoulders. "Oh, Tori. I'm so sorry. You're right. We have to get out of here. We'll figure something out. I promise. Maybe you can go back to your mom and dad."

Tori shook her head. "Nah. I would never go back to my dad."

"Why?"

Tori looked into Joon's face. Her green eyes were sad and tired. "My dad's a drug addict. He probably hasn't even noticed I'm missing."

Joon cringed. "I'm sorry."

"Yeah. The motherfucker never gave a shit about me."

Joon rubbed Tori's arm. "Where's your mom?"

"Who knows?" the girl said. "She and that prick father of mine were too busy getting high to care about me. My mom left one night and never came home. I'm pretty pathetic, huh?"

Joon shook her head. "No, you're not pathetic. We're all damaged."

"Yeah? How are you damaged?"

Joon ran her fingers through her hair. "I ran away from my foster mom who treated me worse than the family pet. Literally."

Tori studied Joon's expression. "Where are your parents?"

"They died when I was little. I went to school one day, and before it was over, they told me my mom and dad were dead. I don't know how or where or anything…just that they died. I was only eight. I got moved to a foster home, and finally, after years of being beaten and starved, I ran away. Now, here I am 'cause I let Quinn trick me."

The two girls sat in silence for a long time. Then Tori grabbed Joon's hand and held it tight. "We're gonna be okay. You know? We're gonna get outta here someday."

"I thought we are all in this alone," Joon teased.

Tori looked at her with a new kind of hardness in her eyes. "Not anymore," she said.

Chapter Forty-Eight

—————————■—————————

By April of the next year, Joon was moved into the house with a new batch of girls. Three black girls around her age now occupied the shed. Joon was immediately turned out to work the street with one of the experienced girls, who showed her "how to lure a john." In the grotesque world in which they all lived, knowing how to lure a john was equivalent to finishing a four year college degree. It was the sole pedigree required for being a successful hooker.

When Joon stepped out of the house and onto the sidewalk that first night, she felt a surge of freedom. She followed Skye, her assigned street teacher, down the block and onto a busy street. There, Skye taught her how to cat call the walking johns and prowl the edge of the sidewalk for driving johns.

Skye pointed to an approaching car. "See how he's slowing down to get a good look at his choices? That's how you know you got a hot one. Follow me."

Joon walked closely behind Skye to the edge of the sidewalk. Skye stuck out her right leg, revealing her long, lean thigh through the high slit in her short skirt. The car pulled over and Skye stepped into the street. She turned around and threw a smile to Joon. "Watch real close now," she instructed.

Skye leaned into the passenger window, exposing her cleavage in her low-cut shirt. It only took a few seconds for Skye's smile to fall flat and for her to turn and look at Joon. She talked to the man in the car again, cocking her hip and jiggling her boobs. She spoke a little longer but eventually turned to Joon again. Skye lifted her index finger and summoned her.

Joon stepped into the street and instinctively tried to pull her Daisy Duke shorts down her thighs. In the house, she wore silk and satin slips, but on the streets, dressing was a big part of how you lured a john. Joon walked up to the car. "What's up?"

Skye looked at her. "This john wants you."

"Why me?"

Skye snorted and a mist of liquid sprayed from her nose. "Exactly. I don't know what he's thinking. I tried to talk the fool out of it, but he insisted it needs to be you. Go on now. Get in and do your thing."

"No. Wait." She dropped her voice to whisper. "I don't want to get in a car with someone I don't know. What if he drives me somewhere and kills me?"

Skye smiled brightly. "Don't be so fuckin' dramatic. You get in the goddamn car, he'll drive a couple of blocks off the main drag for privacy, and you take care of business and walk back here." Skye looked up the block and noticed a few of the Slayers walking toward them. "You best get your ass in that car before those boys reach us and find out you're making a customer wait. Time is money, baby, and right now you're wasting both." Skye turned and walked back to the sidewalk, leaving Joon standing beside the car.

"Hey! You!" the man inside the car yelled. "Either get the hell in now, or I'll find someone else."

Joon looked back and saw the Slayers coming closer. They were watching her, and their strides had quickened. She swiftly opened the door and slid into the passenger seat.

The man ran his hand down her thigh. "I like how you look," he said and gave her a grin that showed his rotting teeth.

Joon cringed and turned her face toward the window. "We can go a couple of streets over," she said.

The man licked his lips. "Yeah, okay."

As he drove away from the active main road, Joon's stomach felt like an ocean current. He drove for six blocks before he decided on a quiet street and parked. Turning on the overhead light in the car, he looked at himself in the rearview mirror and picked his nose. Then he flattened his hair with his hands and gawked at Joon. "Let's get in the backseat."

When it was over, Joon scampered out of the car and stood alone on the dreary, desolate street. She walked back to the place where the man had picked her up. She had just got back onto the main street when another car pulled over. Joon clomped over to it in her high heels, her feet throbbing from the long walk back, and she leaned against the car. Within a few minutes, she was driven off to another random street to repeat her performance. It was one john after another well into the early morning hours of the next day. Exhaustion and pain began to break-through her numbness. She was relieved when Skye approached her and said it was time to head back to the house.

When the girls walked in, Pug was sitting on the sofa, where one of the hooker's was giving him a blow job. He pulled her head up by her hair. "Hold on, bitch. I got business." He stood and crossed the room quickly. Pug pulled on the waist of Joon's shorts. "Where's my money, bitch?"

Joon reached into her purse and pulled out a wad of bills.

Pug looked at the wad skeptically. "You holding out on me, girl?"

She shook her head. "No, that's all of it."

"Oh yeah?" he said. "Give me your purse."

Joon handed it to him and Pug emptied it onto the floor. Relieved the inspection was over, Joon headed for the stairs to her bedroom.

"Where the hell you goin'? Did I tell you to leave?"

Joon's head drooped. "No."

"Exactly. Now take off your clothes, so I know you ain't hiding none of my money from me."

Joon looked around the room at the other girls and a few of Pugs fellow gang members who had gathered to watch. Some girls snickered, while others looked at her with sad, fear-filled eyes.

Pug slapped her. "Hey!" he screamed in her ear. "What did I just tell you to do? Are you disobeying me?"

"No, no. I'm not. I'm sorry," Joon rambled as she stripped naked in the living room.

Pug went through the pockets of her shorts and shook out her clothes. "One place left to check," he said, stepping up to her. He reached between her legs and felt around. Joon's face was bright red. Noticing her discomfort, he grabbed both of her breasts. "Turn around and bend over."

Joon shook her head, and Pug wrapped his hand around her throat. He put his nose against hers. "Turn. Around. And. Bend. Over."

Once Joon did as he said, Pug traced his finger around the opening of her anus and shoved it inside, moving it around and causing her excruci-ating pain. Pug knew he wouldn't find money inside of her, but it was all part of intimidating and controlling what he considered his property. He gained control through fear. This kept his girls in check.

Humiliated and demoralized, Joon lay on her mattress that night thinking about her life. All she had ever wanted was a safe place to live and someone to love her. She had neither.

Chapter Forty-Nine

———————◼———————

"It's Christmas tomorrow," Joon told Tori while they stood outside on the sidewalk waiting for johns. "We are forced to sell our souls to save our lives."

Tori nodded. "Yeah. You know it doesn't really matter anymore. We don't get to celebrate. We don't get no presents. It's just another day in hell."

"Yeah. And, we get to stand out here in the freezing cold with our asses hanging out."

Tori smirked. "We sure do. All these motherfuckers coming outta bars on their way home to be with their families. It ain't right."

The girls looked at their surroundings. Sloppy Christmas lights hung from windows and doorways. The sidewalks were covered in black slush that would freeze when the sun went down.

Joon smiled weakly at Tori, who, through a lot of Joon's hard work and their shared misery, had become good friends over the previous months. "Will we ever get outta here?"

The other girl lowered her head and looked down at her fake patent leather boots as if searching for some profound answer. But eventually, all she did was shrug. "I don't know, Joon. The longer I'm here, the more I think there ain't no way out. Pug belongs to the Slayers. The gang is real strong—everywhere I go I see them on the streets, watching us. How do you get away when you ain't never got no privacy?"

"I don't know." Joon leaned in closer to Tori and whispered, "Sometimes, when I get out of a john's car and I have to walk back, I do something that makes me feel…normal. Like, when I get real scared or lonely, I sit with my back against a house where real people live."

"What? Why?"

Joon pushed her hair over her shoulder. "Because it makes me feel like I'm not all alone. I feel like I'm part of a family. I pretend like it's my house and the people inside it care about me."

Tori squinted at her friend. "Huh. That's good, Joon. Maybe I'll try that sometime."

"Hey," Joon said. "Looks like you gotta go."

Tori looked back at the street and saw one of her regulars sitting in his car, smiling at her. She smiled at the man and as she stepped off of the curb, she turned back to Joon. "I hate all of them. Even the ones that aren't rough. I hate them for wanting me for sex."

Joon shoved her hands into the pockets of her cheap corduroy bomber jacket. She watched Tori get into the car and drive away, then looked up and down the street. There were lots of people out and she knew, within the next few hours, all the girls would be busy. She took a few steps back and leaned against the brick building behind her, pulling out a cigarette and puffing on it. She had started smoking two months prior when Tori explained it would calm her nerves. "Besides," Tori had added, "Pug don't feed us enough and, you know, it makes it so you ain't so hungry all the time. Johns will give you cigarettes and you can buy them with the fifty bucks a month that Pug, the dick, gives us."

Pug gave them a small allowance, but that was to pay for personal hygiene products, makeup and clothes. Luckily, the girls of similar size shared what clothes they had, but the hygiene products were expensive. Joon had gotten her period that year and she couldn't believe how much tampons cost. The only thing that Pug paid for was birth control pills and condoms, but only because, as he put it, "I don't want my bitches diseased or pregnant. I need to make sure my whores can keep selling."

Thirty minutes later, Tori was back standing with Joon.

Joon smiled at her friend. "At least he's a regular."

Tori rolled her eyes. "Yeah, and he smells like he hasn't wiped his ass in years. That dude is a scumbag. He uses all his money for booze, gas, and getting laid. I don't even know if he lives in a house." She gathered saliva and spit onto the ground. "You got any gum? That prick wanted a blow job. He tasted like rotten milk."

"Oh man, they're the worst. Besides, I hate doing blow jobs." Joon scrunched her nose and made a gagging motion. Then she dug in her purse and pulled out a stick of gum.

"Don't we all?" Tori said, taking the gum and shoving it in her mouth. "Anything happen while I was gone?"

Joon rubbed her temples with her index fingers. "Yeah, as soon as you left, a guy collapsed on the street over there. He had some kinda seizure or something. It lasted for a minute or two, then he stopped moving. People are saying he overdosed. His heart stopped. The ambulance came, put him into a bag, and zipped it up. And I stood here and envied that dead guy; I wanted to be him because no matter how much pain he had in those last couple of minutes before death, he's lucky because now all of his pain is gone. I just want my pain to be gone.

Tori put her hands on her hips. "That's so fucked."

"Yeah, the guy died in the filthy street with no one around him."

Tori waved her index finger back and forth at Joon. "I ain't talking about the dead guy. I feel the same as you...that death is better than what we have going on. We ain't living, that's all I'm saying."

Chapter Fifty

On February 3, Joon turned sixteen. She'd been in Kensington just over two years. She had spent her last birthday on the street, and Tori had bought her a cupcake to celebrate.

Joon promised herself this birthday would be different. Her sixteenth year would mark a time when she would take back her freedom.

"Happy birthday, girl!" Tori sang and leaned in for a hug.

"Thanks. I wish I didn't have to work tonight…or any night," she added.

"Yeah, well, today is your birthday, and I say you get to be happy at least one damn day outta the year."

Joon smiled at her. "As if that's possible."

Tori put her arm around Joon's shoulders. "I'm making it possible."

"Oh yeah? How? You gonna buy me another cupcake?" Joon teased.

"Nah, nothing like that. Tonight, when we go out, I got us a bottle of Southern Comfort. I've been saving for it, just so we can celebrate."

Joon pinched her brow and made a gagging face. "You know I don't drink. The only control I have left is over my mind. I don't want to lose it."

Tori leaned her head on Joon's shoulder. "You're such a stiff. Lighten up. It's one time."

"I don't know, Tori. What if I do something stupid?"

"You won't. We'll be together, and I won't let anything happen to you," Tori assured her.

"And our johns?"

Tori puckered her lips. "Those pricks wouldn't care if we were dead as long as they can get a piece of ass."

Out on the streets that night, Tori took the bottle of booze out of her purse. Unscrewing the lid, she held it out to Joon. "Here's to the best girl I know. Happy birthday."

Joon hesitantly took the bottle and raised it to her lips.

"Wait! You gotta make a wish when you take the first swig."

Joon held the bottle and closed her eyes. *Freedom*...she raised the bottle to her lips and took a mouthful. The brown substance burned her throat. "Ew. That's terrible."

"It won't be terrible after a couple more sips," Tori said, taking a big gulp of it.

"That's what Quinn said to me when I drank my first beer."

Tori took the bottle from Joon and raised it into the air. "Well, Quinn is a no-good motherfucker that has a small dick to match his small brain."

Four mouthfuls of Southern Comfort later, Joon was feeling no pain. The two girls were giddy and loud. Their behavior caught the other girls' attention, but they didn't care. After each went with a couple of johns, they were back on the sidewalk drinking more.

"Okay, I can't trink no more. I'm gonna get shick if I keep dis up," Joon slurred.

Tori laughed at her and took another hit from the bottle. The girls were staggering around, laughing and hugging each other.

A meek voice carried through the cold night air. "Hey, guys."

Joon and Tori stopped laughing and looked over.

Joon threw her hands into the air. "Oh my God! Elf! Where the hell ya been?"

Elf pulled in air through her nose. "They moved me to a house in North Philly." The girl had dark circles under her eyes and several scabs on her lips.

Joon moved in closer to get a better look at her. "Hey," she said, swaying. "Are you okay?"

Elf's eyes filled, and she lowered her head. "No. Things are really bad." She shuffled her feet as she looked down the block, eyeing a commercial storefront. "They have me doing...movies."

Tori moved forward. "Porn?"

"Yes," Elf admitted.

"Are you serious?" Joon asked.

"Yeah. They bring guys into the house, and I have sex with them while they film us." Elf hugged herself. "But the guys they bring in have to hurt me."

Joon's heart was racing and the heavy dose of Elf's reality was sobering, literally. She put her arms around Elf's shoulders. "How do they hurt you?"

Elf shook her head vigorously, as though she could fling the images from her mind.

Joon rubbed her hand down the girl's arm. "Tell us, Elf."

"They do all kinds of bad things. Tie me up. Beat me. Burn me with cigars. Give me sex with things that hurt, that are too big to go...in there."

Joon gasped. "Elf, I'm so sorry." She looked at Tori. "We have to help her."

Tori nodded but didn't speak.

Elf looked down the block again. "I gotta get back. If Digger finds out that I left the car, he'll kill me. I came down real quick 'cause I saw you guys."

Elf turned to leave, but Joon put her hand on the girl's shoulder. When she turned around, Joon took her into a bear hug. "It's gonna be okay, Elf. You're gonna be fine. We all are."

Joon and Tori watched as Elf rushed back to the car and slid into the backseat.

Joon turned to Tori. "We have to help her."

Her friend looked away. "There ain't nothing we can do. We have to help ourselves before we can think about helping other people."

"But, Tori, they're hurting her. They could kill her."

"I get that, Joon," she snapped, then shook her head. "But what do you suggest we do? We don't have the power to help. Don't you get it?"

Joon's shoulders slumped. "Yeah, I get it. I just can't live with it."

Chapter Fifty-One

Tori took Joon's arm and they sat on the curb. "Listen, I know what's happening to Elf is really messed up, but you gotta be grateful it ain't you. That's some bad shit she's got going on."

"I know what she's going through though," Joon said. Tori startled, so she continued. "I mean, not the sexual part, but I've been burned by cigarettes and beaten until I was senseless. I know what it's like to be hungry and tired yet still have to endure more abuse. We can't let Elf suffer like that."

"What about our suffering? Ain't nobody helping us. We just need to deal with it," Tori said.

"It's not the same. Being a hooker on the street is nothing compared to being held captive, beaten and sexually assaulted every day."

"Fine, so it really sucks for Elf. What the hell can we do, Joon?"

Joon stood. "I don't know. But we have to figure it out."

As the weeks passed, Joon couldn't stop thinking about the horrible things she imagined were happening to Elf, but there were no opportunities to help, and it was only two months later that the girls in the house were buzzing. As soon as Joon came downstairs, she could see the stress on the girls' faces.

"What's going on, Darlene?" she asked one of them.

"We all heard that Pug is gonna move another girl to the house in North Philly."

Joon's throat constricted. "The one where they make pornos?"

"Yeah."

Joon pulled in a long breath. "Who's going?"

Darlene twisted her hands together. "We don't know yet. All we know is that they need a new girl."

Joon crossed her arms over her chest, trying to look casual. "What about the girls that are there now? Where will they go?"

Darlene met Joon's eyes and held them for several seconds. "You mean where will Elf go? Who told you she was there?"

"Come on, Darlene. We all know. The girls talk."

"Look, I don't know what's gonna happen to Elf and the other girl. They only take one or two girls there at a time. I guess they'll move them into one of the other houses and put them back on the street."

Joon looked around at the worried young faces in the room and asked, "When will we know who's going there?"

"In the next week or two. Pug is out of town for a while. When he gets back, it'll probably happen."

Joon started to walk away, but Darlene grabbed her arm. "Listen, Pug considers the girls at all of his houses. Then he picks one or two he thinks will make him the most money in the films. Elf was picked because she was so timid and he knew that her fear would be a big turn-on. There are men who will pay a lot of money to watch a young girl suffer."

Joon put her hand on Darlene's shoulder. "I'm going upstairs. I think I'm gonna be sick." She ran into the bathroom just in time to throw up.

Hearing the commotion, Tori rushed into the bathroom. "What's wrong? Are you sick?"

Joon wiped her mouth with the back of her hand and laid the side of her face on the toilet seat. In a monotone voice, she said, "No. Pug is sending someone else to the house...the one where Elf is staying. Darlene said that he picks girls that he knows can make him the most money. They picked Elf because she was so shy and...scared, I guess. Anyway, one of us could be next."

Tori went down to her knees and threw her arms around Joon. "It won't be," she whispered.

"You can't know that. I'm a sixteen-year-old white girl and you're a beautiful fifteen-year-old mixed girl. We're the kinda girls that men like to see. Why do you think we get so much more business than most of the other girls in this house? I don't know about you, but it certainly isn't because I'm good at sex. I fucking hate it. I just lay there and let them do their thing."

"Keep your voice down," Tori scolded. "If any of these bitches hear you say that, they'll tell Pug just to save their own ass."

Joon got up and stood in front of the small sink. She threw cold water on her face, rinsed out her mouth, and turned back to Tori. "I'm going downstairs. Are you coming?"

Tori followed her down to the kitchen, where the girls stood at the counter and ate a single slice of bread and a banana each, the breakfast each girl was allocated. Pug said it was to keep them thin, but most girls were so young that weight wasn't an issue.

When they finished eating, Joon and Tori went back upstairs and laid together on a mattress. They were both silent for a long time. Then Joon rolled onto her side.

"What if it's one of us?"

Tori shook her head slightly. "I don't know. I don't think I could survive it."

"Me neither," Joon agreed. Then she put an arm and leg over Tori and the girls held on tight to each other until they drifted into a restless sleep.

Chapter Fifty-Two

The next week, Joon was overwhelmed with anxiety. She kept a low profile, did her work, and acted as if nothing bothered her. She didn't want to bring any attention to herself. Pug had gotten back into town four days after she'd heard the news, and all the girls were stricken with fear.

One night on the streets, a john approached Joon on foot. She followed him a few blocks over to an open lot still covered in snow. Joon trudged through until they got to a private spot.

"Let's go," the man said, gesturing toward his crotch.

Joon bent over to unbutton his pants, and when she did, the man punched her in the back of the head. She fell to the ground in a groggy state. The john kicked her in the back. Then he sat on her stomach and beat her in the face with his fists. Joon, half-conscious, believed he would kill her. He punched her until she slipped into unconsciousness. Then he cut her clothes away and raped her. When he was finished, he dressed and slowly walked away, leaving Joon in the bloodstained snow.

Tori noticed the john come out of the lot and walk in the opposite direction. She waited a few seconds, and when she didn't see Joon return, she hurried into the lot and found Joon lying facedown in the snow. Tori screamed, and within a few minutes, one of the Slayers was running to them.

"You have to help her," Tori cried.

"What the hell happened?" the guy yelled.

"A john brought her back here. I think she's dead," Tori bawled.

The Slayer got on his knees, pushing Tori out of the way, and checked for a pulse. "She's still alive." He rolled Joon onto her back and pushed away the hair that covered her face. The Slayer gasped as he took a long look at her. Maintaining his composure, he said, "Man, he fucked her up. Which house is she in?"

Tori rushed alongside the Slayer as he carried Joon back to the house. Angie was the first one in the living room when the Slayer laid Joon on the sofa. He looked up at Angie. "Take care of her. You understand? If she dies, I'll tell Pug it's your fault and he'll kill you." Then he turned to Tori. "What did this asshole look like?"

Tori was sobbing. "He was a tall white dude with long hair."

"What else?"

"I don't know," Tori shrieked. "He was wearing a long black coat. That's all I remember."

The Slayer gave her a hateful glare and ran out of the house to get one of his fellow gang members to help him look for the man.

In the living room, Angie turned on the overhead light and looked into Joon's face. Her eyes and nose were swollen. Blood dripped from the sides of her mouth. Seeing the deep purple bruises on Joon's bare legs, she lifted the girl's shirt to find more bruises on her ribs, running down her sides, and creeping over her back. Angie couldn't seem to find anywhere on Joon's body that wasn't marred with bruises.

When she finished inspecting Joon's injuries, she looked at Tori. "Help me get her upstairs. I need to clean her up. Then you get your ass back out there before Pug comes back and finds you here."

As the two girls carried Joon upstairs, she regained consciousness and grunted with pain. As soon as they got her on her mattress, Angie dismissed Tori.

Tori obeyed but hesitated at the bedroom door. "Is she gonna be okay?"

Angie nodded. "She'll be fine. Just get moving before Pug kills both of us."

Over the next five days, at Pug's direction, Angie cared for Joon, placing ice on her swollen face and bringing her food allotment into the bedroom so she could regain her strength. A day didn't go by that Pug didn't go into the bedroom to check Joon's condition. Not because he was concerned for her well-being, but because he was losing money.

On the sixth day, he stood over Joon while she was sleeping and kicked the mattress, startling Joon awake. Seeing Pug, she cowered, afraid that he would hurt her.

"Sit up," he demanded.

Joon slowly pushed herself up and looked at Pug.

"The swelling is down and you can cover up the bruises on your face with makeup. You've laid around long enough. Get your ass up, take a shower, and get ready to go out. I have a business to run."

Joon got up from the mattress, and as she did, her head spun. She fell to her hands and knees. "I'm dizzy."

"I ain't your fuckin' daddy. I don't care if you're dizzy. Get the hell up and do what I say," Pug yelled.

Angie rushed forward, grabbing Joon's arm to steady her. Then she turned to Pug. "I got this. I'll take care of it. She'll be ready to go in thirty minutes."

Pug clamped his fingers on Angie's chin and shoved his face close to hers. "You better have this, bitch. 'Cause if you don't, I'll find someone who can do what I need them to do. You ain't no good to me if you can't keep these bitches in line. Got it?"

Angie nodded and pulled Joon toward the bedroom door. She turned on the shower, then instructed Joon to cover her bruises with makeup. Between the beating and all the painkillers Joon took during her recovery, she was feeling a bit out of body. "Girl, you need to get your shit together," Angie said, watching the girl sway on her feet. "Pug ain't playing. Snap out of it."

Joon's eyelids were heavy. "I'm so tired."

"Bitch, nobody cares how tired you are. You're lucky that you got a five-day break. None of us got to stop working," Angie said.

Joon looked around the bathroom confused. "Where's Tori?"

"She's ain't here. All the girls been going out earlier and coming home later to make up for the money you couldn't earn."

"What? They're all going to hate me," Joon wailed.

"No shit. We all been having to pull your share while you were lying around on your back. You owe all of us big time. Better watch you don't get an ass whooping from one of them—maybe me if you don't get your ugly ass moving," Angie said.

Joon hung her head. "I can't do this anymore."

"I think that fucker beat the sense outta ya too. You ain't getting outta here, girl. So pull yourself together. I ain't got no time to put up with your bullshit."

Joon rubbed the back of her skull and a thought popped into her mind. "Who's Pug sending to the house in North Philly?"

Angie stood abruptly. "That ain't none of your concern."

"Oh God! Is it me?"

Angie gave Joon a grave look. "What Pug does is none of our business. Your job is to go out and make money…'cause if you don't, either he'll kill you, or one of us will."

Chapter Fifty-Three

———————◼———————

Joon walked to her usual spot on the street and looked for Tori. She cautiously approached Cinnamon, who had been mean to Joon since her first day at the house.

Cinnamon scowled when she saw Joon approaching her. "Oh look who it is. The motherfuckin' bitch that's had us working extra hours so that she could lie around on her fat ass," Cinnamon said, taunting her.

The other hookers standing close nodded and glared at Joon. One girl flicked her lit cigarette at Joon's feet.

Still groggy, Joon steadied herself. "I'm sorry, but you know it wasn't my fault. I would've done the same for any of you."

Cinnamon stepped closer. "I call bullshit. Just fuck off, bitch. None of us wanna see your pathetic ass or talk to you."

"I just want to know if any of you have seen Tori."

Cinnamon's jaw was clenched. "Do I look like a fuckin' information booth? Huh? I don't know where your lame-ass friend is. Now fuck off."

Joon looked to the others, who glowered at her. She was too weak to persist, so she walked down the street to her and Tori's usual spot. In less than twenty minutes, a car pulled up. A man in a baseball hat and sunglasses jumped out of the driver's side. "Come on, bitch. Hurry up."

The man got back in the car as Joon opened the passenger door and slid onto the cold seat. She turned and looked at the man. "Hey, baby. How are you doing tonight?"

The man ignored her and peeled away from the curb. After he drove five blocks, Joon looked at him. "You can go right at the next street. It's private there."

The man remained silent, and Joon's heart fluttered in her chest. Something wasn't right. Her senses were heightened and her lungs constricted. She had that bad feeling in her belly.

"Hey look," Joon said, in a trembling voice. "I don't know what your deal is, but if you pull over, I'll get out here."

"Just be quiet." The man turned to her and the glow from the dashboard provided just enough light for Joon to see her own petrified reflection in his sunglasses.

Joon clutched the door handle as the man drove onto the highway.

"Relax," he said.

"Where are you taking me?"

He didn't answer, and by the time he exited the highway, Joon could barely take in a breath. He had driven her into the main part of the city and finally, he pulled into an alley where another guy rushed over to her car door. He yanked it open as Joon closed her eyes and retracted.

"Joon, it's okay."

Her eyes shot open and she stared into Tony Bruno's face.

"Tony? What's going on?"

"I'll explain, but not now. There isn't time. We're gonna get you into Center City. We're taking you to a shelter. The guy who runs it is doing us a favor by letting you stay there for the next few nights."

"A shelter?"

"Yeah, away from the Tracks."

Joon rubbed her eyes. "How did you know I was in Kensington?"

Tony turned up his brilliant smile. "Who do you think carried you back to the house the night that sick bastard almost beat you to death? I didn't know Pug had you. Once I saw your face, even swollen five times its size, I knew it was you. I never go around to Pug's houses 'cause that ain't my job. Just so happens that night, one of the guys asked me to cover for him. I'm glad I did."

The man driving the car took off his sunglasses. "I'm Vincent. A friend of Tony's."

"Are you a Slayer too?"

"Nah. I'm just a good friend of this guy's. We've been best friends since we was young."

Tony leaned into the car. "Vincent, get rid of the car. Come on, Joon. We gotta go."

Joon followed Tony to a different car, where another of Tony's friends was waiting. Tony opened the back door and she got in. Once inside, Tony grabbed his friend's shoulder. "Salvatore this is Joon."

Joon's eyes roved over Salvatore, whose olive skin and dark hair enhanced his chiseled face.

Tony continued. "Now look, the Slayers would kill me if they found out I got you outta there. You need to be real careful and not tell nobody nothin'. We told Salvatore's friend at the shelter that you just moved here from Minnesota." Tony turned around and faced Joon. "That bag next to you has warm clothes. I got them at the thrift shop. Get changed while we're driving."

"But I...I...what if they find me? And my friend, Tori—how will she know that I'm okay? I can't just leave her there, Tony. We have to go back for her. Please. She doesn't have anyone but me," Joon cried.

Tony climbed over the seat and sat next to Joon. He rubbed his chin. "Here's the deal. You were the one going to the film house in North Philly. When you got laid up, they sent that girl Tori in your place. When girls are sent there, they don't come out alive."

It hit her like another blow to the chest. "No, Tony. Oh, no. Please don't tell me that. That means Tori's gonna die because of me," she said, barely able to choke out the words.

"If Tori dies it's because Pug is a filthy pig and will do anything to make a dollar. It ain't your fault. And there ain't nothing you can do about it." Tony took Joon's chin lightly in his large hand. "You need to listen to me real careful. What I did tonight would cost me my life if the Slayers ever found out. Pug is gonna be pissed as hell when he finds out you're gone. Don't fuck me over on this. You gotta get yourself together, understand?"

Joon gazed at Tony with red eyes, her nose running. "I'm sorry, Tony. I swear I won't tell anyone. But why? Why are you helping me?"

"You and me have a lot in common. The difference is I always had Salvatore and Vincent, 'cause they've been my friends since we was little. You lost all the people who loved you and that makes me feel like shit. I've always been the type of guy who stands up for people. I can't let bad people get away with hurting good people. I know I can't save everybody, but if I can save a couple of people, then it makes me feel better. Makes me feel like I'm a good person."

"You are a good person," Salvatore said, touched by Tony's words.

Tony met Joon's eyes. "You gotta find a way to be safe. Find yourself some decent people to be around. I wish I could do more."

Joon was happy to be free, but it was tempered with fear. "What if Quinn sees me?"

Tony pinched the bridge of his nose and closed his eyes. "You ain't gotta worry about Quinn. I heard he got hit by a train a couple of days ago. Some shit about him getting high and walking right onto the tracks. Never saw it coming."

Joon let out a loud sigh of relief. "He was an asshole anyway."

Tony climbed back into the front seat as they made their way through the city. When they pulled to the curb, he didn't move to get out of the car.

"See that building on the corner down there?" Tony said. "Knock on the door. Tell them that Salvatore talked to Joey. My buddy here arranged it so you can stay there four nights. You need to find somewhere else to go after that. Whatever you do, keep your mouth shut and don't go back to the places you used to hang out. It's safer if you just start over."

Joon was crying.

"Come on, Joon. You gotta go. This is risky for all of us." Tony reached over the seat and patted her arm.

Joon grabbed the bag of clothing Tony had provided, opened the door, and swung her feet out. Then she leaned back into the car. "Thank you, Tony." She made eye contact with the other boy. "Thanks for helping me."

"Hey, wait a minute," Tony said. He reached into his coat pocket and shoved his hand in Joon's direction. "Take this. You're gonna need it until things settle down."

Joon reached out her hand and Tony put two twenty-dollar bills into it.

"I'll pay you back."

He smiled. "Don't worry about it. Consider it a present."

Joon leaned over the seat, pushing past the pain in her ribs and back, and threw her arms around Tony's neck. "I'll never forget what you all did for me."

Then, she turned around swiftly and walked to the corner as quickly as her injuries allowed. She knocked on the door, and a few seconds later, Tony and Salvatore watched her disappear inside.

***

Salvatore looked over at Tony and smirked. "Quinn got hit by a train? That's the best you could come up with?"

"What the fuck was I supposed to say? I couldn't tell her the truth."

It had been easy to get Quinn alone—Tony only had to get Salvatore and Vincent to say they wanted to buy a large amount of dope. Once Quinn was in the van Salvatore had borrowed from his father, they drove him out to rural New Jersey, where Tony had forced him out of the car at gunpoint. Vincent clobbered Quinn in the back of the head with a rubber mallet, and once the box was in the ground with Quinn inside, Tony nailed the lid shut.

The three of them had stood above the grave and when they had finally heard Quinn awaken and scream and scratch to get out, they'd filled the hole with dirt and drove off.

"Hello?" Salvatore said. "Are you still listening to me?"

"Sorry, man, I was thinking about that night."

The boys looked at each other and shared a smile.

"Well," Salvatore said, "I asked you what really happened to Joon's friend, Tori."

Tony sighed. "Exactly what I told Joon. The girl got sent to the house where Pug makes pornos. I was there the other day, and she was in pretty bad shape. They were fucking her up real bad. Doing shit to her that would leave ya with nightmares. The sooner she dies, the better off she'll be. It's that bad. I would've liked to help her, but there was nothing I could do. Makes me feel like shit."

Salvatore pulled the car away from the curb. "You have to get out of that gang, Tony. They're such a bunch of lowlife pricks."

"You think I don't know that? You know I want out, but getting outta the Slayers ain't so easy."

"I know," Salvatore said. "You're a good man, Tony."

Tony shrugged. "Not really. I just know what it's like to need help. That girl Joon—she needed some help and we gave it to her. It's that simple—it's what real men do."

Tony patted his friends shoulder as Salvatore drove them into South Philadelphia.

Chapter Fifty-Four

When Joon entered the homeless shelter, she stood at the foot of a long, narrow room. There were rows of green canvas army-style cots lined up and down the length of the room. There were people of all ages, genders, and races. She followed the man who led her to the other end of the room.

"You must be Joon," a tall twentysomething guy with black hair said, standing and extending his hand.

"Yes. I am," she mumbled.

"Nice to meet you. I'm Joey, a friend of Salvatore's."

"Yeah, Tony told me you were going to let me stay here." Joon looked around, not knowing what else to say to him.

Joey smiled at her. "Follow me. We saved you a cot." He turned and started walking. "Salvatore's a good kid. His father helps us out with food and other essentials, so when Salvatore called, I was happy to make an exception for you."

As they walked toward her cot, Joey filled Joon in on the shelter rules. "No fighting, yelling, or stealing. Everyone here is in the same boat and going through enough bad stuff. This is a place where you all can find some peace. Might not be the best accommodations, but there are hot showers and two meals a day. Breakfast is from six to seven thirty, and dinner is from five to six thirty. You need to be out of the shelter by eight every morning and can return at four in the afternoon. You're here for four nights, but if you want to stay longer, then I suggest you get here around one in the afternoon. The line is around the building by two thirty."

Joey stopped at a cot next to a woman and her small child. "This is yours. Make sure you keep all your stuff with you, even when you go to the bathroom. Some people get watchers, so they can leave their things safely on the cot, but you have to really trust someone. Have you eaten?"

"I'm not hungry, but can I get a drink of water?"

"Sure thing. I'll bring a cup over to you." Joey picked up the blanket and pillow stacked at the foot of the cot. Lifting the pillow away from the blanket, he grabbed a white pillowcase folded between them. "You can put this on the pillow. We keep things as clean as we can here and expect everyone staying here to do the same. I'll go get that glass of water and you can get settled."

He walked away and Joon stood looking down on the cot.

"This shelter is better than a lot of them. People who volunteer here are really nice and they don't take shit from anyone," said the woman in the cot next to Joon.

Joon met the woman's eyes and gave her a forced smile.

"My name is Madi, and this is my son, Salt."

Joon looked at the small child curled up next to his mother. Her eyes lingered as she took in his pasty white skin and white hair.

Madi smiled at Joon. "Salt is an albino. He was born with a congenital disorder, and he ain't got no pigment in his skin, hair, and eyes. Other than that, he's a perfectly normal four-year-old."

Not wanting to stare, Joon snapped the pillowcase and shoved the foam cube pillow inside. "I'm Joon" is all she could manage.

Madi nodded at her. "First time in a shelter?"

"No. I'm just feeling a little on edge tonight. I didn't...didn't expect to be here."

Madi lay back on her cot. "Beats being out in the cold. Well, welcome. They serve decent meals, but watch out for the older men here. Most are okay, but some of them can be perverts."

Joon huffed out a dry laugh. "Dirty old men are the least of my problems."

Madi studied her more closely. The lines around Joon's eyes and mouth revealed the tension waiting to burst out of the girl. "How long have you been on the streets?"

Joon thought for a moment, wondering how to account for the two years she spent as a prostitute and counted them all rather than explain. "A little over four years. How about you?"

"Almost four years. When Salt was born and my lame-ass boyfriend saw him, he took off running. He said he didn't want no kid that looked like a ghost. He was a real asshole, that one. Didn't even know about albinism, didn't ever take the time to know. Anyway, me and Salt lasted about six months in our apartment before the landlord threw us out. I tried real hard to get a job, but being a single mother and all, it wasn't easy. I waitressed for a while, but one night I got back to my apartment and found my babysitter, the teenager who lived in the apartment a few doors over, smoking crack with her filthy boyfriend while Salt was in the same room. I didn't have anyone else to stay with Salt while I worked so I had to quit my job. Once we got thrown out, I found places to sleep on the street. Then I discovered this shelter, and now my job is to get here every day at one in the afternoon to secure a bed and food for me and my kid," Madi explained.

"That's messed up. How will you ever be able to live in your own place if you spend all of your time here or waiting to get in here?" Joon asked.

Madi leaned onto the edge of the cot to get closer to Joon. "I'm working with Joey, the guy that brought you over here. He said there's a place that'll watch Salt while I find a job. They'll even help me with childcare after I find a job. Joey is calling one of his buddies, and I should hear something in the next few days. There're a couple of programs that watch your kid for you if you're homeless, but they're real hard to get into."

"It's great that Joey can help." Joon rested her head on the foam pillow and pulled the wool blanket over her. "I'm real tired. I've kinda been...um...sick lately, so I'm gonna go to sleep."

"Okay. Good night. I'll see you in the morning. You can meet Salt then."

Joon laid on her cot, her thoughts drifting to Tori. She couldn't hold back her tears, so she let them flow freely as she mourned her friend. Her guilt nearly overwhelmed her, and she knew she'd never get over that Tori had been sacrificed. But as scared and nervous as she had been when entering the shelter, Joon soon fell into a deep sleep, grateful to Tony Bruno for giving her a second chance.

Chapter Fifty-Five

———————————■———————————

Early the next morning, Joon was awakened by an angel singing. The voice was light and steady, and it was singing a song she remembered from when her parents were alive: "Baa baa, black sheep, have you any wool? Yes, sir, yes, sir, three bags full..."

She slowly rolled onto her side toward the voice, and a smile spread over her face.

"Hi, I'm Salt. What's your name?"

Joon sat up slowly, pushing against the pain. "I'm Joon. You sing really well."

"Thank you. My mom didn't even have to teach me. I just knew how to sing. She says I'm smarter than the other kids 'cause I learnt something by myself."

Joon giggled. "Yes, I can see that you're very smart. Don't let me bother you. Go ahead and sing."

She watched the child with white hair and his almost-colorless eyes that vibrated back and forth in quick movements. She thought he was beautiful. His white bangs fell over his eyebrows and his lips were the slightest shade of pink.

Salt stopped singing. "Why are you lookin' at me like that, Joon?"

She shook her head as if coming to her senses. "I'm sorry, Salt. It's just that you're the most beautiful person I've ever seen. You're different than everyone else. That makes you special." She looked around the large room. "Where's your mom?"

"She went to the bafroom. Mom said if anybody bothers me or tries to take our stuff that I gotta wake you up."

"I see. Well, I have to go to the bathroom. Do you want to come with me?"

"No! We can't go to the bafroom. We can't leave our stuff 'cause somebody might steal it. Didn't nobody tell you nothin'?"

Joon chuckled. "Yeah, they told me. I guess I forgot. I'll wait for your mom to come back." She settled back on her cot and looked around her, trying to find someone she knew from the streets, but this shelter was on the other side of the city from where she used to live.

"I'm back, Salt," Madi sang out as she approached. When she saw Joon was awake, she said, "Sorry I left you with him. It's not often I can go to the bathroom without lugging all of my things and Salt with me."

Joon pinched her lips together. "What makes you think that you can trust me? What if I stole your stuff or hurt your kid?"

Madi shook her head and shrugged. "You wouldn't."

Joon sat up and lifted her chin. "How do you know that? You don't know anything about me."

"Okay. You're right, but you're not right. You see, Joon, you don't carry yourself like a badass. Plus, you have a sadness in your eyes. If you were dangerous, I would see anger, not sadness."

"What does that even mean? How do you see sadness in my eyes?"

"I can't describe it. I only know that I looked the same way when Salt's dad left me. I was really sad and confused and scared. I bet you feel that way right now. Don't you?"

Joon flushed and nodded.

"No big deal. Things always get better. Right, Salt?"

"Yeah, Mommy." The boy threw his arms around his mother's neck.

"You better go get washed up, Joon. Breakfast is soon, and then we'll have to get out of here."

Joon stood and looked down at her meager belongings. "You'll watch my stuff for me?"

"You bet. Go ahead and we'll wait right here until you come back."

As Joon walked to the bathroom, her new freedom was overshadowed by deep sadness. She was grateful to Tony for her new start, but as she tried to celebrate her liberation, her thoughts were consumed by Tori—who she had left behind, who had been forced to take Joon's place.

Chapter Fifty-Six

The cold of the early morning hit Joon as she exited the shelter. She looked up and down the street, not sure of what she was looking for and not knowing where to go. Having her freedom was the greatest feeling in the world, but now, out on the streets, she wasn't sure of anything.

"Where are you going?" Madi asked, coming up behind her.

"I'm not sure. I used to live on the other side of the city. I learned where to get food and I had friends. I don't know much about this area."

Madi patted Joon on the back. "The first thing you need to do is make a plan. What's your next step? I mean, after you leave the shelter?"

Joon shrugged. "I haven't had a lot of time to think about it."

"Do you have anyone you can go to?"

Joon thought for a moment. "Not that I can think of...Oh wait! There is one person that I know."

"See. All you need to do is ask for help. Maybe they can let you stay with them for a while."

"Thanks. Maybe I'll see you back here later."

"We'll be here. Right, Salt?"

The child nodded. "Bye, Joon." The child gave her a quick hug. "When we come back, do you wanna eat dinner with us? Maybe I can sing to you again."

As Joon bent down to hug Salt back, she looked into the boy's face. "That sounds great. It'll give me something to look forward to."

Salt beamed and grabbed his mother's hand. "I wanna go to the park. Can we go to the park, Mommy?"

Madi ruffled the boys' hair. "Yeah, baby, we can go to the park for a little while."

Joon watched as the mother and son walked away. Then she walked in the opposite direction.

As Joon walked through the city, the icy air made her whole body ache. By the time she got to her destination, she was certain the blood had frozen in her veins.

Chapter Fifty-Seven

Joon looked up at the building before moving around the back. There, she saw the same thick, blue plastic, covering the doorway. She pushed the heavy plastic aside and entered the kitchen. The room was as she remembered: dark, lost, lifeless. She navigated around the people on the first-floor living space. Joon knew of the pain and suffering of the people around her. She hesitated for a moment, conjuring up the courage to keep moving forward.

Homeless people were everywhere. Some were sleeping. A man in the corner of what was once the dining room looked up at Joon.

"Hey, sweetie. Want me to warm you up?"

Joon stopped and squinted at him, her mouth twisting. "Fuck you, asshole."

She continued to walk through the first floor. A girl no older than herself was leaning up against the wall. Joon couldn't take her eyes off her. She had a belt tied around her arm and a needle in her other hand. She glanced up at Joon but seemed to look right through her. The girl focused on her arm again, slapping at her worn veins. She steadied her hand, inserted the needle, and pulled the plunger of the syringe back. It filled with a little blood, then the girl pushed the magic fluid into her arm. Her eyes closed, and she slumped further, the needle dangling from her arm.

Joon was saddened to see another life claimed by drugs. During her time in Kensington, she'd known a few people who had become consumed by finding their next fix. Nothing else mattered to them, and they didn't care who they hurt to get what they wanted. In Joon's mind, drug addicts were the saddest of those who lived on the streets because they'd rather destroy themselves and everyone around them than face the awful reality of their lives. There was a weakness in drug addicts that she found both heartbreaking and repulsive.

Joon tore her eyes away from the girl and pushed forward, taking the stairs to the third floor. Stepping into the room, she looked around at the group. Then she took a few more steps inside to get a better look. It had been a long time and she'd hoped to recognize at least one person. If she recognized no one, her plan was to make her way into one of the other groups in the house.

"Hey!" a girl yelled.

Joon turned toward the voice.

The girl stood. "I know you."

Joon smiled, recognizing her. "Gia!"

"Right!"

Joon put her open hand on her chest. "Joon. The kid in the subway that stopped that boy who was hitting you. Remember?"

"Oh man! Yes, Joon! How are you? I haven't seen you in…" Gia went silent.

"Four years."

Gia scratched her scalp. "Wow. Time flies. What are you doing here? Did you come in with a group of friends?"

Joon flushed a deep crimson. "No. I'm by myself. I remembered you telling me that you always stayed here during the winter. I'm looking for a place to stay, so I took a chance that you still come here. I thought maybe I could hang out with you."

Gia turned and looked at the other girls. One of them was giving her a hard stare. "What's the problem, Fipple? Why not?"

"I remember that little shit from way back when," she stated as she glared at Joon. "And I just don't like her, so she should go find some other group of people to stay with."

Gia put her hands on her hips. "Fipple! You're such a bitch." She turned to the other girls in her clan. "What does everyone else think?"

The other four girls mumbled and nodded.

"Majority rules. Joon stays."

Fipple threw her empty soda can across the room. "Fine, but I'll tell you right now, she ain't my problem. If she brings us trouble, then she's all yours. I'm tired of bailing your ass outta bad situations 'cause you trust every damn stray cat that crosses your path."

Gia flipped her hair over her shoulder. "Fine. But Joon ain't gonna be a problem. She's a nice girl." She turned and looked Joon up and down cautiously.

Joon moved closer to Gia. "I swear I won't cause any problems. I just don't have anyone." She was desperate to find people she could call family. She knew that, on the streets, the critical path to survival is to have others around her that cared. Fearful Gia would decide to send her away, tears started to flow uncontrollably.

Gia watched Joon for a moment, understanding, as they all did, the loneliness that accompanied homelessness. She embraced Joon. "You're gonna be fine." Gia pulled back and turned to the other girls. "We all stick together like a family. Right?"

A blond-haired, blue-eyed girl with pale skin spoke up. "Come over here and sit next to me. You'll be all right."

Joon sat next to the girl.

"I'm Lulu," the girl offered. "I haven't been here that long myself. I only met these crazy chicks about two months ago," she said loud enough so they could all hear. The other girls smiled. "Anyway, since I'm the newer member, how about if I help you join in? You know, I'll show you the ropes and make sure you know all the rules and shit like that."

Joon smiled at her. "I would like that. Thank you."

"You're welcome. Now, grumpy over there," she said, pointing to Fipple, "won't be able to rag you anymore."

"I ain't grumpy," Fipple argued.

The girls laughed, and Lulu took Joon's hand and whispered, "She's very grumpy, but we love that about her. It keeps us all out of trouble because she's so unaccepting of outsiders. She was brutal when I first joined. She thought I was a plant for one of the pimps." She paused for a moment, then asked, "You're not a plant for a pimp, are you?"

Joon met Lulu's intense stare. The girl wasn't kidding. "No, I'm not. I hate pimps."

"I see. It sounds like you know one personally."

Joon's heart fluttered. "I…I…I've been on the street for a while. I've met all kinds of people."

"Sure," Lulu said, studying Joon carefully. "You're right. We all know assholes."

"Do you have any clothes or anything?" Lulu asked.

"Yeah, but not much. I'm at a shelter right now. I sorta know the guy that runs the place, and he let me leave my stuff in his office today for when I go back tonight."

"Oh, that's weird. They never do shit like that. Usually you wait outside for hours to get a cot."

"Like I said, I kinda know the guy through a friend who got me a bed for a couple of nights. When that's over, I have to leave or wait in line all day to get in. That's why I came here today...because I need something permanent," Joon stated.

"I get what you're saying. So are you staying here tonight?"

"No. I'm gonna go back and stay at the shelter tonight, then I'll come back here tomorrow. You'll be here, right?" Joon asked, feeling at ease with Lulu.

"I'll be here. Why would I ever want to leave this place?" Lulu chuckled, gesturing around the room.

Back in the shelter that night, Joon told Madi all about the group of girls.

Madi's eyes sparkled and she perked up. "Where is this house?"

Joon thought for a moment. "It's not a place that you can bring Salt."

"Oh. Okay," the woman said. She seemed a little disappointed. "Well, I hope you make good friends."

"Yeah, so do I...and that someday I'll meet someone who can help me get off of the streets and into a real house. That would be so great," Joon said with a whimsical tone.

Madi rubbed her tired eyes. "Be careful about the people you meet who are willing to help you off the streets. Sometimes they're pimps or drug dealers. They'll sell you a bill of goods and then fuck you over the minute you've bought in. As for people who don't live on the street, well, they don't understand us, so you need to be careful. Some of them think they can catch homelessness. The only people you can really count on are the people who run the shelters," she said, pointing to the people at the front doors. "They're the only ones that won't judge you 'cause you ain't got all the normal things that regular people have. Now, I know you're still young, but I predict someday you'll be something great. I don't why, but there's something about you that's gentle and...sincere. You hang on to that because it will help you one day."

Joon's brow was furrowed as she listened to Madi's speech.

"You look confused," Madi said.

The girl smiled politely. "Oh, I'm fine. I'm just thinking about everything you said." Joon had always wanted to do good things in her life and Madi's words made her think she might have a chance.

Salt climbed on Joon's cot and sat close to her, and she put her arm around him.

"Joon, does this mean I ain't gonna see you no more?"

"I hope not. I'm sure we'll see each other again."

"Of course we'll see Joon again," Madi yammered, sparing Salt the sadness of never seeing his new friend again. She knew that although they'd only known each other for a day, Joon would be someone Salt would always remember. Most people avoided him because he was so different—Joon had treated him like he was the same as her.

"Do you want me to sing to you?" Salt asked.

"Yes," Joon said. "I was hoping you would sing to me."

Salt climbed back onto his mother's cot and laid on his side, facing Joon. As he sang in a soft, angelic voice, Joon closed her eyes and let herself feel at peace.

Chapter Fifty-Eight

The next morning as Joon entered the abandoned house, there were two twentysomethings yelling at each other. She stood and watched, making sure that it was still safe for her to enter. Pug was always in the back of her mind, and it was as if she expected him to show up at any moment and take her back to Kensington. She stayed close to the door as she watched, for a quick getaway if things turned bad.

"You're a rotten sonofabitch, Frank. You tried to steal my girl from me last night?"

"No, motherfucker! That ain't what happened. I didn't come on to your woman. You couldn't keep it up for her 'cause you were so fuckin' high last night. So your woman gave me a visit. I didn't ask for it. It just happened."

The man spun and looked at his girlfriend, who visibly cowered. "Did you fuckin' come on to him?"

The girl, on drugs herself, jumped to her feet. "Fuck you, Johnny. Every time I wanna little action, you can't do it. So what if I had a little fun last night? I ain't hurting nobody."

Johnny grabbed his girlfriend by the neck, but Frank pulled him off her. "Come on now, Johnny. Ain't no harm done. Just a little bit of fun. Me and your girl, that won't happen again. Okay?"

Johnny let go of his girlfriend's neck and looked into Frank's eyes. "I'll let it go this time, but don't let me catch you two doing it again." For good measure, Johnny pushed Frank into the wall behind him and walked away.

Johnny's girlfriend rushed to him and threw her arms around his waist. "I'm sorry, Johnny. I was feeling real lonely last night. Do you forgive me?"

He looked down at her. "I forgive you this one time. But since you got to be with someone else, then I get to hook up with someone else too...so we're even." He scanned the room and his eyes landed on Joon.

Joon stood tall and shook her head. "I don't think so. You better find yourself some other bitch to be with 'cause it ain't gonna be me. You come near me and I'll kill you."

Johnny laughed at Joon and went about the business of finding another girl.

Joon hurried out of the kitchen and up the stairs. When she stepped inside the room, Lulu rushed over to her.

"Hey," Lulu said, giving her a hug. "What was all the commotion downstairs?"

Joon gave her a sly look. "Two druggies fighting 'cause one of the guys has a druggie girlfriend who slept with the other guy. Asshole who got cheated on wanted to have sex with me, so I had to threaten his life."

Lulu's eyes bugged out. "Then what happened?"

"Then he laughed and went to look for someone else."

Lulu touched Joon's arm. "Weren't you scared?"

Joon shrugged. "A little, but look, you can't let those kinds of people get the best of you. Once they smell your fear, they never leave you alone. Trust me, I know." Joon set her canvas bag on the floor and pulled a brown paper bag out. Then, she reached inside and pulled out a bagel. She held the bag out to the girls. "Joey, the guy I know at the shelter, gave me some extras to-go to share with all of you."

Gia got to her feet, gave Joon a quick hug, and grabbed the bag from her. She and the other girls gobbled down bagels, and Joon handed the bagel she was holding to Lulu.

"Thanks." Lulu reached for the first bite of food she'd eaten since an apple twelve hours earlier.

"Are you okay?" Joon asked, noticing that Lulu's breathing was labored.

"Yeah, I'm fine. I'm getting over a cold and still a little congested."

They sat on the floor with the other girls as Fipple shoved a piece of bagel into her mouth and glared at Joon. "What's your deal? Why don't you have any friends? You've been on the street awhile."

Joon shrugged. "The kids I hung with moved on to other places."

Fipple scowled at her. "I call bullshit."

Lulu leaned in. "What's your problem, Fipple? She just brought you something to eat, and you can't even say thank you. Instead, you're mean to her."

Fipple shifted her glare to Lulu. "I don't have a fuckin' problem, Lulu. And guess what? You've been here about two minutes, so why don't you shut your trap?"

Lulu smiled a brilliant smile that lit up her face. "I'm not afraid of you. None of us are afraid of you, and you don't make the rules—we all decide on the rules together. So here's the deal: stop being an asshole."

Fipple looked at the other girls, but none would meet her eyes. "Fine. You can all go fuck yourselves then. Don't come running to me when you got a problem you can't deal with."

Joon smirked and turned back to Lulu. "Do you wanna hang out today?"

"Sure," Lulu said. "Maybe we can get something hot to eat."

In the afternoon, Joon and Lulu left the abandoned house and headed east, where college dorms and apartments were situated. The cold moisture in the air penetrated their clothing, making their journey torturous.

"I hate living on the streets in the cold," Joon stated. "I'm never dry or warm. My lips are chapped, my skin feels itchy…it's the worst feeling ever."

Lulu glanced at her sideways. "Says the girl who just spent two nights in a shelter with warm food and showers."

Joon blushed. "Yeah, sorry. It's just that I know what's to come. It's almost worse being inside and then having to come out into the cold. When you know how good it feels to be in a heated place, it makes being out here harder."

Lulu poked her elbow gently into Joon's side. "How about we go into the subway? It'll be warmer down there. Begging ain't the greatest, but at least we won't freeze to death trying to get money to buy something to keep us from freezing to death." She chuckled.

Joon looped her arm through Lulu's, and the girls picked up their pace as the wind came at them in heavy gusts. "Very funny. Look, we'll try it for a while, and if it doesn't pay off, we can get back on the street."

By the time they got down in the subway, they were half-frozen. Lulu walked over to a bench away from the crowd and sat. She hugged her body tight, trying to warm herself from the outside in. Joon noticed her pale face had become even whiter.

"Are you okay?" Joon asked, sitting next to her new friend.

Lulu glanced around at the crowd. "Yeah, I'm fine. Just a little tired. I'm so damn cold I can't seem to warm up."

Joon put her arm around Lulu and hugged her tight, trying to generate body heat, but Lulu continued shivering. "Stay here. I'll be right back."

A few minutes later, Joon returned with two cups of hot chocolate. "Here," Joon said, pushing the steaming cup at Lulu. "Drink this. It'll warm you up a little."

Lulu took the cup in both hands, blew lightly on the steaming chocolate, and sipped gently. She felt the liquid warm her insides as it made its way into her belly.

"Mm, this is so good. Thank you," Lulu mumbled. "How did you buy it?"

Joon bit her bottom lip for a moment. "Well, a friend gave me a little money to hold me over. I don't have much..."

Lulu held the cup tighter. "Don't worry. I won't tell anyone. I get it. Sometimes we have to keep a little for ourselves in case we need it. How much you got?"

"He gave me forty bucks."

Lulu eyes bulged. "Wow! That's awesome. I haven't had forty bucks since...well, years ago."

"Well, thanks for not telling the others. I'm gonna keep it in case I need it. Ya know?"

Lulu put her head on Joon's shoulder. "Your secret's safe with me. I don't play that game. I believe that we all get to have our privacy. Some in the group, like Fipple, believe that whatever you have needs to be shared. Mostly because she isn't real good at begging 'cause of her constant scowl. She scares people off, and no one likes an angry, homeless teen."

The girls giggled thinking about Fipple trying to look helpless enough to beg.

Joon brought her feet up onto the bench and faced Lulu. "How did you get here?"

Chapter Fifty-Nine

Lulu closed her eyes. "Well, it's a long story." She looked at Joon again. "When I was six months old, my parents died in a car accident, so I was raised by my father's mom. My gram was something real special. She taught me how to cook and take care of myself. She made sure I went to school, and whenever I brought home my report cards, she'd tell me that I was the smartest person she knew. My gram was a strong woman, didn't take any crap from nobody. I remember one time when I was about five, the kids on our block were picking on me. Gram charged out of the house like a bull, stomping toward us, her hands clenched into fists. And she came up to us, stood behind me, put her hands on my shoulders, and said 'Why is Lulu crying?' When no one answered, her voice got deeper, and she said, 'I asked you children, why is Lulu crying?' By that time, I wasn't crying anymore because I felt the strength of my gram standing behind me—actually, I was starting to get scared for the kids standing around, because when Gram asked a question, you better answer. Everyone in our neighborhood knew that about her."

Lulu twirled her finger into her blond, curly hair as her blue eyes were looking at something invisible. She imagined her grandmother's loving arms around her. She longed to hear her voice and rejoice in the old woman's smile.

"What happened? Did your grandma get the kids to talk?"

Lulu glanced at Joon and smiled. "Right. So, after a long silence, Gram asked them one more time, and one of the girls answered that it was because they were calling me ugly. My grandmother's hands flew from my shoulders to her hips and I could feel the anger getting ready to erupt from inside of her. And she said, 'There isn't any such thing as ugly on the outside. The only ugly that exists in this world is on the inside.

Like all of you—you're being ugly on the inside, teasing my Lulu.' She preached about the good life God gave us and how no one wants to be around mean people and that they would end up old and alone someday. She said, 'I want you kids to think about a time when someone made you feel bad.' The kids just stared at her, but she didn't stop. 'That bad feeling inside when someone is ugly to you, well, that's how you made Lulu feel today. It ain't so pleasant, is it?'

"A few of the kids cried, and she turned and left them standing there, thinking about what she had said. I was so proud that I belonged to her. She told me that there are gonna be all kinds of people in life— nasty people, nice people, weak people, happy people, sad people—and that people need to be loved and know they're special. And that good people will find what's special in each person and help them see it too. She asked me to promise her that I would always feed the good inside of myself and not give my heart over to evil. She said we are all capable of being mean and nasty, and she wanted me to promise I would always feed the good because I was the most special girl she knew." There were tears in her eyes as she thought of how her grandma had teared up that day.

Joon's mouth hung open. "That's the greatest story I've ever heard. You're so lucky to have a grandma like her. Where is she?"

The tears spilled over as she said, "Gram died two years ago, when I was seventeen. She'd been sick for about a year. The doctors said she had breast cancer, and it was too late to do anything to help her. She was so sick in the last three or four months, all I did was go to school, come home, and stay by her side. I would wake up at three every morning, so I could spend more time taking care of her before I went to school. One morning, I went into her room, and she was staring at the ceiling. When she heard me coming, she turned and looked at me...and she was so frail and tired." Lulu took a deep breath before she continued. "But she gave me that smile of hers that always made me feel safe and loved. She patted the side of the bed. 'Lay with me, Lulu,' she whispered. I got onto the mattress and gently lay down with her, and she said, 'Lulu, I have loved you since the beginning. I have taught you all that I know. When I'm gone, I want you to remember that you are very special. I'll be watching you from Heaven, and no matter how bad things get, I will always be with you.' All I could do was cry, and when I looked at her, Gram was crying too, but she was also smiling and she said, 'Because of you, I have lived fully. You gave me purpose—not all old people have such a blessing.'"

Lulu leaned her head back on the bench and let the tears roll down her face as she closed her eyes. "Gram died a few minutes later. She said, 'My little Lulu, I love you more than you'll ever know,' and then I lay there listening to her heart slow until there was silence and she was gone. I held her for a long time, wishing she'd come back." She took a deep, ragged breath. "No matter how bad things are out here and even in my worst experience on the streets, nothing will ever feel as bad as the moment I lost my gram."

Joon swiped the tears from her own cheeks. "You and your gram... you really loved each other. I'm sorry all that happened to you." She paused. "Did you have anyone you could live with after she died?"

Lulu shook her head. "No. Gram was the only family I had. My father was her only child, and she was an only child. I never knew my mom's family. After Gram was gone, I found out she'd taken loans on her house to raise me and owed the bank a lot of money. The day after her funeral, one of our neighbors stayed at the house with me until things got settled, and some lady came over that the school sent, and she said I was gonna have to live in a home until I turned eighteen and finished high school. They were moving me to a bad part of town, and I had to change schools and live with a bunch of girls that didn't have families, and the whole thing sounded awful, and I was so scared. So the night before I was supposed to go with them, I just left the house and started walking. I didn't stop until I reached the city, and I've been making my way ever since, here on the streets...that's my story."

Lulu eyes darkened. "I miss my gram. There isn't a day that goes by where I don't wish she were here. I've been through some really rough shit out here...but even through the worst of it, I was still able to find people who feed the good. Like you, Joon—you feed the good."

Joon ran her fingers through her hair. "I never really thought about it like that, but I guess you're right. I know what it's like to be so broken that you wonder if the pieces will ever fit back together. It's not something that I want others to feel."

"You're a good egg. I can feel it in my heart."

Joon patted Lulu's leg. "Thanks for sharing your story with me."

Lulu shook her head. "I spent a long time grieving the loss of my gram. I know someday I'll be with her again and that she sends good people to me to make up for the bad ones. How about you? How did you get on the streets?"

Chapter Sixty

———————◼———————

Joon looked up to the ceiling. "I became homeless when I was twelve." Joon relayed the short version of her younger life, and when she finished, Lulu put her arms around her and the two held each other tight.

"You know," Lulu said. "All of us on the streets have it hard. I'm sorry you suffered so much and that the system put you with such a bitch. That Aron woman, she'll get hers someday. I'm convinced that mean people suffer at some point."

Joon wrung her hands, thinking of Pug and the despicable acts she'd performed as a prostitute. "I've done some bad shit," Joon admitted. "You know, I had to do things…to survive out here."

"Hooking?" Lulu asked.

Joon nodded and twisted her body away from her friend.

"Hey, you don't have to be embarrassed about it. We all do stuff to get by."

Joon crossed her arms over her chest. "Were you ever a hooker?"

"No. But I've just been lucky in that way. I've always been real careful about the people I get involved with, you know? I mean, I never got myself attached to a guy. Out on the streets, people will do anything to make a buck. So I've stayed single. I've known too many girls who got sucked into a relationship and ended up selling their bodies to keep their boyfriends fed."

Joon pushed her feet out from under her and swung them briskly back and forth. Lulu tried to make eye contact, but Joon looked at the people passing by as if she were waiting for someone she knew.

"Is that what happened to you?" Lulu asked.

Joon's shoulders slumped forward and her hair covered part of her face. "Yeah, something like that. I think the worst thing is that I lost a friend when I was there. At first, we hated each other, but then we became friends. Anyway, we need to make some money today. We better get going." Joon didn't want to talk about everything—not yet at least. She needed to trust Lulu more before she let her in. Plus, she couldn't really talk about Tori—it could get her and Tony in trouble.

Night had fallen by the time Joon and Lulu walked back to the abandoned house. Joon looked up at the moon and watched the cloud of her breath as she exhaled deeply in the bitter cold.

"So, why does Fipple hate me?"

"Because you're strong. She can sense it. We all can."

Joon cocked her head, her eyebrows knitted together.

Lulu shoved her hands into her jeans. "You don't even know it, do you? You give off this feeling of strength and...well, confidence. Until now, Fipple has always been the fearless one. I mean, we're all strong in our own way, but there's something about the way you carry yourself that lets others know that you have arrived. Fipple doesn't like it. She's threatened by you."

Joon let out a distraught chuckle. "You've got to be kidding me. She feels threatened by me? That's such a joke. I'm not any of those things that you think. I'm afraid of everything, and I have nothing to be confident about. In fact, I've never felt comfortable in my own skin. I was raised by a woman who treated me worse than an animal. I met a woman my first day on the streets, and after a while, she abandoned me. Then, I fell for a guy who screwed me over. And, to top it off, I was forced into prostitution. What the hell gives you the idea I'm strong? I am worthless, nothing...I don't matter. That's the truth of me. What you see on the outside doesn't look the same on the inside."

Lulu put her arm around Joon's waist. "You don't see things so clearly. All the things you've been through make you look at life through a different lens. It's not all those things that make up who you are, Joon—it's how you managed to survive all of those things and still be a good person. Those horrible things have given you the ability to see others in a way that a lot of people can't. Do you understand?"

Joon shook her head. She had no appreciation for her own perseverance and resilience. But what Lulu said made sense to her and a small flame of hope ignited inside Joon's heart.

Chapter Sixty-One

J oon's eyes fluttered open. She looked at a broken light fixture in the center of the ceiling surrounded by exposed wood where the plaster had fallen away. She pulled her jacket tighter, but her hands were stiff and her fingers couldn't grasp the canvas tight enough. The girl rolled onto her side and shimmied forward to nuzzle closer to Lulu. Her skin felt iced over, and she curled her body into a small ball.

Lulu stirred and opened her eyes. "It's so fuckin' cold I can barely breathe."

Joon nodded and closed the distance between them.

Lulu got up on her elbow. "Girls, we gotta huddle before one of us freezes to death."

The group of girls all moved closer, a pile of bodies, tightly fitting next to each other perfectly, to generate enough heat to keep them alive. Joon lay there for the next hour, unable to focus on anything but the bitter cold. Her body ached, and as she lay awake, Joon decided they needed to find a better way to get through the winter. A few minutes later, she got up.

Lulu raised her head. "Where are you going?"

"To find us something better than this. I can't last another night freezing. I have an idea."

Lulu quickly joined her. "Great! Where are we going?"

Joon gave her a warm smile. "To find some stuff to make this place livable."

"What kind of stuff?" Lulu whispered.

"The kind of stuff to keep us from freezing to death," Joon said, as she turned and started down the stairs of the abandoned home.

The girls walked carefully on the icy, uneven sidewalks. They remained silent, conserving their energy. Joon walked straight to a sporting goods store and stepped into the warmed building. Pins and needles covered her flesh as she stood at the entryway, waiting for her teeth to stop chattering. A few minutes later, she walked up to a counter where a boy of about sixteen was standing, observing the two girls.

"Hi," Joon managed.

"Hi," the boy said, looking them over and wondering what crime they had committed to bring them to their circumstances.

"We need to buy a tent and some really warm sleeping bags. Do you have anything cheap?"

He just stared at them.

"Well?" Joon asked, uncomfortable under the boy's judging stare.

"Yeah. Sorry. I'll show you what we have."

The girls followed him to the back of the store and listened as he talked to them about their tent options with price tags way out of their range.

"Do you have anything cheaper? On sale? Maybe something that's broken but we can still use?" Joon asked.

The boy nodded and walked over to a shelf of damaged goods.

"This one is thirty bucks," he said, lifting a torn box. "It's missing one of the poles."

Joon wrapped her arms around herself. "How about fifteen dollars?"

The boy shook his head.

Joon leaned in and looked at the boy's name tag. "*Ryan*, please. Just ask your boss," she said.

"Okay, wait here and I'll see what I can do."

A few minutes later, the boy returned with an older man named Mark. Mark's sympathetic eyes roved over the girls, but he kept his arms crossed over his chest and stood at a distance.

"Ryan tells me you're looking to buy this tent for fifteen dollars?"

"Yes, sir," Joon said. "We don't have a lot of money, and...and it's really cold at night."

The man's shoulders drooped, and he ran his hands over his face. "I see. I think we can make fifteen dollars work."

Joon's entire face lit up. "We need some sleeping bags too, ones that'll keep us really warm."

The manager glanced at Ryan and rubbed the back of his neck.

Ryan smiled. "We have the ones in the back that were returned, ones with tears in them."

Mark nodded. "Go get them." He turned back to Joon. "How many do you need?"

Joon scratched at the burning skin on her cheek and softly shook her head. "We need six of them."

Mark put his hands up in the air. "We don't have that many that are damaged. We do have new ones over there..." He stopped midsentence, refraining from doing his normal sales pitch and flushing a deep crimson.

Ryan returned a few minutes later carrying three sleeping bags with feathers trailing behind him from the jagged gashes in them. "This is all we have," he said, pushing the bags toward the girls.

"How much?" Joon asked.

Mark looked down at the floor and shoved his hands into his pockets. "Look these are really good bags. They sell for one eighty a piece. But seeing as how they're damaged, I can sell them to you for fifty bucks a bag."

Joon gasped and Lulu's hand flew to her mouth. Joon rocked back and forth in place. "But they're ripped, so we have to sew them, and, mister, we don't have a hundred and fifty dollars. We don't even have forty dollars. How about we make a deal? You give us everything for thirty bucks and we'll clean the whole store for you?"

Mark put his hand on Joon's shoulder. "I wish I could do that, but I can't."

Joon's body curled forward and she swallowed several times. "Well, what can you do?"

"Look, you seem like nice girls, and I can tell you really need this stuff. I'll sell you the tent for fifteen and the bags for twenty-five each. That's ninety total. It's a great deal."

Joon turned and looked at Lulu and moaned. Then she turned back to the store manager.

"Okay, but two things. We need you to tape the rips on the bags, and we need you to hold all of this stuff until later today 'cause we don't have all the money. Deal?"

"Wait," Lulu said. "Where are we gonna get ninety bucks?"

Joon avoided Lulu's eyes. "We'll get it." She looked hard at the store manager. "Deal or what?"

Mark, feeling helpless, nodded. "Yeah, we're open until eight tonight. Just be back before then."

Outside on the sidewalk, Lulu spun on Joon. "There's no way we can beg for that much money in one day. You have what? Thirty-five or thirty-six bucks in emergency cash left over. I have thirteen dollars. Even if we put it together, and we would be left with nothing, we would still need around forty more dollars."

Joon took Lulu's hand. "We won't spend our emergency money if I can help it."

Lulu pulled her hand away and looked at Joon curiously. "Fine. Then where are we getting ninety bucks? The money fairy?"

Joon looked into Lulu's eyes, hoping her friend would stop asking questions. Finally, she said, "I can earn the money."

"How?"

Joon turned her head, looking away briefly.

Lulu grabbed her by the shoulders. "No, no way. You aren't doing that to yourself again. You can't."

Joon steadied herself and returned her friend's intense gaze. "Yes, I can. I did it for a long time and never saw a dime. I can do it again, and we can stay warm. What other option do we have? It's not a big deal. This is called survival sex. Besides, I'll only sell blow jobs and I won't get into any cars. But you need to stay close, to make sure I'm safe. We'll find a place where I can take them where no one will see me."

Lulu was crying. "You can't do this. I can't let you do this."

"You can't stop me. So either help or go back to the house and I'll see you later."

Resigned, Lulu wrapped her arms around Joon. "I won't leave you alone."

Joon gave her a small smile. "Thank you. Now, let's go."

Chapter Sixty-Two

———————◼———————

Lulu looked around the streets. "Where are we gonna go?"

Joon looped her arm through Lulu's. "When I worked in Kensington there was a girl who talked about how she hooked on Fifteenth Street, between Reed and Federal. We're gonna go there and see what's up."

Joon and Lulu walked the long distance to Fifteenth and Reed. Joon scanned the street, noticing two girls standing at the end of the block. "Come here," Joon said, pulling Lulu into an open lot filled with trash and old appliances.

She led Lulu behind a refrigerator without doors that blocked the sight line from the street. Joon took off several layers of clothing, ripped the T-shirt she wore at the neck to plunge below her breasts, and tied it at the waist to create a midriff. She slipped on her old corduroy bomber jacket, let her hair down, and fluffed it with her fingers.

"Fuck me blue, it's freezing," Joon said.

Lulu pulled off her gloves and gave them to Joon. Then she unwrapped her scarf and wrapped it around her friend, being careful not to cover the girl's cleavage.

"How do I look?" Joon asked.

"Like a ho-bag," Lulu teased.

Joon giggled. "Yeah, it's a skill. Transforming into a slut like Superman, except I hide behind an old refrigerator and I'm not a superhero."

"Anyone who is willing to do what you're gonna do to keep the rest of us warm is a superhero in my mind," Lulu said, pushing Joon's hair behind her ears. "Now, what am I supposed to do?"

"You're gonna stay here in the lot. I'll bring them behind the refrigerator. You sit over there and stay real still. If they see you, they'll just think you're a dope head anyway. But just in case, don't say anything. I'll bring them back here, do my thing, and they'll be gone."

Lulu's eyes clouded over. Her heart grew heavy and she clung to Joon's arm. "I'm so sorry. Maybe there's another way."

Joon shook her head, pointed to the other side of the lot, turned, and walked toward the street. On the sidewalk, she glanced down the block, and two black prostitutes were heading her way. They stood in front of her and immediately confronted Joon.

"Whatcha think you're doin', whitey?"

Joon ignored them.

The girl talking stepped closer. "You dumb or somethin'? I ast you a motherfuckin' question. See, this here is our street, so take your filthy skank ass somewhere else."

Joon took a deep breath and looked at the girl. "I'm not bothering you. So how about you fuck off?"

The girl grinned. There were large gaps between her teeth, and it looked like she had tiny icicles dangling from her long gums. Her brow furrowed, and her nostrils flared. "I know you ain't talkin' to me."

Joon looked her up and down. "Yeah, I am. Just go back to your corner, and I'll stay here."

"Girl, I don't think ya know who you're talking to. I'll whoop your skinny ass up and down this street," the hooker said, pushing Joon in the chest.

Joon almost fell but caught herself. One thing she'd learned from Tori was to never let another hooker see your fear. Joon's face was pinched and her hands clenched into tight fists. She stalked toward the other girl. "Here's the thing," Joon hissed, "I don't want any trouble. I need some cash and I'll be outta here. This shit here," she continued, gesturing up and down the street, "this is fuckin' child's play. I worked Kensington, and if you fucked with another hooker there, you'd be fucking dead without a chance to walk away. So, like I said, *walk away*. Go back to your corner."

The girl let out a guttural, evil laugh. "What? You think 'cause you were whoring in Kensington that you some sorta expert? Bitch, let me tell ya somethin'. My pimp will skin your fuckin' ass alive after I knock the shit outta ya and drag ya back by your hair to one of his whorehouses."

Joon clenched her teeth and screamed, "Then do it. Stop talking about it and try to kick my ass. You don't own the fucking sidewalk."

As the two girls were ready to battle, each waiting for the other to make the first move, a man approached them. He looked the three over and focused on Joon. "How much?"

"Fifteen bucks. I'm only doing bj's today…too cold for anything else," she added. Joon stared into his eyes, her lips pouty and playful.

"Yeah, all right," the john agreed.

As the two walked away, the girl Joon had been fighting with yelled, "Oh, you a cheap fuckin' whore too. Ya dirty, diseased bitch. Dude, ya better wear a condom with that piece of trash."

Ignoring the girl, Joon led the man back into the lot and positioned herself on the side of the refrigerator, where there was privacy. From a distance, Lulu waited, thinking about what Joon was doing. Sadness filled Lulu, and tears rolled down her face. She had been through a lot as a homeless teen and realized even the worst thing that had happened to her could never be as dreadful as what Joon had been forced to do. She couldn't take her eyes off of the refrigerator, anxiously waiting for Joon to emerge. She knew many girls who had prostituted, but she'd never actually been close to it before. Joon was motivated to help friends that she'd known for two days—Lulu was frightened by Joon's casual willingness but also touched by her sacrifice.

Eight hours later and five more men serviced, Joon and Lulu left the lot. As they stepped onto the sidewalk, Joon looked at the hookers who had tried to scare her away. She gave them a broad smile, flipped them a middle finger, and walked the long distance to the store to buy their treasures.

Chapter Sixty-Three

Joon and Lulu lugged the tent and sleeping bags back to the abandoned house, stopping to rest several times. When they entered the bedroom, Gia, Fipple, and the others looked at them with tentative smiles.

"What's that shit?" Fipple asked.

Joon looked her over. "A tent and some sleeping bags."

Fipple sneered. "What are you stupid? You spent money on a tent for inside a house?"

Joon spun on the girl. "Fipple, the way I figure it is, if we can stay close together and keep our body heat inside the tent, we will be able to sleep without freezing to death."

Gia chimed in, trying to defuse the tension between the girls. "Plus, we can store our stuff in there."

Lulu, appalled by Fipple's words, put her hands on her hips. "Hey, Fipple? At least Joon had an idea. She not only got us the tent, but she bought three sleeping bags. You can at least say thank you."

Fipple threw her head back and laughed. "Thank you? I don't think so. And where did you get the money to buy all this stuff?"

Shit, Joon thought. *I didn't think about how I would explain that.* She took a long, steady breath through her nose. "What does it matter how I got the money? If you don't want to sleep in the tent, then you don't have to. No one is going to force you, Fipple."

Fipple stepped closer to Joon. "You didn't answer my question, *Joon.* How did you get the money?"

The other girls, curious to hear Joon's answer, stared.

"I blew six guys," Joon blurted.

Gia gasped and clamped both hands over her mouth. The others looked on with their mouths hanging open, and Fipple gave the girls a wide grin. "I told you all she was trouble. So now we got us a whore that can bring her pimp around here looking for her. None of you believed me. Do you now?"

Lulu moved closer to Joon. "Stop it, Fipple. Joon isn't a danger to any of us. She doesn't have a pimp, and no one is after her. Right, Joon?"

"Yeah, that's right," Joon said, feeling uncomfortable with the lie.

Eventually, Fipple swallowed her pride and followed along with the other girls, placing her things inside the tent. As the sun went down and the temperature plunged, Joon spread the three sleeping bags out over top of the clothes they had used as a layer of additional insulation on the floor of the tent.

"Okay," Joon said, standing outside the tent. "If we sleep two to a bag, we should be warm enough."

The six girls moved into the tent, and by the time they were situated, their six bodies took up every inch of space.

"Wow, this is warmer," Gia said, sharing her bag with Fipple, who huffed at the comment.

The other girls mumbled their agreement with Gia.

"See, Fipple? Joon isn't so bad now, is she?" Lulu pressed.

"Whatever. Fuck you, Lulu."

"Fuck you too. Sweet dreams," Lulu said, nestling closer to Joon.

That night, the group of girls slept together in a tight bundle. In the morning, Joon stretched her arms out to her sides and looked around the tent.

Lulu was smiling at her friend. "I haven't slept that good in weeks."

"Yeah, I think it worked great." Joon pushed her hair away from her face. "Now all we have to do is find a place with lights and running water, and we'll be living."

Lulu laughed and propped herself up on one elbow. "I'm sure if there's a way, you'll figure it out. I'm sticking with you."

"Good," Joon said, crawling out of the tent. "Time to find food. I'm starved."

Chapter Sixty-Four

———————————▬———————————

Joon and Lulu left the house and walked the streets, stopping in front of a popular bakery. They sat on the ground and stared up at people as they came and went. Every time the door opened, Joon got a glorious whiff of the rich coffee aroma and the donuts, cakes, and bagels. She could practically taste the sugar on a glazed donut and the soft, airy center. She would have been happier to eat anything from the small café than receive money.

As the girls sat shivering on the cold sidewalk begging for money, a woman approached the café. As she reached a gloved hand for the door of the café, she stopped short, turning and looking down at the girls. "Girls? How old are you?"

Joon flushed in the bitter cold. "Sixteen."

The woman looked at Lulu. "I'm nineteen."

"I see. You're both rather young. You have your whole lives ahead of you. I suggest you," she said, pointing to Lulu, "get a job. You're old enough. And you"—she looked at Joon—"Get yourself back in school. You'll be stuck here forever without an education."

Joon's jaw clenched tightly. "You know, lady, that all sounds real nice. If it were that easy, don't you think we would be doing that?"

The woman crossed her arms over her chest, and the corners of her mouth tugged downward in disapproval. "Well, maybe it isn't easy, but here's the thing—sitting here, waiting for someone to give you a handout will only get you a quick bite to eat. If you want to make a difference in your life or in the lives of others for that matter, it takes more than begging for leftover scraps and pocket change. Why don't you go to a shelter or something? There are many places in the city that are willing to help people like you."

"People like us?" Joon asked.

"Yes," the woman said, lifting her head and looking down her nose at the girls. "People like you. Children that run away because they don't want to clean their rooms or go to school or because…well, because you prefer to smoke pot and drink beer than apply yourself or live by your parents' rules."

Joon huffed. "You know, lady, wearing fancy clothes and expensive jewelry doesn't make you smarter or better than us. You have no idea how either of us got here." She stood and faced the woman as her anger rose. "I'd rather live on the streets and beg for scraps of food and loose pocket change than be back with my foster mother who beat me, shamed me, burned me with cigarettes, made me eat from the dog bowl, and told me how worthless I was every day."

Joon took a deep breath of cold air, stinging her lungs as tears of anger and sadness slid down her cheeks in a steady stream. "Please, lady, go inside and get your expensive coffee and leave us alone."

The woman smirked at Joon. "This is exactly what I'm talking about. I don't buy any of that story about your foster mother. I'm sure it's one that a lot of you homeless kids use to get what you want from gullible people. And those fake tears of yours…all you kids are so good at turning on the waterworks, then saying the same thing to everyone you encounter: *Do you have any money? I'm hungry. I'll work for food, wah, wah, wah.* You're all lazy brats who want everyone else to take care of you. Go home to your mommy and daddy, little girl, and stop littering our streets with your filthy bodies."

The woman opened the door to the café and stepped inside. Joon watched until she was gone, turned, and sat on the cold pavement next to Lulu. "Wow, that was messed up," Joon said. She paused for several seconds as she wiped her tears away. "I wish I did have a mom and dad to go home to."

"Hey, listen," Lulu whispered. "You're a good person. That lady knows nothing. I mean, most people think like she does, that we're all out here because we're uncontrollable teenagers. You need to let that shit roll off your back."

Joon rubbed her temples with her index fingers. "I know, but she's right too. We're never gonna be anything living like this. I just wanna do something good with my life. I wanna help other people, maybe even kids who got the same shit deal I got."

A few minutes later, a petite woman came out of the bakery wearing an apron and a hairnet. "One of our customers just complained about you sitting at the door. You need to move along."

Joon stared at the woman in defeat.

"Look," the lady said, handing Joon a bag, "take this. It's two donuts and some hot tea. But you gotta move on. We have a business to run, and if we don't keep our customers happy, we'll be out of business."

Joon stood and took the bag. "Thanks for the food."

"You bet, hon. Take care of yourself."

Joon put her hand out and helped to pull Lulu up from the sidewalk. She smiled at Lulu. "Well, at least we have something to eat. We need to find a way to earn money. We can still beg, but maybe we can find someone who will give us real jobs. You know, so we can save money and maybe get a place to live."

The girls walked to a nearby park and sat on a bench in the sun. Joon grabbed the ends of her long hair and looked at them. Then her eyes moved down her own body. Her clothes were oversized and shabby, and she was now self-conscious that she was wearing a man's flannel shirt and jacket.

Lulu took a bite of her donut and sipped her tea. She smiled at her friend. Joon's mouth was downturned and her eyes misty. When she realized Lulu was looking at her, she turned away quickly. Lulu stopped mid-chew. "What's wrong? We have food and the sun is shining. Why do you look like you're gonna cry?"

Joon nudged Lulu with her shoulder. "Look at me. I'm a mess. A disgusting, dirty slob. My hair is matted, my fingernails are packed with dirt, and my lips are chapped and flaky. This is what people see when they look at me. I'm sitting here in the cold, and yeah, the sun is beating on my face, but it doesn't even matter. Being homeless sucks. I'm tired of having nowhere to go, nowhere that I belong. We walk around all day just to keep warm. We beg for money or food so we can eat. We clean ourselves in library and subway bathrooms that are as dirty as we are. My life feels dark. Every day is overcast, even when the sun is shining. I'm sixteen and have no way of getting out of this shit."

Lulu looked at her own hands. There was dirt in the creases of her skin and under her fingernails. Her clothes had stains, and she suddenly recognized that she too was a harrowing sight.

She placed place her food and tea on the bench and leaned her elbows on her knees. "At some point, we all feel the way that you do now. And yeah, we're dirty and smelly and gross. But I want you to remember that we're living on the streets because it seemed the best option. And there is something about living on the streets that is unique—we take care of each other. Sure, there are some assholes out here, but there are assholes everywhere. What makes the nice homeless people so special is that we do shit for each and don't expect anything in return 'cause we already know they ain't got nothing to give back. Look at you and me—we make each other feel better, and you did all that horrible stuff with those men yesterday so that our group could sleep through the cold nights. That kind of giving you can't find in a wad of money. That's the stuff we're made of, ya know? Living in a home with a shower and clean clothes doesn't give you love, and it sure as hell doesn't make you a good person, you know that more than I do. So, look around you and see the beauty that's right within your reach. And if you want something or you wanna be somebody, then you go for it. I wanna be somebody too. I decided last week I'm gonna go to the library and figure out how to take the GED. After that, I'm gonna go to college, maybe be a nurse or even a doctor. Just because you ain't got shit now doesn't mean you won't have everything you want someday."

Joon tilted her head and gently rested it on Lulu's shoulder. "You're smarter than you look." Both girls chuckled. "Are you really gonna take the GED?"

"Yep."

"I would like to do that too. On my first day of kindergarten, my dad told me that someday I was going to be something really special when I grew up. I've learned a lot since then...I learned the hate of a woman, abandonment, being forced into sex; I've learned hunger, pain, suffering, humiliation, embarrassment. The list goes on and on." She took a deep breath and shook her head. "And I regret that I didn't learn enough from books and teachers and history. I haven't been to real school since I was twelve. I read a lot—thank God for the library—but I'm not sure I know how to learn anymore. It's not easy to see past all the bad things and believe there's much good out there...and, sometimes I just wanna give up. Just roll into a ball and die. I know I sound like a coward, but really, Lulu, what's the point if this is all there is?"

"The point is that we deserve better. Nobody is gonna swoop in and give us something for nothing. If we want something, we're gonna have to go after it. I say we both try to get our GEDs. We can help each other. What do you say?"

"Sure, if you think it'll make a difference." Joon put her hand over Lulu's. "Thank you for being my friend."

Lulu placed a gentle kiss on Joon's temple. "There's nothing to thank me for. You and me...I think we were meant to be sisters."

The girls sat on the bench for a while. When they weren't talking, Joon thought about a future that could be filled with happiness and decided to do what was necessary to change her life and become the person her parents would have wanted her to be.

Chapter Sixty-Five

As Christmas approached Joon and Lulu were busy begging on the streets. The holidays were when people were most generous, and homeless teens took to the streets because, after New Year's, no one wanted to part with their money.

On Christmas Eve, Joon was in good spirits.

"What are you so happy about today?" Lulu asked. "Expecting Santa to bring you a bag of twenties or something?"

Joon laughed. "Yeah, I wish. I don't think Santa's coming this year. But you and I are gonna stay inside a warm place tonight. We'll get food, a place to sleep, and breakfast."

Lulu slid into her sleeping bag and pulled it tight. Although it was the middle of the afternoon, she hadn't been able to shake the cold in her bones for three days. "Where are we going?"

Joon winked at her. "I know a place. We might even get to take a real shower. How's that sound?"

Lulu's teeth chattered. "Like the best fuckin' thing I heard in days. Aren't you cold?"

"Not any more than usual. Maybe you're getting sick," Joon said, leaning over and feeling Lulu's forehead. "Your forehead is warm."

"Just what I need...to be sick. Do we have any more aspirin?"

Joon opened the small community box that the group of girls left inside the tent. She searched through the contents. "Nope. None in here. I'll go and buy some. You stay here."

Joon hated leaving Lulu with none of the other girls there but figured she wouldn't be long, and having Lulu out in the cold wouldn't help matters. She picked up her own sleeping bag and laid it over Lulu for extra warmth. "You try to sleep. I'll go get some aspirin and come right back."

Upon Joon's return, she found Lulu sleeping.

"Wake up, girl. I have your aspirin."

Lulu opened her eyes slowly. "I feel like shit."

Joon lifted her eyebrows. "You look like shit."

Lulu closed her eyes again and let out a soft laugh. "You smell like shit."

Joon brushed Lulu's long curls away from her face. "Well, I can't deny that one. We need to get going if we're gonna make it inside tonight."

Lulu moaned. She sat up slowly and rubbed her eyes. "My head is pounding." Her hands clamped over her stomach. "I feel nauseous and everything hurts."

Joon moved closer. "Maybe you have the flu. You're over eighteen. Do you wanna go to the emergency room?"

Lulu considered it, but she shook her head. "Nah. I'll be fine. Let's get through Christmas. I don't wanna spend tonight in the emergency room with a bunch of drunks. Help me up and we'll get going."

An hour later, Joon and Lulu stood on the steps of Saint Monica Roman Catholic Church.

Lulu had her arm weaved through Joon's. "How did you hear about this place?"

"I came here years ago. I was alone on Christmas Eve. I couldn't find Ragtop, so I came here and they were really nice to me."

The doors to the church opened, and as the homeless teens entered, Joon focused on the altar at the front of the church. She leaned into Lulu. "That's Father John."

"How do you know that?"

"I told you, I was here before. Anyway, he's real nice and likes to help us."

"Too bad he ain't around all year. Hell—" Lulu said, covering her mouth and looking up waiting for a lightning bolt to zap her. "I mean, it would be nice if there were more churches where we could go on nights other than Christmas Eve."

Joon laughed. "Be quiet before you damn both of us to the fiery pits of Hell."

The homeless group was ushered to the back of the church and into the kitchen, where they ate before mass.

"Father John?" Joon said.

"Yes. Oh wait. You've been here before."

"Yeah, four years ago," Joon said, fidgeting under his intense gaze. "How did you remember?"

"Your eyes. I remember those angelic eyes. How have you been?"

Joon touched her dirty, matted hair. "Well, I've been good. I mean, what do you mean? Like, how have I been acting?"

Father John smiled. "No, Joon. I mean, how has life been treating you? How are you feeling?"

Joon sighed. She pulled on the bottom of her oversized coat. "Life's treating me crappy. I mean, I'm okay, but, you know, living on the streets ain't easy."

Father John nodded and rested his hand on Joon's shoulder. "May I say a prayer for you?"

"I guess so." Joon looked over at Lulu. "Can you say one for my best friend, Lulu too?"

Father John put his other hand on Lulu's shoulder and closed his eyes. "Dear God, watch over your children Joon and Lulu. Keep them safe. Fill them with the Holy Spirit and guide them to a better life, provide them with love and happiness in all of their days. Amen." The priest opened his eyes. "Now, you girls go find a seat. Mass is about to begin."

Once seated in a pew, Joon took hold of Lulu's hand and asked, "Do you believe in God?"

Lulu's eyes remained fixed on the cross above the altar. "I don't know. I mean, when my gram died and I was left all alone, I was confused. Gram believed there was a God and Heaven and all of that stuff. I believed it then because she did. But after she died, I wasn't so sure. Then, living on the streets and…"

"And what?"

"Nothing."

"No, tell me. What happened to you?"

"Not now. Mass is gonna start."

Joon slid her hand gently up and down Lulu's arm. "You can tell me anything. You stood watch while I blew guys for a tent and sleeping bags," she whispered.

"Oh my God, Joon. You're so crude. We're in church," she said, laughing.

Joon smiled. "Do you feel better?"

"A little. Being inside and eating helped. You don't need to worry. It'll pass."

Father John started the mass and the girls fell silent. Later, as they lay in the church waiting for sleep to claim them, Joon flung her arm over Lulu's waist. "We did good coming here tonight, right?"

"Yeah, Joon, we did real good. You're pretty smart for such a young 'un."

The two girls snuggled closer and closed their eyes.

"Merry Christmas," Joon whispered.

"Merry Christmas, my friend."

Chapter Sixty-Six

———————◼︎———————

Joon and Lulu left the church after mass on Christmas morning. With their bellies full, Joon led them to the homeless shelter where Tony Bruno had taken her.

Joon made her way to the man who'd helped her. "Hey, Joey. I don't know if you remember me. I'm a friend of Tony...um, well, his friend Salvatore talked to you so I could stay here."

"Sure," Joey said, stacking more juice boxes on a table. "I remember you. How's it going?"

"It's going all right. I was hoping that maybe you could help us."

Joey pinched his bottom lip between his thumb and index finger. "Hey, look, I'd love to help you out, but I'm already over capacity. I don't have any beds left and..."

"No, I'm sorry," Joon interrupted. "I was hoping you would maybe just let us take a shower. This is my friend Lulu. We stayed at a church last night and they didn't have showers we could use. It's just that it's been a while. Ya know?"

Joey patted Joon on the back. "Yeah, I know. Follow me. I can help you with that. Sorry there isn't space for you to stay."

After Joey gave the girls towels, he left them in the shower room. They undressed, laying their clothes on a bench. It took a while before they had stripped off the multiple layers of clothing.

Joon looked at Lulu, in a pair of hipster panties and sports bra, and her eyes were drawn to a huge scar, the shape of a capital L next to her rib cage. "What's that?" she asked, pointing.

Lulu looked down at herself. "I lost a kidney."

"What do you mean lost a kidney? Like you misplaced it or like something happened to you when you were a kid?"

"No. Like, someone took it."

"Wait. What are you saying?"

Lulu let out a loud huff. "I'm saying that last year, I was at a party. You know, a friend of a friend of a friend that had a party in their apartment. So, I went. I was talking to this guy. He was real cute, and he wasn't homeless, so that was a bonus. Anyway, he went into the kitchen and grabbed me a beer from the keg. The next thing I knew, I woke up in a hospital bed."

"I'm so confused. I don't get it."

"The dude was a fraud. Showed up at the party with a couple of his friends. No one really knew them. He must've put something in my drink. Apparently, I left with him and his buddies. The rest is just pieced together. They must've taken me somewhere and stolen one of my kidneys and left me on a bench in Rittenhouse Square. A guy walking through the park with his wife noticed I was naked from the waist down, and they saw blood as they got closer to me. Then they saw the staples—bastards used a staple gun on me, but hey, it probably saved my life. Anyway, things were bad for several months. I stayed in the hospital for a while. I was lucky that couple walked by when they did. The kidney doctor, Dr. Becker, rushed me into surgery once I got to the hospital. He fixed me up as best he could."

Joon sat on the bench with her mouth agape. "Why didn't you tell me this before?"

"Just something I keep quiet about. You know as well as I do you don't let other people know your weaknesses. I figured if Fipple found out, she definitely wouldn't want me to stay with the group. She would see me as broken, a 'liability' as she puts it."

Joon was shocked—and worried. Her new friend was dealing with missing an organ. "Well, are you okay now? I mean, do you have to do anything?"

Lulu grabbed her towel. "Yeah. I go see Dr. Becker every three months. So far, I've been doing fine with one kidney. The assholes that took my other one hacked into my body. I got an infection...a really bad one. I was sick for a long time. Fuckers almost killed me. I know this would freak the other girls out—Fipple would make sure of it. I hope you won't tell them and that you're not scared to be around me now that you know."

Joon took her bra and panties off slowly and deliberately, held her arms away from her body, and slowly turned in a full circle. "The scars on my back and legs are from where Aron whipped me. She would whip me with a belt until I bled and then she would whip the bleeding welts. She used to tell me I needed to really feel the pain because that's what punishments are all about. The pinky toe missing on my left foot?" she continued, pointing to it. "That's where Aron cut my toe off because I collapsed when I couldn't stay in my squat position for one more minute. She hacked it right off in her kitchen, then took a lighter and burned the skin together. The bite marks on my boobs are from Pug letting men 'sample' me. In the beginning, when I was first taken to Kensington by my so-called boyfriend, I was fairly innocent. I fought against those bastards as hard as I could—so hard that after the first night, Pug or one of his goons would tie me to the bed. The marks around my wrists and ankles are where the ropes held me to the bed. Those marks from one shoulder blade to the other are from cigarettes and cigars that Pug let the johns torture me with...helped them get their rocks off." She took a deep breath as she looked down at her own ruined body. "These are the scars you can see. I have many more, but they're hidden. I look great on the outside compared to the damage on the inside."

She stopped talking, lifted her head, and stared steadily into Lulu eyes. "Do you still worry I'm scared to be around you?"

Tears slid down Lulu's face. She walked over to Joon and took her hand. Together, each of them, perfectly flawed humans, walked into the shower and let the hot water wash over them. As the dirt fell away and the weight of their secrets lifted, they both felt a literal and figurative lightness.

"I've never told anyone all of that before," Joon said, breaking the silence. "I guess when I was with Ragtop I was too young. Then, I never wanted any of the other hookers to know 'cause that would have made me seem weaker, and eventually, they'd have used it against me."

"Yeah, I had a kidney stolen and you had your innocence and a toe stolen." Both girls cracked a smile at the toe comment. "We make a good team. I bet if we stick together, we'll get off the streets and live a half-decent life. We may be missing big parts of ourselves, but we have so much heart between the two of us we're unstoppable."

When the girls returned to the bench where they'd left their clothing, each found new panties and socks.

"Joey must've left these for us," Joon said, lifting them in one hand and holding the soft cotton close to her bare chest. "Lulu, do you really think that we can get off the streets?"

"Sure. Why not? We've survived some really horrible shit. We must have some luck, right?"

Joon would have never considered herself lucky, but Lulu was right. They both could've been dead. Her thoughts roamed to Tori. It'd been several months since she thought about her old friend, and her belly churned with guilt. She hoped that Tori had also been lucky.

Chapter Sixty-Seven

————————————◼————————————

A few weeks later, close to ten at night, Joon and Lulu were just over a mile from their abandoned house when they noticed a tall boy with long hair fiddling with the lock on a parked car. As they drew closer, the boy eyed them.

"You guys looking for a place to sleep?" he asked.

"Who wants to know?" Joon replied, slowing her pace.

The boy chuckled. "I wanna know. Hell, girl, I'm trying to be nice is all," he said, putting his hand to his heart.

"Hm. Why? What are you looking for? We don't have any money," Joon said, taking a small step backward.

"Come on, Joon. Let's just go," Lulu said, tugging on her friend's jacket.

"Hang on," the boy began. "Look, I just wanted to know if you needed a warm place to sleep. That's all." He looked at the pavement and shook his head slowly.

Joon frowned. "Whose car is it? I know it ain't yours," she said, looking him up and down.

"No shit it ain't mine," he responded. "I break into cars and sleep in them, so I don't freeze my balls off at night. Don't you know anything?" he snapped, turning his back on the girls.

Joon crossed her arms over her chest. "Why are you being an asshole?"

"Hey, look, I'm sorry. I get jittery out here sometimes...okay, most of the time. My name is Skinner. What are your names?"

"I'm Joon and this is Lulu."

Skinner lifted his chin in a swift nod. "Good to meet you guys. So? Do you wanna sleep in the car tonight?"

Joon looked at the car apprehensively. "Maybe."

Skinner gave her a smirk. "Maybe isn't an answer. That's a way of stalling instead of making a decision." He dug into the car window. "See, if you get the hanger down in the window like this, you can unlock the door." The lock clicked, and he pulled the door open, put his hand on his hip, and jutted it out to the side. He cocked his head and lifted his eyebrows. "Are you getting in or not?"

Joon pulled Lulu to the side. "Do you wanna?"

Lulu shook her head. "Why would we?" she said in a low voice, so Skinner couldn't hear her. "I mean, we have our stuff back at the house. Besides, what if he's some kind of weirdo?"

Joon thought for moment. "Well, it's freezing out, and we still have a while to walk. Besides, you never know how shit goes down, right? I mean, our life out here can change in a second. Couldn't hurt to learn something new."

Lulu shrugged. "Fine, but this guy better not be some ax murderer."

Joon squeezed Lulu's hand and slid into the front seat while Lulu crawled into the back. She looked over at Skinner. "This doesn't feel much warmer than the sidewalk."

"Well, princess, that's because I haven't done this yet." He leaned down under the dashboard, and a couple of minutes later, the engine hummed quietly. Then he turned the heat on full blast. A short while later, hot air blew from the car heater.

"Ah," Joon cooed. "That feels great."

Lulu stretched out across the backseat, while Joon and Skinner reclined their seats over her.

"Sweet dreams," Skinner said.

Joon sighed. "Yeah, sweet dreams. I want you to show me how to turn on cars...you know whatever you did with the wires. That way, if we're ever freezing to death, we have an option."

In the morning, just as the sun was rising, Skinner showed Joon how to hotwire a car, and when Lulu woke, Joon opened the passenger door. "We gotta beat it. Whoever owns this car could be coming soon."

The three teens stood on the sidewalk, looking at each other until Joon spoke. "It was nice meeting you, Skinner. Thanks for the warm sleep last night. Maybe we'll see ya around sometime."

"Sure thing," Skinner replied, edging into their personal space.

Joon shot Lulu a look, and they cackled. "Listen," Joon said, "we're not laughing at you. It's just that neither of us are looking for a boyfriend."

"Well, that's good 'cause I am. In case you haven't noticed, I'm gay. I was just looking for someone to keep me company. It gets…it gets lonely out here when you don't have anyone. It ain't easy when there's nobody to connect with. So I try to give myself pep talks, try to convince myself things will get better, that I'll meet someone. You know, it helps for a few days, but then I'm still alone and I feel like I'm falling into this deep, dark, wet, smelly hole that I'll never climb out of. "

Skinner's description made Joon's stomach twist. "Hey," she said, feeling wretched. "I've been where you're at. I know how it feels. We're gonna go to Broad Street to beg. You wanna join us?"

He brightened. "Yeah, I'd love that. Well, not that I love begging or anything, but I'd really like to hang out with you guys."

As they walked, Joon turned to the boy. "So, you're gay? Like you have sex with guys?"

Skinner gave Joon a small smile. "Well, only one guy when I was in high school. We had a pretty good thing going until some of the other kids found out. The rumors spread fast, and then my mom and dad found out, and they flipped their shit. They told me that I was an embarrassment. Well, my father wouldn't talk to me and my mother wanted me to see a shrink. She said all I needed was to get my head straight."

Joon played with her long strands of hair as they walked. "Is that why you left home?"

Skinner nodded. "My parents thought it was best for everyone. They didn't want my younger brother and sister to be 'infected' by me." He did air quotes and shook his head. "My father tried to beat the gay outta me. He fucked me up real bad. I was scared outta my mind. He broke my nose and sprained my wrist. So after I healed, I did what any respectable, gay sixteen-year-old would do. I wrote a letter to my parents, letting them know how fucked up they were, packed a bag, took all eighty-three dollars of my life savings, and left. I've been on the streets just under three months. There have been days out here that make me wonder what's worse: living somewhere you aren't wanted or wanting somewhere to live."

Joon threaded her arm through Skinner's. "I think that living somewhere you aren't wanted is way harder. Don't get me wrong, street life can be some real hard shit, but not being wanted is a different kind of pain—a physical and emotional pain that runs so deep you don't care if you live or die. That's the way it was for me living with my foster mother. I didn't care if I died. There were times when I prayed I would die. But out here on the streets, I'm fighting to live. We're all doing whatever we need to do to survive. I think that fighting to live is a whole lot better than hoping to die."

Skinner turned to her and smiled. "I think you're right." He looked at Lulu. "What do you think?"

Lulu shrugged. "That's a hard one. I lived with my grandmother, who loved me to death. After she died, I had nowhere else to go. But I totally get how you two can feel that way."

"Lulu's a feeler," Joon joked. "She can feel others pain."

"Yeah, that's me...I'm a real feeler," Lulu said, clutching and stroking Joon's arm.

"And a creeper," Joon laughed, shrugging her off and running ahead.

"Hey, fuck you, Joon!" Lulu sang.

"Fuck you, back, Lulu. I thought you kept that just for Fipple."

Lulu swung her hips from side to side. "I've decided to expand my circle. I'm trying to be more inclusive."

When Lulu and Skinner caught up to Joon, she was twirling around, head back, eyes closed, soaking up the morning sun. Lulu put her arms around Joon's waist and pulled her close, and the girls held hands as they continued walking toward Broad Street, Skinner chattering the whole way.

They begged all day, and in the early evening, just before sunset, it was time to leave the streets. Joon reached into her coat pocket and counted out the money they'd earned and split it in thirds.

Joon handed money to her new friend. "Here's your share, Skinner. We gotta get back 'cause the other girls are gonna wonder what happened to us, since we didn't show up last night."

Skinner took the money and shoved it into his pocket. "Maybe I can go with you guys. You know, stay where you're staying for a little while?"

Joon looked at her feet and shifted from foot to foot. "I really wish we could bring you back, but the girls we're staying with aren't open to new people, and since you're a boy, it would make it even harder. I'm real sorry."

Paige Dearth

Skinner's mouth went slack, and he ran his fingers through his tangled hair. "Yeah, I get it. Well, it was nice hanging with you." As he turned and walked away, Joon faced Lulu.

"I feel like a piece of shit. I know how it feels not to have anyone, and so do you," she said with conviction.

Lulu nodded as they watched him getting farther and farther away. Joon, unable to bear the pain of Skinner's loneliness, sprinted to him. When she caught up to him, she grabbed his shoulder and Skinner spun around.

"Here's the deal," she said. "You can come with us but don't expect it to be easy. I doubt the other girls are gonna welcome you in, but we can try, right?"

He beamed at her as he nodded. "Yeah, we can try. Thanks, Joon."

The three teens began the walk back to the abandoned house, and on the way, the girls filled Skinner in on Fipple. When they were standing outside the house, Joon gave him a lame smile. "Remember, just be yourself. No wait, scratch that. Just be quiet," she said, and poking him lightly in the sternum.

Chapter Sixty-Eight

Inside the house, Skinner looked around the first floor. People were partying. There was a couple against one wall, openly having sex as if they were alone.

"Well," Skinner whispered. "I guess they don't care that people can see them going at it."

Joon glanced at him. "They're a nice couple. They love each other, and this is all they got. Doesn't seem to bother anyone but you."

"I didn't say it bothered me. I just couldn't imagine having sex in front of other people."

Joon shrugged. "Happens all the time on the streets. Some do it for love and others do it for money."

Skinner followed Joon and Lulu upstairs. When they entered the room, they found the other girls inside the tent with the flap open. The girls stared at the threesome. Joon was wringing her hands as she approached the tent and knelt.

She glanced from one girl to the next. "Hey. So, Lulu and me met this guy on the streets last night. He let us sleep in a car with him. Ran the heat all night long. Anyway, he doesn't have anywhere to go, doesn't know anybody on the streets. He wants to hang with us for a while, you know, until he finds a better place to stay."

Gia smiled. "Well, I think—"

Fipple put her hand over Gia's mouth. "Shut up, Gia. Everyone knows you make bad decisions especially when it comes to guys." Fipple turned to Joon, eyes blazing and nostrils flared. "The answer is no. Tell your asshole friend that we don't want him here. You're a fuckin' idiot for even showing up with him." Fipple turned to the other girls in the tent. "This is the shit I've been saying, haven't I? This stupid bitch," she yelled, pointing to Joon, "is gonna get us hurt or kicked outta here or both. It's time for her to go. You agree with me, right?"

The other girls, caught between their respect for Fipple's leadership and admiration for Joon's creativity and kindness, remained silent. Fipple spun back to Joon. "Listen, you little shit. Tell that stray dog," she growled, pointing at Skinner, "to take a fuckin' hike. The answer is no. He can't stay here with us. And if you had a brain in your head, you would've known that."

Joon's hands were on her hips, elbows jutting out like wings. She puffed out her chest and glowered at Fipple for several seconds. "Who the fuck do you think you are? It's clear that you're no genius. You're just an ugly bitch with a big mouth."

Fipple lunged at Joon and the two rolled on the floor outside of the tent. Joon got the upper hand, and soon, she was sitting on Fipple's stomach pinning her hands above her head. She put her face close to Fipple's. Teeth clenched, she spoke in a hushed voice. "Here's the deal, Fipple. Skinner is staying with us for a while. If you don't like it, I'll take my tent and my sleeping bags and move to another floor. Maybe you can explain that to your following over there," she said, gesturing toward the girls in the tent watching with bulging eyes.

"You don't scare me, skank." But Fipple said it quietly.

"I'm not trying to scare you. I'm letting you know what's gonna happen. You get to decide." Slowly, she moved off of Fipple and turned to Skinner and Lulu. "Fipple said it would be fine if you stayed with us for a while," she announced.

Skinner whispered through a smile, "No she didn't."

Joon elbowed him. "Shut up and go with it. Sheesh, you're dense."

"Oh. Right. Sorry," he said in an undertone.

Inside the tent, Joon unzipped the sleeping bag she shared with Lulu, and the three of them lay next to each other and pulled the bag over them. They made Skinner sleep against the wall of the tent, the colder spot. "After all," Joon teased, "You're the newcomer. Lulu and me have seniority."

Skinner shook his hips back and forth. "Girlfriend, I wouldn't care if I had to sleep on top of the tent if it meant I wasn't by myself."

The seven teens laid side by side, crammed in the small tent; Joon was on her back between Lulu and Skinner with her eyes closed.

"You sleeping?" Lulu asked her.

"Does it matter? You would've woken me up anyway." Joon turned toward Lulu. "What's up? You got something important to tell me?"

Lulu looked deep into Joon's eyes. "I think that what you did for Skinner was really brave. You stood up for someone you hardly know. I don't think I would've done that."

"It's not brave, Lulu. It's being on the side of right. It's not fair to push someone away 'cause you don't know them. I mean, did you see how scared he was when Fipple started yelling?"

Lulu nodded. "That's why I would have backed down. I wouldn't have wanted to fight Fipple."

"Fuck Fipple," Joon said, leaning up and flipping her middle finger to the sleeping girl on the other side of the tent.

Lulu draped her arm over Joon as she lay back down. "I just wanted you to know. That's all. You're a good egg and I'm glad I have you."

"Me too," Skinner whispered.

Joon whipped her head toward him. "Were you listening the whole time?"

Skinner snapped his wrist and flung his hand forward. "Baby girl, I heard every word. I wasn't all that scared."

"Yes you were," Joon protested quietly.

"Okay. Fine. I was a little scared. But not of that bulldog. I was scared I'd have to spend more time on the damn street by myself. I hate it out there. People ain't kind to homeless teens and nobody likes a gay homeless teen."

Joon pushed her fingers through Skinner's hair. "Stop whining about being gay. You're just trying to get sympathy," she said, rolling her eyes.

Skinner stuck his fingers in her armpit and Joon let out a squeal. The other girls stirred, and Joon smacked him playfully. "Shhhh, do you wanna get us both kicked out?"

Skinner pulled the sleeping bag up on his shoulder. "Well if the three us do get kicked out, at least we'll all have our own sleeping bag. These bitches don't know who they're fucking with. We'll take our damn tent and sleeping bags and move on."

Joon puckered her lips. "Oh, will *we* now? Since when is this 'our' tent and sleeping bags?"

Skinner tapped his chin with his index finger. "Well, let me think... since you adopted me."

"Please, I didn't adopt you. Don't get too comfortable, big guy."

"This is the most comfortable I've been in a year," Skinner said, putting his arm over Joon's waist.

"Wow. That's nice of you to say. I like helping people."

"Baby girl, you can keep on helping me all you want," Skinner said.

"Me too," Lulu added, putting her arm over Joon.

Joon closed her eyes. She felt relaxed and blissful that she could make a small difference for her friends.

Chapter Sixty-Nine

It was in mid-February and one of the coldest winters Philadelphia had seen in a decade. Even the tent and sleeping bags couldn't keep the group from freezing.

"It's too cold," Joon said inside the tent. "We gotta get outta here. Maybe go to a shelter like the others. The house is practically empty."

Lulu shook her head. "I'd risk freezing to death before I'd stay in a hellish shelter. You all know that the chances of getting beaten, robbed, or stabbed inside those places is high. I say we stay here and huddle under every fucking piece of clothing we got."

"Really? It's that bad?" Skinner said.

The girls looked at him as if he was nuts. Joon lifted her eyebrows and rolled her eyes. "Right. You haven't been on the street long enough to know. If you've ever been in a shelter, you'd know that you're practically taking your life in your hands. You know, there are a lot of crazy people and others that are real desperate to get their hands on anything of value. I mean, regular people stay in them too, but we're definitely outnumbered by the insane and criminals."

"Oh. Who knew? Okay then. I guess we'll just keep our girly asses here and freeze. Makes good sense to me," Skinner said.

Joon and the other girls laughed, but Fipple's face shrunk into a tight knot. She glared at Skinner. "If you haven't noticed, you're not a girl. I know you think you are 'cause you're 'gay,'" she said, throwing air quotes at the word, "but you ain't. So how about if you stop acting like you belong here? You're only here 'cause Joon's a stupid ass, but as soon as the weather is warmer and we don't need this shit to keep us warm, your faggot ass is outta here."

Joon squeezed her hands into fists. "What the hell's your problem? You don't speak for everyone here." She paused and looked at the other girls. "Does she?"

None of them made eye contact with Joon. She turned to Lulu, who put her hands in the air and shrugged. "Did you know they were waiting until it got warm to kick Skinner out?" she asked Lulu.

Lulu cocked her head. "No, I didn't fucking know. I mean really, Joon, I would've told you."

"You're right. I'm sorry," Joon said. Then she turned to the others. "You don't need to worry. We'll be outta here as soon as possible."

"Wait," Gia said. "It's not you, Joon. We just aren't comfortable having a guy around all the time. It makes it hard to get changed or go to the bathroom or all the other stuff we do in front of each other."

Joon leaned forward to be closer to Gia. "I thought that you were different, but you're just like the rest of them." She shook her head. "It's no big deal, Gia. We'll clear out when we can, I promise." She stood and left the room, going down the dark stairs and out the back door off the kitchen. She shivered as the wind whipped around her.

A minute later, Lulu and Skinner joined her. "You can't stay out here. It's too cold," Lulu said.

Joon chattered a response. "I kn...n...n...ow."

"Come on," Lulu said. She grabbed her hand and led her into the kitchen.

"I'm sorry, you guys," Skinner said. "I didn't mean for all of this to happen. Maybe I should try to stay at a shelter tonight. I mean," he said with a brilliant smile and pulling his jean pockets inside out, "I don't have anything to fucking steal."

"No. You're not leaving," Joon stated definitively. "You're staying here with us. And we'll figure something out. Let's go back upstairs and sleep. We can make a plan tomorrow."

Chapter Seventy

It was almost two in the morning when Joon started coughing. Her lungs felt like they were on fire and she sat up slowly. Seeing that everyone was coughing, she crawled outside the tent and lit her lighter. The room was filled with smoke.

"Get up! Get up! Wake up! We have to get outta here!" She rushed into the tent, where the others were sitting up, coughing.

"Move it!" she screamed. "I think the house is on fire."

Panic set in, but Joon pushed it down deep inside of her. She grabbed Lulu's hand and pulled her out of the tent, Skinner following right behind, and then the others. All seven of them were holding hands, forming a human chain as Joon led them into the hallway.

The smoke was thick and there was no visibility. Joon's mind shifted back to first grade, when she'd learned fire safety. She yelled at the group. "Drop to your hands and knees. We need to stay below the smoke."

Joon sat on the first step and eased her way down, screaming instructions to the others. When they got to the first floor, she quickly assessed the situation. The kitchen and the room that was once the formal dining room were engulfed in flames. The sitting room, where they all were at the bottom of the stairs, was the only room that hadn't caught fire yet.

"We need to get over to the front windows," she yelled. "Stay on your bellies. We have to keep low."

Joon crawled to the spot where she remembered the window being. It was impossible to see anything, and she also knew they had to contend with the plywood that covered it. "Lulu," she said, reaching for her hand, but her friend didn't respond.

"Lulu!" she screamed, pulling on the girl's limp arm. Still no response. "Skinner! We gotta get Lulu outta here. I think she passed out," she yelled.

For a moment, Joon was motionless, thinking of what to do next. It was only then that she could hear the wood burning around them, the crackling of the upper floors as the house shifted and the wind behind the boarded-up windows letting a little air through. The open back door was pulling the smoke through the first floor in a frantic rush, and she could hear the girls in her group crying, even though she couldn't see them.

"Skinner, we have to get the wood off of the front window…fast!"

Skinner let go of Lulu and moved a few feet to be close to Joon. "Get your fingers under the wood," Joon shouted.

"Fuck, Joon. The fire is spreading," he said.

"Fingers. Wood. Pull," she hollered. "Ready, pull. Pull! Pull!"

The plywood gave an inch with the third pull. "Again," she demanded.

Less than a minute later, the plywood gave way from the rotted windowsill and they had a glimpse of the outside.

"Fuck! We need to break the glass," Joon roared.

"I got this," Skinner yelled, pulling off his boots and handing one to Joon. She held it in her hand and looked at him questioningly. "They're steel tipped," Skinner shouted.

The two of them beat at the glass until it shattered, and the smoke inside the room was sucked out, bringing the raging fire quickly behind it. They hoisted Lulu from the floor and placed her outside. After climbing out, they grabbed her arms and legs, and moved her farther from the burning structure, the other girls following.

Joon and Skinner were coughing and gagging, their faces and clothes covered with soot and ash. Fire engines were pulling up as the group sputtered and struggled to breathe, and Joon crawled over to Lulu.

"Lulu?" Joon looked into her friend's face and put her hand on her chest, feeling the shallow rise and fall of her chest. She staggered to her feet and ran to a fireman. "My friend, I think she's dying."

The fireman ran with Joon over to Lulu and thrust an oxygen mask over Lulu's face before he checked her vital signs. Before he was done, an ambulance pulled up to the curb. They got Lulu into the ambulance quickly as other first responders rushed around the group, checking everyone's condition.

Joon climbed into the ambulance with Lulu. "Is she gonna be okay?" she cried.

The male paramedic met Joon's sad eyes. "She's breathing. The oxygen's helping. Does she have any health issues?"

"She only has one kidney. The other one got stolen," Joon blurted.

The paramedic looked toward the driver. "Call for another ambulance. We have to get this lady to the ER." Then he turned to Joon. "We're taking her to Penn," he said dismissively.

"I'm not leaving her. I'm coming with you," she stated.

"Fine," he said. "But I need you to sit there and put that oxygen mask on. You've inhaled a lot of smoke."

Joon sat back and put the oxygen mask over her mouth as the sirens sliced through the cold night.

Chapter Seventy-One

Inside the emergency room, Joon refused treatment and insisted on staying with Lulu.

"I'm fine," she told the ER nurse, Becky, who made her sit in a wheelchair. "My friend hasn't woken up since we got outta the house. I need to be with her."

Becky put her hand on Joon's shoulder. "Honey, I understand you're worried. But the doctor hasn't seen her yet, and I want to get you cleaned up so we can take a look at you. Would that be all right?"

Tears began to fall down her cheeks, and flesh-colored streaks appeared in the black soot on her face. "What if she needs me?"

Becky sat down, so she could be eye level with Joon. "I want you to listen to me. You have some nasty burns on your face and arms."

Joon put her hand on her cheek and flinched. Then she looked down at the large, black blisters on her arms. She had felt nothing. Her eyes widened and her mouth went slack as she looked back at Becky.

"Sometimes, when we're in fight-or-flight mode, our adrenaline is so powerful that we can't feel anything when we get hurt. Now, I want to get you cleaned up and checked out. I promise I'll stay with your friend while you're gone. If she wakes up, I'll come and get you. Okay?"

Joon nodded. Becky stood and guided the girl out into the open nurse's area. "Candice? Can you take Joon down to bay eight? I want you to get her face and arms cleaned up. She has several burns, so be careful. Then we'll get the doctor to take a look at her," Becky instructed. "Oh, Candice, Joon is a priority. She needs to get back to her friend in bay three who is still unconscious."

Candice moved quickly, taking Joon to the assigned bay and cleaning the soot from her eyes, nose, mouth, and skin as the young nurse chatted away. Joon couldn't focus on anything she was saying but welcomed the distraction. The doctor checked Joon over, bandaged her up, and left.

Candice came back into the bay and asked, "Did the doctor explain everything to you?"

Joon nodded. "How's Lulu?"

"Becky's still with her and I'll take you over there in a minute. Listen, you have second-degree burns on your face and arms. Now, it's important you keep those areas clean and use the ointment we're going to give you so that they don't get infected. I'm gonna give you a tetanus shot," she said, uncapping the needle tip.

"What's that for?"

"Well, you said you haven't seen a doctor since you were five, and that means you haven't had a tetanus shot in a long time. I need to give you one to help prevent you from getting tetanus," she explained.

Joon closed her eyes. "I don't understand what you're saying."

"Your wounds can make you really sick. It's called tetanus. It's a precaution, but one that is very important."

Joon opened her eyes. "So if you were me, then you'd get that needle?"

"You bet," Candice said. "Now, I'm going to put the needle into your arm. It's going to hurt, and your shoulder may feel stiff and sore for a couple of days. That's all normal."

Back in bay three, Joon pulled one of the extra chairs to the side of Lulu's bed. She took her friends limp hand in her own and stroked it gently. Soon, a doctor came in and smiled. "You must be Joon."

She nodded.

"Lulu told me about you at her last visit. I'm Dr. Becker. Her kidney doctor. I got to the hospital early this morning, and when they saw she was my patient, the ER doctor called me."

Joon gave him a small smile. "She told me about you too. Is Lulu gonna be okay?"

"Yes, the ER doctor that checked her out said she'll be okay."

"How come she isn't waking up then?"

Dr. Becker pulled the other chair up beside Joon. "With Lulu's condition, she can have fluid buildup in her lungs, which makes it difficult for her to breathe. That combined with the smoke inhalation was too much for her."

Joon stared at her dirty fingernails and quickly curled her fingers into her palm to hide them. "She's gonna be okay, right?"

"Yes. We gave her some medication that's making her sleep. We want to make sure she gets lots of oxygen in her system. We're going to keep her here for a while."

Joon looked at her own bandaged arms and then at Lulu's. "She burned her arms."

"Yes, she did." Dr. Becker leaned forward in his chair. "Listen, they will admit her tonight. You can stay with her here. Once she's assigned a room, I'll ask the nurse to let you know where you can find her. Is it safe to assume you have nowhere to go tonight?"

"Yes. We lost everything in the fire. One of my other friends, Skinner, is still out there somewhere."

"The paramedics brought seven of you in tonight. Which one is Skinner?"

"The boy."

"I'll let him know where to find you. Okay?"

"Thank you," Joon said. "Dr. Becker, if we're real quiet, can Skinner stay in here with me too?"

He smiled at Joon. "Yes, but only if you're real quiet."

Only a short time had passed when Skinner entered bay three. Joon stood and gave him a hug. His hand was bandaged, but he didn't have signs of any other injuries. She stared at the white gauze when they broke the embrace.

Skinner followed her gaze. "I broke two fuckin' fingers pulling that damn board off the window. I think that's kinda manly," he said with a cheesy smile. "And I have first-degree burns on the top of my hand." He assessed the bandages on Joon's face and arms. "Looks like I made out way better than you."

"Yeah, the nurse told me I have to keep the wounds clean. Looks like I'll be in the library bathroom every day until this shit heals."

Skinner sat down. "You know, if it wasn't for you, we all would be dead."

"Luck. I woke up in time. That's all."

Skinner wiggled his finger at her. "No, it wasn't all luck. You kept your cool. You made us do all the shit we learned when we were young. It was pretty fuckin' fantastic. Thanks."

Joon flushed. "You're welcome. I didn't do it on purpose though…it just sorta happened. I didn't think it all through, you know?"

"Then I'm grateful for your instincts. Those other ugly bitches better kiss your ass from now on," he joked.

Joon rested her head on the side of Lulu's gurney. "I'm done with them. We've lost everything we had, and when Lulu gets out of here, we won't be staying with the other girls."

"Is that because of me?" Skinner asked.

Joon considered before she answered. "It's because I want to be around people who care. And even if it's only Fipple that's an asshole, the others aren't disagreeing with her. It's not because of you but because I got to see the kind of people they are—one bully and three cowards."

The curtain was pushed to the side and Becky walked into the bay. She was carrying two pillows and two blankets. "Here you go. I thought these would be useful."

"Thank you, Becky," Joon said.

The nurse turned to walk away. "Oh, and I ordered a pizza from a twenty-four-hour joint. It's not the best, but it isn't the worst either. It'll be delivered within an hour. Dr. Becker thought you two might be hungry."

Joon and Skinner settled back into their chairs with the pillows and blankets. Joon focused on the rhythm of Lulu's heartbeat on the monitor until her eyes slowly closed and her body relaxed into the softness of the fresh, comfortable pillow.

Chapter Seventy-Two

It was almost nine the next morning when they moved Lulu from the ER to a regular room. A different nurse, in for the day shift, shook Joon gently to wake her.

"Hey, Joon. The night nurse asked me to wake you when we move your friend. Dr. Becker got her a room. We're going to be moving her up as soon as transport gets here."

Joon stretched and stifled a yawn. "Can I go with her?"

The nurse smiled and nodded. "You bet. We stopped giving her medication, so she'll wake up soon enough, and I'm sure that she'll want to see you."

When transport arrived, Joon grabbed her coat and moved out of the bay. Skinner was standing next to her. She grabbed his hand. "You need to find a place to stay tonight. After you figure it out, come back and tell me where you are, so I have somewhere to go when I leave here later."

Skinner nodded. "Okay, I'll be back." He moved forward and took Joon into his arms. "Everything's gonna be okay. Lulu is going to be fine, and I'll figure something out."

"You better. Otherwise, you're worthless to me," Joon teased.

Skinner put his hand on his hip and flicked his wrist in her direction. "Oh hell, girl. I've been worthless my whole fuckin' life. That ain't nothing new for me."

Joon pulled him into her. "I know you're trying to be funny, but from the look on your face, you believe that shit. You're a good person. It doesn't matter what people think. It took me a long time after I left Aron to find out that I wasn't so bad. I believed everything she told me. I was raised on hate and anger. I thought I was stupid and ugly and a total piece of trash. Look," Joon said, rubbing Skinner's arm. "It doesn't mean I don't have bad days. You know, times when I think that I'm never gonna find a way outta this shit, and on those days, the only thing I got left is hope. My life has been pretty fucked up to this point. I met awesome people on the streets, but I've also been with some evil ones. There are plenty of assholes out there to bring ya down, so you have to raise yourself up as much as you can."

Skinner pushed Joon's hair behind her shoulders. "You're right. I'm gonna get going. Figure out where we're staying tonight." He leaned over and kissed her on the forehead. "Tell Lulu that I'm thinking of her."

Joon followed the transport person to the fourth floor of the children's unit, the place where Dr. Becker had specifically requested for her. Inside the hospital room, Joon stared at Lulu's roommate, a young girl sleeping in the other bed. Once Lulu was settled, Joon plopped down on the padded chair and turned on the television.

"Hi," a small voice said from across the room.

"Hi," Joon said. She stood and walked over to the young girl's bedside.

"My name is Molly. Is that your sister?" she said, pointing to Lulu.

Joon nodded. "Yeah, something like that."

"Why is she here?" Molly asked.

"Our house burned down last night. Lulu has some burns, but she's here because she had a hard time breathing." Joon took in the girl's almost-translucent skin and the dark circles under her eyes. "Why are you here?"

"I'm always at the doctor or in the hospital. I've been sick for a lot of years. I have a bunch of different things wrong with me. Right now, my kidneys aren't working the way they should, so the doctor decided to keep me here."

"Oh. Have you been sick since you were born?"

Molly shook her head. "It all started after I turned eight. All of a sudden, I was sick all the time. I've had surgeries and take lots of different medicine, but the doctors can't figure out what's wrong with me. Sometimes, I even feel good, but then a few days later, I start feeling crappy again."

"That sounds awful. I'm really sorry that you don't feel good." Joon moved at the sound of Lulu waking and rushed to be at her side. "Hey, Lulu. It's about time you woke up."

Lulu smiled weakly. "What happened?"

"Remember the house caught on fire?"

Lulu grimaced. "Oh yeah. What the hell died in my mouth?"

Joon laughed and relief washed over her. "I think it's from the smoke you breathed in."

"Can you get me a drink?"

Joon filled a cup with water from the pitcher on Lulu's table. "Drink slow." She pressed the red call button for the nurse.

A few minutes later, the nurse came into the room. "Well, hello, Lulu. I'm glad to see you're awake. How do you feel?"

"My throat is sore and my body hurts. Other than that, I can't stand the smell of smoke in my hair." Lulu looked Joon up and down. "And her hair too."

Joon smiled. "I'm sure it's my clothes too. As soon as I go back to the penthouse, I'll change and shower, Princess Lulu."

The nurse checked Lulu's vital signs and left the room. She came back within ten minutes carrying several towels and two pairs of clean scrubs. She sat everything on one of the empty chairs and turned to Joon. "There's a shower in the bathroom. You go first and then I'll help Lulu."

Joon's mouth dropped open. "Me?"

The nurse nodded. "You need a shower, right? I understand you've been here all night. So go on and do your thing. I can help you rebandage your arms and face when you come out."

Later on, cleaned and feeling better, Joon settled on the bed next to Lulu, and the girls curled up together.

Lulu grabbed Joon's hand. "What happened to the others?"

"Everyone got out. We all got burned and breathed in a lot of smoke, but you're the only one they admitted." Joon paused. "I met Dr. Becker in the emergency room."

Lulu brightened. "What did he say?"

"Only that he wanted to admit you."

"I love Dr. Becker," Lulu said.

Molly used the button to raise the bed. "Dr. Becker is my doctor too."

Lulu looked over at the young girl and gave her a smile. "Oh yeah? Then you're as lucky as I am."

Molly smiled and nodded. "I'm Molly and you're Lulu."

"I am," Lulu said. "How long have you been here?"

Molly counted on her fingers. "Six days so far. I usually stay for at least a week or two."

Joon sat up and swung her feet over the edge of the bed. "That sucks. How often are you here?"

"Whenever I get so sick that Mama doesn't know what to do. She tries to take care of me at home 'cause she thinks I hate being in the hospital, but I don't mind it so much."

Joon looked at Lulu and raised her eyebrows, then turned back to Molly. "I don't get that. Being sick is annoying."

Molly raised the back of her bed a little more and leaned toward Joon. "Being sick is awful. But in the hospital, I get to eat things that I can't have at home. When Mama isn't around, the nurses give me things like water ice and ice cream. Mama thinks that stuff is bad for me, so I almost never get sweets or anything that she doesn't make from scratch."

Joon lay back next to Lulu, who was drifting off to sleep. "Yeah, that makes sense. Although having home-cooked food sounds really good to me."

Molly leaned back into her pillows. "That's because you never ate Mama's cooking."

As the morning melted into the afternoon, Joon dozed on and off, exhausted from the night before. Around dinnertime, Skinner showed up.

"Hey," he sang as he walked into the room.

Joon stood and gave him a hug. "She's sleeping. Let's get going. I don't want to bother her. Did you find us a place?"

Skinner looked down at the floor. "I found us a way to get through the night."

Joon's belly swirled. She could see the concern in Skinner's eyes and hoped wherever they were going would be safe.

Chapter Seventy-Three

When they left the hospital, Joon followed Skinner to Suburban Station.

Joon grabbed Skinner's arm. "What are we doing here?"

"The station never closes. It's warm, and I spent most of the day inside and nobody bothered me. There are a lot of homeless spread throughout the place. It ain't the greatest thing, but its way better than being outside. And," he said, taking a bow, "there are bathrooms in there, thank you very much."

Joon slipped her arm through his. "I'm impressed. You did real good for a clueless newbie."

"Who are you calling clueless? I'm becoming a real veteran in living this shitty life."

Once inside the station, Joon and Skinner walked until they found an empty bench. Joon sat down with a thud. "I just realized we don't have shit. No blankets, no clothes—we are the most pathetic homeless people I've ever seen."

Skinner gave her a sheepish smile. "I thought about that too. Tomorrow, we'll go into the parking garage at the hospital and take a look around in those cars. We can break into a few and get some of the stuff we need."

Joon lay down on the bench and put her head in Skinner's lap. "That's brilliant. What are we gonna do about tonight though?"

"We're gonna curl up on this bench together and keep each other warm. So get up and let me lie down too, Queen Joon," he said, brushing his hand softly over the top of her head. When the two were spooning on the bench, Skinner cleared his throat. "When will Lulu get released?"

Joon shrugged. "Don't know yet. The doctor didn't come in today. He'll probably stop and see her tonight."

"All right. Good. You know, we gotta get some money together," Skinner said.

Joon adjusted on the bench. "I have some money. It's the only thing I didn't lose 'cause I keep it on me at all times."

"How much you got?"

Joon closed her eyes. "Thirty-seven bucks. I've been saving it for a while. It ain't enough to help us much, but it'll get us started. Maybe we can find some temporary work tomorrow."

Skinner laughed. "Yeah, like selling my body on the streets."

"Maybe," Joon remarked.

Skinner pulled her shoulder down so he can look into her face. "What do you mean, maybe? We can't do that. I can't do that, and you certainly can't either. I was joking."

Joon pulled her shoulder out of his grip and refused to look at him. "I wasn't. It's not like I never had to do it before."

"What are you saying, Joon? You were a hooker?"

"Yeah, I was a hooker. It wasn't by choice…I mean, they wouldn't let me leave."

Skinner ran his hand through his hair. "Who wouldn't let you leave?"

"It doesn't matter. The point is, we gotta do what we gotta do. It's freezing cold, we don't have anything left, and we gotta get through this winter."

"I'm not comfortable with you doing that."

"I never asked you to be," she said. "My body, my choice. We'll see how things go. All right? Now, can we get some sleep? I have a feeling there'll be a lot more people here as it gets later, so we should sleep now, while we can."

Several minutes later, Joon's breathing became steady as she fell asleep and dreamed of a life where she had all the things she wanted.

Skinner stayed awake, too stunned by what Joon had said. He'd never imagined that she had gone through something so dreadful, and his heart ached with images of her being forced to have sex.

Chapter Seventy-Four

———————◼———————

Lulu stayed in the hospital for three more nights, and Joon remained by her side during the day while Skinner begged for money. He managed to get two manual labor jobs at a small hardware store; the owner paid him twenty dollars a job to move a wood pile and stock shelves. With almost fifty dollars in his pocket, Skinner felt like the threesome could get a fresh start. Skinner had broken into five cars, and they now had three blankets, a box of tissues, two sweatshirts, a pair of sunglasses, and a few hand tools. He had also taken a large canvas bag from one of the cars to carry it all in. One night, back in Suburban Station, Skinner showed Joon the things he'd acquired and the two shared a sense of comfort.

"I feel like we lose all of our humanity living on the streets. It's weird how having a few things makes me feel like I'm human again," Joon shared. "When I lived at Aron's house, I didn't have anything, not even food or water when I wanted it. It makes these *things* feel more important." She picked up a blanket and wrapped it around her shoulders. "See? Like this. To be able to wrap myself in this blanket is a treat, you know? People who have things probably don't appreciate these little things, things that make us comfortable…things that make us feel like we exist."

"I know," Skinner agreed. "I know it isn't right to steal from people, but I'm glad I did it. At least it makes us both feel better."

On the morning of Lulu's release, Joon went to her hospital room.

"Can you leave now?" she asked Lulu.

"Nah. I have to wait for Dr. Becker to come see me. Then he'll let me go," she explained.

"I wish you weren't leaving," Molly said. "I like having you two around."

299

Joon walked over to the young girl's bed. "Yeah, it was fun being around you too. Your mom is kinda weird, but you're a cool kid."

"My mama is a helicopter—she hovers." Molly thought for a moment. "I need to ask you a favor."

Joon looked at her questioningly. "Sure. What do you need?"

Molly reached under her pillow. "I want you to keep this for me," she said, producing a small diary and thrusting it at Joon. "If anything happens to me, I need you to give it to my dad. It has all of my last wishes."

Joon gave her a curious look.

"I can't give it to my mama because she won't talk about me dying. My daddy's a real nice person, and he works really hard so that me, my mom, and my little sister are taken care of. He would want to know my wishes. You know, like who should have my stuff."

Joon took the small diary from Molly. "How will I know if anything happens to you? We'll probably never see each other again once Lulu gets out today."

"You can ask Dr. Becker. He'll know."

"What if he doesn't?" Joon said, feeling uncomfortable with the enormous responsibility.

"If he doesn't, then you can read it. My address is written on the inside cover."

Joon held the diary against her heart. "Fine. But I can't promise that I won't fuck this up." She clapped her hand over her mouth. "Sorry. I didn't mean to curse."

Molly giggled. "It's okay. Sometimes I curse in my head, like when I can't have candy." She paused for a moment looking at the older girl. "Joon?"

"Yeah."

"Thanks for doing this for me. I don't have any friends, and there's no one else I would trust with my diary."

Joon gave her a dazzling smile. "So you decided to trust someone you've known for less than a week."

"Yeah, I did. I can tell that you do things to help people and that you'll help me *if* the time comes."

Joon felt a warmth spreading in her chest—like Lulu had said, maybe it was clear to people that Joon was a good egg. "Okay. Sure."

"You promise to keep it safe and not lose it?"

Joon brushed Molly's arm. "I promise."

"And, you can't read it. Okay? It's for my dad."

"Yep, got it."

"Unless you have to read it, like I said before."

"Yep, I got that too."

She smiled. "Thank you, Joon."

"You're welcome." Joon leaned over the bed and kissed the girl's forehead. "You're gonna get better. I just know it."

Molly smiled, and her heart filled with hope. "Do you think so?"

"Yeah, I do," Joon said.

Just as the two were finishing their conversation, Dr. Becker walked into the room.

"I see you've enjoyed Joon's and Lulu's company," Dr. Becker said to Molly.

"Yeah, they're great," she said.

Dr. Becker made his way to the other side of the room, where Lulu was lying with her eyes closed. He put his hand on her foot. "How are you doing today?"

Lulu opened her eyes and gave him a faint smile. "I'm okay. I'm tired, but ready to get outta here. You know how much I hate hospitals."

"Yeah, yeah, I know. I wanted to talk to you about your test results," he said, pulling a chair next to her bed.

Joon was already sitting in the other chair across from him, and Dr. Becker looked at Lulu, then at Joon.

"It's fine. You can say whatever in front of her. She'll get it outta me anyway," Lulu joked.

"Okay. Well, your results show that your remaining kidney is failing. We'll need to increase your dialysis treatments, and I'd like to keep you overnight for observation each time."

"Aw, man. Come on, Dr. Becker. You made me get on insurance from the state and you talked me into coming for dialysis every three months, now this?"

Dr. Becker nodded. "Your condition has worsened. You're on the organ donor list, and I'd feel better if we took more aggressive steps to keep you stable."

"What does that mean? She's on the organ donor list?" Joon interrupted.

Dr. Becker looked into Joon's eyes. "We put Lulu on the list for a kidney donation several months ago. The kidney she has left is failing. We are hoping to find a donor that will be a match for her soon."

Joon came out of her chair and grasped the bed rail tightly. "I'll give her one of my kidneys," she said firmly.

"We'd have to see if you're a match. How old are you, Joon?"

Joon pushed hair away from her face. "Eighteen," she lied.

"You'd have to be able to prove you're eighteen. Can you do that?"

Joon shook her head. "I left home without anything. Just test me, okay? Please." She stared at the doctor without blinking. "I'm not fucking around. You're a doctor. We need you to figure something out."

"Okay," he conceded. "I'll order a blood test. I'll see if I can get the kidney organization to pay for it. If not, I'll figure out how to get it taken care of."

"Thank you," Joon said.

He stood and patted Joon's shoulder. "Go on and sit back down." The doctor turned back to Lulu. "You're in end-stage kidney failure. It's serious this time, Lulu."

Lulu glanced at Joon but diverted her eyes quickly.

Joon took Lulu's hand. "You knew. You knew that you were getting worse. That's why you've been so tired and cold all the time. Why didn't you tell me?"

"Because I want to live as normally as I can. I didn't want you to worry about me."

Joon looked back at the doctor. "What do we do now?"

"We make sure that Ms. Lulu comes in for every treatment and stays overnight for observation. In the meantime, I'll contact the National Kidney Foundation and we'll have your blood tested." He turned back to Lulu. "Given how young you are and that your condition has worsened, I'll request to have you moved up on the list."

Tears slid down Joon's face. She looked at Lulu. "Please. You have to do everything he says. You will, right?"

Lulu leaned forward and hugged Joon. "Sure. I'll do it. You don't need to worry. I'm gonna be fine."

Joon let her head fall back and she closed her eyes. "Yeah, you have to be and I'm gonna take good care of you."

Later in the day, when Lulu was released from the hospital, Skinner joined them.

"I was thinking that we could rent something for the night," he said, looking at the other two for approval. "I mean, Lulu just got outta the hospital, and I have fifty bucks in my pocket. What do you say?"

Joon and Lulu stared at him for a moment.

Finally, Joon threw her hands up in the air. "Hell yeah."

Chapter Seventy-Five

"Where are we gonna get a room though?" Joon asked. Skinner waved his hands through the air above his head. "Abracadabra, give us a room."

Joon stopped and put her hands on her hips. "I'm serious, Skinner. If we don't know where we're going, we should head to Suburban Station. I'm worried about Lulu getting too cold."

"Helloooo?" Lulu said. "I'm standing right here. I can hear you and I don't need you worrying about me. I'll be fine. Don't be so serious all the time."

"Ha! I have to worry about you 'cause you don't tell me everything," Joon huffed. She turned back to Skinner. "Well?"

"Well, I met this guy today, and he told me about a woman who rents rooms in her house. I went over there and paid for tonight."

"Who is this woman?" Joon asked.

"Don't know. Just some woman who wants to make money. She charges twenty bucks a night. She doesn't keep the heat real high, so it's sorta cold in there, but we won't freeze. Plus, there's a bed we can all cram into. It even has nasty sheets and an old quilt on top."

"You sure know how to impress the girls," Joon teased.

"Girls? Let me tell you about the guy who told me about this place. He's so damn hot. He has thick, black hair and dreamy, green eyes. His name is Gunther," he said, grinning.

"Gunther?" Joon laughed.

"Yeah, his name's Gunther. Now shut up and listen. *Gunther* is real tall and lean, and he's got a small waist and broad shoulders, and wait until you get a look at his ass. *And* I think he's got a crush on me."

Joon laughed. "Oh really? How do you know he's gay?"

Skinner lifted his chin and shrugged his shoulders. "The same way you know when a guy is coming on to you. It's something you just feel. Anyway, he's really good-looking. Oh. My. God. He was so nice to me. He shared his soft pretzel and soda. Now if that ain't a crush, I don't know what is."

Lulu laced her arm through Joon's. "I think it's great you met someone. Just be careful you don't get hurt."

Joon tilted her head and her eyes were twinkling with mischief. "Did you tell him about us?"

"Um, duh. I told him everything—that you can be bitches and you both smell."

Joon smacked Skinner's arm. "Very funny. How did he end up out here?"

"He lived with his mom and sister. One day when he wasn't home, someone broke into their apartment and murdered them. He didn't have anybody or anywhere else to go. He's been living on the streets since he was fifteen."

Lulu gasped. "That's really messed up."

Skinner nodded. "At first, I was nervous when he told me his family story. But then as we got to talking, I realized he's just a normal dude. I told him all about what happened to me and how I ended up on the streets. When I finished, he was actually crying."

Joon wrapped her arms around herself as the wind whipped through her clothing. "We're really happy for you, but its freezing. How far is this place?"

"Just a few more blocks."

When they arrived at the three-story row home, they rang the doorbell and anxiously waited to be let in from the cold.

When the door finally opened, Skinner took charge. "Hi, Mallory. This is Joon and Lulu."

The lady who had opened the door appeared to be in her upper fifties. She was fifty pounds overweight and wore tight pants and a T-shirt two sizes too small. Her brown hair was stringy and hung around her large, bloodshot eyes. She looked over the girls and stepped aside so they could all enter.

Mallory crossed her arms over her chest and leaned back. "Let me be real clear since you're all new here. I don't take no shit. You smoke, do drugs, or sell sex in my house, and you're outta here. I need my money every morning if ya expect to leave your stuff in the room. Every day you wanna shower, I need two bucks a person. If I find out you stole a shower, I'll kick your asses out in the middle of the night if I have to. How long you plan on staying?"

"We'll probably stay here tomorrow night too," Skinner said, his voice shaky.

"Then I need another twenty bucks in the morning. Another thing: don't go in my kitchen, 'cause it's my kitchen. I'm renting you a room with a bed. That's it. Nothing else is included. If I catch ya in my kitchen or touching any of my stuff, I'll kick your asses out in the middle of the night if I have to. You don't want to test me on any of this, trust me. Another thing: no music, no loud talking or laughing after ten at night. I go to bed and I don't like to be woken up. If you disturb me when I'm sleeping, I can't be held responsible for what I'll do to you. I like my routine and none of you little shit stains will fuck with it. If you break any of the rules, I'll kick your asses out in the middle of the night if I have to."

Mallory tapped her index finger on her forehead. "Hm, let me think, did I cover everything?" she said to herself. "Oh right. If you need to use the shitter to take a piss, I require three pisses before a flush, so do your damnedest to all piss at the same time. There ain't no toilet paper in the bathroom, so you better buy your own if you expect to wipe your ass. If you clog my toilet, I'll shove your fucking arm down there to plunge it. You got any questions?"

The three of them looked at each other, and Skinner answered, "No. I think that was pretty clear."

"Good. Then go ahead and show your...what are these girls to you anyway?"

Skinner stood straighter. "Oh, this is my sister, Lulu, and our cousin, Joon."

"Lulu and Joon," Mallory said aloud. "What kind of names are those?" She held up her hand to silence them before they could think about answering. "Never mind. I don't give a shit. Go show them the room and get outta my way."

Skinner led the girls up to the third floor and opened the door of the last room on the right. The room had a yellow haze from a small lamp sitting on the floor. The only furniture was a queen-size bed. The quilt on the bed lay crooked, and the thin pillows were bare, revealing the drool stains from other occupants. The only window had been covered with newspaper.

The three laid across the bed. Joon covered her eyes with one hand. "That lady is crazy. I'm not sure we can make it here one night without breaking a rule."

Skinner rolled over on his side and propped his head in his hand. "Gunther said Mallory can be a bitch, but as long as we follow the rules, we'll be fine."

"Did you see how big her boobs were?" Lulu asked and giggled.

"I know," Joon jumped in. "I couldn't tell where her boobs stopped and her stomach started. She's a bruiser. I wouldn't mess with her."

"Yeah," Lulu said. "Did you see the skull tattoo on her arm?"

"I did, right above the knife dripping with blood," Joon added. "Anyway, where's Gunther? Is he here? We wanna meet him."

Skinner stood quickly, tucked in his shirt, and fluffed his hair. "He's staying across the hall. I'll go see if he's in his room."

"Go get 'em, lover boy," Joon teased.

"Listen, honey, you can't rush love. Besides, I'm not sure I like him yet."

Joon rolled her eyes as Skinner pulled the door shut behind him.

A few minutes later, Skinner came back into the bedroom with Gunther. He was as good-looking as Skinner had said. Joon studied the new boy closely for signs he liked Skinner, and sure enough, when Gunther spoke, he'd put his hand on Skinner and kept smiling and laughing a lot.

After a while, Lulu curled up on the bed, and Joon pulled the worn quilt over her. "We gotta get some sleep," Joon said, trying to let Gunther know it was time for him to go. "Lulu just got out of the hospital today, and the doctor said she needs to rest."

Gunther looked at Skinner and raised his eyebrows. "Do you wanna come across the hall for a while? We can play cards."

Skinner nodded a bit too enthusiastically. "Yeah, that sounds great." He pranced to the door and turned back to Joon. "I'll be back later," he said.

She smiled and nodded. After the boys were gone, she turned to Lulu. "I hope Skinner found a boyfriend. He wants intimacy so bad I think he can taste it."

Lulu winked at her friend. "What about you? Don't you want to find love?"

"I have found love; I love you like a sister. Besides, all I want is stability and happiness."

Lulu lay back on the bed, took Joon's hand in her own, and within minutes, was sleeping. Joon lay awake for most of the night, worried sick about her friend and facing the fact that she may have been losing Skinner to the new boy.

Chapter Seventy-Six

On their last night at Mallory's house, Joon invited Skinner to take a walk around the block.

"So you really like Gunther?"

Skinner smiled. "I like him a lot."

"I noticed. You spent both nights in his room." Joon glanced at her friend out of the side of her eye. "We're leaving here tomorrow morning. Do you think you're coming with us or going with Gunther?"

He sighed deeply before responding. "I guess I'm gonna go with Gunther. Listen, I don't know if him and me are gonna work out," he said, rushing to finish, "but I have to give it a try. Gunther's a good man, and he's really smart."

"Sounds serious already."

Skinner let out a long breath. "It's not like I love him or anything, but I'm real damn close. I adore being with him. The past couple of days have been a blast. Gunther is so much fun to be around. I have an idea though. What if you and Lulu come with us? We can all find a place together."

Joon shook her head slightly. "I appreciate the offer, but it will be too hard to find a place for four people. I think we go our own way, but we should make a plan to meet up somewhere once a week. That way we can stay close."

Skinner lowered his head, and his long hair fell over his face. "I'm sorry, Joon. I didn't expect to meet anyone. I know you have a lot on your mind with Lulu being sick and all. I feel like a total asshole, abandoning you."

Joon thought about being separated from Skinner and shuddered as gloominess swept over her. "It's okay. We'll be fine. Lulu is going to do great. She has to go for dialysis more often to make her better. And it's almost spring. The weather will be getting warmer, and then we'll have more options."

Joon and Lulu decided to stay close to Mallory's house. It was still in the city, but it was more residential, with lots of apartment buildings.

"Where are we going?" Lulu asked as they walked.

"You see those three buildings down the way?" Joon said, pointing. "Well, Gunther told Skinner they're apartment complexes. They have open hallways to access their apartment from the inside. We're gonna sleep in those hallways for a while."

"You think we're gonna get away with that?"

"Sure. If we go in when most people are either in bed, or watching television for the night, no one will notice us. We'll have to get out early in the morning though. During the day, we can spend time at Suburban Station or the library."

"You've thought of everything," Lulu remarked.

"I'm worried about you. Dr. Becker is worried about you too."

Lulu shook her head a bit. "I get it. I know that you're worried, but this is why I didn't tell you in the first place. Unless I get a new kidney, I can die. I knew that all along. I wanna live what life I have left the best that I can." Lulu stopped walking and took both of Joon's hands in her own. "I've never been close to anyone since my grandmom died. You're the only one. I need you to relax about my health so that it doesn't make me worry. Okay?"

"Okay. But only if you promise that if you start to feel bad, you'll tell me, so we go back to the hospital. Besides, my blood test will be back soon, and then I can give you one of my kidneys."

"I hope you're a match, but if not, Dr. Becker will figure something out."

Over the next week, Joon and Lulu slept in the hallways of various apartment buildings.

One morning, Joon turned to Lulu. "We're not freezing to death in the hallways, but we need to camp out somewhere during the day. We need a place to store our shit, so we don't have to carry it around all the time. I know this guy in South Philly. His name is Tony and he works at a bakery. We could go see him. Maybe he knows where we could squat."

As they stepped through the doors of the bakery later that morning, the aroma of the homemade cakes, cookies, and pies hit them in the face.

They both breathed in deeply. Joon walked up to the woman behind the counter and said casually, "Hi, Donata. Is Tony here?"

"Where the hell have you been?" the woman asked, a broad smile on her face. "It's been too long since I set eyes on you."

Joon tilted her head and gave the woman a sweet smile. "I know. I've been out of town for a couple of years. It's good to be back though."

"Well, it's good to see you again. You wait here and I'll get Tony."

When Donata returned, Tony was right behind her, and he rushed at Joon, so they could hug.

Joon pulled back a little and looked at him. "We didn't know where else to go. I thought maybe you would know of some place we can stay for a while...just until winter is over."

"Who's your friend?"

"Oh, sorry. This is Lulu. We met several months back. She's cool though."

"Nice to meet ya," Tony said, extending his hand. "I'd love to help ya's out, but I'm still staying in North Philly. I know there's an abandoned warehouse on the nine-hundred block of Poplar Street. A place called the Quaker Storage Building. Some department store used it for storage a long time ago. I ain't never been there myself, but I heard about it. People stay there in the winter. It ain't too far and is probably worth going over there to check it out. Where were you staying before now?"

"We were staying in an abandoned house. It caught on fire and we lost everything."

"Jesus. That's a lot to go through. Hey, look," Tony said and turned to Donata. "Can we get these two a bag of goodies to go?"

Donata twisted the ring on her finger. She looked up at the girls with a heavy heart that shone through in her gaze. "I'm sorry things are so bad for you girls. I'll keep you two in my prayers." Then she grabbed a paper bag and filled it with pastries, cookies, and bread.

Before leaving the bakery, Joon gave Tony a hug. "Thank you, Tony. I would be dead right now if it weren't for you," she whispered.

"I'm always around if you need me," Tony whispered back.

As the girls went back out to the cold, Joon thought about Tony's offer and it comforted her to know there was someone willing and able to protect her.

Chapter Seventy-Seven

T he girls spent most of the day at Suburban Station, begging for money. Just before dusk, they walked to the Quaker Storage Building. The dirt-caked brick building was many stories tall, and there was a fair number of windows that remained intact on the upper floors. Several of the lower-level windows were boarded up or smashed out, leaving gaping holes in the building's façade. The girls circled the structure until they came to an open entrance. They entered slowly, being hypervigilant as they walked into a large, open room. Several homeless groups were camped out in different places on the first floor.

"Do you smell all the pot in this place?"

Lulu nodded and held her nose. "I also smell the piss and shit."

"Come on," Joon said. "Let's go upstairs. Maybe there're fewer people up there."

When the girls reached the second floor of the building, they found more groups. As they turned to walk back to the stairs, to check out the third floor, a girl ran toward them yelling.

"Hey, you can't go upstairs," she said.

Joon's eyes narrowed as she looked at the young teen. "Why not?"

"A lot of criminals and assholes stay on the higher floors. We have like an unspoken rule that us regular homeless people keep to the first and second floors. The dickheads on the higher floors don't bother us, and we don't bother them."

Joon flipped her hair over her shoulder. "How do we know you're not lying?"

The teen scoffed. "You don't. Look, my name is Scarlet. My group is over there in the corner. If you wanna stay here, you should find a group. It's safer than being by yourselves. I'm trying to help, but you can do what you want. Just don't say I didn't warn you."

Joon and Lulu watched as Scarlet went back to her group.

"What do you think?" Joon asked.

"I think we should probably go hang with Scarlet and her group." Lulu looked around the room. "It's not like we have a better option. And if she's right about the people on the upper floors, we need to be protected. Two girls on their own make an easy target."

"All right, but here's the deal. If they're anything like Fipple and the girls we just got rid of, we find another group. Okay?"

Lulu put her arm over Joon's shoulder. "Okay, whatever you say, boss. You know, technically, I should be the boss because I'm older than you."

Joon rolled her eyes. "Whatever. I'm the boss because I have the bigger mouth. Besides, I'm taking care of you, remember?"

The girls approached the group slowly. Once they were in their space, the others all turned to stare at them.

Joon stepped forward. "So I'm Joon, and this is Lulu. We thought you might let us join your group."

Scarlet smiled brightly. "They were gonna go upstairs, and I stopped them. Told 'em they could stay with us."

A boy stood and walked over to them. "I'm Rick. You're welcome to stay as long as you agree to our laws. We share our beer, cigarettes, and pot. We all gotta bring in food or money. If any one of us is in trouble with another group in the building, we all fight. No stealing or fighting within our group. That's about it."

Joon glanced at Lulu to show solidarity, but the rules made sense, so she quickly nodded. "That's fine with us." She held out what was left of the bag of baked goods Donata had given them. "We got these this morning."

Rick reached out, took the bag from her, and glanced in it. "This is great. Thanks."

The two joined the group, and once introductions were done, they all settled into their spot. Most of them were between fifteen and seventeen-years-old, and many had been on the streets for several years.

Joon and Lulu lay together, attempting to generate body heat under the blankets that Skinner had given them. In the morning, Joon woke with stiff muscles. She pushed Lulu's hair from her face and looked at her friend's pale skin and the deep circles under her eyes. "How do you feel?"

Lulu's teeth chattered. "Like a fucking popsicle."

"Yeah, me too. Today we gotta get some better gear."

"Fine," Lulu said. "We'll rob a bank and buy everything we need." She smiled a bit ruefully.

Joon gave her a dry look before she started getting up. "Let's get moving. It'll help warm us up."

As the girls left the warehouse, Lulu asked, "Where are we going today?"

"I'm not sure. I figured we'd go to the library. Warm up a little. It'll give us time to think."

They walked for a few minutes before Lulu broke the silence. "Joon, sometimes I get tired of having nowhere to go."

Joon glanced at her friend. "I know. It makes me feel lost. I don't let myself think about it too much, but when I do, I feel like shit. I think about what life would have been like if my parents hadn't died, and then I get pissed off. I didn't do anything to deserve this shit and neither did you."

Lulu pulled her coat collar up. "The bright side is we have each other."

Joon looked at her friend again, a bit more intensely this time. "You and me are lucky that we met. I...never mind."

"What? What else were you gonna say?"

Joon wiped a stray tear from her cheek. "I'm worried about you. About you being sick. What if I can't take care of you? What if something bad happens?"

"I'm going to be fine. I don't want you to worry about me. You and me will always be together, even when we're old and gray and walking with canes."

Joon wanted to believe her, but she didn't know how to have hope about this. In place of optimism, Joon had learned how to retreat from her dark reality and focus inward, to maintain her sanity.

She pulled the door to the library open, and the warm air hit them like a soft summer breeze. "I don't think about what my life is gonna be like when I'm older. I've tried," Joon said, "but I can't see anything but all the nothingness I have now."

Lulu sat at the nearest table and took several deep breaths, trying to stabilize her breathing. "You have to think about where you'll be when you grow up."

Joon laid her head on the table as she sat across from Lulu. "I don't know how. Every day I live on the streets, all I can think about is how I'm going to eat or stay warm or get clean. Regular people don't see us, ya know? They only see dirty people who must've done something wrong. People like Aron get to go on with their lives, and I get to live like an animal. I could've stayed at Aron's house, and she probably would have killed me. The system failed me. People failed me. But what really bothers me is that I failed myself."

"How did you fail yourself?"

Joon inhaled deeply and sat up. "Because when I ran away from Aron, I left so I could have a better life. Somewhere along the way, I lost focus on getting to something better. Instead, I've done things I'm ashamed of, I live minute to minute. I don't even own a blanket to keep me warm enough at night, and I have no clear way of getting out of this. That's how I failed myself."

Lulu folded her hands on the table in front of her and sat up straight. "Everything you're saying is true. But you need to remember that you were just a kid when you got here…you're still a kid. I see it differently. It is people and society who have let you down. You couldn't turn to the system because they'd already fucked you over and left you with that whore, Aron. You couldn't turn to other kids, because look how Quinn betrayed you. Even Fipple was a total bitch to us. I think you need to know what you wanna do or what you wanna be and then figure out how to get there. I always wanted to be a nurse. So, to do that, I gotta graduate high school and go to college. Even though I don't know how I'll do it, I just gotta start. I told you before I'm gonna take the GED. As soon as the weather warms up, I'm gonna figure out how to do that. I'm nineteen. Maybe the government will give me money, so I can rent a cheap place, and then you can come and live there with me. The point is, nobody's gonna hand us anything—if we want something, we gotta work through all the stuff needed to get it."

"You make it sound so different. You have a way of taking awful things, like your kidney problem, and being so sure that everything will work out the way it's supposed to. I don't think like that. I wish I did. I'd probably be happier."

Lulu leaned on her elbows. "Someday, you're gonna figure it out. You'll do something and you're gonna know that you're a good person, someone who other people will look up to."

Joon shook her head. "I think you're crazy, but whatever. Let's hit the bathrooms and clean up."

As Joon stood over the sink in the library bathroom, she watched as the flesh on her face started to appear from under the mask of dirt. It always amazed her how dirty she could get, to where she looked like she was someone different. As the new face emerged, Joon hoped that some-day a face she could be proud of would look back at her from the mirror.

Chapter Seventy-Eight

———————————— ■ ————————————

The following week, Joon accompanied Lulu for her first overnight dialysis treatment.

When they arrived at the hospital, the nurse let Lulu take a hot shower before getting into her gown. Once in bed, she was covered with warm blankets, and two needles were inserted into the tube implanted under her forearm. Joon, who had reclined in the leather lounge chair next to the bed, watched her friend intently. After what seemed like an agonizingly long time, the dialysis machine was started, and the girls watched television until they both feel asleep.

In the morning, Lulu was released with medication she had to take every day. Before they left, Dr. Becker stopped in to see her and to confirm things they'd covered in their previous conversation. Then he added, "You'll need to have dialysis three nights a week."

"No way, Dr. Becker. I don't wanna be here that much," Lulu said, tears running down her cheeks. "If I'm in here, then I ain't living."

Dr. Becker gave Lulu a long, serious look. "I understand that this is something you may not want to do. Right now, I'm trying to save your life so that you *can* live. Haven't I done everything to make you comfortable?" He paused and glanced at Joon, who stared at him wide eyed. "I would encourage you to look at this like a place for you and Joon to sleep three nights a week. Sometimes it's how we view things that makes all the difference."

Lulu was still crying, but she looked over at Joon, who smiled weakly and nodded. "Are you sure?" Lulu asked the doctor. "Hospitals kill people."

Dr. Becker put both hands over his heart. "Thanks, Lulu. Now that really hurts."

Lulu let out a nervous giggle that turned into a belly laugh and ended in deep sobs. Joon leaned into the bed and held her friend until the crying subsided.

"It's okay," Joon told her. "Dr. Becker is right. We need to look at this like a gift. It's going to help you feel better, and as a bonus, we have a warm, dry, safe place to sleep three nights a week."

Lulu hugged Joon tighter and looked up at Dr. Becker. "Fine. I'll do it, but only because Joon agrees."

Dr. Becker stood and smiled. "Good. I'm happy that's settled."

Lulu grabbed Dr. Becker's arm. "One more thing though. You gotta tell these nurses to let Joon take a shower 'cause she smells like shit."

"Hey, I don't smell."

"Um, yeah, you do. You smell really bad."

The two girls laughed.

"Done," Dr. Becker said, chuckling with them.

"Dr. Becker?" Joon said. "Can Lulu take one of my kidneys?"

Dr. Becker's eyes darkened. "I'm sorry, Joon. You weren't a match."

Her heart felt like it stopped beating, but she regrouped quickly. "We have some other friends. Can they get tested too?"

"Sure. We can do that," Dr. Becker said.

In spite of the news, when Joon and Lulu left the hospital later that morning, they were in good spirits. Lulu was feeling better than she had in a while.

"For the first time, I think in my whole life, I have something to believe in," Joon said.

"Oh yeah? What?"

"That you're gonna get better."

Chapter Seventy-Nine

Joon's nights at the hospital became a much-needed distraction from her life in the abandoned warehouse. She was grateful that she could take a shower regularly. After a month of showers three days a week, even the black around her fingernails faded.

When they weren't in the hospital, Joon spent time at night trying to talk the other teens and adults in the warehouse into getting tested to donate a kidney. She was desperately trying to find a match for Lulu. Several had agreed, but by the middle of summer, there still wasn't a viable kidney donor. Skinner and Gunther had been tested and, not being a match, tried get others to be tested, but for many homeless, jeopardizing their health was enough to keep them from helping.

As the months wore on, Joon recognized that Lulu was declining. She had a difficult time walking, which made moving around the city nearly impossible, and she had more bad days than good ones. The skin around her eyes swelled to where she became unrecognizable. Her feet filled with so much fluid she could no longer wear shoes. Joon was forced to buy her men's slippers from the Salvation Army store. The sick girl was plagued with nausea and vomiting, and Joon spent whatever money she had trying to make Lulu comfortable, but she never felt like it was enough. In the warehouse, the others in their group became protective of Lulu, always making sure someone stayed with her when Joon had to be out on the streets, finding food or money.

One night in late August, Joon returned to the warehouse to find the group crowded around Lulu. She rushed over to see what was happening, and in the middle of the circle of kids, she found Lulu sleeping on her back, her breath rattling around in her chest.

"What happened?" Joon shrieked.

Scarlet spoke first. "We were hanging out like normal and Lulu was lying there. She was even talking a little. Then she sat straight up, and it was like she couldn't breathe." Scarlett rubbed the back of her neck. "Her eyes were bulging, and her lips turned purple. We were all freaked out 'cause we didn't know what to do, so we helped her lie back down." Joon started pacing, and Scarlett took a few steps away. "Rick kept telling her to breathe in and out. He did it for a long time, until she calmed down and could breathe normal again. Then she just fell asleep, and we've been watching her. It scared the shit outta all of us."

Rick was sitting next to Lulu, and he looked up at Joon. "I'm not sure we can handle this, Joon. We're not doctors. You know...we all talked about it, what would we do if she dies here?"

"Shut up!" Joon screamed. "She isn't dying. Okay? Lulu's just going through a hard time right now. But she isn't dying." She looked into the faces of their new friends around the circle. They looked sad, but no one would meet her eyes. Joon's adrenaline was pumping through her veins as she demanded, "What are you saying? Are you kicking us out of the group 'cause Lulu's sick?"

Rick's mouth turned downward. "We're really sorry, Joon. But Lulu has been getting worse for weeks now. We all see it even though you can't. None of us knows how to handle this, and we all agreed it would be better for Lulu if she was somewhere more, you know, comfortable."

Joon put her hands on her hips. "No! What you mean is you all would be more comfortable if we weren't here." She looked at Scarlet for support, but the girl turned away from her.

Joon was so angry that her tears seemed to have been released by a faucet. "Fine! I need a little time to figure out where to take her."

Rick's chin dropped to his chest, and his shoulder's slumped forward. "How long?"

Through tears, Joon gave him a bitter smile. "I'll figure something out tomorrow."

That night, while waiting for sleep to claim her, Joon lay nestled next to Lulu. Her friend hadn't woken since Joon had returned to the warehouse. By morning, Joon had come up with a short-term plan. As the others woke, she was moving about the space, gathering the small amount of items they had collected. Finally, Lulu's eyes opened slowly, and she gave Joon a weak smile.

Joon hurried over and brushed the hair from her face. "How are you feeling?"

"Weak, but I think I'm okay."

"I heard you had trouble breathing last night when I wasn't here."

Lulu broke eye contact with Joon. "Yeah, but I'm fine now." She pushed herself up on her elbows.

Joon extended her hands to help pull Lulu up into a sitting position. Then she maneuvered herself to sit behind her, so Lulu could lean against her.

"Here's the thing," Joon said, looking up and seeing the others listening. "We need to move outta here."

"Why?" Lulu said, looking around and sensing the shame and guilt the others were feeling.

"Well, because I think we need to be somewhere more comfortable. I don't think all the dirt in this shit hole is helping you—probably why you couldn't breathe last night. Besides, I wanna be closer to the hospital, in case you don't feel good."

Lulu looked around the group and read their faces. "You all don't want me here," she said.

"It's not that we don't want you here," Rick said, "We were all really scared last night. It's like we told Joon: we aren't doctors, and we don't know how to take care of you. We thought you were gonna die."

"So you think making us leave is the answer. I get it." Lulu, fueled by embarrassment and disappointment, got to her knees. "Let's get outta here."

Joon put her hand up. "You're gonna stay here. I have a plan. I just need a few hours, and I'll be back to get you. I want you to save your energy for later today."

Lulu tensed, getting ready to argue, but Joon put her hands on the girl's shoulder and moved her face closer. "We aren't arguing over this. It's my final decision."

"Fine," Lulu said, disappointed but relieved at the same time. "But hurry up. I want outta here."

Joon left shortly afterward with a calm determination. She was no longer angry at the others—she had shifted her energy to making her plan work.

Chapter Eighty

———————————◼———————————

J oon made it to the river where Skinner and Gunther were staying for the summer. As she skidded down the embankment Skinner looked up and smiled.

"Hey, girl, what the hell are you doing here so early?"

"I need your help," she said breathlessly.

"Is everything all right?"

The simple question unleashed her emotions, and Joon broke down and cried. Skinner took her into his arms, and Gunther held both of them.

"The group wants us out. Lulu couldn't breathe last night, and they don't want us around in case anything bad happens," she sobbed.

Skinner stroked her hair. "Well, aren't they a cheery group. I told you to stay here with us."

Joon pushed her face into his chest. "We can't. At least at the warehouse she doesn't get wet in the rain. She needs as much shelter as I can find."

"Okay, but now you have nowhere to go. Do you want to come here with us? We can figure out something to give her shelter. Right?" Skinner said, looking at Gunther.

Before Gunther could answer, Joon refused the offer. "No. I have another idea. I wanna take her back to the apartment complex. Remember when we slept in the hallways for a while? I need you two to help me get her there."

"Sounds a little dangerous," Skinner commented. "I mean, the last time you were there, you were out all day and only sleeping there at night. It doesn't sound like Lulu feels good enough to be out all day."

Joon looked down at the dirt and rubbed the back of her neck. "She's not. But I thought if you two came over in the mornings, you could help me get her to Suburban Station. She can stay on a bench and I can pan-handle. It's all I can think of right now. Will you help?"

"Of course we'll help. Let's get moving."

When they arrived at the warehouse, Lulu was sitting up, and relief washed over her face when she saw her friends coming toward her. "Where are we going?" she asked, sounding chipper.

Joon handed the few bags they had to Gunther. "We're heading to Suburban Station for the afternoon. I gotta get some money together."

"Then where?"

Joon gave Lulu a smile. "You know, you ask a lot of questions."

"I need to keep my eye on you," Lulu said, grabbing Joon's hand.

"Suburban Station, then to the apartment complexes," Joon said, avoiding eye contact.

Lulu stifled a moan. "And if we get caught there?"

"We won't."

Lulu held on tight as Joon steadied her. "What? You have a crystal ball now?"

Joon looked at Lulu and rolled her eyes. "You are the bossiest person I know."

"It's my job. I do it well, don't you think?"

"I think that you are the biggest control freak I've ever met," Joon joked.

"Ha! Whatever. Let's get going."

With Joon holding one of Lulu's arms and Skinner holding the other, the group of four walked away. After only a couple of steps, Lulu said, "Wait." She turned back to the group of teens they would probably never see again. "I know that I scared you last night, and it's okay. I get it. Nobody wants to be around the sick girl. I'm not mad at you guys, and I hope that someday, if you're ever sick, you have a friend like Joon." With that, she turned, and they left the warehouse.

In Suburban Station, they sat Lulu on a bench. Even though it was hot outside, the weak air-conditioning in the station made Lulu shiver. Joon covered her with their blankets and turned to the two boys.

"Thanks for your help. Can you come back around eight to get us?"

"Yeah, we'll be back," Skinner said, putting his arms around her. "Everything is gonna be okay. You're one strong bitch."

Joon cracked a smile. "Yeah, I don't feel so strong right now," she whispered. She watched as the two boys walked out of the station hand in hand. When they were gone, she turned back to Lulu, who had drifted off to sleep again. With a loud sigh, she settled herself on the ground next to the bench and begged.

That night, as they approached the apartments, Joon insisted they go to a specific building.

"Why are we going to the one farther away when all these other buildings are closer?" Skinner asked her.

"Because when we stayed here the last time, I noticed the buildings in the back are filled with old people, and they don't come out of their apartments as much."

"Oh," Skinner said. "That makes sense."

Inside one of the battered buildings, they moved to the end of the long hallway on the second floor. They were as quiet as they could manage, hoping they would go unnoticed. With Lulu in the corner, Joon turned to the boys. "See you tomorrow?" she said quietly.

"Yeah, we'll see you tomorrow. When is her next treatment?"

"Monday."

"Oh hell. That's two more days," Skinner said.

"No shit. We'll be fine. Just come back in the morning."

Skinner and Gunther gave Joon a hug, and as she watched them leave, she felt the first rip in her heart.

Chapter Eighty-One

———————————◼——————————

During the night, Joon felt someone standing over them, and her eyes snapped open to find an angry black woman looming over her. The woman was holding a broom over her head, and Joon instinctively put her body over Lulu to protect her.

"Get your drugged-up asses outta my hallway," the woman growled.

Joon peeked at her and mumbled, "We don't do drugs."

"Oh really? Then how come your friend there looks like she's stoned outta her mind?"

Joon positioned her body so she could look at the woman. "She's sick. Please put the broom down. We just need a place where she can sleep." Joon turned to Lulu and tucked the blanket under her chin.

Slowly, the woman lowered the broom. "Is that so? What's wrong with her then?"

"Her kidney. She only has one and it's failing." Joon took in a long breath to hold back the tears that stung her eyes. She looked back at the woman. "Someone stole her other kidney."

The old woman bent to put her face close to Lulu's. She drew in a deep breath through her nose, then looked directly into Joon's eyes. "Just 'cause I don't smell no alcohol on her doesn't mean you two ain't high on something else."

Joon stared at the woman, and her anguish flowed freely. Her body quivered, and she raked her hands through her hair continuously. "I told you, we don't do drugs. My friend is sick. She's the only person in the world I have. Please just leave us alone. We won't bother you. Okay?" Joon babbled.

The woman put her hands on her round hips and watched Joon as she broke down and sobbed.

Her chest heaved and the weight of having nowhere to go crashed in on her. "I can't move her on my own. Please, lady, cut us a break," she pleaded.

The woman turned and walked several feet to her apartment door. Joon was worried she was calling the police but was too exhausted and numb to attempt waking and moving Lulu. She could only sit and wait. A few minutes later, the apartment door opened, and the woman returned.

"Here," she said, handing Joon a pillow and another blanket. "I figure you can use these."

Joon looked at the woman. "Th-thank you."

"Never let it be said that Nellie didn't help someone in need."

Joon just stared at the woman as tears dripped from her chin.

"My name is Nellie. I've lived here almost twenty years. I spend most of my time in my apartment now, but when I was younger and, I got out more, I helped everyone I could. Even volunteered at the Red Cross for a spell. Now, I know when I see someone in need, and it seems to me that you could use a little kindness right now. You go on and stay here tonight. I ain't gonna bother you, but don't make me regret it."

"We won't," Joon mumbled.

"Good. Now, sleep tight." Nellie walked back to her apartment.

"Wait," Joon said. "Nellie? I'm Joon and this is Lulu."

Nellie lifted her chin in quick acknowledgment and turned back around.

"Thank you, Nellie," Joon said.

"You're welcome," Nellie said as she disappeared into her apartment.

Lulu woke early the next morning and gently shook Joon awake.

"Morning," Lulu said with a smile.

"Hey. How are you feeling?"

"A little better. You were right—I slept like a rock in here."

Lulu sat up, her hand brushing the pillow where her head had laid. "Where did this come from?"

Joon pointed to the door a short distance away. "An old lady named Nellie. She thought we were high. I told her you were sick, and she brought out a pillow and this other blanket for us. I was freaking the fuck out that she was gonna call the cops."

"Aw, that was nice."

"Nice? I about shit my pants. I'm only seventeen, remember? If the cops came, they'd probably send me back to Aron."

Lulu rested her forehead against Joon's. "But Nellie didn't call the cops, and they didn't take you away and send you back to Aron."

"Smart-ass," Joon remarked.

"I gotta pee," Lulu said.

"Really? You're like a fucking camel. You never have to pee, but you gotta pee right now?"

"Yep. Let's go outside and pop a squat."

Joon moaned but stood up and pulled Lulu to her feet. The girl threw her arms around Joon. "Fucking hell, I'm so dizzy. Give me a second."

Joon held her upright as Nellie's apartment door opened.

Nellie stuck her head out and looked at them. "Are you two trying to wake the whole floor up? Ain't nobody ever teach you how to be quiet?"

Joon bit the inside of her lip. "Sorry. Lulu has to take a whiz and when she stood up she got dizzy."

Nellie walked up to the girls. "So you're Lulu?"

"Yes, ma'am."

"Your friend Joon here tells me you're sick."

"Yes, ma'am, but I'm gonna be fine."

Nellie cocked her hip out and pursed her lips. "You don't look too fine to me." The older woman turned to Joon. "Let's bring her inside my apartment. You can use my bathroom."

Joon and Lulu exchanged a wide-eyed look.

"Thanks a lot," Joon said. "That's really nice of you."

Nellie glanced at Joon, then at all of their items in the corner of the hall. "I'll help Lulu and you gather all that stuff up and bring it inside. If my nosy neighbors see it, they'll be calling the authorities."

Joon and Lulu followed the old woman into her apartment and closed the door behind them.

Chapter Eighty-Two

As Joon stepped inside the small apartment, she saw a tiny kitchen with two cabinets hanging above the sink and three drawers between the sink and a miniature gas stove to the left. Perched on the three-foot-wide countertop was an old coffeepot and a bowl with a few overripe bananas. Joon placed their belongings to the side of the door, went over to Lulu, and took her hand.

"The bathroom is on the right," Nellie said, pointing to the short hallway. Nellie sat on the love seat, the only place to sit in the small living area, and picked up her knitting.

Inside the bathroom was a tub, a narrow sink with a mirror above, and a toilet crammed between the tub and the outside wall. Lulu was on the toilet as Joon stood staring into the mirror. "I look awful."

"Yeah, you do," Lulu said, teasing her.

Joon spun on her. "What? You think you look any better?"

"No, but I'm sick. What's your excuse?"

"I'm too busy taking care of your ass," she teased. "If I wasn't spending all my time doing that, I might even have found my prince charming by now."

"Oh, pleeeease. Spare me the theatrics. You don't want a man any more than I want my kidney to stop working."

Joon scratched her scalp. "That may be true. Do you think I'm a man hater?"

Lulu ripped off several squares of toilet paper and wiped herself. "You're such a freak. You are not a man hater. You just had a really bad experience with that asshole Quinn. I hope that someday we both meet great guys and our kids can grow up together."

Joon fantasized about how good it would feel to have a family of her own. "Yeah, that would be cool." She looked at Lulu and shrugged. "Are you gonna get up and let me go or are you gonna sit there all day?"

When the girls were finished, they walked back out to where Nellie was sitting.

"Thanks for letting us use your bathroom," Joon said.

"Did you wash your hands?"

Joon smiled. "Yes, ma'am."

"Stop calling me *ma'am*. My name is Nellie. You can call me Miss Nellie. I put a box of cereal on the counter and there's milk in the fridge. You girls go eat something. You can help yourselves to a banana if you like them. I ain't got much, but I don't mind sharing what I have."

The girls sat on the floor next to Nellie's love seat and ate their cereal. Joon practically inhaled hers, while Lulu ate with uncertainty.

Nellie kept a close eye on Lulu. "Why ain't you eating, sugar?"

Lulu took another small mouthful. "Most of the time after I eat, I get sick. So I'm taking it slow 'cause I don't wanna puke."

Joon stopped eating and looked at Nellie, afraid she'd make them leave if Lulu threw up in her small living space. Instead, Nellie waved her hand in the air. "No worries, sugar. Joon, go get Lulu the plastic basin from under the sink. That way, if she's gotta spew, she can use it."

Joon was relieved that Lulu didn't complain of nausea when she finished her food. She got a blanket and put it over her friend, who was still on the floor leaning against the love seat. Joon wanted to stay in Nellie's apartment for as long as they could, so she didn't volunteer to leave and was on pins and needles waiting for Nellie to tell them it was time to go. When they heard voices in the hallway, Joon stood and turned to the old lady. "I think that's our friends. They came to help me get Lulu to Suburban Station."

"Oh yeah?" Nellie said nonchalantly. "You going on a trip?"

"No. Our plan is to stay at Suburban Station during the day and sleep in the apartment hallways at night. We did it before and no one ever caught us."

Nellie glanced up from her knitting. "Go on and open the door, so your friends know you're safe."

Joon pulled the door open just as Skinner and Gunther were leaving the floor. "Hey. Skinner."

"What the hell are you doing in there?" Skinner asked, walking toward the apartment.

"This nice lady," Joon said, pointing to Nellie from the doorway, "let us use her bathroom. Give us a few minutes and we'll be out."

With the door open, Skinner waved at Nellie. "Hi."

Nellie pinched her lips together and glared at the boys. "You boys mind yourself."

"They're our friends. They're good guys, and they don't take drugs either," Joon said, giving the woman a grin.

"Good for them. Shut the door and come back over here," Nellie said.

Joon approached the old woman, and Lulu watched silently.

Nellie put her knitting down and hoisted herself from the love seat. "I don't see the sense in taking this sick child out all day just to come back and sleep in the hallway at night. I'm gonna let you two stay here for a day or two 'cause I wanna keep an eye on this child."

Joon's mouth dropped open. "Really? You don't even know us."

Nellie's chin went to her chest as she leered at Joon through narrowed eyelids. "You're right, I don't know you. So I'll warn you now: don't disappointment me or you'll find yourself on the other end of my broom handle, and that is one place you don't ever wanna be."

Joon felt a chill run through her. She felt like a trapped child again. Her chest tightened and her skin prickled under her clothing. Not that she thought Nellie was evil, but she realized the old woman would make good on her word.

"I...I...I won't disappoint you," Joon promised.

"Good. Go out in the hallway and tell your friends that you and Lulu are staying here for a few days."

When Joon explained the situation to Skinner, his jaw tightened. "I don't know about this. What if she does something crazy to you or Lulu?"

"She won't."

Skinner's eyes narrowed. "How do you know that?"

"Because I've seen evil in my life and she ain't it."

Skinner rubbed his chin with his thumb and index finger. "Well, I'm sorry, but you're gonna have to prove it, 'cause I'll worry my pretty, little head off thinking about the two of you. And if anything happens, I'll spend the rest of my life buried in guilt 'cause I should've done something."

Joon laughed a little and shook her head. "You're such a drama queen. It'll be fine. I'll find you in Suburban Station every day. I have to make money. The old lady ain't gonna pay for our food. She barely has anything in there. I'll be down there later today, after I get Lulu settled."

"Fine, girlfriend, but you remember that I don't like it. Not one little bit."

"You know, Skinner, you should trust people more," Joon said jokingly.

"Beotch, you're the one who taught me not to trust anybody. Hell," he said, running his finger down Gunther's arm, "she didn't trust you for shit. Yep, my girl wasn't happy that she didn't approve of you before we took off on our own."

Gunther kissed Skinner on his neck. "That makes her a good friend."

Skinner gently pushed his boyfriend away. "Whose side are you on?"

"He's on the side of right, you ninny," Joon said. Then she got on her tiptoes and planted a kiss on Skinner's cheek, turned, and did the same to Gunther. "I'll see you two lovebirds later. Stay outta trouble."

Joon walked back into the apartment, and Nellie looked up at her.

The old woman stood from the loveseat and started toward the small kitchen. "You take care of your business with those boys?"

"Yes, Miss Nellie."

"Good. Me and Lulu are gonna have a cup of tea. You want one?"

"Yes, that would be great."

Joon joined Lulu on the floor. "How are you?"

"Fine, mom. I'm feeling a little better now."

It wasn't lost on Joon, however, that Lulu refused to make eye contact.

Chapter Eighty-Three

———————————————————

"**M**iss Nellie, I need to go out for a couple of hours."

"What for?"

"So I can earn some money to buy food," Joon explained. "Can Lulu stay here with you? If she wakes up, just tell her I went to panhandle."

"Yeah, I can do that. Now, when you go out and beg, do people get mad with ya?"

"Some people do. They'll yell at us and say that we need to go back to school or go home to our parents. But there're a lot of people who will throw their change in your collector and keep walking."

Nellie's eyebrows raised. "Your collector?"

"Yeah, that's what we call the hat or can or basket or whatever we're collecting money in."

"Oh, I see. And these people who are mean to you, does it make you feel bad?"

"Sometimes. Mostly when it's rich kids that are our age. Some of them will throw trash in my collector or throw water or soda on me or just make fun of me." Joon paused, looking down at her worn hands. "They tell me I'm dirty and that I smell. I've heard it all before though, when I was a kid."

"A kid?"

"Yeah, it's a long story. I was raised in a foster home. That's where I learned that the devil ain't a man. The devil is a woman, a nasty bitch named Aron." Joon covered her mouth with her hand. "Sorry, Miss Nellie. I didn't mean to curse."

The old woman grinned at her. "It's okay." She winked at Joon. "Miss Nellie is known to spew a few cuss words when I get irritated too."

***

Joon returned to Nellie's apartment in the early evening. She had stopped at a small local grocery to buy a few items, and Nellie watched as she unpacked the few items. She admired that the girl had contributed to their basic needs, her gut telling her that Joon was a good kid with a big heart—and Nellie always followed her gut.

Joon sat on the floor next to Lulu. "Did you sleep most of the day?"

Lulu looked at her sheepishly. "Yeah. But me and Miss Nellie watched television too. She makes the best grilled cheese sandwiches."

"Uh-huh," Nellie chimed in. "Until she threw it up all over herself."

Joon put her head back on the love seat cushion. "I bought saltine crackers for you." She turned to Nellie. "She can keep them down pretty good if she doesn't eat them too fast." She turned back to Lulu. "On Monday, we'll ask Dr. Becker for some more of those anti-nausea pills. They helped you for a while."

Lulu stared at the television. "This is not at all how I pictured my life. Hell, I'm not even old enough to drink. I'm tired of being sick."

"I know you are, and I know it's been hard on you. But I think the treatments help. Right?"

"Truthfully?" Lulu said, looking at Joon. "Not really. The last few weeks have been horrible. I've been thinking about stopping the treatments."

Joon was up on her knees. "What? No. You can't do that. Without a kidney transplant or dialysis, you'll die. Dr. Becker said so. You're just gonna have to keep doing the treatment until you feel better."

Lulu sighed. "I'll try a little longer, but look at me, Joon. I'm sick and weak all the time. I can't eat, and when I do, I throw it up. I rarely pee, my body hurts, and I'm always swollen like a tick. Oh, and to top it off, I'm freezing no matter how hard I try to warm up."

Joon grabbed their other blanket and laid it over top of her friend.

Lulu smiled sadly. "I know you love me and that you do everything you can to take care of me, but, Joon, I'm not living right now, and neither are you."

"Stop it, Lulu. Just stop talking. I don't wanna hear it. You promised that you would do the treatments and you can't go back on your word."

"I know I promised you, Joon. But that was months ago. And even though you don't want to face it, I've gotten worse, not better. Even Dr. Becker sees it."

Nellie was sitting at the dinette in the kitchen, watching the two girls in silence.

Joon had gotten up and was pacing the small space. Then she stopped abruptly, crying, and spun on Lulu. "So what? You wanna just give up? Is that what you're saying?"

"No, Joon. I mean, I don't know what I wanna do. I'm always trying to hide how bad I feel from you. I feel so guilty that I'm not getting better, so I lie to you."

Joon fell to her knees in front of her friend. "Oh, please, Lulu. You have to keep trying. I'm gonna find you a donor, I just know it. I can feel it." She hadn't been able to save Tori, and now she wouldn't even have the chance to save Lulu. This could not be happening to her again; she wouldn't let it.

Lulu smiled and gently put her hand on Joon's cheek. "I didn't say I was gonna stop treatment now, but at some point, if I can't get a transplant, I have to think about it. I'm in pain all of the time. If my body doesn't hurt, then my brain hurts thinking about all of the things I can't do. Can you understand?"

Joon curled up against Lulu. "I don't wanna understand. I need you. You're all I have in this world."

The young women fell silent as they sat leaning on each other. Finally, Nellie stood from the table. "I think a nice hot bath will warm you up, Lulu," she said.

"That would be great."

"Joon, baby. Do you wanna go get a bath ready for her?"

Joon hopped up. "You bet," she said as she rushed into the bathroom. *Miss Nellie will help me fix Lulu, I just know it,* Joon thought.

Chapter Eighty-Four

Once Lulu was in the tub of warm water, Joon walked into the other room and sat next to Nellie. The old woman put her arm over the girl's shoulder, and Joon collapsed against the woman's large chest.

"You know, Joon, there comes a time when we have to do things in our life that feel really bad to us, but make other people feel good. Take Lulu for instance. She's trying her best to get better and be strong. Can you see that?"

Joon nodded. "But I'm not ready for her to give up," she said quietly. "I know she's gonna come through this okay."

"You can't know that, child. You and her are like sisters. I ain't known you for more than a day, and I can see how you are with each other. And that poor girl is trying to tell you that she don't wanna fight no more. Sometimes people get tired, you know? They wanna just lie their head down and let God take care of 'em." The woman was saying everything in a firm but quiet voice as she rocked Joon a little with the arm that was around her. "You need to listen to what she's saying to you. I'm afraid if you don't listen to her real close, she'll leave this world and you won't have told her the things she needs to know. The things she's begging to hear from you 'cause you're the only person on this earth who matters to her."

"But I'm afraid. I want her to get better and if I give up, then so will she. If she can get a kidney transplant, then she'll be okay. It can happen any day." Joon slid her arms around Nellie's broad waist. The woman was hitting a nerve. Joon knew in her heart that Lulu's health had worsened, but the thought of losing her was unbearable—she preferred pretending not to know than admitting to where the future was clearly headed.

"Listen, God talks to people, and maybe He's talking to Lulu. Calling her home. She probably don't realize it, but she has the desire to be somewhere else. Lulu's a young girl. She don't wanna live her life sleeping and feeling sick. Hell, I'm an old woman and I don't wanna live like that. You're too busy trying to make her better to realize that all she wants from you is the safety and comfort of your love." She took a deep breath. "All I'm saying is you need to listen a little closer to what she's sayin' and you need to put what you want aside. That's what real love is about— helping others get what they need."

Joon was crying again. "I know you're right, but I don't wanna lose her."

Nellie stroked Joon's hair. "If God's ready for her there ain't nothing you can do to stop it. But what you can do is help her get ready. You need to give her permission to go with grace and dignity. She don't wanna leave feeling like she disappointed you, so it's your job to release her of the guilt she's holding in her heart."

Nellie held Joon for a while longer. "You best go check on her. If the water cools, she'll be freezing in there. There are towels in the hall closet."

Lulu had a towel wrapped around her as Joon followed her out of the bathroom. Nellie was in her bedroom across the hall.

"Come here, girls," Nellie said. Inside the dreary bedroom, the woman held out a flannel nightgown. "Put this on, Lulu. I think it'll fit you. It used to be my daughter's."

Lulu took it and Joon helped slip it over her head.

"It's so soft and warm. Thank you," Lulu said.

"I got another one of those if you wanna wear it tonight," Nellie said to Joon.

Joon took the garment from Nellie and undressed.

Nellie's eyes narrowed. "What do you think you're doing?"

"Putting on the nightgown?" Joon sputtered.

"Child, go in that bathroom and get your ass in that tub. You need to clean yourself up."

"Really? I can?" Joon said.

"Oh Lord. Yes, you can. Lulu and me don't wanna smell your ass all night," she said, breaking into a smile.

Lulu held her nose. "Yeah, girl, go wash off that stank."

The three laughed. Lulu and Nellie watched as Joon crossed the hallway and closed the bathroom door behind her.

Lulu gazed at Nellie with a pained expression, waiting for the woman to speak.

"Joon's gonna be okay and so are you. You got dealt a bad hand, and your friend don't wanna accept that, but she will. Baby, you gotta do what's right for you. Ain't nobody else living your life, and only you know what's best. Don't mean it ain't gonna be hard—always is for the people left behind—but life goes on. It doesn't stop for nobody." She walked over to Lulu and wrapped her in a warm embrace. "Let's get you settled in, so you can rest. You go in for your treatment tomorrow and talk to your doctor about all of this. You tell him how you're feeling and don't hold back. Joon will understand. It may not seem like it now, but she will."

Lulu wrung her hands together. "I feel so selfish just thinking about stopping my treatments. Joon and me, we're a team. We were alone until we found each other. On the streets, it ain't easy to find another human being that you can trust with your life. Everybody is competing to survive, so it's the worst competition you'll ever know. I mean, it's not all bad, but in the end, it's about survival, so sometimes we gotta do things that hurt other people, like steal their food or money. Not Joon and me though. We take care of each other because our love is stronger than our need to survive. Our love is our survival. It ain't easy to find love out on the streets."

Nellie pressed her fist to her lips while she got ahold of her emotions. "That's some kinda love. I know people who live their whole lives without finding it."

Lulu put her arm through Nellie's. "Can I ask you a question?"

"Sure, baby."

"Where's your daughter?"

Nellie put her hand over her own heart. "She died. She was addicted to drugs and it finally got the best of her. Police found her on a bench, overdosed."

"I'm sorry, Nellie."

"I'm sorry too, baby. I'm sorry I couldn't help her. Lord knows I tried. That's why I wanted to help you and Joon. You see, I just got myself a bed in a nearby nursing home. Gonna be going there in a few weeks. It's hard for me here by myself, and now I can live around other people, so I won't be so lonely. Besides, it's getting harder to go to the store and cook my own food. The nursing home will take care of all that. A bed finally opened up." She was silent for a moment before she continued. "I'm scared. I've been independent my whole life, but I figure I can make some friends and be happy. Maybe I'll find a friend in there like you have in Joon."

Lulu kissed the woman's cheek. "I hope you do. You're a good lady and you deserve to be happy. Not too many people would have taken us in."

"I felt like it was my last chance to do something nice to help another human being. I'm glad I did and, for the time that you're both here, maybe we can help each other accept what comes next in our lives."

Lulu and Nellie walked into the living area together and waited for Joon to join them. Now Lulu knew their friendship with Nellie would be short-lived. When Joon came out, they crawled under the covers together.

Lulu and Nellie didn't know that Joon had overheard everything.

Chapter Eighty-Five

On Monday, Joon prepared to take Lulu for her treatment. They spent the day relaxing with Nellie, and by late afternoon, Joon had packed their belongings and placed them by the door.

"Where will you girls stay tonight?" Nellie asked Joon while Lulu napped.

"We'll stay in the hospital. She gets her treatment overnight. The weather is supposed to be nice tomorrow, so I think I'll take Lulu to Rittenhouse Square for a while. It's real nice there. Lots of people to watch. It helps pass the time."

"I'll be staying here for a while longer, just about two weeks, so if you need a place, you can come back," Nellie offered.

"Thanks, I'll keep that in mind. I heard you tell Lulu you were going into a nursing home." She had considered going back to Nellie's but couldn't bear getting closer to the woman just to deal with yet another loss. Her emotional state was fragile, and in her heart, Joon knew there was only so much she could endure.

Nellie nodded. "Best thing for me now. Took a long time to get a bed. Can't say I'm looking forward to it, but seeing as I ain't got no family, it makes sense."

Joon wiped her palms on her pants to dry the puddle of sweat that had collected. "I'm happy for you, Nellie. You're gonna make lots of friends there."

When it was time to leave, the girls hugged Nellie and thanked her for being so kind. Joon picked up their bags and Lulu held on to her arm. When they opened the door to leave, Skinner and Gunther stood in the hall, and Joon's heart felt like it would explode when she saw them there.

Skinner stepped forward and grabbed their bags. "We thought you might want company walking to the hospital."

Joon released a loud sigh as some of the tension drained out of her, and together they began their walk to the hospital. When they arrived, Joon and Lulu went to the overnight treatment center. Once Lulu was in bed receiving dialysis, Joon drifted off to sleep.

In the morning, Dr. Becker came in to talk. "Morning, girls. Sleep well?"

Joon stretched her arms and legs while Lulu put her bed up, so she could talk to the doctor. Her expression was serious, and Dr. Becker pulled a chair up next to her.

"What's on your mind, Lulu?"

The girl glanced at Joon quickly, then proceeded. "Dialysis isn't working. I'm getting worse every week. I've thought about this for a long time." She took a long pause. "I'm thinking about stopping."

The momentary silence in the room lay over them like a heavy wet blanket. Joon wanted to argue with Lulu, but before she protested, she remembered what Nellie had told her.

"That's a big decision, Lulu," Dr. Becker began. "However, it is your decision to make."

"What do you think?" Lulu asked him.

"Your kidney is worsening, and you're getting weaker. The sicker you become, the less likely a transplant will be successful."

Lulu fixed her eyes on Joon, who was staring out the window. "Joon?"

Joon slowly turned back toward her.

"Give me your hand," Lulu said.

Joon placed her hand in Lulu's.

"This is a really hard decision. I know what you want me to do, but I'm losing the fight. I know this, and in your heart, you know it too. I don't want to hurt you, and I don't want to be a burden anymore."

Joon was on her feet, leaning over the bed to hug her friend. "You're not a burden." A sob caught in her throat. "I love being with you. I would do anything for you."

Lulu clutched her friend. "I need you to make this okay for me. I need you to understand my decision."

Joon held her tighter. "I will do whatever you want," she said solemnly.

Lulu gave Joon another squeeze, then pulled back a little to look at Dr. Becker. "I'm going to stop dialysis."

Dr. Becker nodded. "It's your choice."

Joon was wrecked. She clung to Lulu as they cried and tried to console each other. "What…what happens now?" she asked the doctor.

"We will keep Lulu as comfortable as we can."

"How long? How long before…?" Joon couldn't finish her sentence.

"There's no science to this. It could be weeks or even months. However, based on Lulu's health, I'm more inclined to say weeks."

"Oh God," Joon moaned. She felt like a piece of her was dying too. She took several gulps of air. "Will she stay in the hospital? I don't know where I can take her." She touched Lulu's forehead with her own. "I won't let you die on the dirty streets. I'll sell my body to get us a room if I have to."

Dr. Becker cleared his throat. "Lulu, you'll stay here. I'll put you in hospice care. That way we can keep you as comfortable as possible. I know you hate being in the hospital, but I think it's the best thing. Is that okay?"

"Yeah," Lulu conceded.

Dr. Becker stood. "I'll make the arrangements. I'm sorry, Lulu. I'm sorry that we couldn't do more to help you."

Together in the hospital bed, the girls shared a misery that neither could have imagined.

"I'm sorry I can't fight anymore," Lulu said, her voice barely above a whisper.

Joon's heart twisted in her chest. "I'm sorrier that I can't save you."

Chapter Eighty-Six

Just ten days later, Lulu was struggling to stay alive. Joon hadn't left her side since she'd entered hospice. Skinner and Gunther had visited every day, pretending to be cheery in an attempt to dissipate the grief that filled every nook of the room. Lulu's breathing was labored, and Joon watched over her like a mother with her newborn child.

"Do you want your oxygen mask on?"

"No," Lulu said in a weak voice. "I want to talk to you. I don't have much time. I can feel death coming at me."

"What does death feel like?"

Lulu gave a genuine smile. "It feels like pins and needles at first. Then, there's this deep blackness that takes over. Suddenly, all the pain is gone, and I can see clearly, with laser focus. I remember all the things that made me happy and see the faces of all the people that loved me. I see them like they're right here with me. Then everything begins to fade from black to gray to white, and that's how I know I'm going home—to the only home that I'll ever need."

"You make it sound...nice."

"It is nice, Joon. I'm not afraid anymore."

Joon looked at Lulu, her mouth turned downward and eyes rimmed in red. "I'm so scared, Lulu. I want to die with you. I don't think I can take more pain and loss. I'm losing one of the only people who ever loved me. I always lose the ones I love."

"I'll be with you always."

Joon rubbed her hand gently up and down Lulu's arm.

"I'm afraid, Lulu."

"Of what?"

"Of being alone," she sobbed.

"You'll never be alone. You're too easy to love."

Lulu opened her eyes, and Joon could see her friend was free in a way she never had been before. There was a peacefulness that Joon envied, but she focused on the present, on what was happening right then—she wanted Lulu's last moments to be filled with love and safety.

Joon climbed into bed with her friend, and the two turned toward each other and, in a moment, were wrapped in each other's arms. "I love you," Joon said.

"I love you too," Lulu whispered back. Then she closed her eyes, and two minutes later, she was gone.

Joon remained in the bed, holding Lulu's lifeless body, and felt her heart breaking. She howled loudly and uncontrollably until Dr. Becker came into the room and tried to gently pull her off the bed.

"No. Please. Just leave me."

Dr. Becker's heart broke for the girl. "Lulu's gone, Joon. Let me help you."

"No. No one can help me. Not you. Not anyone. Don't you know she was all I had? I'm alone now. I have no one. I might as well be dead too."

Dr. Becker sat with Joon for a long time, eventually coaxing her away from Lulu. As she sat in the chair across from the doctor, she bawled. The doctor leaned over and took her hand. "You're not alone. You'll never be alone. You're one of the most remarkable young women I've had the pleasure of knowing. Will you promise to come back and visit me?"

"Ohhhh God, Dr. Becker, I'll never get over this," Joon wailed.

"No, you won't. But you have to remember how much you meant to Lulu. She didn't have to face this alone because of you. You tried so hard to save her, and in the end, you gave her the gift that every person needs when they are going to die—you shared her pain and suffering and made her death your own. I'm proud of you, Joon. You made a big difference in her life and you should carry that with you forever."

Several hours later, Joon had pulled herself together enough to leave the hospital, and as she walked through the lobby, she heard a familiar voice call her name.

"Tony," Joon said in a flat voice.

"Are you okay?" he asked.

"My best friend just died," Joon managed to choke out before a sob took her words.

Tony took her into his arms and let her cry on his shoulder for several minutes. After Joon gathered herself, she stood up straight. "I'm sorry, Tony. Why are you here?"

"You know Donata. Well, these two sorry assholes came into the bakery today and beat her granddaughter, Ruth. You remember her?"

"Yeah, she's a sweet kid. Is she okay?"

"She will be, but they fucked her up pretty bad. Anyway, I was just heading back to Donata's to take care of some things."

"Is there anything I can do?" Joon asked.

"Nah. Well, yeah, there's one thing."

"What's that?"

"If you need me, I want you to find me. Understand?"

Joon nodded and sniffled as she wiped her still-damp face.

Tony lifted her chin with his index finger. "I know what it's like to lose everyone and everything you got. I know exactly how you feel. It feels like life handed you a big shit sandwich and you had no choice but to eat it. That's why I'm telling you to come and find me if you need my help. 'Cause you and me, we're the same like that, you understand?"

"Yes. Thank you, Tony. I promise to find you if I need anything," she said, leaning in to hug him again.

As they embraced, Skinner and Gunther approached. When Joon turned to face them, Skinner's eyes were brimming with tears.

"She's gone?"

"Yeah. It's over."

Skinner put his arm around Joon's shoulder. "Come on, girl. You're coming with me and Gunther."

With a quick wave, Joon and Tony parted ways, Joon following the two boys as if in a trance, not knowing what would come next.

Chapter Eighty-Seven

———————————■———————————

Once they left the hospital, Joon followed the boys to Mallory's house, where they had rented a room for five nights. Joon walked into the room and dropped onto the bed, where she cried silently until sleep overrode her ability to grieve. When she woke, Skinner was on the bed watching her.

"Hey," he said gently.

"Hey. How long did I sleep?"

"Almost ten hours. How do you feel?"

Joon rubbed the tears from her eyes. "Like I'm drowning in a puddle."

Skinner put his hand on her shoulder. "It's hard and we're all sad. But things will get better. I promise."

"You sound like Lulu. Before she died, she kept telling me that I had to believe my life would get better after she was gone. I don't know how she could think that anything would be better without her."

Skinner scratched his five o'clock shadow. "I think she knew her death was going to be hard on you, but that, in time, your life would change, and you would adjust. It's not that you won't miss her, but you'll learn to go on without her and live in a way that she wanted to live. That's what she wanted for you. I heard her say that to you lots of times in the past week. You have to look to the future, sweetie. Remember, you're not alone. You have me and my stallion to keep you company."

Joon and Skinner looked over at Gunther sitting in a chair, scratching his crotch and giggled half-heartedly.

"I talked to Dr. Becker before I left the hospital. Lulu's gonna be cremated. I have to go back for the ashes, but the doctor is taking care of everything. I need to have a funeral for her."

"Of course we will. In fact, Gunther knows this religious dude, and he asked him to say some prayers or something."

Joon shook her head. "No, just us. She needs to be with the people who loved her."

Skinner nodded. "Whatever you want."

"I want Lulu to be alive and healthy," Joon said. She had a twisted, rotten feeling in her gut.

"I wish I could give you that, but I can't."

"Thanks for coming to get me today...or yesterday or whenever it was. I appreciate it."

"Sure thing. Remember, you're the one who couldn't leave me on the street by myself and had to deal with the wrath of that bitch whore Fipple for bringing me into the house."

Joon smiled at the memory. "Lulu was sick then, but she didn't tell me."

"I know." He looked at her for a moment. "Hey! Gunther and I are springing for burgers and milkshakes for dinner tonight."

Joon tilted her head and closed her eyes. "Thanks for everything you're doing. I don't know what I'd do if you weren't here. You're spending a lot of money."

"We've been saving up." Skinner lowered his head. "We talked about it. We knew this day was coming, so we begged, stole some stuff, sold some stuff, you know...all the things us homeless people do to stay alive. We wanted to be able to take care of you, so we did what we had to do to make that happen."

"Thank you."

"You're welcome. We washed your clothes while you slept."

"You're a good friend."

"Oh, when we emptied your bags, we found a diary. I mean, we didn't read it, but I never knew you kept one."

"I don't. I've had it for a while now. A little girl that shared a hospital room with Lulu gave it to me...asked me to give it to her father if anything happened to her. Her 'last wishes,' she said."

"Well, that's odd...and a bit intense. Okay then. It's back in your bag."

Joon thought about Molly and hoped the girl was doing better than Lulu. She made a mental note to ask Dr. Becker about her when she went to pick up Lulu's ashes.

Chapter Eighty-Eight

"Joon, how are you holding up?" Dr. Becker asked after a nurse showed her into his office.

She shook her head. "I feel like I'm in a fog. I keep telling myself things will get better, but I can't see how that's ever going to happen."

"Losing people we love is the hardest thing in life. But I believe that every loss we suffer comes with a life lesson, and if we open our hearts and listen closely, we find a way to make our grief meaningful."

Dr. Becker stood from his desk and carried a small, thick cardboard box over to Joon. He handed it to her and put his hand on her shoulder. "Lulu was lucky to have you. You be good to yourself, and if you ever need to talk, come back and see me."

After talking to the doctor a few more minutes, Joon hung her head and left his office. Skinner was waiting for her in the hospital lobby, and as she approached, he eyed the box but remained silent. The two walked to the place where they would lay Lulu to rest.

After a long walk, Joon and Skinner stood staring at the burned structure. They hadn't been back to the abandoned house since the fire. The brick row home stood stark against the overcast sky. The roof of the front porch sagged and the black shingles had melted and re-formed into grotesque shapes. Inside, all they saw through the glassless windows was black. They made their way around to the back and stepped into the gaping hole once covered with blue plastic. Inside, they looked up into a cavern of charred ruins. The floors above them were gone; stairs, walls, and rooms no longer existed. It was one big, empty space covered in black. The smell was unbearable, but Joon didn't seem to mind as she looked around and carefully picked her way through the debris covering the floor.

Skinner held her hand. "It's so...so...black."

Joon looked into the darkness. "It's the way my heart feels—hollowed out, covered in soot...dead."

Skinner put his arm around her waist in an effort to comfort her. "We should take care of business and get outta here. This isn't a safe place for us to be."

They found a small spot where the dining room was when the house was first built. Joon knelt in the gray and black ash. She opened the cardboard box and pulled out the plastic bag that held Lulu's remains. Her hands shook as she untied the bag, and a puff of Lulu's ashes floated into the air in a small plume. Grabbing the bag, Joon stood and looked at Skinner for support.

She turned the open bag upside down, scattering Lulu's ashes onto the scorched floor. Then she dropped to her knees and scooped up a handful of ashes. "Oh, Lulu, I'm so sorry that I couldn't help you. I'm sorry that my stupid kidney didn't match. I'm sorry that I couldn't find anyone to give you a kidney. If I had just found one person, you would still be alive. Please forgive me for failing you." Joon let the tears fall. Her chest heaved as sobs gripped her from the depth of her soul.

Skinner was leaning over her, trying to steady and soothe her. "Come on, Joon. We should go now."

"No! I'm not finished."

"Okay," he said, stroking her matted hair.

Joon took a deep breath of burnt, rotten air. "Lulu, I hope you're with your gram. I hope she's holding you and loving you. I will miss you so much. I'll miss the way you shined your light on the dark times. I'll miss you believing in me and telling me that I'm worth something. Most of all, I'll miss sharing my life with you. It may be a shitty life, but we were in it together. I hope that someday I can make you proud and that you watch over me and help me find what it is I'm supposed to do with my life. I will never forget you, and I'll think of you every day, I promise. Please stay with me, because I don't know if I can make it on my own. I will love you forever."

"Come on now. We need to go," Skinner said. "Lulu's at peace. She feels good again, alive, and she's with her gram. You've done everything you could do."

Joon curled her body into a tight ball and grasped at the ashy floor. "I can't leave her here by herself. I don't know what to do. I can't think straight. I just want to lie here until I die too."

"No, look," Skinner said, picking up the bag that held Lulu's ashes. He shook it, and the remaining ashes piled into the corner of the plastic. "You can take this part of Lulu with you. We'll find something to put her ashes in and you can keep them."

Joon studied the corner of the plastic bag for a few seconds before she reached up and closed her fist around the small amount of ashes that had collected there and held them against her heart.

"Let's go," Skinner said, pulling her to her feet.

As she clung to the plastic bag, Skinner guided her to the hole in the building where they had entered.

Right before Joon stepped out of the house, she looked back at the spot where Lulu's ashes were scattered, then down at the bag in her hand. "I really loved her," she said.

"I know you did. She loved you too," Skinner said as he led Joon outside. He looked at his friend, tears streaming from her unfocused eyes. For a moment, he worried that she wouldn't recover, but he knew that Joon was a strong person. Thunder cracked overhead, and Skinner looked up at the darkening sky. He took a tighter grip on Joon's hand and walked her back into the heart of the city.

Chapter Eighty-Nine

Months had passed since Lulu died, and Joon spent some of her time with Skinner and Gunther, but mostly she was alone. "I don't know why you're staying at the warehouse by yourself again," Skinner said. "You should stay with me and Gunther."

"Because I hate riding the train all night. There are too many creeps lurking around. Besides, you don't need a third wheel around all the time."

"You're right, the train is a pain in the ass, but at least it's heated. In that warehouse you're all by yourself," he argued.

"I told you a million times, a group took me in, so I'm not alone." Joon tied her hair up in a ponytail. "I never realized I'd be this lonely without Lulu," she sighed. "I'm empty, ya know? I'm having a hard time moving on, and the group at the warehouse doesn't expect anything of me. I mean, I have to bring in food or money, but they don't expect me to be happy."

"That's exactly why you should be with us. Because those bozos don't expect you to be happy, and we do. You're taking the easy way out. If you don't have to face reality, then you get to keep walking around in your hopeless fog. Lulu would be disappointed."

"Well, Lulu isn't here, is she?" Joon snapped.

Skinner sighed. "I'm sorry. I shouldn't have said that. So, okay, you're staying at the warehouse with a big group of losers. What are you gonna do for yourself?"

Joon smirked. "There are two things I need to do." She kept her eyes glued to the ground below her.

"Are you gonna tell me?"

"Actually, I was going to ask if you'd help me."

"Okaaaay, do you wanna tell me what these two things are?"

"Yeah, of course. When I went back to pick up Lulu's ashes from Dr. Becker, I asked him about Molly," Joon said, staring at Skinner oddly.

"Who the hell is Molly?"

Joon sighed. "The diary you found. The little girl who shared a hospital room with Lulu."

"Oh, sorry. How is she?"

"She died a couple of days before Lulu. Anyway, I promised Molly that I would take her diary to her dad." She pulled the diary from her bag and opened the front cover. Joon pointed to the address Molly had written. "She lived in Villanova. It's west of the city. Anyway, I thought I could take a train out there, and you know...drop it off to him."

"Okay, that's reasonable. I'll go with you. What's the other thing?"

Joon took in a loud breath. "I want to stop at Tioga-Nicetown."

"Isn't that a real shit section of town? What do you have to do there?"

"I want to go back and see the house where I lived with Aron."

Skinner gasped. "I don't know if that's a good idea. I mean, what if she sees you?"

"Yeah, what if? I'm not the little girl I was when I ran away. I'm gonna be eighteen in two months. There's nothing she can do to me." Joon paused. "Especially not if you're with me."

Skinner rubbed his temples. "What do you expect to get out of it?"

"To face my greatest fear. That woman still gives me nightmares. When I dream of her, I feel like I'm a little girl being tortured again. I can go months without thinking of her at all. Then, I see someone who looks like her or sounds like her, and I spiral into this dark hole. Lulu and I talked about her a lot. She said that someday, we would go back to that house together, and she'd show me that the big, bad Aron isn't so scary." Joon chuckled. "Lulu would say the only thing big and bad about Aron is her breath. That always cracked me up...but she didn't know Aron and how evil she could be. No one really believes me when I say that she's the devil." Joon looked into Skinner's eyes. "I need to put her behind me once and for all. Face my fear. See that she's nothing more than a sick woman. Maybe even spit on her if I get close enough."

"Okay. When are we doing this?"

"Tomorrow."

Chapter Ninety

The following day, Joon and Skinner took a train and two buses to reach Aron's house. It was almost three thirty in the afternoon when they arrived. They sat on a curb where they could see Aron's house.

"Is she home?" Skinner asked.

"How should I know? When I lived there, I would get home from school around this time. She was always at home then. But who knows what her routine is now?"

The two sat there and Joon looked around the neighborhood. She'd never spent much time out of the house, except to go to school, but she remembered how scary the neighborhood was to her when her caseworker drove her here so many years ago. Skinner lit a cigarette and passed it to Joon, who took a few drags and handed it back to him.

"Do you wanna get closer?" he asked.

"Yeah," Joon answered, standing up and brushing off her pants. As they walked toward Aron's house, they heard the brakes of a school bus squeaking behind them. The two turned around and watched as seven kids bolted off the bus. Then a few seconds behind them, a young girl lumbered off the last step. Instinctively, Joon grabbed Skinner's arm.

"What?" he said, leaning into her.

"I don't know. Something's weird about that kid."

"You're spooking yourself out because you're standing so close to that bitch's house."

Joon shook her head. "Let's wait and watch her…make sure she's okay."

The two of them stepped back as the girl approached. Joon smiled at the child, who looked away quickly. As the girl got closer, Joon said, "Hi. Um, we're lost. Do you know where the closest bus stop is?"

The little girl hesitated for a split second. "No," she said in a whisper.

Joon looked the girl over. Her jacket was old, and her pants were three inches too short for her. The girl's hair was dirty and matted to her head, and she was so thin. Joon smelled the child's fear—her anguish was coming off her in waves. As the young girl kept walking, Joon followed at a distance. As the girl turned and walked up the porch to Aron's house, Joon's mouth fell open.

When the child got to the door, it opened, and there stood Aron with her hand on her hip and a scowl on her face.

"That's her," Joon croaked.

Skinner watched the woman intently. She didn't look evil. In fact, she looked normal aside from her expression. Then as the child walked past her, Aron gripped the girl's filthy hair at the nape of her neck and dragged her into the house, slamming the door behind them.

Skinner sprang forward. "Come on, Joon. We gotta help that kid."

Joon remained planted on the sidewalk. Seeing Aron had made terror wash over her. Her limbs felt weak and her ears were ringing.

She'd always imagined that she would get even someday when she saw her foster mother. But seeing the woman had nearly crippled her with apprehension. She thought quickly and stopped Skinner. "No. We can't. You don't know what Aron's capable of. She'll kill us and bury our bodies in the backyard. She's an emotional vampire. Sucks the life outta you and then beats your corpse until there's nothing left."

Skinner put his hands on Joon's shoulders and shook her gently. "Snap the fuck out of it, Joon. Didn't you see her grab that kid's hair when she walked by her?"

Joon nodded. "That's nothing compared to what she's gonna do."

"And we're gonna stand here and do nothing?"

Joon's knees felt weak. Before she arrived, she fantasized about confronting Aron. But now, seeing the woman made her want to get far away. "We can't do anything now. I have to think. I...I just gotta get outta here. Please."

Skinner looked at her carefully—the blood was drained from her face and she was visibly shaken. "Okay, we'll come back. All right?" he said, trying to calm her.

"Yeah, we'll come back and help that little girl. I promise. Let's go. I wanna be waiting for Molly's dad when he gets home from work. I don't know what time that is, but we'll just have to wait. Even if we have to stay there all night."

On the train to Villanova, Joon thought about the horrors taking place inside Aron's house. Guilt pressed in on her, and she felt a surge of remorse for not being stronger, but she also knew that Aron was clever, a manipulative woman who couldn't be trusted.

"You okay?" Skinner asked as the train hummed along.

"No, not really. I know what's going on in that house. I've lived that little girl's life."

"One thing at a time, Joon. Let's get this diary delivered and head back to the city."

Joon and Skinner got off the train at Villanova just before five in the evening. Spotting what she needed, Joon headed straight to the map behind glass hanging on the wall. She and Skinner mapped out their route to Molly's house, and seeing that it was less than two miles from the station, they walked.

When they arrived, Joon stood on the sidewalk for a moment, looking across the manicured lawn at the beautifully kept home—Molly's home.

"Let's sit and wait," she said.

For the next two hours, the two friends sat and talked about the little girl that lived at Aron's house. Then, as they were growing tired, a car turned into the long driveway.

"Here we go," Joon said, standing and walking toward the car.

As the man got out of the car, he noticed Joon and Skinner coming toward him. As they got closer, he could see they wore tattered clothing, and he adjusted his stance, his feet spread apart, his back erect, not knowing what to expect, but wanting to be prepared. "What do you want?"

"My name is Joon. I met your daughter Molly when she was in the hospital."

Sadness flashed across the man's face at the mention of his daughter. "Like I asked, what do you want?"

Joon held up the diary. "Molly asked me to give you this. She said, well, she said that she wanted you to know her last wishes."

Molly's father grabbed the diary and flipped to a random page. Recognizing his daughter's handwriting, his posture relaxed slightly. Then he looked at Joon and Skinner. "Okay, now I have it. Thanks."

"Sir, Molly said it was important for you to read it by yourself," Joon explained, feeling a bit odd dictating what the man was supposed to do with his deceased daughter's thoughts. "She said it would upset her mother too much and she didn't want to put her through any more pain."

The man turned the diary over in his hands, thinking. Then he leaned into the car, pulled out his briefcase, and stuck the diary inside. "Anything else?" he said, sounding annoyed.

"Yeah," Joon said, trying to be compassionate, "I'm sorry about Molly. She was a really nice kid. She was smart, and we laughed a lot together. She was funny. I just want you to know I'm sorry Molly died."

Molly's father shoved his hand in his suit pocket as he felt heat spreading across his chest and into face. "Thanks...I appreciate that." He looked Joon over from head to toe. "Do you need some money to get back home?"

Joon shook her head. "No. We're fine. I hope that whatever Molly's last wishes were that you can make them happen. I know that would've made her very happy."

"You didn't read it?"

"No. It's her diary and she asked me not to."

He gave her a sad smile. "Thanks. And good luck...to both of you."

Joon and Skinner sat on a wooden bench as they waited for the train to take them back to Philadelphia.

"You know," Joon said, smiling at Skinner, "it feels really good to keep a promise. I actually feel useful."

On the train, Joon slept while Skinner kept alert to the people around them. Back in the city again, they met Gunther at Suburban Station and spent the rest of the night tucked between two Dumpsters in an alleyway.

Chapter Ninety-One

"What if she does something crazy?" Joon asked.

Tony Bruno turned to look at her. "Maybe you'd be better off waitin' in the car."

"No. I can't."

Tony rubbed his hands on his jeans. "Then ya need to calm down."

Joon fell silent. She had asked for Tony's help, and now she needed to listen to him.

After walking another block, Tony turned to Salvatore and Vincent. "It's the next block. We ready?"

"I was born ready," Vincent replied. "My ma used to tell me that when I was little. She said, 'Vincent, you was born ready to get in trouble.' It made me feel really good when she said that to me."

The four teens stood on the sidewalk and looked up at the battered house. "I'm gonna take Joon up to the front door. Once we get inside, you two follow."

Joon stood at the front door. Her legs felt like rubber. Tony stood off to the side but still close enough to keep her safe. She lifted her hand and knocked.

A minute later, the inner door opened, and she stood staring down at Aron. Her pulse quickened as the woman stared into her eyes. "Well, look who it is. Looney Jooney. What the fuck are you doing here?"

Joon's heart pounded against her ribs. "You're not as tall as I remembered," she managed.

Aron was looking up at her. "Bitch, I don't need height. I will fuck you over in a minute."

At the outburst, Tony stepped in front of Joon and placed a gun against Aron's temple. In a low, deep voice, he said, "I suggest you step inside and let us in, or I'll blow your fuckin' brains out right here on your broken-down porch."

Aron glared at him. Joon was disturbed that the woman didn't seem at all alarmed by having a gun to her head and realized the woman was crazier than she'd originally believed. Watching Aron was like viewing a horror movie where you're screaming at the screen for the actor to be smarter. As Joon stepped into Aron's house behind Tony, she waved Salvatore and Vincent in.

"Sit the fuck down," Tony said, gesturing for Aron to sit in the recliner.

"What do you want? I don't have any money," Aron growled.

Tony glared at her. "What we want money can't buy. Who else is in the house?"

Aron remained silent. Tony turned to his two friends and nodded toward the other rooms. A few minutes later, Salvatore and Vincent came back pushing Deen ahead of them.

"Joon? Who else lives here?"

"She has two sons, Deen and Dobi. That's Deen."

Tony kicked the recliner Aron was sitting in. "Where the fuck is Dobi?"

Aron huffed. "That little prick moved out. Stupid son of a bitch joined the navy. Couldn't wait to get outta this town."

"Couldn't wait to get away from you," Joon spat.

Aron jolted off the recliner, but before she could get to Joon, Tony punched her in the nose, and she flew back into the chair in a heap.

Joon laughed as she looked at Aron's bloodied, stunned face, but it was mostly bravado to irritate Aron because her insides were quivering. Being in the house, around the people who had ruined her childhood, was overwhelming. Fear and revenge were warring against each other inside her head. It left her confused and partly detached from what was happening. She shook her head to steady her thoughts. Then Joon turned on Deen.

"Tony, did I tell you that Deen was going to rape me the night I ran away?"

Tony played her sidekick perfectly. "I think you mentioned that to me." He walked over to Deen who was still standing between Salvatore and Vincent. "Is that what you was gonna do to her, *Deen*?"

Deen's upper lip curled in a snarl. "Fuck you, you little Guido."

Tony rubbed his chin. "Oh, we got us a smart-ass. You think you're a badass? Is that it?"

Deen sneered in response.

In one swift move, Vincent grabbed the back of Deen's head and slammed his face into the doorjamb.

Tony grabbed Deen by the collar and put his nose to the other boy's. "Right now, you're playing wit fire. You don't know who we are or what we're willing to do. But I'll tell ya this, ain't none of us got tolerance for little rapists. I suggest you shut your motherfucking mouth and open up your Dumbo ears," he said. Then, he slapped Deen full force on the side of his head.

Joon felt a twinge of guilt as she looked from Aron to Deen. Both were bleeding and seemed helpless against the might of Tony, Salvatore, and Vincent. She even felt scared for them and considered asking Tony to dial it back—but then she remembered why she'd brought Tony and his friends to Aron's house, and she turned on Aron with renewed rage.

"Where's the little girl that lives here?"

Aron pursed her lips, her mouth cocked to the right side. "Don't know what little girl you're talking about. We don't have anyone else living here."

"You're lying. I was here a couple of weeks ago. I watched you grab her by the hair and drag her into the house. Where is she?"

Aron's mouth edged up into a twisted, sick smile.

Joon turned and headed straight into the kitchen. She went to the cellar door, found they had put a deadbolt on it, and returned to the living room. "Where's the key to the deadbolt?"

Aron shrugged. "I have no idea what you're talking about. Have any of your boyfriends here told you that you smell really bad? Look at you," she said, exaggeratedly examining her from her head to her toes. "You're a disgusting piece of shit. I see nothing has changed."

Joon rushed the woman and the recliner flipped backward, spilling both of them onto the floor. Joon moved with graceful quickness as she got on top of Aron, straddling her. She wanted to hit the woman, smash her face in with her fist, rip the wiry hair out of her head, cut her big ears off…but given the opportunity to physically harm Aron, she couldn't do it. Instead, she spit in Aron's face and stood up.

"The little girl is in the basement. That's where she kept me too. We need that key to the deadbolt," she stated.

Tony nodded. "Hey!"

Salvatore and Vincent looked over at him. "Take that piece of shit into the kitchen and help him find the key to unlock the basement door."

"Keep your fucking mouth shut, Deen!" Aron hollered.

Tony kicked Aron in the shin, and she yelped. "You better watch your fucking mouth. I ain't a man who hurts women, but if there was ever a broad I'd like to beat the shit outta, it's you."

Joon covered her ears as Deen screamed in agony from the kitchen. She didn't know what Salvatore and Vincent were doing to him, but whatever it was, she was certain it was very unpleasant. It wasn't long before Salvatore walked into the living room, smiling, a key resting in his palm.

He walked up to Joon and gave her the key. "You better go down first, and we'll follow. If there is a kid down there, she'll be scared to see us. This way, you can let her know it's okay."

Tony pulled Aron off the floor, and they all walked into the kitchen. Joon opened the door and threw on the light switch. A dim bulb came on, and at the bottom of the steps, she could see the little girl huddled in the corner, staring up wide-eyed and fearful. It was like looking at herself several years before, and Joon was relieved she'd come back to find the child.

Chapter Ninety-Two

J oon walked down the steps calmly. When she got to the bottom, she stooped in front of the little girl.

"Hi. I'm Joon."

The little girl's eyes welled with tears, and she buried her face in her hands. It wasn't until that moment that Joon noticed the girl was naked. She quickly took off her coat and wrapped it around the child. "Are you okay? Are you hurt?"

The girl looked up and shook her head, changing her mind suddenly and nodding.

"You're hurt?"

The girl nodded again. "Are you going to hit me?" the girl mumbled.

"No. Of course not. Why would I hit you?"

The girl looked up at the top of the stairs where Tony was standing. "Aron hits me. And…she lets them hit me too."

"Who is them?"

The child looked up at Tony again. "The men."

Joon sucked in a breath so hard she couldn't handle the sudden rush of air into her lungs and started coughing. "There are no men here that are going to hit you. We came to get you outta here, far away from that monster bitch."

The girl smiled.

"We're gonna go upstairs so we can leave," Joon said. She reached for the child's hand, but the girl shrunk away.

"What's your name?"

"Lily."

"Take my hand, Lily. I need you to trust me, okay? You're going to be fine." Joon followed Lily's eyes to the top of the stairs. "That guy up there is a friend of mine. His name is Tony. He came to help take you away from here."

After more coaxing, the child stood and Joon wrapped an arm around her as they ascended the stairs together. In the kitchen, Lily saw Aron and turned to go back down the stairs. Joon gently held her arm. "You don't have to be afraid of her anymore. She's never gonna hurt you again." Joon swiftly moved Lily through the kitchen and into the bedroom where she'd once stayed. She opened the dresser drawers until she found clothes that Lily could wear. Once the child was dressed, Joon and Lily met Tony in the living room.

"Here are the keys to the car. You and..."

"Lily," Joon said, smiling down at the girl.

"You and Lily go outside and wait for us. We won't be much longer."

Taking the car keys from Tony, Joon headed for the door but took one final look over her shoulder to find Aron staring at her. Joon gave her a beautiful smile, mouthed *fuck you*, and left the house with her head held high.

"Well," Tony said, "I'm glad they're gone. Now we can get down to business." He turned to his friends. "Where's the shit?"

"It's on the porch," Vincent said. "I'll get it."

By the time Vincent returned, Aron and Deen were tied up in the basement. Tony stood over them. "You know, I didn't wanna kill ya. I mean, I hardly know ya."

"There's no reason to kill us," Aron said, trying to keep her cool.

"Sure there is. I mean, you two was really mean to my friend Joon. And by the looks of that little girl, you was mean to her too. Anyway, here's what we're gonna do. First off, my friend Vincent has a little surprise for both of you."

Vincent walked downstairs and stood over Aron. She tilted her head back to give him her nastiest look, and as she did, Vincent emptied the glass of acid into her face.

Aron's screams indicated the pain level of her torture, and, satisfied with her reaction, Tony moved to Deen. The young man was shaking his head and sweating profusely.

"Please. I swear. I'll do anything you want. Please don't hurt me."

Tony tapped his own forehead with his index finger. "Funny. I think Joon told me that she said something just like that to you when you was torturing her." Tony bent down and cut Deen's pajama bottoms away. Then Vincent walked up, leered at Deen, and poured a glass of acid on his crotch.

Aron and Deen were both yelling as Tony bent down in front of Aron, whose face was melting off and hanging in a mangled mass of flesh. "I know you care a whole lot about looks—you know, always telling Joon how ugly she was and all. So we thought you needed a little attitude adjustment. Now, we can't leave ya here like this. If someone finds you, who knows? You could talk. So just to make sure..."

Tony slit Aron's throat with a hunting knife. The three boys stood and watched as the life slipped out of her and she gurgled her way into hell. Then Tony did the same to Deen. Once both were dead, Tony, Salvatore, and Vincent left the house and closed the door behind them.

"We did good work here tonight," Salvatore said, patting Tony on the back.

"Yeah, it's easy to kill people like that. They ain't doing this world no good," Tony said.

As the boys got into the car, Joon looked at them with anticipation. "Well?"

Tony slid in the car next to Joon. "Everything's been taken care of. They ain't never gonna bother you or Lily again."

Joon's stomach flip-flopped. She didn't know what the boys had done but figured whatever it was had been painful and permanent. A tinge of guilt hit her in the belly, but she soothed it by remembering they had saved a child.

One Year Later

J oon walked into the small waiting room outside Dr. Becker's office, gave the receptionist her name, and looked around for a seat. There were three chairs sitting side by side, and she settled into the chair on the end. She sat staring at her hands, which rested in her lap. Her fingernails were black. She brushed her fingers on her oversized jeans as if she could get rid of the grime. Self-conscious, she ran her fingers through her hair, trying to make it look as though it were combed. She let out a loud sigh.

I'm covered in filth. Maybe Dr. Becker won't notice. Not that he cares. Dr. Becker never judges...I wonder how bad I smell. Oh God, I know I smell like shit and sour piss. Okay, stop it.

As Joon waited, the door opened and a couple entered with their small daughter. They didn't seem to notice her while they gave the receptionist their name, but as the couple turned back to the room, they looked directly at Joon. She saw the mother wince.

They slowly made their way over to sit, the mother taking the seat on the other end of the row and pulling her child onto her lap, leaving the chair between herself and Joon empty. The husband hovered in front of his wife and daughter.

"Hi," the little girl said, leaning from her mother's lap into the open chair between them. "My name is Christy. What's yours?"

"Christy," her mother said sharply. "Leave that lady alone."

Joon smiled at the girl. "It's okay," she said to the mother. "My name is Joon."

Christy smiled back at her. "Are you sick?"

"No."

Christy's mom tried to pull the seven-year-old back onto her lap, but she kept trying to wiggle away.

"How come your clothes look like that?" Christy asked.

Joon readjusted in her chair. "Well, I didn't get a chance to wash them."

Christy pointed at Joon's hands. "You forgot to wash your hands too?"

Joon flushed. She wished the child would stop pointing out the obvious. Her parents were becoming visibly more uncomfortable.

"Yeah, I forgot to wash them," Joon said, making two fists to hide her fingernails. Then she tried to ignore the child for the sake of her parents.

Against her mother's will, the little girl moved off her lap and climbed into the chair next to Joon. The child's mother grabbed the girl's shoulder and held her away from Joon. Finally, the father had his wife stand up, and he lifted her chair and moved it against another wall.

"Come on, Christy," her father instructed. "Come over here and sit with Mommy."

Christy obeyed her father and moved across the room, where her mother held her tight, as if to protect the child from the germs and disease of Joon. The couple whispered a few times and looked over at Joon, who wished she could fade into invisibility. Joon could sense that Christy's parents were repulsed and even scared of their child being near her. It wasn't often that Joon spent time around "normal" people in small spaces, and today, she wasn't prepared to handle the rejection and repulsion that the couple couldn't hide. They were huddled around the chair as if they could filter the air, so Christy wouldn't breathe in Joon. Joon glanced up and again found them staring at her. Their brows furrowed and mouths pinched.

For fuck's sake, it's just dirt. I'm not gonna give your kid the plague, Joon thought.

She breathed a sigh of relief when the door next to the receptionist opened and a nurse came out. "Joon?"

She stood up quickly and rushed over to the nurse, who seemed not to notice how filthy she was. All Joon wanted to do was get on the other side of that door and leave her shame in the waiting room. But to Joon's horror, the nurse didn't move.

"Mr. and Mrs. Herr? You can come back too."

The nurse opened Dr. Becker's office door and stood to the side. "Go on in and have a seat."

Joon followed her instructions and was relieved to see Dr. Becker's bright smile as she entered his office. She sat quickly and peeked back at Christy and her parents as they waited to be led to another room.

The nurse gave the Herrs a bright smile. "You can go in and have a seat too."

Dr. Becker greeted them as they entered.

"Dr. Becker, I think we'd rather wait until you're done with this," Mr. Herr said seriously, "um…this…young lady and then we can see you. We don't mind waiting."

"Daddy, her name is Joon," Christy interrupted.

"That's right, Christy. Her name is Joon," Dr. Becker confirmed.

"Seriously, Dr. Becker," Mrs. Herr said. "We want our privacy."

Dr. Becker stood from behind his desk. "You're absolutely right. You deserve your privacy, so I'll get my nurse to take you back to the waiting room." The couple stood and crossed to the other side of the office with Christy, as Dr. Becker turned to Joon. "Mr. and Mrs. Herr have a foundation that helps children and adults fund the cost of kidney transplants."

"Dr. Becker," Mrs. Herr said. "May I speak to you for a moment?"

The doctor approached, and Mrs. Herr leaned close to his ear. "You know that Christy's susceptible to germs, and that girl is, well, I assume she's homeless. Her fingernails alone are carrying a small country of germs; our foundation was created to help people who are in dire need, not for lazy people who choose to live in squalor."

Dr. Becker turned away for a moment to gain his composure. When he looked at the couple again, his mouth was open, and his tongue was pushing slightly forward, as if he was having a battle with the words that wanted to escape. "You're a smart, successful couple. I'm sure you're aware that not all homeless people are lazy or choose to live on the streets. Sometimes life isn't kind to everyone like it has been to the three of us."

Dr. Becker looked back at Joon. He could see her sorrow in the deep creases around her eyes and mouth. She had literally shrunk herself into the corner of the sofa as she sheepishly looked at her own appearance.

The doctor turned back to the Herrs, shoved his hands into his pants pockets, and tilted his head back. "Before I call my nurse to take you back to the waiting room, I thought you'd like to meet the person who saved Christy's life. You said you wanted to meet her." He turned and walked across the room and sat beside Joon. "This young lady, Joon, is the person who gave Christy one of her kidneys."

Mrs. Herr put her hand over her mouth and tears sprung to her eyes. "Oh my God."

Christy pulled her hand away from her mother's and walked over to Joon. The child climbed onto the sofa next to the young woman. The moment was bittersweet. Joon was thrilled to see the healthy child and started to cry, but her thoughts also drifted to Lulu. Though she hadn't been able to save her friend, Joon had vowed to herself that she would help someone who could use her kidney. She looked up at Christy's mother.

Dr. Becker knelt in front of them. "Christy, Joon gave you her kidney. Because of her, you will live a long and healthy life."

Christy threw her arms around Joon as Dr. Becker turned to the couple and raised his eyebrows.

Mr. and Mrs. Herr walked over to Joon, their shame palpable, and the mother put out her hands to help Joon off the sofa. She pulled Joon up and embraced her, Mr. Herr wrapped his arms around both women.

"We are so sorry," Mrs. Herr began. "There is no excuse for what we just put you through. We are both mortified and deeply humbled." Her voice was wavering with emotion as she spoke. "Thank you for sharing your life with our daughter. Because of you, our child is well again. We can never thank you enough. If there is anything that you ever need..."

Joon shook her head and bent down to look into Christy eyes. Through her tears, she said, "We will always be related. No matter where we are, you and me, we will know that we share something very special. I'm a part of you and you're a part of me now."

Joon and the child embraced again for several moments, and Mr. Herr put his hand on Joon's shoulder. "You're an amazing young woman. We had waited so long for a matching donor, and...we don't know how to thank you."

"You already have thanked me," Joon said. "I've done something good with my life. If it's the only thing I ever do, I already know that I, little, old, homeless Joon, changed one person's life. I did something remarkable. I made a difference. That's all I ever wanted—to make a difference."

When it was time to leave Dr. Becker's office, Joon gave him a tight hug. "Thank you," she whispered.

As she turned to leave, the Herrs offered to take her to lunch, but she declined. "I'm way too emotional to eat right now. I'm sorry."

"Can we walk you home?" Mrs. Herr offered. "We would like to spend a little more time with you."

Joon looked at Dr. Becker, who gave her a quick nod. "Sure. You can walk me back to where I sleep. My home is everywhere…and nowhere." She smiled at the family. "That's the way it is when you don't have a real home," she said, feeling comfortable with her situation. She had given Christy something her parents' money couldn't buy, and this gave Joon a sense of peace.

Joon and Christy walked hand in hand. The Herrs followed behind them as Joon led them to the place under the bridge where she had first slept with Ragtop. She had moved back there after her recovery, and since the weather was still warm, she planned to stay under the bridge for as long as possible. Joon looked at the Herrs and then up at her space, she raised her hands into the air, and said, "This is it. Home Street Home."

Joon shimmied up the concrete and pulled Christy along with her. Mrs. Herr slipped out of her high heels, and together, she and her husband climbed onto the ledge and sat down.

Christy was sitting next to Joon and tugged on her arm. "Do you actually live here?"

"Yeah, I do," Joon said, taking the girls hand. "You see a home doesn't mean anything. That's just a place to live. It's making your mark in the world that really matters. Sharing what I have with you was the best thing I have ever done. If I wasn't here tomorrow, that would be okay because you will live a long life, and I will always be with you."

When the time came for the Herrs to leave, they hugged Joon and promised to see her again. Joon watched until the family walked out of sight, then she sat under the bridge and smiled for a long time.

Later that afternoon, when she went to visit Skinner and Gunther, she could barely contain her excitement as she told them what had happened with Christy and her parents. Gunther had secured a construction job and moved them into a low-income apartment. The two young men had taken Lily in and were raising her as their own. Joon had wanted so much to raise her but knew that Lily would be better off with them. Lily had been deeply scarred by Aron, but Skinner made it his sole purpose in life to help heal the child. It wasn't perfect, but it was a life that Skinner,

Gunther, and Lily loved. Joon visited for a while, then she returned to her concrete home.

That night, Joon thought about Christy. The child looked so healthy. She had tried for months to donate her kidney, and when Dr. Becker said he'd found someone, Joon had been so happy. As she fell asleep, she held on to an image of Lulu. In Christy, Joon saw what could have been for her friend, and the gratifying peace of helping another person washed over her.

Two Weeks Later

―――――――――――――――――――――――

I t was early on Tuesday morning, and Joon was sleeping soundly—she had slept well since she'd met the Herrs and saw with her own two eyes the good she'd contributed to the world. As she dreamed, she felt blissful and smelled something wonderful. Still sleeping, she breathed in deeply...there was that smell again. She opened her eyes and blinked.

I must still be dreaming, Joon told herself.

"Hey, baby," the silky voice sang. "I got you a hot chocolate. Just like the one I got you on your first morning in this very spot."

Joon sat up, rubbing her eyes. "Ragtop?"

"Alive and well," Ragtop said, beaming.

Joon studied the older woman. Her hair was in perfect, long braids. She wore clean clothes that fit her, and she even had makeup beautifully applied to her dark skin. Before she knew what was happening, Joon was crying.

"You don't have your bandana anymore."

"No, baby. I got myself all cleaned up," she said proudly.

Finally, Joon threw her arms around the woman's neck. "What happened to you?"

"Got myself fucked up on drugs. I left you alone, and I'm so sorry. I've been looking for you whenever I'm not working. For the first couple of years after I got outta rehab, I came back here a lot looking for ya. Then, today, something told me to check again. When I saw ya sleeping here, my chest got tight and I could hardly breathe. I thought maybe I was seeing things, but seeing you again for real made me so happy—it made me feel whole again. So I went and bought you a hot chocolate...a stupid-ass peace offering, but to let you know I never forgot about you."

"Thank you," Joon said, looking at the cup in Ragtop's hand. "What did you mean by working? Are you still prostituting?"

"No, sugar. I got myself a real job. I work and live in Camden. After rehab, they helped me get a job and a place to stay. I've been employed for over three years. Got an apartment that has enough room for two people. That's why I've been searching for you. Came to see if you wanna come back and live with me. Can't think of a better roommate than you," she said, smiling at Joon.

Joon bowed her head and cried.

Ragtop put her arm around her shoulders. "Is that a yes?" she asked quietly.

Joon looked at her, the blue of her eyes blazing with life. "Yeah. It's definitely a yes."

As the two waited for a bus that would take them over to Camden, Joon started telling her about how she'd donated a kidney and how surprised the family was that she, a homeless person, was the donor, and as she thought of Lulu and why she'd done it, she realized just how far back the story began. "I have so much to tell you," she said.

"We'll have a lot of time to talk, and I want you to tell me everything," Ragtop said, taking Joon's hand and drawing in a long breath. "I'm really sorry I let you down. I promise it won't happen again."

Joon couldn't have been happier. She was back with the only mom she'd ever known since her own mother had died. The future looked bright for the first time in as long as she could remember, and Joon was genuinely optimistic.

She squeezed Ragtop's hand. "I wanna make something good out of my life, and I've already started by donating my kidney. Now, I wanna go to school and learn. I don't know exactly what I want to do yet, but I know I want to do something to help others. I know it's gonna be a long road, but I'm willing to travel that road until it leads me to the life that has always belonged to me."

Ragtop hugged Joon tight to her chest. "You're home, baby. We're both finally home."

Continue Reading...

Read about Tony's story and how he became the man who helped Joon, from my novel, Mean Little People. Read a sample of Mean Little People here…

The Beating Path

———————————▬———————————

Seven-year-old Tony Bruno feared the dark hands of death were reaching for him. His small feet pounded against the hot pavement as he tried to get away from the boys chasing after him.

In midstride two of the seven-year-old boys snatched Tony by the back of his worn-out T-shirt. His arms flailed spastically. He tried to make contact with his small fists. One boy got angry and yelled, "Knock it off, Bruno, ya little queer."

Tony was dragged through the trash that lined the sidewalk.

"Leave me alone," Tony cried in a high-pitched voice.

"Shut up, Bruno. I swear if ya open your mouth again, we'll kill ya," Vincent snapped.

Tony twisted and pitched against the boys. He fought with everything he had in him, but he was no match for the kids who used bullying as an after-school activity.

Tony's eyes fixed on his surroundings as if he were seeing them for the first time. He looked into the open lot, taking in the small patch of trees and overgrown grass. On either side of the lot were brick buildings with broken windows that revealed the lifeless blackness within. Vines clung to the exterior as if they'd grown there from the inside out. Tony never walked between the buildings. It was taboo. This place scared him. This was the place where the monsters lived. He'd heard the groan of drunks coming from deep inside the cavity of the broken-down buildings when he'd walked by months before with his mother.

Tony fixated on his mother's words now.

"There are googamongers that live in that place. Do ya know what a googamonger is?" Teresa had said.

Tony had shaken his head, scanning the trees and buildings, waiting for a humanlike creature to come after him.

"They're real big. Bigger than your father. They got long claws for fingers and real pointy teeth. They like to eat children 'cause every time they eat a kid, they grow stronger. So you keep your skinny ass outta there."

Tony was paralyzed with fear thinking about the googamongers. He kept fighting against his tormentors, but they dragged him deeper into the forbidden lot. Vincent and his friends forced Tony into the shadow of a small grouping of trees. Tony peed himself, imagining the googamongers watching him, getting ready to eat him. His stomach turned with a wispy emptiness. Tony made one final attempt to free himself and got one arm loose. Vincent punched Tony in the gut, and a few seconds later, Tony's head slammed against a large oak tree.

Vincent poked his index finger into Tony's sternum. "Give us all your money."

"I ain't g...g...got no money." Tony stared into Vincent's rich brown eyes through the jet-black hair that fell in front of them.

Frankie grabbed Tony around the waist and threw him to the ground. Then he pulled Tony's T-shirt over his head and threw it off to the side.

"Look!" Frankie stood over the boy. "Bruno peed himself."

The boys stood in a circle around Tony and laughed.

Vincent turned to his best friend, Patton. "Grab the bucket we left in the grass."

Patton stared for a moment as if he was trying to read Vincent's mind. He jumped up and down and clapped his hands together. "Yeahhhhhh..." he sang as he ran into the tall grass.

Patton raced back to the noisy circle of boys. Vincent pulled the old plastic clothesline they had stolen from the neighbor lady they called Mrs. Mean. He handed the line to Patton, who threw it over a tree limb while another boy turned the bucket upside down.

A few minutes later, Tony was standing on the bucket with the plastic cord around his neck. His fingers clawed at the cord with frantic desperation. His body shook. In the heat of the day, Tony's teeth chattered. He couldn't think. His mind went blank. While Tony didn't comprehend the possible consequences of the boy's actions, he felt he was in grave danger.

Vincent looked at Tony and smiled. "He looks just like that cowboy in the movie. They hung 'im from a tree; then one of the guys kicked the horse he was sittin' on, and the guy fell off. He was swingin' by his neck. It was so cool—his legs were movin' like he was ridin' a bike, and he was twitchin' and stuff."

The energy in the small group of boys was a blend of morbid curiosity and fear of the unknown. Tony's motions were jerky. His tongue stuck to the roof of his mouth. The more his fear showed outwardly, the higher the energy level rose through the circle of boys.

"I need to go home," Tony cried. "My ma will be lookin' for me."

"You'll go home when we say ya can," Patton hissed. Then he picked up a long stick and whacked Tony on his bare back. The rough, bark-covered branches dug into his tender flesh and left bloated, red welts.

"Wow! Let me try that," Vincent said, picking up a branch and slashing it across Tony's abdomen.

Tony continued to pull at the cord around his neck. Each time one of the boys whacked him with a stick, he flinched, and the rope tightened. After a short time, Tony's muscles went limp, and he welcomed the numb feeling inside his head. His eyelids drooped, and he stopped fighting. His shoulders flopped forward, and his head hung. With a lack of oxygen, death crept upon him, bringing him the closure he longed for.

"Hey! What the hell are ya boys doin' over there?" A male voice boomed.

Vincent turned and saw a delivery-truck driver at the edge of the lot; he was coming toward them.

Vincent screamed, "Run!"

The boys took off in different directions, but Patton hesitated for a moment and kicked the bucket from under Tony's feet before he took off.

The cord was just long enough so Tony landed on his tippy-toes, but the initial fall tightened it around his neck, jarring him awake. Tony tried to suck in a breath, and when nothing came through, his panic heightened, and he lost his balance. He lost his battle against the strangling cord. His windpipe betrayed him, and the lack of oxygen gave him comfort again.

The deliveryman reached Tony right before he slipped out of consciousness. He lifted Tony's small body and held him on his hip, as though he were a toddler. The man quickly loosened the rope around

Tony's neck. Tony gulped air into his lungs, and the bluish color in his face shortly returned to normal.

"What the hell happened here?" the deliveryman said. He pulled a knife from his pocket and cut the cord.

Tony rubbed his neck with his fingertips. He looked around with a pinched expression. Then he remembered. "Vincent and his friends followed me. And...and...they made me come here and..."

Tony sobbed from the memory that rushed into his mind.

"OK, big guy. What's your name?"

"Tony."

"Well, I'm Mac. Let's get ya home. Where's your shirt?"

Tony looked around the tall grass in a daze. It was gone. Carried off by Patton.

"Forget the shirt. Ya all right?"

Tony nodded.

"Ya think ya can stand?" Mac said, placing Tony on his feet.

Tony wobbled at first but then gained his footing.

"Where do you live?"

"Over that way," Tony said, pointing in the direction of his row home.

Mac slowly walked Tony to his house and stood at the front door with him.

"Everything will be fine," Mac said and softly rapped on the front door.

"What the hell did ya do now?" Tony's father, Carmen, yelled, when he flung the door open.

"Nothin'," Tony replied timidly.

Carmen looked at Mac, whose mouth hung open.

"What the hell are ya starin' at, and who are ya, anyway?" Carmen barked.

Mac adjusted his stance. His legs locked at the knees and his chest pushed forward. "I just found your kid being hung from a tree. A group of boys were hurtin' him. Those boys ain't got no scruples. Your son almost died."

"My *son* almost died 'cause he ain't got no backbone. Now, go on and deliver your packages. Stay the hell outta other people's business."

Mac stared at Carmen for a moment. Then he bent down and looked into Tony's eyes. "You take care of yourself. Stay away from those boys. Ya hear?"

Tony nodded. "Yeah, I wish they'd just leave me alone."

"Oh, for cryin' out loud! Get the hell in this house before I give ya another beatin'."

Tony knew from Carmen's squinty eyes that his father was having a worse day than normal. For a passing moment, Tony wished that he could go live with Mac. He didn't want to face his father, not alone, not again.

After Carmen slammed the door, he turned to his son. His eyes poured over Tony's gangly body, and he bent slightly at the waist to look closely at the purple mark that the cord had left around his neck.

Carmen's upper lip lifted. "Where's your shirt?"

Tony sniffled, his fear ignited by his father's venomous stare. He took a few steps backward and crossed his arms over his abdomen.

"I asked ya a question, boy."

"The kids stole it from me."

"Why did ya let 'em steal it?"

"I didn't let 'em. They made me."

"That's 'cause you're a little weasel. Ain't got no man in ya."

Carmen grabbed a handful of Tony's thick brown hair and pulled his head back to look into his son's green eyes. "You're pathetic. Go to your room, and don't come out till I say so. While you're up there, I want cha to think about how much ya embarrass me. I swear your ma cheated on me with another man, 'cause ya ain't no son of mine. Look at ya! Covered in all those scratches and bruises. The sight of ya makes me sick. Get outta my livin' room before I slap the shit outta ya."

Tony gimped up the steps as quickly as he could manage and shut his bedroom door gingerly. He pulled on a clean T-shirt and lay on his bed, waiting for his mother to come home. He rubbed his arms and legs with open hands. Pulling the blanket from his bed, he wrapped himself tightly and waited. He put his hand up to his forehead, expecting it to be on fire, but it was cold and clammy.

Then his bedroom door flew open. He sat up quickly, and the blanket dropped to his sides when he saw the belt in his father's hand. Carmen's hand lifted into the air, and the belt came down on Tony with a hard crack. The beating went on for several minutes, and when it stopped, Tony lay in a ball wishing the boys had killed him.

Chapter One

Tony's father, Carmen, had been placed in a Catholic orphanage after his mother died, when he was barely three years old. The nuns who ran the facility had believed in the saying "Spare the rod; spoil the child." When Carmen turned six, his father brought him back home after marrying another woman. But his stepmother, with three children of her own, didn't take to Carmen. She complained about his appearance and lack of manners. Over time, Carmen's father beat him, trying to make his son into what his new wife wanted. But the more beatings Carmen withstood, the greater the anger the child stored inside. Many days of his childhood, Carmen walked around with black eyes or bruises on his body. Immediately after graduating high school, Carmen was thrown out of his home and out of his father's life.

Carmen took a job as a roofer. He hated the labor-intensive work, feeling like it was below him, and a year later, after marrying Tony's mother, Teresa, he was hired by a large rigging company in Philadelphia, where Tony's family lived.

Teresa and Carmen had met in high school. Teresa had followed in her mother's footsteps and had become a seamstress at a small bridal shop.

Ten years into Carmen and Teresa's rocky marriage, with two kids, Carmen was laid off from his job and fell into a deep depression. To ease his sorrows and worries, he let his casual drinking become excessive, sloppy, and repulsive. The neighborhood watched the transformation, and he became a big joke to those who knew him. Because his rigging skills weren't in high demand, Carmen couldn't figure out what to do to earn a living.

Teresa bore the brunt of Carmen's anger over what he considered a failed life. Tony remembered the first time his father had struck his mother. One of the neighbors had just left the house after dropping off pants for Teresa to hem.

"Why do ya have to let the neighbors in here?" Carmen had growled.

"Because I'm tryin' to earn some extra money. What kind of question is that?"

"It's the kinda question a man asks when his wife is actin' like some sniveling beggar lookin' for a couple of dollars. Look at cha—ya look ridiculous wit' that measuring thing hangin' around your neck, kissin' that bitch's ass so ya can make a couple of dollars."

"Well, if ya got a real job, maybe I wouldn't have to take in side work," Teresa had fired back.

Tony had been lying on the floor in front of the television with his sister, Macie, who was three years younger than he was. He pretended like nothing was wrong, but Carmen's anger escalated, and his father rose from his worn-out recliner. He thudded over to Teresa and punched her hard in the belly.

"Stop it," Tony cried.

Like a grizzly bear drawn to a new noise, Carmen turned toward Tony and took a few steps in his direction.

Teresa grabbed on to Carmen's shoulder, and he flung her off.

"You little bitch. Don't cha ever try and get in my way," Carmen yelled. He grabbed Teresa's arm and twisted it behind her back, sending her to her knees.

"Carmen, stop! Please stop!"

"That's where ya belong, on your knees suckin' me off."

As Carmen let go of her arm, he grabbed a handful of her hair, and she rose to her feet. Carmen put his face close to hers.

"Now get in the fuckin' kitchen and do your fuckin' job before I break both of your arms."

Teresa was crying as she looked over at Tony, with Macie wrapped in a tight embrace. "Come on, Tony. Come help me in the kitchen."

Tony cautiously walked by his father with Macie behind him. Her small arms were fastened around her brother's waist. As Tony slunk by his father, Carmen jabbed him in the temple with his thick fingers.

"Get the fuck outta my sight. I can't stand any of ya."

Tony pulled Macie toward his mother as she started for the kitchen. When they were alone, Teresa grabbed her children and held them tightly.

"It's gonna be all right," Teresa said in a low, shaky voice.

"I'm scared," Tony said. "What if Dad hurts us real bad?"

Teresa looked into her son's eyes. "I'm scared too, baby. We just gotta keep 'im happy. That means doin' what he says and stayin' outta his way."

Teresa swallowed hard. "Just make sure you're a good boy."

"But I didn't do nothin', and he hit me in the head just now."

"That's 'cause ya was lookin' at him. Don't even look at 'im no more. Not when he's mad like that."

"Why can't we just go live with Grandma?"

"'Cause her and Grandpa don't need our problems. We just gotta deal wit' 'em on our own."

Now, as he lay on his bed nursing the welts from his father's beating, Tony rubbed his face with his hands. He kept looking toward the doorway for his father to appear while his mother started dinner. The room closed in on him until the small space made his breathing ragged. *What are we going to do now? How can I help my family?* Tony thought.

Chapter Two

The day after the hanging incident, Tony crouched low in the corner of the brick building in the schoolyard. His arms were crossed over his head to protect himself. The schoolyard was filled with children, playing and laughing, several watching him from a distance. The teacher and her aide stood across the long stretch of blacktop, unable to see through the crowd of rowdy second graders to where Tony was being bullied.

"Get away from me," Tony whimpered.

"You're such a dork. Maybe if we kick your butt again, we can knock the dork outta ya," Vincent said. Five of Vincent's friends stood around in a semicircle, egging on the harassment.

Vincent laughed wholeheartedly, and then he kicked Tony in the leg. Instinctively, Tony grabbed the spot where Vincent's sneaker had landed, and Vincent smacked him on the top of the head. Tony put his hands up to cover his face, but Vincent didn't let up. He kept on slapping and kicking Tony until all of his own rage was spent.

"You're an idiot, Tony. Ya ain't even smart enough to be in school. Ya should just stay in your house and never come to school," Vincent said.

"Maybe we can hang him again," Patton said.

Vincent smiled. "Would ya like that, Bruno? Gettin' hung again?"

Tony hyperventilated. Tears stung his eyes. He held his breath and curled his hands into tight fists. He feared the boys; he feared his father. His life had become lightless. He felt as though he were in a deep, dark, wet hole filled with sticky hatred.

As Tony's anguish escalated, he could no longer hold back his wails of sorrow. The group of boys watched him for a moment; then they walked away, satisfied. Tony lay in a fetal position on the pavement, wishing that someone would come to his rescue.

After several minutes, Tony sat up cautiously and looked around, embarrassed. Groups of children on the playground stood motionless, watching him. Several small clusters of children were giggling and pointing. Others wore faces of relief, happy that Tony's fate was not their own.

In kindergarten and first grade, Vincent and his friends had stuck to verbal assaults. But now, in the second grade, they had become physically abusive with Tony, turning their teasing into torment.

Tony was scared to move but even more worried the boys would come back and make good on their promise to hang him again. He got to his feet and walked slowly toward the door that led into the building.

"Hey, Tony," Brian, another second grader, said in a friendly tone, approaching him. "Here, do ya wanna drink?"

Tony turned toward the boy. He watched Brian for a moment; then a smile played on his lips. Tony's throat was dry. He looked at the condensation on the soda can and imagined the cool liquid sliding down his scratchy throat.

"Thanks a lot, Brian," Tony said, reaching for the can.

Tony put the can to his lips. The liquid splashed over his tongue; then, as he swallowed, he tasted the dirt.

Tony choked on the contents and spit the foul mixture onto the ground.

"You're such a moron," Brian taunted, as the other kids laughed. "You're so easy to pick on," he added.

Tony fell silent. His head hung, and his shoulders drooped forward. He walked fast toward the doors of the building. He wanted to get inside, to hide from his peers.

Miss Cassidy, Tony's teacher, scanned the schoolyard, and her eyes stopped on Tony. She rushed over to him as he gripped the door handle.

"Tony, what happened to you?" Miss Cassidy asked. Instinctively she gently touched his red cheek. Then she discreetly wiped away the saliva and dirt stuck on his chin.

"Nothin', Miss Cassidy," Tony said, his voice barely audible.

"Nothing, huh? Well, it doesn't look like nothing to me. Come on. Let's go inside and rinse your face with cold water."

Miss Cassidy looked around and spotted Vincent and his friends gawking at her. She lifted both eyebrows and pinched her lips together at the moment that Vincent made eye contact—a sign to let the boy know she was onto him. Miss Cassidy took Tony by the hand and led him into the building.

Once they were alone, she knelt down and placed her hands on Tony's shoulders. "Were Vincent and his friends picking on you?"

Tony shook his head slowly, but he wouldn't make eye contact.

"Are you sure?" she pressed.

Tony nodded. He thought about snitching, but the bees buzzing around in his belly reminded him there would be consequences.

"How did you get that bruise on your neck? It looks like someone was choking you."

"I ran into somethin' at my house."

"Tony, are you telling me the truth? Is there something you need to talk about?"

"No, Miss Cassidy. Can I go to the bathroom?" Tony said.

Inside the boy's bathroom, Tony looked at himself in the mirror. He was repulsed by the hollow person who stared back at him.

"You're a dork," he said out loud. "Everybody hates ya. Why can't ya fight back?"

Tony's impulse was to bust the mirror to pieces and smash the pathetic reflection that glared back at him, judging him.

"I hate ya," he said to his reflection. "I wish ya would disappear. Nobody likes ya. Not even your father."

After a few minutes, Tony washed his hands and purposely took his time walking to his classroom. Every second in the hallway was time away from the mean kids. He opened the classroom door and stepped inside. The room fell silent; then several children snickered.

"Wah! Wah! Wah! I want my mommy," Patton bellowed.

Tony wrapped his arms around himself as if he could ward off the cutting words and scathing stares that sliced through him and settled in the center of his heart.

"Patton! You stop that this instant," Miss Cassidy said.

Patton looked at Miss Cassidy innocently. "What? I didn't do nothin'."

"I want you to go straight to the principal's office," she demanded.

Patton smiled at his friends but didn't move out of his chair.

"This instant!" she yelled, surprising everyone, including herself.

As Patton slid past Tony, he whispered, "You're gonna be real sorry for this, ya stupid jerk."

Tony cringed and edged his way to his seat. He walked through the aisle of second graders cautiously. Only a few feet from his desk, one boy stuck out his foot and tripped him. Tony flew into the desk of one of the popular girls. She looked at him sympathetically at first, but realizing the other kids were watching her, she quickly pinched her nose with her thumb and index finger and turned away.

"Ew," she said, pushing Tony away from her, "you smell bad, and you're ugly."

The other kids laughed, and Tony wished he could disappear, be invisible.

Finally sitting at his desk, Tony gazed at Miss Cassidy as she lectured the class about how to treat each other. Her voice was a constant buzz of white noise in his ears as she droned on about the importance of kindness, an alien concept to him. Tony's thoughts wandered to his father. Carmen would never let people push him around; Carmen had mocked Tony for being weak since the bullying began in kindergarten. The thought of going home with more bruises boosted his anxiety. His heart thudded in his chest; he could feel every heartbeat. Tony knew his father would "give it to him" when he saw Tony's swollen lip. It was the same cycle of insanity. After his peers beat him down, he would stand before Carmen for judgment. Meanness and cruelty seemed inescapable.

When the last bell of the day rang, Tony hurried to the bus and sat in the front seat behind the bus driver. As Vincent and his friends entered, they poked, slapped, or pinched him on their way to the back of the bus. When they arrived at his bus stop that day, he ran as fast as he could until he was rushing through the front door of his house.

Teresa looked up from her sewing machine. "What's the rush? Hey, come over here—let me take a look at ya," she said.

Tony walked over to his mother, and she lifted his chin.

"Those no-good little shit stains do this to ya again?" Teresa asked.

Tony nodded.

"Go upstairs and wash up before your father gets home."

Tony hesitated. "Ma, Dad's gonna be real mad when he sees me, huh?"

Teresa closed her eyes and lowered her head. "Don't get all worked up. Your face will get more swollen, and then for sure your father will know ya got an ass whoop…Those boys were pickin' on ya again."

To Tony's delight, his father didn't make it home before he'd gone to bed that night. As he drifted off to sleep, he imagined being the strongest boy in the world and hurting every single person that had hurt him.

Buy here: Mean Little People

More books by Paige Dearth:

Believe Like A Child

When Smiles Fade

One Among Us

CPSIA information can be obtained
at www.ICGtesting.com
Printed in the USA
LVHW041635181119
637699LV00001B/89

9 781983 422843